Th...
the...
exp...
res...
tra...
the...

At first she was concerned that here, in the hall of the very hotel where she lived, they might be discovered, and she thought to resist. But then she felt new spirals of ecstasy racing through her, leaving her mouth burning with fire, and she knew she would offer no resistance whatsoever. She could no more break off this kiss than she could fly, and though a weak cry, far back in her mind, warned her against going too far, every emotion and sensation in her body silenced that voice.

Critics adore Sara Luck's bl... **hot Western roma**...

TALL...

A *Publishers W*... ...2012

The dangerou... ... *r a genteel British novelist f*... ... *one plucky lady embraces the spirit o*... ... *nd captures the heart of her new hero, a daring* ... *er with big dreams of his own.*

"The Wild West retains its appeal in *Tallie's Hero*."
                                        —*Publishers Weekly*

"Steamy Western romance."
                                        —*Fresh Fiction*

More praise for Sara Luck and her novels

CLAIMING THE HEART

*As the Texas and Pacific Railroad expands across the wild
frontier, a spirited young woman experiences the triumphs
and tumult of building a part of history . . . and loving a
track man bound to a politically powerful family.*

"Terrific. . . . Sara Luck provides an enjoyable
nineteenth-century Americana tale starring two
fabulous protagonists."

—*Genre Go Round*

"Luck captures the true essence of the Texas
frontier, the expansion of the railroads, and the
determined men and women of the West. . . .
Well-researched. . . . A fast-paced story with
plenty of action and engaging characters."

—*Romantic Times*

SUSANNA'S CHOICE

The acclaimed debut novel from Sara Luck!

*In a dusty Nevada mining town, an aspiring
newspaperwoman crosses paths with a wealthy
entrepreneur from San Francisco, and everything changes—
including her own uncertain destiny.*

"An exciting read. . . . A passionate, adventure-
filled historical romance."

—*Shadowfire Press*

ALSO BY SARA LUCK

Tallie's Hero

Claiming the Heart

Susanna's Choice

RIMFIRE BRIDE

SARA LUCK

Pocket Books

New York London Toronto Sydney New Delhi

Pocket Books
A Division of Simon & Schuster, Inc.
1230 Avenue of the Americas
New York, NY 10020

This book is a work of fiction. Names, characters, places, and incidents either are products of the author's imagination or are used fictitiously. Any resemblance to actual events or locales or persons, living or dead, is entirely coincidental.

First Pocket Books paperback edition February 2013

POCKET and colophon are registered trademarks of Simon & Schuster, Inc.

For information about special discounts for bulk purchases, please contact Simon & Schuster Special Sales at 1-866-506-1949 or business@simonandschuster.com.

The Simon & Schuster Speakers Bureau can bring authors to your live event. For more information or to book an event contact the Simon & Schuster Speakers Bureau at 1-866-248-3049 or visit our website at www.simonspeakers.com.

Manufactured in the United States of America

10 9 8 7 6 5 4 3 2 1

ISBN 978-1-4516-7389-0
ISBN 978-1-4516-7392-0 (ebook)

RIMFIRE
BRIDE

ONE

Highland, Illinois—September 1882

Jana Hartmann had just released her class and was wiping the chalkboard when she heard a young voice behind her.

"Miss Hartmann, you are the bestest teacher I've ever had," six-year-old Stanley Fickert said.

"Well, thank you, Stanley," Jana replied. "And even though I'm the only teacher you've ever had, I do appreciate your thoughts. But I'm sure you meant to say I am the *best* teacher you've ever had."

"Yes, ma'am, that's what I said. You are the bestest teacher in the whole world, I bet."

Stanley ran to Jana and buried his head in her skirt as he squeezed her around the legs, then, with childlike embarrassment, turned and ran out of the classroom.

She smiled as she watched the boy disappear through the door, then she picked up the feather duster and began cleaning chalk dust off the oak desk that sat at the front of the room.

Jana enjoyed teaching youngsters. Hearing the praise that Stanley had just given her was a huge motivator to carry on with her exhausting day. She arrived at the schoolhouse before seven each day, where she taught more than fifteen children, ranging in age from Stanley's six, to three young ladies who were nearly fourteen. She smiled when she thought of "her girls," as she called them. Any of the three was capable of taking her job, and she called upon them often to act as tutors to the younger children who were enrolled. She found teaching to be pleasant, at least pleasant enough to take her mind off her second job.

Glancing up, she saw that the big clock above the blackboard showed a quarter to three. She was going to be late, and that wasn't good.

Quickly, she put away her duster and grabbed some composition books that she would grade before turning in for the night. Putting them into her knapsack, she hurried out the door, setting the latch as she left. When she reached the road, she began to run with an easy lope. Being even a minute late was all it took to incur her stepfather's sizable wrath.

Jana's father, Johann Hartmann, had died when she was three years old, and Marta, her mother, had remarried, to Frederick Kaiser, within a few months of Johann's death. That happened in Geldersheim, Germany, twenty-one years ago. In truth, Mr. Kaiser was the only father Jana had ever known, but Jana found it telling that, for her whole life, she had never called him anything but Mr. Kaiser.

Mr. Kaiser had a small farm in Germany, and in five years he and Marta, working both on his own farm and hiring out to others, saved enough money to emigrate to America. Jana, as a child, was left to care for her sister, Greta, who was four years younger. By the time Jana was five, she could build a fire and make eggs and toast for both herself and her sister, which allowed her mother to labor in the fields during the growing season.

Jana was eight when they arrived in America. At first the family settled in St. Louis, with its large German population, but Frederick soon moved his wife and children thirty miles east to a small farm near a Swiss settlement that also had a large complement of Germans.

Marta insisted that both girls get an education, and thanks to Sister Mary Kathleen, the kind old mother superior at St. Paul's Catholic School, Jana excelled. When she arrived at St. Paul's, she spoke no English, but within a year she was not only speaking English, but French and Latin, too. She also insisted that Jana not only continue to speak German, but learn to read and write it as well.

Sister Mary Kathleen taught by dwelling on the good things the children did, and she seldom resorted to the switch for discipline. Now, in her own classroom, Jana tried to follow the old nun's methods of seeking the good and sparing the rod.

Even though Jana earned a salary from teaching school, she still lived and worked on the Kaiser farm just outside town. Because of Sister Mary Kathleen, Jana had been one of the first recipients of the state's coveted township scholarship to go to Illinois State Normal College. But Mr. Kaiser had refused to allow her to travel the 150 miles to the school.

Again, Sister Mary Kathleen had interceded. She arranged for Jana to use her scholarship to attend McKendree College, just sixteen miles away in Lebanon. That way, she could easily return home to help out in the fields when she was not in school. Jana had stayed with a doctor and his family during the week in Lebanon, and in exchange for her room and board, she was expected to do housework. But her room was not furnished, so her mother paid for that. When her stepfather found out that his money was going to Jana, he made her sign a contract with him to repay every cent with exorbitant interest. Now that she had returned to Highland and was living at home, he insisted she pay room and board.

"You must hurry. Your *Vater* and Greta are in the field now, and the light, it will be gone soon," Marta Kaiser said when Jana got home. Jana's mother had lived in America for sixteen years, but still spoke English with a heavy accent, often throwing in German words.

"He is not my father," Jana replied in a low voice.

"Ssssh . . . he has been your *Vater* since you were a little girl. There is much work to do."

Jana changed quickly into a faded denim dress, then pulled on a bonnet and tied the strings under her chin, covering her ash-blond hair. After pulling on gloves, she grabbed a cane knife from the back porch and hurried out into the field. There, her stepfather was cutting cornstalks while Greta stood them in shocks.

Greta looked like a somewhat frailer version of Jana, with the same ash-blond hair and blue eyes. When the two young ladies were dressed up for church, they turned the head of every young man in Highland and were universally declared to be "the two prettiest young ladies in town."

Frederick, who was slightly shorter than Jana's five foot eight inches, looked up as she approached the field. Frederick was strong from a lifetime of physical labor, with a round face and a misshapen nose, which was broken when he was a boy.

"It is late you are, and this field we must finish before dark," he said angrily.

"I'm sorry, I had to clean my classroom."

"It is here your work is, not the *Schule*. And not the pictures you draw."

"I earn the money to pay you for my room and board at the school. And I paint on my own time."

"If you work hard like you should, you would have no time for art. No more talk now. Work." Frederick motioned with his cane knife. "Your sister, since morning she has worked. You, you work only three, four hours today."

Frederick and the two young women worked in silence, chopping the cornstalks then standing them upright to allow thorough drying before storing them for feed for the livestock. The final task was the most irritating to Jana—twisting twine around the shock, taking care to prevent the errant dry leaves from cutting her arms and face.

She looked toward Greta and noticed that she

had fallen behind. Her sister was frail and suffered from a malady that made it difficult for her to breathe, and the dry corn silks made it nearly unbearable for her. Jana could hear her wheezing and gasping.

"Papa, please," Greta pleaded, "I cannot work anymore."

Frederick stopped and looked first at his daughter, then toward the setting sun. "We have maybe thirty more minutes. Then we quit."

Greta worked a few minutes longer, then with a groan, she dropped her cane knife and fell on her hands and knees gasping for breath. Jana hurried to her.

"Get up!" Frederick yelled, dropping his knife and striding angrily toward them. "You lazy girl. Get up and finish this field before I give you a reason to crawl in the dirt!"

"Leave her alone!" Jana said defiantly, her eyes staring pointedly at Frederick. "I'm taking her back to the house."

"She stays, and she works," Frederick said as he attempted to grab Greta's arm.

Jana raised her cane knife. "Don't you dare touch her!"

Frederick stared at Jana, his face contorted by anger, then he turned away. "We will stop working for today." He turned and started for the house, leaving Greta on the ground.

"You shouldn't have done that," Greta said between gasps for air.

"How many hours have you worked today?" Jana asked as she helped her sister to her feet.

"It doesn't matter."

Greta leaned heavily on Jana as they slowly made their way back to the farmhouse. When they arrived, Marta met them at the door, helping Jana get Greta to a bench.

"I'll get her a drink," Marta said as she unhooked the dipper from the lip of the water bucket and filled it.

While Greta drank, Jana massaged Greta's lower chest with one hand and her back with the other. Eventually, Greta's breathing returned to normal—not deep breaths, but at least no wheezing.

"Mama, Greta can't work in the field. Doesn't he understand that she's not well, and the corn silk is making things worse?"

"Ich gab ihm keine Söhne."

"You're right. You gave him no sons, but he can't make boys out of us. Come, Greta, you need to lie down."

"But supper?"

Just then Frederick came into the house, his hair wet from a dousing at the outside water pump. He went to the table without comment and took a helping from the bowl of noodles and cabbage that Marta had prepared for the evening meal. Jana noticed that he had taken at least three-fourths of the available food.

It didn't matter. Tonight, she would refuse to sit at the table with her stepfather.

When Jana and Greta got up to their room, Jana helped Greta out of her dress. Jana went to the washstand and poured water from the pitcher into the bowl. With a soft cloth, she began wiping her sister's face with the cool water.

"Thank you," Greta mumbled as tears began to run down her face. "I'm so sorry."

"It's not your fault," Jana held her sister in her arms. "Tomorrow you rest, and I'll let my girls take over the class. I'll come home as soon as I can get them started, and the corn will be shocked lickety-split."

Greta lay back on the bed and soon fell into a troubled sleep. Jana picked up a candle and her knapsack, then sat down on the window seat. She needed to correct the compositions, but she wasn't ready to do that just yet. She was so tired. If only she could fall asleep right now.

Jana raised the window, putting a stick under the sash to keep it open. A gentle breeze was blowing, causing the still-green leaves on the maple tree to rustle. A large, yellow moon hung over the barn, bathing the farm in silver and shadow. As a child she had sat in this spot many times, watching the stillness of the night. She had never known anything but life on a farm, and the beauty of moments like this soothed her like a balm.

But whatever beauty there was to see was spoiled by the thoughtlessness of the man who had governed her life for the last twenty years. At one time Frederick had a hired man to help him, but over the last few years money had been so dear that he had let the man go. She would have thought he would be pleased that she had a source of employment, but at times she thought he actually resented it.

Sometimes Jana felt that he treated her as he did because she wasn't his natural daughter. But in truth, he showed no favoritism with his cruelty. He treated Greta, his biological daughter, as harshly as he did Jana.

After a light knock on the door, she heard her mother calling quietly, "Jana? Greta?"

Jana hesitated for a second. She wouldn't put it past Frederick to use his wife as a means of getting Jana to open the door.

"Jana?" her mother called again. a little louder. "Are you awake? *Ich habe Lebensmittel.*"

Taking a deep breath and bracing herself, Jana walked over to the door and jerked it open. Her mother was standing there, but no one else.

"I don't need any food, Mama. I'm not hungry."

"But take. Maybe later you are hungry." Marta handed a burlap bag to Jana. "How is *deine Schwester*?"

"She is sleeping."

"Can Greta go with you?"

"What do you mean, can Greta go with me? Go where?"

Marta looked up and down the hallway. "Today it was bad." Marta shook her head. "If Greta stays here, I think she might die. You can save her if you leave and Greta *geht mit Ihnen.*" Marta reached into a pocket of her dress and pulled out a cloth drawstring pouch, which she handed to Jana.

In the dark, Jana could feel coins, and when

she slipped the drawstring, she felt a roll that she assumed was paper money.

"This is a lot of money, Mother. Where did you get it? If Mr. Kaiser discovers it is gone . . ." Jana let the sentence hang.

"It is not Frederick's money, it is my money. It is *Ei Geld* about which he knows nothing, and for a long time I have kept it."

"Mama, I can't take the egg money you have saved for so many years, and I can't leave you here alone with Mr. Kaiser. When he discovers we are gone, he will be very angry, and he will make you work even harder than you do now."

"He is very—*wütend jetzt*—angry now," Marta repeated, finding the English words she was looking for. "I am an old woman. If I die, it is my time. Greta is *jung,* but twenty. It is not her time. You must take care of her, Jana, just as you did when you were *ein Kind.*"

Jana looked back at Greta as she lay sleeping, the moonlight causing the shadows of the maple leaves to make eerie patterns on the wall. She knew her mother was right. Her sister would die if Frederick Kaiser continued to work her like a hired hand.

"Oh, Mama, how do we do this?"

"You are a strong woman, *meine Tochter.* You will find a way. Today I talked to Dewey Gehrig at the market. Go to him tonight. Early in the morning, he will take his pigs to the stockyard. He will take you and Greta with him and leave you at the depot. Dewey says there is a train *nach* Chicago. In Chicago *ist meine* cousin Marie. In there is a letter for her." Marta pointed to the little cloth bag.

Jana put her arms around her mother and held her close. She felt moistness on Marta's cheeks. Jana could not recall having ever seen her mother cry. Jana knew then what a sacrifice her mother was making. She was sending away her two daughters, which meant she might never see them again, just as she had left her own mother when Frederick brought her to America sixteen years ago. Jana hugged her mother tighter and felt her mother's arms around her. She felt her mother shudder; then Marta dropped her arms, recognizing the urgency of the moment.

"*Gehen jetzt schnell!* He must not see you go."

"Aren't you going to tell Greta good-bye?"

"*Ja.* I will tell her."

Jana stepped out into the hall to keep her eyes and ears alert for the sight or sound of her stepfather. Behind her, she heard her mother's voice, quiet and anxious. She heard, too, Greta's voice, questioning at first, then acquiescing.

Finally, wiping the tears on her apron, Marta stepped back into the hallway.

"Mama, the school! I can't just leave without them knowing what happened to me. You must send word that I will not be coming back."

"I will. Hurry, *mein liebes Kind.*"

Jana went back into the bedroom and found Greta sitting on the edge of the bed.

"Jana, are we leaving tonight, as Mother said?"

"Yes. Get packed, but only take what we can carry in one case between the two of us."

"I'll light the lamp," Greta said, reaching for the matches.

"No, the light will be too bright. Light a candle. That's all we'll need. Hurry now."

As Greta was packing, Jana withdrew a wooden picture frame from her drawer in the chest. It contained a wedding picture of Johann and Marta Hartmann, a happy young couple with no inkling of the sorrow to come. She held the picture, wanting to take it with her, but then she decided against it. It would just take up much-needed space in the case, and if she left it, she would have a good reason to return someday. Turning the picture around, she withdrew seven $10 bills she had managed to save from her salary last year. She stuck that money into a pocket of her dress. Then, helping Greta pack, Jana put in her own packet of paper and charcoal pencils for drawing.

"Do you really think we should do this? We may never see Mama again."

Jana stopped and looked at Greta, who was standing in the light of the candle. She looked so fragile, so delicate, and Jana was hit with the enormity of the situation. Her mother had asked Jana to take on the responsibility of what both women thought was necessary to save Greta's life, but no one had asked Greta if she wanted to do this.

"Greta, you've had no say in this, so I ask you now. Do you want to do this? Or would you rather stay?"

"I'm sad to leave Mama, but I'll go wherever you take me."

Jana gave her sister a hug, then picked up the

case, handed the bag of food to Greta, and quietly they left the house.

Marta stood in the dark upstairs hallway and watched through the open window as her two daughters walked down the lane, then turned on the road toward Dewey Gehrig's farm. She knew that she would likely never see either of them again, and she wiped the tears from her eyes before she went back to her bed. Frederick's heavy snoring told her that he knew nothing of the girls' escape.

She crawled into the bed beside him, then said a quick and silent prayer that she had done the right thing, and that *Gott* would look after her two daughters.

Bismarck, Dakota Territory—September 1882

Drew Malone stood in his law office and poured two cups of coffee. He looked back at the rather stout woman who was sitting on the other side of his desk.

"Ma'am, do you take cream or sugar?" he asked.

"I can't always get cream or sugar, so I always drink it black."

Drew handed her the cup of coffee, then sat down behind his desk. He held his cup in both hands for a moment.

"Tell me a little about yourself, Mrs. . . ." He glanced down at his paper. "Considine, is it?"

"Yes, sir. Elfrieda Considine. Well, I've been in the Dakota Territory for almost ten years now— came when they opened Fort A. Lincoln. My husband was proud to bring the best laundress Fort Riley ever had."

"Your husband was Sergeant Considine?"

"No, sir. Martin was my second husband. He was killed with General Custer, rest his soul, but John Dalton was killed by a civilian in a drunken brawl. Do you drink, Mr. Malone? Because if you do, there's no need for this conversation to continue."

Drew's eyebrows raised in amusement at the turn the interview had taken. This woman, who stood close to six feet tall and weighed at least 230 pounds, was interviewing him!

"I've been known to take a drink now and then."

"I didn't ask if you took a drink. I asked you if you drank. Believe me, there *is* a difference."

"I am not a drunk, Mrs. Considine."

"Good. Then when do I start?"

"Don't you want to know what your duties will be?"

"I expect you want me to take care of the two little boys that you've been shufflin' from pillar to post since your wife died."

"Are you sure you were a laundress and not a detective?" Drew laughed openly.

"A woman alone in the world can't be too careful about who she takes up with. I've buried two husbands, or rather, the army has buried two husbands for me, and, Mr. Malone, I want you to understand right now, I'm not in the market for another man."

"That's good to know, and I'm not in the market for another wife, so we should get along fine.

Besides looking out for the boys, I'd like you to do some cooking, some housekeeping, and laundering. Are you agreeable to that?"

"Your ad in the *Tribune* said as much, so I'm expecting to do that. My cooking's not fancy, but it's tasty, and I run a clean house."

"That's all I ask. When can you start, Mrs. Considine?"

"Tomorrow will be right fine. My friends call me Elfrieda, and I would be honored if you would call me that as well."

"And you may call me Drew."

"No. While I never wore stripes, bein' married to two soldiers and doin' laundry for the bunch of 'em, I was in the army same as if I stood reveille ever' mornin'. And the army taught me that rank has its privileges. You will be *Mr. Malone* to me." Elfrieda stood and offered her hand for a shake. "I'll see you bright and early tomorrow morning."

"Yes, ma'am."

When Elfrieda left, Drew stood and watched her from his window.

What a strange interview. She hadn't asked him where he lived, what her living accommodations would be, how old the boys were, not even how much money he would be willing to pay her. He smiled. Something told him that with the introduction of Elfrieda, his household was about to be a whole lot different.

Drew hoped that was so. He had just put Rose Denton on a train back to Chicago. Rose was Addie's mother and had come out to Bismarck to take her grandchildren back to "civilization," as she called it. Thank God he'd gotten her on the train without his boys.

What business was it of hers how he raised his children? They were healthy and seemed happy. Maybe Sam couldn't read as well as she thought he should, and maybe Benji said "son of a bitch" too often, but they had the love of every cowboy who rode the range at Rimfire Ranch, and the attention of every single woman in Bismarck. To get Rose to leave, he had agreed to hire a full-time nanny.

He laughed. Could Elfrieda Considine be considered a nanny?

The boys and he had been without a woman's presence for two years now. Two painful, lonely years, he thought, and returned to his seat behind the desk.

TWO

July 4, 1880

From the *Bismarck Tribune*:

FOURTH OF JULY

The committee on grounds has prepared what is pronounced by competent judges to be the finest race course in the territory, and the speakers' stand, seats, refreshment booths, official headquarters, the barrels for ice water, the bandstand, decorations, etc., are so nearly completed as to afford the most positive assurance that nothing will be lacking by July the 4th.

Cannon from Fort Lincoln will be fired at intervals during the day, and the combined bands of Bismarck (eighteen pieces) will furnish excellent music.

At 10:00 p.m. the grand pyrotechnic display will be held. The citizens of Bis-

*marck can expect a glorious birthday
celebration, as it has been reported
that the good merchants have put up
$1,000 for this extravaganza.*

When the marshals were assembling to head the
parade, Drew Malone, who was one of the parade
marshals, took his place beside Clement Lounsberry, the editor of the *Bismarck Tribune,* and
Sheriff Alex McKenzie.

"You've done a great job promoting this celebration," Drew said to Lounsberry. "Look at all the
people. They're everywhere."

"I'm doing my damnedest," Colonel Lounsberry
said. "I want the Territorial Legislature to move the
capital from Yankton to Bismarck, and it's events
like this that will get the word out. Anybody here
will spread the word that we're the town to watch."

"I've got a bad feeling having so many folks in
town. I'll bet there's at least twenty-five thousand
people here, and when that many congregate, you
know there's going to be trouble," Alex McKenzie
said.

"I think you and your men can handle it," Drew
said.

"That's why we keep electing you sheriff," Lounsberry added.

"But this is different. You get all these people
liquored up and bunched together. I don't like it,
not at all."

When the marshals had walked the length of the
parade route, Drew hurried back to join his wife,

Addie, and their two children, who were sitting on a quilt spread out on the boardwalk in front of Drew's office. A sign in gold leaf was painted on the door: PARTNERS, FRANK B. ALLEN & ANDREW B. MALONE, ATTORNEYS AT LAW.

Four-year-old Sam was sitting patiently, watching everything that was going on, while Benji, who was two, was making the acquaintance of a stray dog that had wandered up on the boardwalk.

"Stop it, Benji. Leave that mangy old thing alone," Addie said as she moved the boy to another spot. But as soon as she sat down again, Benji went after the dog.

"Here, doggie, here, doggie," Benji said as he jumped off the boardwalk, falling onto the street. When he did, his face puckered up, but he did not cry.

"Now look what you've done. Can't you sit still like your brother?" Addie helped Benji to his feet and began to brush the coal cinders off his knees. "Where's your father?"

"I'm here," Drew said as he approached his family.

"Good. You take him. I should have kept them both at home," Addie said.

"But Sam would have missed seeing the callithumpian band if you would have done that." Drew picked up his younger son and put him on his shoulders. "Now you can't get in any trouble, little man."

Benji began to run his hands through Drew's thick brown hair, making it stand up in stiff tufts.

Addie shook her head as she watched her son.

"What am I going to do with him? He's going to be the death of me yet."

Drew put the boy back down. "You stay here with Sam, and Benji and I'll go find something to eat. I'll bet someone has ice cream. What do you think?"

"Don't give him ice cream. That'll be all he'll eat if you do that."

"Addie, it's the Fourth of July. That's what you do. You eat ice cream and you have a good time. Don't worry, we'll bring you some, too," he said with a wink.

Just then a stovepipe cornet band, a washboiler drum corps, and a squeegee orchestra passed in front of them.

"Sam, look. The callithumpians. Clap your hands."

Sam flashed a big grin at his father and began clapping as the men passed in front of him. One of the squeegee men ran over to the young boy, as if attempting to wipe his face, eliciting a squeal of laughter from Sam.

"Boys, come with me. You can help me find ice cream."

Drew and his sons began moving through the crowd, speaking to first one person and then another. Drew was well-known in Bismarck. He had come out from Evanston, Illinois, in 1878 to handle land claims for the Northern Pacific Railway and had joined Frank Allen in a law partnership. Now, with more and more talk of statehood for the Dakota Territory, Clement Lounsberry and Alex McKenzie were talking to Drew about the possibility of his standing for Congress.

His father had long been a congressman from Illinois, and Drew had grown up going back and forth to Washington. He was particularly interested in it now, especially since Addie had just made it known that she was pregnant again.

When Benji came along, he was truly a handful. Drew had already decided he would surprise Addie by hiring a full-time girl to come live with them. Many upstanding immigrant girls were coming into Bismarck every day, some wanting to homestead themselves, and others just wanting to earn money to help their parents prove up their claim. Addie would like that he'd been thoughtful and love the help.

When the parade was over, Addie joined Drew and the children near the refreshment stands. Addie's prediction had been accurate; after the ice cream Sam wasn't interested in eating anything else, but finally accepted a piece of pilot bread and some cheese, while Benji was eagerly eating a cruller that was slathered with a sugary glaze.

"Andrew Malone, I'm not going to let you take care of them ever again. You just give them anything they want."

"I'll be good, Mama, I'll never do it again," Drew said as he gave Addie a kiss.

"Drew, someone will see you." Addie looked around to see who might be standing nearby that would know her.

"I can kiss my wife anytime I want to." He kissed her again as he drew her to him and held her.

Drew had never thought of any woman but

Addie. They had known each other since childhood, having grown up next door to one another. Drew's father, Samuel Malone, was a US congressman who spent most of his time in Washington, and Addie's father, Eli Denton, was a professor at Northwestern University. Drew and Addie's relationship was, and had always been, comfortable because it had been assumed by both families that they would marry someday. They were married soon after Drew graduated from law school at Northwestern, and Sam, their perfect child, was born within a year. Then Benji, their wild child, was born two years after that. They were a happy couple, a happy family.

"I want that," Benji said as he grabbed at Sam's hardtack. "It's mine." He tried to take the cracker as Sam, with much patience and practice, kept turning away from his brother, protecting his food.

"I think he's had enough. If he's going to be up for the fireworks tonight, he'd better take a nap," Drew said. "Come on, let's go home."

"I'll take him. I know how much you like this stuff."

"Let me go with you. If I carry him, Benji may fall asleep on the way home and then we can just put him in bed."

"All right. Sam and I may lie down, too, when we get home, right, Son?"

"Yes, ma'am," Sam answered.

When the family was within a block of home, they were met by an excited Sheriff McKenzie.

"Drew, you'd better get over to the glass-ball

shoot. When I left, Major Bates was closing in on the record Fritz Kimball shot at St. Paul," the sheriff said.

"How many has the major hit?"

"When I left, it was 236, and the record is 245. This is the first time we've used Mole's trap to throw up the balls. That's the key. If we keep that thing and practice, our team will beat Mandan every time."

"I'd love to see him break the record, but . . ." Drew looked to Addie.

"Go ahead. I can get them home from here, and if Benji has to walk the rest of the way, he'll be really tired," Addie said.

"Thanks, honey." Drew put Benji on the ground. "I'll be home as soon as the major misses."

"You don't have to. Like I said, I need to lie down, too."

Addie took Benji by the hand and started to lead him down the street.

Drew and the sheriff had walked no more than half a block away when Drew heard Sam's scream, the scream that had brought him and the sheriff back to the scene. Addie lay prostrate on the ground, blood gushing from her neck, as Sam cried, "Mama, Mama, Mama," over and over. Benji was, uncharacteristically, trying to comfort Sam. "Shuuuu, Sam, Mama's sleeping."

Drew cradled the dying Addie in his arms, her blood soaking his shirt as he applied pressure to the wound, trying to stop the bleeding. He remembered Alex saying, "Your boys need you, Drew, I'll take care of Addie," but Drew, tears flowing down his cheeks, would not put his wife down.

Her final words were: "Get a good woman to take care of my boys. I love you." And then she died.

They never found out whose stray bullet hit her.

Chicago, Illinois—September 1882

Early Sunday morning, the Illinois Central rolled into Chicago's Great Central Depot, where Jana and Greta left the train. The depot was crowded, and for an instant Jana was terrified. Chicago was a city of over half a million people, yet her mother had confidence that she could find one person among the multitudes. What if this cousin—this Marie Gunter, whom her mother had not seen in fourteen years—didn't even live in Chicago anymore?

Jana felt for the cloth pouch that contained the savings that she was sure had taken her mother years to put aside. It was safely in her pocket. If she couldn't find her cousin, she had more than enough money to go back home.

No, she had enough money to go back to Highland. She would not think of the farm as her home ever again. If she dwelled on that, she could not do what she knew she had to do. She would protect Greta no matter what it took.

Greta was staring at everything around her much as a child would, and when they stepped out into the crisp autumn air, Greta smiled. "Look, Jana." Greta pointed toward the sun rising over Lake Michigan. "Isn't it beautiful? I know when we find Mama's cousin, we're going to love Chicago. Could we walk down to the water right now?"

Jana looked up at the street signs and located them on Randolph Street and Michigan Avenue. She withdrew the money pouch from her pocket and looked at the letter her mother had asked her to give to Cousin Marie. Marie's address was on the envelope.

"Let's wait until we find Cousin Marie. Maybe she doesn't live too far from the lake and we can come here for a picnic sometime." Jana checked the address on the envelope. "Mama says she lives on Forty-Seventh Street. All we have to do is find someone who will take us there."

Several cabs were standing in front of the depot, and when the two women approached one of them, the driver stepped off the box.

"Where to, ladies? I'm happy to have you grace my humble hack." The driver opened the door and Jana and Greta climbed in.

"Thank you. We're not sure where we're going, but the address is 1724 West Forty-Seventh Street near Ashland Avenue. Can you take us there?"

The expression on the driver's face changed from an open smile to one of what Jana thought was pity. "Oh, miss, I can't take you there."

"Why not?" Greta asked.

"Taking folks where they want to go is how I make a living, and it would take me a long time to get you there, and if I did get you there, no one would want to pay me to come back. I'll tell you what I'll do though. I'll take you to the horsecar line on Ashland, and you can ride it until you get to Forty-Seventh. Then you won't have far to go."

The driver closed the door and climbed back up on the box, flicked the lines, and the horse pulled away from the depot and headed down Randolph.

Greta reached over and squeezed her sister's hand. "Thank you, Jana, thank you for taking me away from all that work. I know you'll find a school that will have students that are smarter and cuter than you would ever have in Highland, and I'm going to find a job—oh, what will I be? Do you think I could be a telegrapher? Or maybe I'll work in a tearoom or maybe I'll be a milliner. I just can't wait to get to Cousin Marie's."

When the driver got to Ashland Avenue, he stepped down and opened the door for Jana and Greta.

"Here it is, ladies. There'll be a horsecar going south on these tracks before you know it. Just get on it and ride until you come to Forty-Seventh Street. Once you get there, it'll just be a couple of blocks until you get to the seventeen hundreds."

"Thank you, sir. You have been most kind to us. What do we owe you?" Jana asked, withdrawing her pouch.

"Nothing."

"But that can't be. This is how you make your living," Jana said.

"Let this be my gift to you, so that you always remember the first person you dealt with in Chicago was a kind man."

A smile crossed Jana's face. "That is very nice of you, sir, and I will gladly accept your kindness."

Just then a horsecar appeared.

"Here's your ride, ladies, and good luck." The driver tipped his hat and turned his rig around, waving as he did so.

Several men were sitting on benches around the sides of the car, but no women. One man approached them to take their fare, which they learned was a nickel no matter how far they rode. Jana and Greta chose a bench near the front so they could observe all the sights along the way.

When they first left the depot, they had been filled with awe over the magnificent buildings and the well-dressed people going about their business. But after they boarded the car, the scenery began to change, and not for the better.

The fine stone-faced brick buildings gave way to crowded buildings, some of brick, many of wood. As they traveled farther along Ashland Avenue, most of the men on the car got off, to be replaced with more men, big, burly men with solemn faces. They barely spoke to one another, and when they did speak, Jana didn't understand the language, except for the occasional German words.

The scenery was upsetting. The sky became darker and darker. It was almost as if storm clouds had come up, but the darkness was caused by billowing smoke, gushing out from tall smokestacks on industrial buildings.

"Jana," Greta said, "this can't be right. Mama wouldn't send us to a place like this. We've made some mistake."

Jana took out the letter once more. "It says she lives on Forty-Seventh Street, two blocks from Ashland." Jana looked at Greta, who was fighting back her tears. "We're on Ashland, and I've been watching the numbers go by. We just passed Forty-First Street, so it can't be too far now. I promise you, if it's this bad, we won't stay any longer than we have to."

"I don't want to go back to Papa," Greta said.

"And we won't. In a city the size of Chicago, we'll find something we can do, but it will cost money, so if we can, we will stay with Cousin Marie for a while."

Just then Greta began to wheeze. As she had done so many times before, Jana began to rub Greta's back trying to comfort her.

"It's the smell. It's horrible. What is it?"

"I'm not sure, but it's like a barnyard only a hundred times worse."

"It's the stockyards, woman. What do you expect a slaughterhouse to smell like? Roses?" The man who was sitting on the bench beside them laughed at his own joke. These were the first words spoken in English for the last fifteen or twenty blocks.

"Oh," Jana said, her only word. She knew about the stockyards in East St. Louis because, if the conditions were just right, the smell would reach the farm in Highland, but it never stayed for more than a day or two. This constant smell, almost like a rancid odor, was burning her throat. How could Greta breathe at all?

The horsecar stopped, and Jana saw that it was Forty-Seventh Street, so she stood and helped Greta off the car. Several of the men also got off, and they began walking toward a commercial area with large, ugly buildings. A heavy, oily smoke gushing from towering stacks colored the sky black as night. Here, too, were scores of railroad tracks crossing and recrossing, on which chugging locomotives were pulling long lines of rattling freight cars loaded with cows, all bellowing loudly.

"Jana, it's awful," Greta said, a shocked expression on her face as she looked around.

Jana grabbed her sister's hand and held it tightly. "We'll get through this, Greta. I promise you, we'll get through this."

They began walking away from the stockyard, seeing rows upon rows of ugly tenement houses all connected. Scattered among these buildings were a few open lots with tall weeds, strewn with trash. Clusters of poorly dressed, dirty children congregated in the lots, often darting into the hard-packed-dirt street, which was at least two feet lower than where the houses sat. Sewage, mixed with the cart-horse droppings, was flowing through the street, and the children ran through this filthy water as if it were a brook in a farm.

God in heaven, what were they getting into?

At last they reached a door with the number 1724 above it. Jana took a deep breath and then knocked. She smiled wanly at Greta, hoping to hide her own trepidation.

"What do you want?" a large woman with straggling hair asked as she jerked the door open.

"We are looking for Marie Gunter. Do you know her?" Jana asked.

"Who wants to know?"

"I am Jana Hartmann and this is my sister, Greta Kaiser, and Mrs. Gunter is our mother's cousin—her name is Marta Saathoff. Can you help us find her?"

A smile crossed the woman's face. "*Ja,* I see the resemblance. You do look a bit like Marta did when she was a youngun. I grew up just two miles from her in Niederwerrn, I did. I long to go home, but . . . come in if you will."

Jana and Greta stepped into the small room that was Marie's home. Once inside, Jana saw that it was surprisingly clean, the stench of the outside air somewhat ameliorated by the smell of lye soap.

"I have always thought Marta and her husband lived among the Swiss. What brings her daughters to this place?"

"Mama sent you a letter." Jana withdrew it from her pouch and gave it to her mother's cousin.

Marie took the letter and looked at it, then handed it back to Jana. "Could you read it to me? My eyes aren't what they used to be."

Jana took the letter and began to read in careful German:

> *Cousin Marie, I ask that you please look after my daughters for a while until they can get settled in Chicago.*
> *My girls are good girls, but my Greta is sickly. It is important that she have some time away from my husband because I fear he does not look favorably upon a weak child. I have enclosed some funds for you, should you have a need for it. I will forever be indebted to you should you do this for me.*
> *Your cousin, Marta Saathoff Kaiser*

"How much money?" Marie asked.

Jana handed her the paper bills that Marta had inserted in the envelope. Marie began to count them out, then she looked at Greta.

"Does he beat you?"

"He does not," Greta answered.

"Then why has she sent you to me?"

"It is the work. He has no sons, and he hasn't enough money to hire help," Greta continued.

"And you think the work will be easier in Chicago?"

THREE

The first night was miserable because if a window was opened, the stench was unbearable, but without an open window the heat from the September evening was stifling. Once Jana got up and stepped out onto the steps that led to Marie's front door. She was surprised to see that people were sleeping on pallets on the sidewalk. Why did people choose to live like this? There had to be a better way.

The sleeping arrangements inside were considerably less than comfortable, and it wasn't just because of the heat and the smell. Marie strung a hammock between two hooks on adjoining walls with the idea that one night Greta would sleep in the hammock while Jana slept on the floor, then the next night they would switch. But because of her frailty, Jana knew Greta would not be able to sleep except in the hammock, so Jana would be spending every night on the floor.

Jana soon discovered that she had to endure

more than just the discomfort of a hard floor. The apartment crawled with mice, and Marie's cat, which was not a loving pet, but a mouser, did his most productive hunting in the night, often awakening Jana when she was able to fall asleep.

The next morning, even before sunrise, Marie Gunter put on one of the two dresses that she owned and covered it with an apron that was near threadbare from washing. She had told Jana and Greta to stay in her home for the day while she found out if there were places for them in her shop. If so, they could start working the next day.

A job was necessary because part of their arrangement with Marie was that they would pay rent, as well as their share for the food. Marie did get the two a job in the butcher shop.

Greta swept and mopped the floors and cleaned the meat cases, but Jana had to actually cut up the meat, a job she found so loathsome that she actually considered returning to Highland. She knew, though, that she wouldn't be able to get her job back at the school, and if she had no money to give to Mr. Kaiser, he would make things even more difficult for her. She would like a teaching position in Chicago, but without a convenient place to live, and with no time off from the butcher shop to look for the job, she had no opportunity to apply.

But to Jana's surprise she found that she was making $4 more a month working in the butcher shop than she had as a teacher in Highland. Greta was earning an income as well, and since they didn't have to pay Marie as much for rent and food as Jana had been paying her stepfather, they were able to save what money they had brought with them and even add to it.

The girls had been in Chicago for almost two months, and as the hot summer waned with the approach of fall the smell became more bearable.

"Do you want to stay in Chicago?" Greta asked as they were walking home from the butcher shop.

"I don't know what choice we have right now. I'm thinking, if we just stay where we are, by spring we'll have saved enough to find a room and then look for something else," Jana said.

"Would you leave right now?"

"What do you mean, would I leave right now? If we did leave, where would we go?"

"To Dakota Territory."

"Where?" Jana asked with a little laugh.

"To Dakota Territory. Someone left this pamphlet in the shop today, and I put it in my pocket. Read it."

The girls stopped in a circle of light that was coming from one of the dingy gaslights. Jana began to read the pamphlet, put out by the Northern Pacific Railway.

IMMIGRANTS ARE INVITED TO DAKOTA TERRITORY

RAILROAD TO GIVE GREATLY REDUCED RATES FOR PASSAGE

*Those who wish to better themselves would
do well to examine the opportunities offered*

by moving to the Dakota Territory. It is not a false statement to say that the young and vigorous settlers of Dakota are drawn from the best of America, and the energy, capacity, and enterprise of these settlers are bringing about a rapid accumulation of riches in the shape of active capital, pushing the development of Dakota. It can truly be said that Dakota is drawing from the older states the best blood that flows in the veins of American men and women.

The soil is from three to six inches deep and is the most fertile to be found anywhere. The cutting plow, going down three inches deep, turns over a ribbon of black dirt as rich as butter. Breaking commences in the latter part of April and continues until June. Farmers can raise vegetables, flax, and fodder grain.

The Northern Pacific is currently plotting out a new town to be known as New Salem, located approximately thirty miles west of the Missouri River. It is to be settled by the German Evangelical Synod of North America. A colonization bureau has been organized in Chicago under the leadership of Pastor G. L. Kling, and plans are under way to take no fewer than two hundred immigrants to New Salem, where anyone, man or woman, who is 21 years of age, or the head of a household, qualifies for free land.

Northern Pacific is giving special reduced rates for those travelers who would settle in the Dakota Territory.

"What do you think, Jana?"

"Oh, Greta, I don't know. What if we got out there and, uh, something happened? I mean, what if you got really sick?"

"What you're actually asking, is if I'm up to doing this."

"Well, are you? Coming to Chicago was a big change for us, but going to Dakota—that would be an even bigger move. Here, at least we have Cousin Marie if something happens, but out there we'd have no one," Jana said.

"That's not true. We'd have each other. And the answer is, yes, I am up to doing this."

"Dakota is a long way from Highland."

"And Geldersheim is a long way from Highland. At least the Dakota Territory is on the same continent. It says man or woman twenty-one years of age. That's you. We know how to farm. We can do this," Greta continued.

"It's cold there."

"And it's not going to be cold here? Look around you. Do you think Cousin Marie wants to live here? No. She's stuck here. Let's get out before something happens and we can't go either," Greta pleaded.

"You really do want to do this, don't you?"

"Yes," Greta answered enthusiastically.

"All right, I'll find Pastor Kling's church," Jana said.

Greta threw her arms around her sister. "Oh, thank you, Jana, I know it's the right thing to do."

◈

Sunday morning, as Jana sat through Reverend Kling's service, she studied the man—tall, hawk-nosed, with an eminent brow, sad eyes, and a mouth that, unless he kept it tightly shut, was apt to be quivering. He had a look as if he had just been startled.

Dear Lord, she prayed silently, *I am about to put both my life and my sister's in the hands of this man. Please don't let me make a big mistake.*

"Do you speak German?" Reverend Kling asked Jana when she spoke to him after the service. "It's not necessary, but if you do, it will be helpful."

"I lived in Germany until I was eight. That's when my family moved to America, so, yes, I am quite comfortable speaking German."

"Good. The next question: Do you know anything about farming?"

"The village where I was born was a farming community, and I've lived and worked on a farm since coming to America. I've also taught school."

Pastor Kling smiled broadly. "Then I know you'll be welcome at New Salem. A young woman who can both work the fields and teach the minds of the young. Yes, you'll be welcomed by our group."

"Thank you. I am honored. Oh, and my sister will come with me."

"Wonderful, and is she also a schoolteacher?"

"No."

"That is okay. There's always room for one more, especially a young woman who wants to join our flock."

"When do we leave?" Jana asked, her enthusiasm over the project growing even as they were talking.

"We plan to leave next spring."

Jana felt her spirits tumble as she thought of the prospect of having to spend the winter at Cousin Marie's. "Next spring?"

"Yes. We want to be there in time to break the sod and have something in the ground for the growing season."

"Reverend Kling, next spring is too late. I, that is, my sister and I, need to go now."

"Oh, dear. Young lady, you aren't in any sort of difficulty, are you? Something that you haven't told me?"

"No, sir, it's nothing like that. It's just that we are living with our cousin—on Forty-Seventh Street—and we would like to, that is, we need to, find some other living arrangement. My sister found a pamphlet describing the Dakota Territory, and we got very excited about the prospect of owning our own land."

"I see. Perhaps I could offer a suggestion. Do you have any money at all?"

Jana was skeptical of the pastor. "Why?"

"Because if you have enough to sustain yourselves for the winter, you could go on to Fargo or Bismarck now, and then you could join us at New Salem when we arrive in the spring."

Jana took a deep breath. "That's a wonderful idea. If we're frugal, we could do that."

"If you do decide to go ahead of us, I'll expect

you to let me know by the end of February if you plan to join us at New Salem."

"Oh," Jana said, putting her hand to her mouth. "We won't be able to go now because the pamphlet said the reduced fares were for those going to New Salem. I know we don't have the money to pay the regular fare."

"Oh, my dear, you needn't wait for us. The Northern Pacific is giving reduced fares to anyone who will go to Dakota. It's a penny a mile for a one-way ticket."

Jana smiled at the news. "Thank you! Thank you very much! Then, my sister and I will go right away. Where's the Northern Pacific depot?"

"In St. Paul, Minnesota."

At the Chicago and North Western Depot, Jana waited in line at the ticket cage. The ticket agent on the other side of the barred window wore a visor and wire-rimmed glasses.

"Yes, miss, where to?" His voice reflected the weariness of someone who had been standing all day, and no smile was in his greeting.

Jana showed the ticket agent the pamphlet. "This says that the Northern Pacific is giving reduced rates to all who would take passage to Dakota."

"Madam, this is the Chicago and North Western."

"Yes, I realize that. But I was told that your railroad will connect to the Northern Pacific in St. Paul. And that I can buy a through ticket here."

"That's true, but you do understand, the Chicago and North Western does not give the cheap fares from here to St. Paul?"

"How much would a ticket be from here to Dakota?"

The ticket agent let out a long-suffering sigh. "Dakota is a big territory, madam. You will have to be more specific. Where in Dakota would you like to go?"

Jana tried to remember the names of the cities Reverend Kling had mentioned, but the only name that came to mind was Bismarck, which had stuck in her head because of Chancellor Otto von Bismarck of the German Empire.

"Bismarck."

The agent checked a chart. "Will you want palace-car service?"

"No, I want the least expensive service."

"You'll be one full day and night on the train between here and St. Paul. I assure you, madam, that the emigrant car won't be very comfortable."

"I realize that, but cost is more important than comfort."

"The total cost will be sixteen dollars. Twelve dollars from here to St. Paul, and four dollars from St. Paul to Bismarck."

"I shall require two tickets."

After saying good-bye and thanking Cousin Marie for her hospitality, Jana and Greta left Chicago the next evening at 6:00 p.m. Because Jana had bought the most inexpensive tickets, they walked by the palace cars and the sleeper cars, which shone with varnish and colorful trim, until they reached a dull car without any trim at all. This was one of several emigrant cars, a long, narrow box, with a stove at one end and a convenience at the other end, with but a hanging curtain to provide privacy. The car was quite dark in the dim glimmer from its lamps, but Jana could see wooden benches, with straw-filled cushions. By maneuvering through the people already filling the car, she found a spot near the corner that was large enough for her and Greta to sit together. They placed their small suitcase on the floor and put their feet up on it.

Jana was grateful that their chosen spot was in a corner, because for the entire night she could lean against the wall and cushion Greta's head on her shoulder.

The next morning the train stopped for barely thirty minutes as it took on water and fuel. With such a crowd of people, Jana was only able to buy a single biscuit, which she and Greta shared for their breakfast. The lunch counter at their noon stop was equally crowded, and again they had no time to get anything resembling a meal, but they bought an apple apiece from a vendor who was doing a brisk business on the depot platform.

To pass the time during the day, Jana made a long and detailed sketch of the car they were in, filling it with the passengers she observed. She drew a bald-headed, bearded man eating a meal of sausage and bread; a little girl with pigtails sitting on the floor as she played with a cat; another child asleep on the seat; a man snoozing with his hat pulled down over his head, his wife resting her chin on her hand as she stared through the window; an elderly woman wearing a kerchief knitting; a man standing in the aisle leaning back against the seat, speaking to the people in the seat across the aisle from him.

"I'm tellin' you, these trains are goin' to be the ruination of this country," the standing man was saying. "The steam that comes from 'em wilts the grass, and that spoils the pasture. The stink off the train will poison all the fish in all the creeks, the whistles scare the deer and turkey and keep the cattle from eatin' so's the cows will give no milk. The sparks start all kinds of fires. And here's another thing. There's telegraph wires runnin' alongside the track, and who knows what's goin' to happen with all that electricity runnin' loose ever'where."

"And yet, sir, you are riding on the very contraption you condemn," the man across the aisle replied.

"Yes, sir, well, it's the best way to go a long distance, for all its faults."

Jana looked at Greta, who had been listening to the conversation, and the two sisters shared a smile.

For a while Greta watched as Jana's drawings took on the personalities of her subjects. Someday, when the two women were old, Greta hoped they could look back on this trip and enjoy a laugh together as they recalled this adventure.

But would this adventure be something they remembered with fondness or with horror?

Greta turned her attention to the passing land-scape. She had tried to be brave for Jana, but inside she was afraid. What if she became a burden for her sister? What if the work proving up a homestead was something she absolutely couldn't do and all the responsibility would once again fall upon Jana?

But wasn't that how it had always been? From childhood on, Greta had always turned to Jana to take care of her, but as Greta stared out the window, she vowed right then and there that she would not allow that to happen—not this time. She would shoulder her part of the responsibility. Somehow, some way, she would find a way to be a productive partner in this endeavor. Tentatively, she reached for Jana's hand and squeezed it.

Jana smiled. She could feel the uncertainty and anxiety that Greta was feeling because it mirrored her own. Looking around at all these people, who were doubtless on the same quest that she and Greta had undertaken, among them there were bound to be failures.

The strong man who had complained about the trains—what made her think she could succeed when perhaps he would not? The woman knitting? Was she with a man or was she going West alone? And the child sitting on the floor? Was she afraid of what lay ahead of her?

All of these people—all of these thoughts—gave Jana some comfort. If others thought they could do this, then she could, too.

She put down her pencil and drawing pad and clasped Greta's hand firmly. Without words, she was conveying a strength that came from deep within her. Greta had to know that her big sister would never let anything happen to her.

They reached St. Paul at eight o'clock that evening. There, they learned that they would have to spend the night in the depot because the train to Bismarck, which was to be an all-emigrant train, wouldn't leave until nine the next morning. That night they had supper, but Jana didn't want to waste any money on lodging, so she was pleased when she saw that others would be spending the night in the waiting room of the Northern Pacific Depot.

Some of the other passengers were placing boards between two benches to sleep on. She went to one of the ticket windows.

"Yes, ma'am, what can I do for you?"

"I see that some of the passengers have boards that they've laid between the benches. Where'd they get those?"

"I rent 'em. Would you like a couple?"

"My sister is with me. I'll need four of them."

"That's ten cents. Jacob, grab four for the lady," he called over his shoulder.

"Thank you," Jana said as she gave the man a dime.

Jana smiled at Greta when she returned. "Have some cheer, little one, we'll be able to sleep tonight. It won't be a comfortable bed, but at least it'll be better than last night. We'll be able to stretch out."

A moment later a boy of about sixteen arrived, carrying four boards. "These are for you, ma'am?"

"Yes."

"I'll put them down for you. If you wad up your coat, it makes a pretty good pillow."

"Thank you, we'll do that. Are there any blankets?"

"They're all gone."

The boy put the boards in place, then stood there for a moment, and Jana realized he was waiting for a tip. She gave him a nickel.

"Thank you, ma'am," the boy said with a smile.

"We can make do. We'll use one coat as a pillow, and the other as a blanket," Jana suggested.

Greta rolled her coat into a bundle, then she got on one side of the boards and stretched out. "Oh, this will do just fine."

Jana lay down beside her sister, and placing her money pouch under her chemise next to her breasts, she pulled her coat over the two of them. In spite of the hard boards and the various noises from the other weary travelers, she was asleep within a few minutes.

Jana didn't know how long she had been asleep when she felt something on her hip under her makeshift blanket. Her skirt had been inched up and she felt her leg exposed to the air.

"Ahh!" she said, as she forced her elbow back into the gut of the person behind her.

"What the hell are you doin', woman? Can't a body get any sleep?" a man asked in a loud voice, awakening many who were sleeping nearby.

Looking around, she saw that two more boards had been stretched between the benches, and a man was lying beside her. It had been his hand on her hip.

"Keep your hands off me!" Jana said angrily as she pulled her skirt down to restore some of her modesty.

Just then, Greta sat up and opened her eyes with a squint.

"What happened? Is it time to get on the train?" Greta asked.

An official-looking man came over to them. "Ladies, please, you'll have to keep it quiet. People are trying to sleep."

"Who are you?" Jana asked.

"I am G. K. Barnes, the Northern Pacific passenger agent here in St. Paul."

"Well, Mr. G. K. Barnes, I was trying to sleep until this . . . this beast tried to assault me."

"Why, I did no such thing." The man looked to be in his thirties and was dressed not unlike any of the other emigrants. "I was sleeping when you suddenly called out and elbowed me in my stomach."

"Are you going to deny that you . . . you *groped* me?"

"That's exactly what I'm going to do."

"Then you, sir, are a liar." Jana pointed to his two boards. "Why are those things so close to mine?"

"I sought only to take up as little space as possible, so that others may have a place to rest."

"Move them!" Jana demanded.

"Madam, I assure you, if I, uh, touched you, it was unintended, something that I did in my sleep."

"I think, sir, that you should put your boards elsewhere," Barnes said.

"I shall," the man replied petulantly. "I certainly have no desire to be attacked in my sleep again by this crazy woman."

Jana watched until the man was on the far side of the waiting room.

"I'm sorry, ma'am," Barnes said. "I hope you'll not be disturbed again."

"I hope so as well."

"Are you all right?" Greta asked after Barnes left.

"Yes, I'm all right now. Try to go back to sleep."

Within a few minutes Greta was asleep once more. But sleep for Jana was fleeting, not only because she feared a return of her would-be assailant, but also because she was afraid she might sleep so soundly that they would miss their train to Bismarck.

What would happen to them if they did miss the train? It might be a week before the next emigrant train departed. If she had to sit here all night long with her eyes forced open to keep herself from going to sleep, she would do just that. They were not going to miss the train. They couldn't afford it financially, or emotionally.

The next morning Jana picked up a pamphlet from the Northern Pacific. It listed the names of all the officers of the railroad, the distances on the various divisions, and, according to the heading at the top of the page, "Important Information for Settlers and Tourists." The pamphlet gave information about each of the towns along the route, and Jana looked to see what had been written about Bismarck. Up until now, the only thing she knew about the place where she and her sister were planning to spend the next four or five months, depending on the schedule of Pastor G. L. Kling and the German Evangelical Synod of North America, was its name.

> *Bismarck—Population, 2,500. Two first-class and eight second-class hotels, seven churches, two banks, a public hall, a daily and two weekly newspapers, courthouse and town hall, an artesian well, and all branches of trade represented. Products are wheat, oats, and potatoes. Shipments same. Game: antelope, deer, elk, prairie chickens, and ducks. Four lines of steamers receiving and discharging general merchandise and supplies to and from Upper Missouri River forts, posts, and landings. The Chamber of Commerce with the push of its enterprising businessmen will make Bismarck one of the most prominent points on the Northern Pacific line. An iron bridge is just completed across the Missouri, costing $1,500,000. Fort Abraham Lincoln is three miles distant on the opposite side of the river.*

Seven churches. That was a comforting thought. If there were churches, the town couldn't be all bad.

By the time they boarded the train, Jana had recovered some of her optimism. When she chose a seat for them this time, she made sure they were sitting close to another woman.

"Hello," Jana said.

"Halla," the woman replied. *"Sverige."*

"Sweden," a man sitting next to her said with a wave of his hand and a broad grin.

Jana nodded and smiled. No wonder no one spoke to one another.

They had been under way for only a short time when the train was moved to a sidetrack. The conductor, without explaining the reason for the stop, pushed the door to the emigrant car aside and said that any who wanted to do so might step outside for a breath of fresh air.

Jana weighed the situation. The potbellied stove was warming the car, making it almost too hot. The heat caused the car to reek of body odor, as the people were forced to sit shoulder to shoulder in the crowd. Added to the body odor were the strange smells of various sausages and cheeses that others had brought, but the worst stench was from the curtained "convenience."

Outside the air would be clean, but it was also quite cool. She decided that a breath of fresh air was worth the cold, so she and Greta stepped outside.

They were near no station, and as far as Jana could see, no town was anywhere on the horizon. All she could see was gently rolling country that stretched away upon all sides. The scene did, however, have a sparkling freshness, with not a cloud in the sky, and it smelled of clean earth. It was pleasant, but still a mystery as to why they had stopped.

Soon the mystery was solved as another train, going east, appeared on the main line. It roared by at tremendous speed, its cars shining bright with varnished wood, accenting paint, and polished metal fittings. The passengers looked out upon the occupants of the emigrant cars who were standing along the tracks as if they were observing an inferior species.

The scene would be repeated often during the next twenty-four hours, for every train on the line took precedence over the emigrants.

Soon after the train passed, the conductor shouted, "All aboard!" Jana and Greta went back into the uncomfortable closeness and foul air of their car, and like everyone else on the train, they tried to grab a catnap when they could.

Thirty-four hours after leaving St. Paul, their trip interspersed with at least a dozen interruptions as they pulled off onto a sidetrack to let another train pass, they arrived in Bismarck. It was seven o'clock in the evening, and since it had now been three nights since either Jana or Greta had enjoyed a real night's sleep, they checked into the Custer Hotel, which was only a short distance from the depot.

Jana was awakened the next morning by a knock on the door. For just a second, she had no idea where she was, then she remembered that she and Greta had checked into a hotel the night before. The room was bright with sunlight, and she knew that it was much later than she was used to awakening. Greta was still sleeping soundly beside her.

Again there was a knock, this time much louder.

"Yes?" Jana called.

"Miss," a man's voice said from the other side of the door, "if you stay past noon, it'll cost you for another day."

"What time is it now?"

"It lacks ten minutes of eleven."

"Oh, my heavens!" Was it possible that she had slept until almost eleven o'clock? Evidently it was, because she was still in bed.

"Well, will you be checking out?"

Jana knew she needed to find somewhere for them to stay more permanently. And she had to find some sort of employment so they could afford to stay in Bismarck until spring, when Reverend Kling and the New Salem group would be coming to the Dakota Territory.

But until she found a place for them, they would have to stay in a hotel.

"We'll be here another day," she called back.

"That's good. Just come on down to the desk before noon and ask for Tom McGowan. I'll be there, and, miss, if you plan on staying a week, I can rent you a cheaper room."

"Thank you."

"Uhmm," Greta said groggily. "What is it? What's going on?"

"Nothing," Jana said. "You just stay in bed until you rest up. As cold as it is, and as much sleep as you've lost in the last few days, you have no business moving around until you're rested."

"I am tired," Greta mumbled as she rolled over and pulled the covers up over her shoulders.

Jana got out of bed, padded across the floor to stand in front of the steam radiator for a moment to warm up, then walked over to the suitcase, where she took out a rose-colored dress with a white collar. If she was going to be meeting people today, she needed to look her best. She dressed quietly and then put a dollar on the dresser.

"Greta, I hope I'm gone for most of the day, looking for a place for us to stay. I left you some money if you get hungry," Jana said as she opened the door to leave. "I think I saw a place downstairs where you might get a bite to eat, but don't go wandering about on your own. I'll see you sometime this afternoon."

"All right," Greta said, not opening her eyes.

Jana felt a little guilty leaving Greta all alone on their first day in Bismarck, but if they were going to survive until Reverend Kling's group arrived, she had to find an income. Besides, Greta had to be as exhausted as Jana was after the long train trip. She hoped Greta would be able to sleep for most of the day and gather her strength.

FOUR

Stepping out of her room at the Custer Hotel, Jana walked down three flights of stairs until she reached the lobby. She had been so tired when they arrived last night that she hadn't paid any attention to the lobby, so she took it in now. The floor was wide, unvarnished planks of wood, and much of it was covered with a patterned carpet of rose and gray. A leather sofa and several comfortable chairs were scattered about. At least three steam radiators were pumping out heat, though no fire was burning in the fireplace.

Jana walked across the lobby to the front desk. A man standing behind the desk appeared to be checking the hotel register.

"Is it Mr. McGowan?"

"It's Tom." The man smiled as he extended his hand toward Jana. "Especially if you're going to be our guest for a while."

"Well, that all depends . . . Tom. It depends on

whether I get a job or not. Right now, I just want to make arrangements for my sister and me to spend another night here."

"In Bismarck there's plenty of work, especially for a pretty woman like you. We've got way too many men for the number of women we have. Oh, I should ask, do you have a man waitin' for you?"

Jana almost answered immediately, but then she thought better of it. She didn't want to complicate her stay until she was ready to move on to New Salem.

"I don't have a man waiting for me, but I'm waiting for a man to arrive." Jana's answer was truthful, as far as it went, since she was waiting for Pastor Kling, though not in the way she supposed Tom meant.

"When will your man be here?"

"He'll be here in the spring. I need to send him a telegram to tell him we arrived. Can you tell me where the telegraph office is?"

"It's that little building just across from the railroad depot. Charley Draper can fix you right up. Now, how many nights do you expect to stay at the Custer?"

"At least for tonight. How much will it cost?"

"Like I said, it's cheaper if you stay by the week."

"And how much would that be?"

"I could let you and your sister stay here for five a week."

Jana's eyes opened wide, and a big smile spread across her face. "That settles it, Mr. McGowan, we'll stay a week. Now I see your restaurant is closed. What time does it open?"

Tom looked down and began filling in the guest register to reflect the longer stay. "All right, it's all taken care of."

"Good. Now what about the hours for the restaurant?"

"Oh, Miss Hartmann, that's not a restaurant, it's a saloon."

"Really? I've never been in one. May I look inside?"

"Sure." Tom stepped out from behind the counter and led her to the swinging doors that opened into the saloon.

She saw about a dozen tables with chairs, and a long, polished wooden bar with a large mirror behind it. Shelves containing bottles of liquor ran across the bottom of the mirror.

"Why don't you serve food?" Jana asked.

"We just never have."

"Well, you should. Can you tell me where I can go to get a bite of lunch?"

"The Sheridan House has a restaurant. It's that big building on the corner of Main and Fifth."

"Thank you, Mr. McGowan. You've been most helpful."

"It's Tom."

Jana smiled. He was her landlord, at least for the time being, so there was no harm in being nice to him.

Tom watched the pretty young woman leave, hardly able to believe that he had offered to let her and her sister stay for $5 a week. The usual rate was $2.50 a night, or $12.50 if you stayed all week.

He had just let this woman stay in his hotel for practically free because he thought that an attractive young woman would bring customers to his saloon if he could convince her to be friendly to some of the men. Nothing untoward, not every man was looking for a woman to bed. Some just wanted a woman to talk to. But quite obviously he had misjudged the situation. They were sisters, but they didn't have the same last name. One of the women must be married, and this one said she was waiting for a man.

Well, at least he would have the pleasure of seeing her, and even speaking to her on occasion, over the next week.

The Sheridan House, where Tom had directed Jana, was also a hotel, and the huge, three-story brick building covered an entire block. An elegant, columned porch was in front. Jana stepped inside and bought a copy of the *Bismarck Tribune* before going into the dining room. She decided that reading the local paper would be the quickest way of learning more about the town, and perhaps there would be advertisements for openings.

Just inside the dining room, a slate board listed the lunch specials, and she had a hard time deciding if she wanted an elk steak, antelope stew, or fricasseed prairie chicken. She finally chose the prairie chicken since all the meat was new to her and perhaps the sauce that smothered the chicken would make it more to her liking.

The dining room was quite crowded, but she saw an empty table right in the middle of the room and moved to it. A waiter approached as soon as she sat down, and Jana ordered the prairie chicken. As she waited for her food, she began reading the newspaper.

She saw in the paper that tomorrow, Tuesday, November 7, was Election Day. When she was in Chicago, with its half million people, she had heard no mention of an upcoming election, but here in a town of less than three thousand people, it seemed to be the topic of conversation at every table within Jana's earshot.

When Drew Malone entered the Sheridan House, he was greeted by a waiter, who escorted him to the table already occupied by his partner, Frank Allen. Frank looked up from his paper.

"Have you decided how you're going to vote?" Drew asked as he pulled out a chair and sat down across from his partner.

"Not yet, but if we're to believe the colonel, we shouldn't vote for the Republicans or the Democrats. Have you read his editorial today?"

"I haven't seen it yet. Is it bad?"

"Bad? Well, yes, it is bad. But it's also truthful. Lounsberry put in print what we've all known for years. Both Richards and Griffin are pretty smart. They are business partners, but one runs as a Republican and one runs as a Democrat. That way no matter who wins, their gambling outfit won't be touched."

"Well, it's got to stop. I'll bet this Citizens' Ticket Clement is pushing wins the whole shebang."

"If it does, it'll go a long way toward cleaning

up the politics and . . ." Frank stopped in midsentence, then leaned closer to Drew. "Well, I'll be damned. Guess who just walked in."

"Colonel Lounsberry?"

"No, it's the good justice of the peace himself, Mr. Richards in person. Let's just watch and see whose votes he buys today."

A rotund, swarthy man stopped for a moment just inside the door, looking around the dining room. Then he proceeded to every table, calling each person by name, smiling broadly, and shaking hands. At each of the tables, he left several tokens that could be exchanged for five cents in trade at the Palace Saloon, his place of business.

"There you go, boys," he said magnanimously. "Stop by and have a beer on me."

"Are you gettin' a little worried, Judge?" someone called.

"About the election? Not at all."

"You've got Colonel Lounsberry and the *Tribune* against you."

"Why, if I didn't have the paper against me, I'd think I wasn't doing my job properly," Richards replied, and a few of the customers laughed.

Richards started toward the table of an attractive young woman who was sitting alone, engrossed in the pages of the newspaper.

"Frank, who is that woman Richards is approaching? Do you know her?" Drew asked, tossing his head toward Jana.

"I've never seen her before, but I like the way

she looks. I'd say she'd make a good mama for Sam and Benji," Frank quipped.

Chuckling, Drew shook his head. "I don't know why I stay friends with you. You keep pushing, pushing, and pushing when you know I've got that taken care of. Mrs. Considine has been with me for almost two months now, and she's working out just fine."

"Oh, yes, the giantess," Frank teased. "But then she's not in the market for a husband, or so I was told. . . ."

Both men laughed uproariously.

Jana looked up from her paper when she heard the laughter. She saw two men sitting at the table nearest her, but she had been reading and hadn't noticed them before. Of the two men, one in particular caught her attention. He had dark brown hair, was clean shaven, and had, from what she could tell from here, an athletic build. He was, she thought, a most attractive man.

Even as she was considering his attributes, a rather plump man approached her and stuck out his hand.

"How do you do, ma'am. I'm Jason Richards, and I'd like to ask for your vote for me in tomorrow's election. I'm running for justice of the peace. Can I count on your vote?"

"I'm afraid not."

"Oh? And why not? I assure you, I can take care of any problem you might have."

"You can't solve my problem, sir."

"Oh, but I can." He reached into his upper

breast pocket and withdrew something and placed it under Jana's plate. "Now can I count on your vote?"

Jana looked down and saw a folded bill.

"No, sir." She handed the money back to the man without looking at the amount. "Your money won't buy my vote, because I can't vote. I just arrived in Bismarck last night, so I'm not a resident."

"Oh, my dear, in Bismarck, that's not a problem. Take the money, and, remember, I'm Jason Richards, running for justice of the peace."

"Thank you, but no. Even if I could vote, I don't think I'd vote for you. If buying votes is the way Bismarck is run, I'll find another place to live. Good day, sir."

The smile left Richards's face and he glared at Jana. "You've just made a big mistake, girly. Yes, sir, a big mistake, and you'll be sorry. Because you see, I *will* win, and if you so much as step into the street in the wrong place, I'll have you before my bench."

"So be it. You're not buying my vote. Good day, Mr. Richards."

Jason Richards put a stub of a cigar in his mouth, then turned and stomped out of the dining room.

At the neighboring table, Drew had watched and listened with amusement to the entire exchange between the young woman and the rotund, despicable politician. He couldn't help but think of the fairy tale he had read to the boys just a few evenings ago. Except in *The Beauty and the Beast,* the beast had some redeeming qualities. As far as Drew knew, Richards had none.

When Drew realized that she was turning down Richards's attempt to buy her vote, his interest in her went beyond just finding her to be exceptionally pretty. He got up from his table and walked over to her.

Jana saw the handsome man from the other table come toward her, and she wondered if he, too, was going to try to buy her vote.

"Ma'am, I'd like to shake your hand, and on behalf of the honest people of Bismarck, I'd like to welcome you to our city. You are exactly the type of citizen we need in this town. I'm Drew Malone."

"What are you running for?"

Drew laughed. "Why, nothing, ma'am. I overheard the way you handled our least favorite politician, and I wanted to tell you that I liked how you did it."

"In that case, Mr. Malone, I'm Jana Hartmann." She extended her hand, and when she looked up, she was struck by the man's captivating blue eyes. For an instant, her gaze locked with his.

The other man who had been sitting at the table with Drew had approached, and he spoke to her, breaking the spell.

"Would it be an affront to you if we joined you? I'm Frank Allen. Mr. Malone and I are partners in the Allen and Malone Law Firm, and I believe I overheard you say you had a problem."

"Did I say that?"

"You'll have to excuse Frank, Miss Hartmann.

Sometimes he tries to horn in on other people's affairs when he has no business doing that." Drew moved toward his seat at his own table.

"No, wait. You said you were lawyers?"

"Yes, we are," Frank said as he grasped Drew's arm to keep him from returning to their table.

"Then maybe you can help me."

Both men moved to her table and sat one on either side of Jana.

"What can we do?" Frank asked.

"As I said to the rather disagreeable Mr. Richards, I just arrived in Bismarck. My sister and I came last night on"—she paused for a second before she continued, knowing that what she was about to say would speak volumes about her economic status— "the emigrant train. It is our intention to go next spring with a group of like-minded people to form the community of New Salem."

"New Salem? Have you heard of that, Drew?"

"I believe it might be in Morton County, about thirty miles west of here. Would that be the place, Miss Hartmann?"

"I'm not sure. We are waiting for Pastor Kling from the German Evangelical Synod to arrive in the spring, and then we will find out."

"Miss Hartmann, wait a minute, let me get this straight. You don't have any idea where you're going?" Drew asked.

"No."

"But you do know this man who is in charge, do you not? Pastor Kling, I think you said?"

"I've met him."

"But you don't know him."

"Ease up on her, Drew. She's not in a court of law." Frank laughed nervously.

"He's right, Miss Hartmann, I'm sorry."

"Well, you may have a point. I wanted to leave Chicago so badly that I really didn't delve into all the particulars about New Salem."

"You wanted to leave Chicago? Do you have a legal problem?" Drew asked. "Maybe we could help you."

"No, it's nothing like that." Jana lowered her gaze, breaking any eye contact with either man. She took a deep breath. "I left because of something I read. The Northern Pacific Railway published a pamphlet that said a woman could homestead in Dakota, and I thought I could do that."

A broad smile spread across Drew's face. "Well, now, that I can understand. There are hundreds of other women right now in Burleigh County proving up their claims. And if that's your problem, we can help you."

"Before I do that, I have another problem."

"And that would be . . . ?"

"I need a job."

"That shouldn't be a problem. Bismarck is a boomtown right now with all the people moving in, and if we get to be the capital of the territory, there'll be even more jobs. Have you ever worked before?"

"I taught school for three years."

"You're a schoolteacher, but you want to homestead? Proving up a homestead plot is hard work. Do you know anything about farming?"

Jana laughed.

"Did I say something funny?" Drew asked.

"I haven't told you everything. I've been on a farm my whole life, except while I was away at college, but then I worked on the family farm anytime I was at home. My sister and I both know how to work."

Drew smiled sheepishly. "That was my fault for making such an assumption. But as for a teaching position, I'm afraid all our teachers for this term are already contracted."

"I thought as much," Jana said, "but I'll take whatever job I can get."

"Maybe she can work at the new telephone exchange," Frank suggested.

"That's a good idea," Drew said. "I can take you to see Charley Draper if you'd like. He has a crew out putting up wires now, and the exchange should be up and running in a couple of weeks."

"Charley Draper? Is he the telegrapher?"

"Yes, have you already met Charley? He runs the Western Union office, and now he's started the telephone exchange."

"No, I haven't met him, but I need to send a telegram, and when I inquired, his name was mentioned. I'm surprised that you are getting telephone service in Bismarck," Jana said. "I wouldn't have thought that."

"We aren't exactly uncivilized out here," Drew said, perhaps a bit more sharply than he'd intended, as he thought of his mother-in-law's constant harping that either he move "back to civilization" or that she be allowed to raise the boys in Evanston.

"I'm sorry, I didn't intend to suggest otherwise," Jana said.

"No, it was me. 'Civilization' is a sensitive subject right now," Drew said. "As soon as we have our lunch, why don't I take you to see Charley? I know he said he was looking for someone to help him run the exchange."

"That sounds wonderfully kind of you. As I said, I planned to send a couple of telegrams, anyway."

At well past noon, Greta Kaiser came down the stairs of the hotel with the dollar Jana had left clutched in her hand. She saw a man standing behind the front desk, but he was conversing with an elderly man, so Greta went to what appeared to be a restaurant. She stepped through the bat-winged doors, stopping immediately as she looked around in confusion.

This didn't look like any restaurant she had ever before seen, though if she had to admit it, she hadn't been in many restaurants. Not a soul was sitting at any of the tables in the room.

She wondered if she was too late. Had lunch already been served, and had she missed it?

A man wearing a white apron came through a door that led to another room. He was carrying a tray of glasses, and he stopped short when he saw Greta standing there, almost dropping the tray.

"Girl, you gave me a start. Who ya lookin' for?"

"I'm looking for dinner."

The man laughed as he set the tray down and began putting the glasses under the polished counter. "I'm afraid you're not going to find that here."

Greta walked on into the room, stepping up to the bar to address the man as he continued to put the glasses away. "Has the restaurant already closed?" Greta looked around the empty room.

"Restaurant? Is that what you think this is?"

"Well, yes, I was told there was a place to eat off the lobby, so I came here."

"Well, miss, this ain't no restaurant. It's a saloon. We don't serve nothin' here but drinks," the man said with a broad smile.

"No food?"

"No, ma'am."

"Why not? This is part of the hotel, isn't it? Don't you think some of the people who are staying here might want to eat?"

"You'll have to talk to Mr. McGowan about that. He's the one that runs the place."

"Where will I find this Mr. McGowan?"

"Right now you'll find him behind the check-in desk."

"Thank you."

Tom McGowan looked up when the pretty, young woman approached his desk. At first glance he thought it was the same woman he had spoken to earlier, the woman who had booked the room for a week. Then he realized this must be the sister. He looked at the register to check her name.

"Yes, Miss Kaiser, may I help you?"

Greta looked surprised. "How do you know my name?"

Tom chuckled. "The only two young ladies staying in the Custer Hotel are you and your sister. She made arrangements this morning for the two of you to stay for the rest of the week. Now, what can I do for you?"

Greta pointed toward the saloon. "Why don't you serve food in there?"

"Well, Miss Kaiser, we don't serve food in there because it's a saloon. It's where people come to drink."

"When it's time for dinner, or supper, where do they go?"

"We have restaurants in town. Nice ones. The Sheridan House probably has the finest dining room in the territory. I sent your sister there when she asked where she could go to eat."

"Is the Sheridan House a hotel?"

"It is."

"Let me ask you something, Mr. McGowan. When the people leave the—saloon—to go eat, aren't they taking their money to another hotel? What if you served a meal here? Wouldn't they stay for the meal? And if they stayed, wouldn't you make more money?"

"I don't know, I suppose so," Tom agreed. "I've never really given it any thought."

"She's got you there, Tom," the old man, who was now sitting in one of the chairs, chimed in. "I've been asking ya to feed us ever since I been staying here, but, no, not the Custer. No food here."

"Hank, you know the reason we don't serve food. Where would we put a dining room and a kitchen?"

"Oh, pish posh," Greta said. "You could serve in that saloon. You already have the tables, and what does it take to prepare and serve a meal but a stove, a pot, and a few bowls?"

"She's right," Hank said. "Think about how we do it on a steamer. We feed a whole crew with a lot less space than you got here."

"A pot and a few bowls, huh?"

"Yes. You could serve a stew or a soup every day. And if I were you, I'd give it away for free. You'd make up the difference by selling more drinks."

"By damn, listen to the woman. She's makin' a lot of sense," Hank said.

Tom stroked his chin as he studied the young woman who was standing before him.

"I don't suppose you have any suggestions as to who I might hire to fix this stew, do you?"

Greta thought this would be her opportunity to take some of the load off Jana's shoulders. If she could convince Mr. McGowan to hire her, she could not only help with some of the expenses, she could prove to Jana—and to herself—that she wasn't entirely helpless.

Greta smiled. "I have the perfect person in mind."

Jana and Drew left the dining room of the Sheridan House. On this chilly November day, as they walked toward the Western Union office, she noticed that Drew hadn't even bothered to put on an overcoat over the brown town coat he was wearing. But how he was dressed wasn't the only thing she noticed about him. She noticed his physique, perhaps as much as six inches taller than her own five feet eight inches, and she found he was a most attractive man. She had been drawn to the deep blue of his eyes in the restaurant, but here in the sunlight they seemed to be almost magnetic.

Just then, Jana's foot caught on a loose board in the walkway and she stumbled.

"I should have warned you about that," Drew said as he grabbed Jana to prevent her from falling. "These boardwalks are quite new, and I'm afraid the carpenter didn't do his job as well as he should have. Would you like to take my arm?"

Jana thought it strange how easily this man offered her his arm, as if it was expected. An aura of strength and self-confidence seemed to emanate from Drew. But there was something else.

No man had ever had such an effect on her, and she felt what she could only describe as magnetism, drawing her toward him. But with no real experience in such a situation, she didn't know if this was normal.

She accepted his arm as if she had taken the arm of a gentleman hundreds of times before, and they continued down the street until they reached the Western Union office.

"I'll be right with you," a man said without looking up as he continued to write rapidly while the telegraph key tapped out its message.

At the back of the building, Jana saw an upright cabinet with wires hanging from it. A telephone with three oak boxes was attached to the wall beside the cabinet.

She turned her attention back to the telegrapher until the instrument quit clicking. Draper put his own hand on the key, sent a brief message, then turned toward Drew and Jana.

"Mr. Malone, what can I do for you, sir?"

"Charley, this young lady is Jana Hartmann, and she just arrived in Bismarck. She's well educated, and she's looking for employment."

"Can you jerk lightning?" Draper asked.

"I beg your pardon?"

Draper smiled. "I asked if you knew telegraphy. Since you didn't understand the term, I can only assume that you don't."

"No, I'm not a telegrapher."

"I thought perhaps you might hire her to help with the new telephone exchange. Back East, a lot of women are handling the calls, and from what I've read, they're doing a good job," Drew suggested.

Draper shook his head. "I'd love to help you out, miss, but I just told Lucy Griffin she could start working a day or two a week. That is, if we ever get all the wires in place."

"Are you getting a lot of subscribers?" Drew asked.

"I'll say. I got so many I'm going to have to start giving 'em numbers just to keep track of 'em all."

"You should do that right from the start anyway, because I know that's how it's done in bigger cities," Drew said.

"That's what old Troy Laundry said, but he just said that 'cause he was the first one to sign up and he wants to be number one. Are you and that partner of yours going to subscribe anytime soon?"

"I think we'll have to, don't you? As a law office, we should have all the modern conveniences."

"Do you want to sign up now?"

"I'd be willing to, but Frank wants to wait a couple of weeks, just to make sure everything works right. Maybe you'll get so many customers you'll need to keep the exchange open at night. Then you could hire Miss Hartmann."

"I'll keep that in mind," Charley said.

"That's all we can ask. Come on, Miss Hartmann, I know a couple of other places we can try."

"Wait," Jana said. "I'd like to send a telegram. What does it cost?"

"Ten cents a word," Draper said.

"Oh, my. That is quite dear." Jana had never sent nor received a telegram before, so she had no idea of the cost. However, she did need to let the Reverend Kling know that she and her sister would be wintering in Bismarck.

"Do you still want to send it?"

"Yes, I suppose so."

Draper gave her a pencil and a piece of paper. "You write out your message, and I'll send it on."

Jana began to write: *My sister and I have arrived safely in Bismarck. When you come to New Salem, please contact us. Jana and Greta Hartmann.*

Draper counted the words. "If you send it like it's written, it'll cost you two dollars and twenty cents. Would you like me to save you some money on your message?"

"Oh, yes, please do."

Draper rewrote the message: *Contact me Bismarck when you reach DT. Jana Hartmann.*

"There you are, miss. The same information for ninety cents instead of two twenty."

Jana read the message and smiled. "Yes. Thank you very much."

"Who is the recipient?"

"Pastor G. L. Kling of the German Evangelical Synod of North America, in Chicago.

"And now if you don't mind, I'd like to send another one. This one is to Mr. Dewey Gehrig in Highland, Illinois."

"Would you like me to write the message for you?"

"No, thank you, I think I got the idea." Jana wrote a second message.

Tell mama safe in Bismarck DT. Jana.

Draper counted the words, then smiled. "That'll do it, and you can send both telegrams for less than the first one would've cost you."

"I do appreciate your help," Jana said, smiling at the kindly telegraph man.

Jana and Drew waited as Draper sent the two messages. After each one, the telegraph key clacked on its own.

"Both messages got through," Draper said with a smile.

"Thank you," Jana said. Then she turned to Drew. "You said you knew some other places we could try?"

"Yes, and I have a good idea where to start."

Greta, Tom McGowan, and the bartender, whose name Greta learned was Carl Meunch, were in a small storeroom just off the saloon.

"I think this would work fine as a kitchen," Tom said. "What about you, Greta?"

"I think it will be fine, as soon as we can get a cookstove in here."

"Oh, that's no problem. We can go see Ollie Beal," Tom said. "He'll give us a good price on a stove, and he'll even deliver it and put it up for us."

"Good," Greta said. "That's the most important thing we'll have to get."

"What about dishes and such? What ya gonna cook in?" Carl asked.

"Greta says we won't need very many," said Tom.

"That's right," Greta said. "If we're only going to serve one thing, all we'll need is a couple of pots, a frying pan, some serving bowls, and an equal number of spoons."

"Don't forget a dishpan, and a water pail. You can't use mine."

"Oh, Carl, since I'm here, maybe I'll wash your glasses, too. Would you mind that?"

Carl smiled. "All right, I'll get the storeroom ready for you."

"I know just the place to buy our supplies," Tom said. "Greta, you go out the front door of the hotel and turn right. About three doors down you'll find a place called Cheap Jake's. Pick out everything you need and have Jake deliver it for us. If we can get everything put together in time, do you think you can fix something for tonight's supper?"

"I'm sure I can. I used to put something on the table in just an hour when my mama was out in the field. I was best at putting together a soup when it seemed like there was nothing in the house to eat. Even my father didn't complain about that."

"That's good to know, because if this hare-brained idea you and Hank cooked up about givin' the food away doesn't work, we may have to resort to stone soup."

FIVE

I t's too bad Charley already hired Lucy.
That would've been a great job for you,"
Drew said as he and Jana left the West-
ern Union office.

"Maybe it's for the best. Did you hear him say
she was only going to work a couple of days a
week? I really need more than that."

Drew smiled at Jana. Somehow this smile, no
more than a friendly smile, connected as it was to
the confident, almost possessive way he had held
her arm, caused her pulse to race.

"Don't worry, we'll find something for you to
do." Drew unconsciously took her hand in his, then
immediately dropped it. "Oh! I'm sorry."

Jana didn't respond. The feel of his hand felt
intimate, if only for a moment. She thought that it
might have been the first time any man had taken
her hand in his, other than in a handshake. In
college, she had been determined to get a degree

as quickly as the school would allow it, so all her time was spent in study. Her responsibilities had always come first, so she had never taken the time to be interested in a man.

"You said you had an idea of where to start looking?" Jana asked so as to break the disquieting connection she was feeling toward this man

"Yes, I do. How about working in a shop? Would you be willing to do something like that?"

"Oh, I don't . . ." Jana started, thinking of the butcher shop where she had worked in Chicago. But no shop in Bismarck could be as bad as that place. "I don't know why not."

"Then I know just the place. I've done some work for Walter Watson, and he's an honest man. He might be a little peculiar though." Drew again flashed a broad smile.

The two walked down Main Street, with Drew speaking to almost everyone they met, until they reached a brick building with a large green sign, upon which, painted in gold, was the name of the establishment: W. B. WATSON, LADIES' EMPORIUM.

The building had a rather large, three-sided bay window in front that projected out onto the boardwalk. A platform was built to elevate a dress form that was draped in a beautiful green silk dress.

"Oh, my." Jana stopped for a moment to look through the window. "I've never seen a dress like that. It's so beautiful."

"It is pretty. Let's go see what Mr. Watson has to say." As Drew opened the door for Jana, a small bell dinged to announce their entry.

"I'll be right with you," a man's voice called out.

"That's all right, Walt, we'll come to you," Drew replied.

In all her life, Jana had never seen so many ready-made women's clothes in one place. Highland had fewer than two thousand people in the whole area, and the one store that handled ready-made clothing never had more than a dozen dresses at any time. Everyone usually stitched her own.

When Drew and Jana found Walter Watson, he was bent over a counter writing something.

"Hello, Drew."

"What are you doing, adding up all your money?" Drew teased.

"No, I'm trying to come up with an advertisement to run in tomorrow's paper. You see all this merchandise?" Walt swept his hand in an arc. "You can barely walk now, and the missus keeps ordering more and more stuff. She says I'll sell it by Christmas, but nobody can find anything in this place."

"Well, I've got the answer for you," Drew said.

"Unless you want to be a hawker on the street corner, I don't know what that answer would be."

"Miss Hartmann, meet Walter Watson. This young lady, who has just arrived from the East, has the answer."

"And what would that be, madam?"

Jana was speechless. She had no idea what Drew had in mind.

"Ah, Mr. Watson," Drew said, holding up his hand, "at the present time, my client isn't at liberty to tell you, but I can assure you that your stock will be greatly reduced by Christmas if you'll consent to hire her."

"Oh, Drew, I don't know. I'm spending all my money on inventory. I'm afraid I can't afford a salesgirl."

"It's your loss, Walt. Come on, Jana," Drew said, taking Jana's arm and turning toward the door. "Let's go down to Sig Hanauer's establishment. I thought Mr. Watson would be more receptive to your talents, but perhaps he is not."

"Wait just a minute. What are you telling me she can do?"

"First, will you hire the young woman?"

Walter expelled a long sigh. "I'll hire her."

"How much will you pay?"

"Not much, I'm afraid. Would you take ten dollars a week?"

"Walter! That's an insult," Drew said. "She needs at least twenty dollars a week and a percentage of whatever she sells, say two percent."

"All right, all right, but it's only till Christmas."

"You won't be sorry. She'll start tomorrow."

"Thank you, Mr. Watson. I appreciate the opportunity to work with such beautiful clothing."

"Humph. Twenty dollars a week. We'll see what you can do."

"Good day, Walter." Drew took Jana by the arm and escorted her out of the store.

"Whew," Jana exclaimed when they got outside. "I'll bet you're a very persuasive lawyer. I feel sorry for poor Mr. Watson."

"Why? He needs to clear that store out. He's got so much stuff in there, no one can find anything."

"But twenty dollars a week. That's twice the amount I made teaching school!"

"Welcome to the frontier, my friend. We're used to paying higher prices for everything."

Jana's arm was still snugly hooked over Drew's, and she didn't try to withdraw it as they walked along together.

"Mr. Malone, I can't thank you enough. I couldn't have gotten a job today without you."

"Mr. Malone, is it? Didn't you hear? You're my client." Drew flashed another devastating smile. "Please, from now on when I see you, call me Drew. Now, may I walk you to your abode?"

"That's not necessary. I'm just around the corner at the hotel."

"At the Sheridan House?"

"No, at the Custer."

The expression on Drew's face changed suddenly, as he dropped her arm. "Where are you staying?"

"At the Custer Hotel. Why? Is there something wrong with that?"

"I've never known a woman to stay there. That's for railroad workers and transient army officers. It's not a place for a woman."

"For the rest of this week, it's the place for two women. Mr. McGowan has gone out of his way to accommodate my sister and me. Again, I can't thank you enough for what you have done for me today. Good day, Mr. Malone."

Jana turned to walk away from him, but he caught her hand. "You've forgotten already. It's Drew."

He held her hand for a moment, a moment like none other Jana had ever experienced. The day was chilled, and his hand and fingers were cold.

Or were they?

Oddly, she felt a strange heat diffusing through her body. She looked at him with a questioning expression on her face, and she thought she could read something in his eyes, a sense of connection that was beyond verbal. Finally, after a time that stretched out for an eternity, but ended much too quickly, he withdrew his hand and touched his fingers to his hat as if in salute. "I'd better be going," he said as, with a final smile, he turned to leave. "Oh, buy some gloves tomorrow. Dakota nights get pretty cold."

"Greta, I've got a . . ." Jana stopped in midsentence as she looked around the room and saw no one was there. She checked to see if Greta had left her a note, but there was no note anywhere.

"I told her to stay here," Jana mumbled as she hurried down the stairs and across the lobby.

"Hold on there, little lady, where're you goin' so fast?" an older man who was sitting in the lobby called out. A couple of the others laughed.

With her cheeks flaming in embarrassment, Jana slowed down, but continued to walk purposefully and with long strides to the front desk.

No one was at the desk, but a small bell could be rung by slapping the palm of your hand against it, which she did.

"Mr. McGowan!" she called out while hitting the bell again and again.

McGowan came from a side room and, see-ing her, smiled. "Miss Hartmann, have you had a pleasant day in the banner city?"

"Mr. McGowan, my sister is gone. Have you seen her?"

"Greta hasn't gone anywhere. She's back in the kitchen cookin' up a stew for supper."

It did not escape Jana's attention that McGowan had called Greta by her first name. But what most got her attention was what he said.

"In the kitchen? What kitchen? You say she's cooking?"

"Maybe you'd better let Greta tell you herself." McGowan pointed toward the door that led into the saloon. "She's in there."

"My sister is in the saloon?"

"Yes, ma'am. She's been there all afternoon."

"What?" Jana gasped.

Spinning away from the desk before McGowan could say another word to her, Jana hurried across the lobby and through the door into the saloon. Unlike this morning when she had looked in, the saloon was now filled with men. Some were playing cards, several were smoking, most were drinking, and all were conversing, as the room rang with their voices, occasionally punctuated by laughter.

"Hello, miss," a man called from one of the tables. Standing, he pulled out a chair. "Won't you join us?"

"No, thank you," Jana said, though she didn't say the words harshly. She looked around the room to see if she could locate Greta, but didn't see her. Then she walked up to the bar.

The bartender came down toward her. "You must be Miss Hartmann."

"Yes, how do you know?"

"Greta told me you'd be in here lookin' for her."

"Where is she?" Jana asked anxiously. "Where's my sister?"

"I'll show you. She's back here." The bartender walked down the length of the bar.

Jana was aware of scores of eyes on her as she traversed the length of the bar. When she got to the far end, the bartender walked over to a door and pushed it open. "Here she is."

Jana stepped in through the door and saw Greta peeling potatoes.

"Greta! What are you doing?"

Turning, Greta greeted Jana with a big smile. "I've got a job, Jana!" she said excitedly. "Every day I'll make a pot of soup or stew, and Carl will serve it to his customers."

"Carl?"

"Yes, Carl, the bartender."

"You've never cooked for this many people," Jana began to protest.

"No, but I always cooked for our family while you and Mama were out working, so how hard can it be to cook for a few more?"

"I admire your confidence, but believe me, cooking for four people and cooking for a crowd of hungry men is a lot different."

"Mama always said she liked my cooking, and now I've made up my mind to be the best cook the Custer Hotel has ever had."

Jana got a challenging expression on her face.

"I'm under the impression that the Custer Hotel has never had a cook before."

"Then it won't be hard for me to be the best they've ever had, will it?" Greta questioned, and they both laughed.

Jana went over to sniff the large kettle that sat on the stove.

"Doesn't the meat smell good? It's elk," Greta said. "I've never tasted elk before, so I'm anxious to see what it's like. I put in some potatoes, and some carrots and onions and I've got some turnips, but I don't think I should put them in. What do you think?"

"I—no, I wouldn't put turnips in. Greta, how'd you get this job?"

"It was easy. When I came down to go to the restaurant you told me about, I found out it was a saloon. I told Tom he was missing out on business by not having food in this place, so he asked me if I would cook if he fixed a kitchen. When I said yes, we went right over to Ollie's store and bought a stove, and then Cheap Jake's brought the pots and pans and all the dishes we'll need."

"My gosh, Greta, it didn't take you long to get acquainted."

"You'll never guess what else has happened. Tom says we can stay here for free as long as I cook. Isn't that wonderful? Oh, he's going to give my soup to everybody for free, so that means we can eat free, too."

Jana listened to her sister and had to admit she was divided as to how she felt. Part of her wanted to scold Greta for doing something like this without even consulting her. But Greta was so proud of what she had done that Jana couldn't find it in her heart to scold her in any way. And if they had a place to stay for free and their meals were furnished, too, it would make it easier to save money for when they began their homestead. She smiled at her little sister.

"I'm proud of you, Greta."

"Oh, I'm so glad," Greta said, relieved that her sister agreed with what she had done. "I didn't know how you would take it."

"You did the right thing."

"You can take your time finding just the right job because now we won't be spending our money for anything."

"I already have a job. I got it today."

"You did? Why didn't you tell me?"

Jana laughed. "When could I have told you? You're so excited."

"I am excited. Will you be teaching school?"

"No, all the positions are filled for this year. Starting tomorrow, I'll be working at Watson's Ladies' Emporium. Greta, you have to see the dresses in this store. They're the most beautiful dresses I've ever seen."

"Oh, Jana," Greta said, her expression growing serious, "what will you wear?"

"Oh, my." Jana put her hand to her mouth. "I hadn't even thought of that. Right now we only have four dresses between us. Until I figure out something, we'll just have to share our clothes."

"You'll come up with something, I know you will. You're so smart." Greta brushed a fall of hair back from her forehead. "I think it was a good idea for us to leave home and come out here, don't you?"

Jana chuckled. "Yes, I do, but I certainly can't take credit for it. It was Mama's idea that we leave home, and it was your idea that we come out here. But I agree. It was a wonderful idea."

"Oh, poor Mama. She has no idea where we are."

"Yes, she does."

"She does? How does she know?"

"I sent her a telegram."

"Oh, Jana, if Papa finds out . . ." Greta let the sentence hang, uncompleted.

"I didn't send it directly to Mama. I sent it to Mr. Gehrig."

Greta smiled. "Yes, that was a good idea. He'll know what to do, and I'm so glad Mama won't be worried."

"Daddy!" Sam and Benji yelled as Drew stepped into the house. Drew returned their greetings.

"Have they been behaving themselves, Elfrieda?"

"Yes, sir, Mr. Malone, they've been very good."

Drew smiled at the two boys. "Good. That makes me very proud."

"Daddy, do you know how many states there are?" Sam asked.

"No, how many states are there?"

"There are thirty-eight," Sam said proudly. "If we become a state, we'll be number thirty-nine."

"Oh? How do you know that?"

"I learned it in school," Sam said.

Drew reached out and rubbed the top of Sam's head. "Well, you're learning so much in school that pretty soon you'll be smarter than I am. Then what will I do?"

"You'll just have to ask me questions when there's something you don't know," Sam said with a broad smile.

"I suppose I will."

"You boys go wash up for supper," Elfrieda said.

Sam went off to do Elfrieda's bidding, but Benji didn't move.

"Oh, Mrs. Considine, look, I didn't get my hands very dirty today." Benji held them out for her inspection. "Don't you think they're clean enough for supper?"

"Hmm, you're right," Elfrieda said, examining them. "They do look clean enough for supper. But they aren't clean enough for the apple pie I made for dessert."

"I'll wash 'em," Benji said, running to the washbasin.

"How was your day, Mr. Malone?" Elfrieda asked.

"It was—interesting," Drew replied without further explanation.

As Drew sat by his hearth after dinner, he couldn't get Jana Hartmann out of his mind. Elfrieda's question had stayed with him through the meal. Jana was attractive, yes, but other pretty women were in Bismarck, and in Burleigh County. He had met many of them, most often as a result of Frank Allen's none-too-subtle attempts to find a wife for him.

But Drew was definitely not looking for a wife. He didn't need a woman for his children; Elfrieda was taking care of that for him. If he took on a wife now, it would simply complicate things. So, if he didn't find Jana interesting as a possible spouse, what did so arouse his interest and curiosity?

Ha! Drew thought. That was it. He was curious, that and nothing more.

What sort of woman, who was clearly as educated as she was, would want to come to Dakota to homestead? Was this story about going to New Salem with a preacher the truth? And if it was, why was she staying at the Custer Hotel? Something just didn't seem to ring true about Jana Hartmann. He would find out more about her. After all, how else could he satisfy his curiosity?

She had said she was in a hurry to leave Chicago. Why the hurry? And if she really was joining this German church group, why didn't she wait until the whole group came? Two women coming alone to spend the winter? That seemed unlikely, unless they were running away from a husband or the law.

Then, an unbidden thought came to his mind. What if the two women were prostitutes? Was Jana Hartmann a prostitute? She didn't act like one. She hadn't flirted with him, and she had certainly handled Jason Richards with integrity.

But then, she was staying at the Custer. Why would she be staying there, of all places? Women simply didn't stay at the Custer Hotel. Yes, he was curious about this woman, and he was determined he would find out more about her. After all, wouldn't any good lawyer want to find out about a new citizen of the town?

As Jana lay in bed that night, she thought back over her day and smiled. Her first day in Bismarck had been busy. Both she and Greta had gotten jobs, she had seen much of the town, and she had met Mr. Drew Malone.

How did that thought get in there? she wondered. He wasn't the only person she'd met today. She'd met Frank Allen, Jason Richards, Charles Draper, and Walter Watson. And Walter Watson was certainly the most important person she met today, because he was to be her employer.

But as she drifted off to sleep, the last image of which she was aware was not of Walter Watson. It was the smiling eyes of Drew Malone.

SIX

The next morning, Jana donned the best of the four dresses she and Greta had brought with them, a high-necked wool navy with a removable white lace collar. She pulled her long, ash-blond hair straight back, coiling it into a knot at the back of her head. When she left the hotel, she thought she epitomized the matronly store clerk who would not offend anyone who came into the store.

She arrived at the emporium at exactly nine o'clock. Before opening the door, she took a deep breath. This was not like teaching a group of children who were eager to listen to every word she told them. In this job you had to convince women to buy dresses or shoes or accessories that were undoubtedly quite expensive. And Drew Malone had insisted that she was just the person who could sell the mounds of clothing that Mr. Watson had in his store.

Jana was nervous, but then she smiled when

she thought of Greta. Greta, the cook, and Jana, the saleslady.

She opened the door, listening to the tinkling of the bell.

"Your first day, and you're late, Miss Hartmann," Mr. Watson said sternly.

"Oh, sir, I'm sorry. You didn't say what time to come."

"The sign says 'open at eight.'" Mr. Watson went to the counter at the back of the store and pulled out a sign from under some papers.

"I didn't see it, sir. I'll be here at eight tomorrow morning."

"That will depend on how much you sell today. And I can tell you right now, it won't be much."

"Why do you say that?"

"Look at you. You look like a schoolmarm."

Jana's eyebrows lifted at Mr. Watson's comment. "Is there something wrong with a schoolmarm?"

"Of course not, in a schoolroom. But this isn't a schoolroom, Miss Hartmann. This is a ladies' emporium. The ladies who come into this store want to see someone who appreciates the merchandise, someone who wears the clothing I sell."

"Sir, I will tell you right now, I cannot afford the clothing you sell. But I have an idea. If you will allow me to wear one of your dresses, for say an hour, then perhaps when a woman comes in, she will see me wearing the dress and want to buy it."

"Now, why would I . . . ?" Watson stopped in midsentence and looked at Jana. "Turn around slowly."

"I beg your pardon?"

"Turn around, turn around." Watson made a circular motion with his finger. As she did so, he looked at her as if he were buying a horse. "I think that is probably a pretty good idea, Miss Hartmann, but I'm wondering, how you will get the women to come into the store?"

"You have a mannequin in your window. What if I put the dress I am wearing on the mannequin?"

"No, that won't work, you'll spend all your time dressing the mannequin. I know." He smiled and held up his finger. "We'll have a living mannequin. Miss Hartmann, *you* will stand in the window."

"What? No, I can't do that! Why, that's perfectly scandalous!"

"Why? What's the difference between wearing the dress in the store or wearing it in the window? The way I see it, there *is* no difference. Except that, if you are standing in the window, more people will see you, and that might bring them into the store."

"Mr. Watson . . . I think I'd better find another job."

"No, now wait a minute. This was your idea and it's a very good one. We'll have you stand in the window for fifteen minutes. Then you come in and help any customer who might want the dress you're wearing. The next hour you'll put on another dress and do it again. Will you try it for today?"

"All right, but I'll only stand in the window for ten minutes," Jana said, thinking that this was most certainly *not* her idea.

Mr. Watson smiled broadly. "That'll be fine, but

if that's the case, I get to choose the dress you'll wear. And one other thing: do something else with your hair."

What had Jana gotten herself into? Had she actually just agreed to stand in a window in order to sell something? At least she was trying to sell clothing, not herself. She had read English novels where the heroine, an illicit woman perhaps, would find herself in a window offering herself to the highest bidder, and then the handsome prince would ride by in his elegant carriage and, seeing her exquisite beauty, would whisk her away to his castle, where she became his princess and the two lived happily ever after.

Jana laughed. Perhaps a prince would see her and take her away to his ten-by-twelve-foot sod shack where he was proving up his homestead. Then she wouldn't have to go to New Salem.

The dress that Mr. Watson had selected for her was by far the finest garment she had ever worn. The slate-gray velvet walking suit was trimmed in red cashmere frieze. The jacket had long coattails in the back and short points at the waist in front. The frieze, with its soft fiber curls, was gathered at the neck and then topped with a gray velvet collar. She had used wire hair rolls to help her arrange her hair in puffs, and when she put on a red hat with dyed red feathers and red kid gloves, she had to admit the ensemble was beautiful.

When she stepped out of the dressing room, Mr. Watson's face displayed his approval.

"Jana, it's perfect. If this doesn't sell clothes, I

don't know what will. I put a chair in the window, for you to steady yourself, but I don't want you to sit down. We can't get any wrinkles."

"All right." Jana walked toward the front of the store and stepped up onto the window ledge. She placed her hand on the back of the chair and stood as still as she could.

The first person who passed by the store didn't even glance toward the window, but the next person was an elderly man who was shuffling along leaning on a cane. When he came to Jana's window, he stopped. Then he began to rap on the window, trying to get her attention, but she stood as still as she could. Within a minute, he was joined by a small crowd of men.

Standing across the street, leaning casually against a post, Jana saw Drew Malone. He was grinning the way she imagined the Cheshire cat grinned in *Alice's Adventures in Wonderland*, a book she had read to her students. Although she had not acknowledged any other gentleman who had stood in front of the window, she met his gaze directly and smiled discreetly as she nodded her head in his direction. In response, he tipped his hat and walked away.

For the rest of the day, Jana changed outfits every hour and got back in the window for ten minutes, before coming back into the store as a salesclerk. The crowds grew larger both outside and in the store. Also, and this was important, women began to be a part of the crowd.

Before the end of the day, Jana had sold eleven dresses, ranging in price from $3.50 all the way up to one gown that cost $14. The store brought in $96 that day, which was more than Watson had made for the entire week, up until this date. "This is wonderful," Mr. Watson said. "I've never had anything that created so much attention. But don't expect sales to be this brisk tomorrow."

"Why do you say that?"

"Because today is Election Day and all the folks will be caught up in that frenzy. No, I'm afraid tomorrow will be a dead day for sales."

"We'll just have to choose some of your most spectacular dresses to entice customers to come in tomorrow," Jana said.

"I tell you, they won't be up this way. Everybody will be hanging around the courthouse tonight, waiting to see if this Citizens' Ticket Colonel Lounsberry is pushing is going to win. They'll all be tuckered out tomorrow."

Jana was quiet for a moment, then said, "What if the dresses went to where the people are? Rather than standing in the window for ten minutes, why couldn't I walk down to the courthouse and mingle with the people who are there?"

"That would be fine, but how would they know the dresses were from the Emporium?"

"Promotion, Mr. Watson. Promotion. Everybody loves a sale. We could offer a discount for any dress sold between Wednesday and Saturday of this week. Have some cards printed up that would have to be brought to the store to get the ten percent off or whatever amount you choose to give. Maybe we could even have a jar with lots of cards in it and one would be as high as fifty percent off. That way people could draw their own discount. I know I would want to come to your store if I thought there was a chance I could get a new Christmas dress at half price."

Mr. Watson was smiling broadly. "Remind me to buy a big steak dinner for Drew Malone. You, my dear, are a born merchandiser. Take care of the store while I run down to the *Tribune* office to have some cards printed up. When I come back, you can start wandering around, but I expect you'll do the most good tonight, when they start posting the returns."

"What time do you think the biggest crowd will be there?"

"Around ten o'clock I would say. By then most of the vote counting will be done."

"Will you be at the courthouse?"

"Of course, everybody will be there."

"You know, I'm looking forward to this. It sounds exciting," Jana said.

"Oh, it is." Watson picked out another dress and held it out for her to see. "And this is the dress I want you to wear tonight."

"I couldn't wear that one. It's too beautiful. If there's a big crowd, what if someone spilled something on the dress? Then we wouldn't be able to sell it."

"Jana, I don't intend to sell the dress you'll wear tonight. It's yours."

"Mine?" Jana asked, as if not sure she had heard him correctly.

"Yes. You've done such a good job, you've earned it."

"Thank you, sir." Tears glistened in Jana's eyes.

"Did you vote?" Clement Lounsberry called to Drew as he passed by the *Tribune* office.

"Of course I voted. It looks like we had a big turnout, thanks to all the hard work you've done. Tell me, Clem, do you think the Citizens' Ticket has a chance of winning? I mean, you are going up against the establishment."

"Yes, I do. And it'll be thanks to the registry law you drew up. A riverboat landed down at the river this morning—all her passengers thought they were going to get to vote, just like the last time. You remember two years ago when the crew of the *Butte* voted at the landing and then some of them voted in all three wards?"

"Yes, of course I remember."

Lounsberry chuckled. "Well, that didn't work for them this time. I think both the Democrats and the Republicans are going to be in for a rude awakening come tomorrow morning when they're all out of a job."

"I hope you're right, Colonel, but a lot of money has changed hands. It just depends on how fed up the citizens of Bismarck are with all the chicanery that's been going on around here."

"Will you be at the courthouse watching the returns tonight?" Lounsberry asked.

"If I can get the boys settled down and in bed in time, I'll be there."

"I thought you hired Mrs. Considine to take care of those boys."

"I did, and she's doing a pretty good job with them, but I try to spend as much time as I can with them. You know Sam's in school now, and I try to listen to him read every night."

"Is young Sam doing all right? I mean, everybody was so worried about him after . . ."

"He's doing his best. He's talking again, and that's good."

"Frank's right you know. You need to find—"

"Oh, no, not you, too." Drew chuckled.

"It never hurts to look. That's all I have to say. I'll see you tonight."

"I'll be there."

Drew usually walked all the way down Main Street, turning over on Eighth Street to get to his home on Thayer, thus avoiding the spot where Addie had been killed, but tonight for some reason he went up Fifth, then turned down Meiggs, the street that passed by the Custer Hotel.

He smiled as he passed the hotel, and his mind wandered to Jana Hartmann. It pleased him that she had broken her pose for him when he had watched her tableau in the window this morning. When he met her in the Sheridan House, he had thought she was an attractive woman, but seeing her dressed in the latest fashions with her hair artfully arranged, he had thought she was more than attractive. She was beautiful.

A goodly number of his fellow citizens apparently agreed with him. Several times throughout the day he had looked down the street toward Watson's Emporium, and every time he looked, he had seen a crowd gathered in front of the window, fully as many men as women.

And why not? The beautiful and stylish dresses, Drew had to admit, were somewhat daring. Watching her bravery and good humor today, he had felt a strong attraction toward her, but he didn't know what to think about that attraction. It seemed sexual, as if to a wanton woman. But was he being unfair?

No, it wasn't just her physical appearance that drew him to her. She was a spunky lady; she'd showed him that in the way she'd reacted to Jason Richards's attempt to buy her vote at the Sheridan yesterday at lunch. She also had a good sense of humor; he could see that today, by the way she was reacting to the people who had gathered around Watson's store window.

Many people would be intimidated when they were the center of attention, but Jana's smiles, body posture, facial expressions, and eye movements showed her to be at ease with herself. That was a most admirable trait.

As Drew approached the Custer, he slowed his pace and looked into the lobby. He didn't see Jana, or anyone else, not even Tom McGowan. At just that moment, two gentlemen left the bar and came out onto the street.

"I don't know how Tom can make money doin' that, but I'll be coming back tomorrow, sure thing," one man said.

"Good eats at the Custer—and for free—that'll bring more people to the bar."

"That stew was right tasty, and that little ole gal they got cookin', why she's a sweetheart, don't ya know. A pretty little thing, too."

The two men, who were not in any way drunk, crossed the street and Drew could no longer hear their conversation. He wondered who the "little ole gal" was, but he had a pretty good guess. Maybe he would have to stop by the Custer some evening and sample the free food.

Shaking his head at his own folly, he hurried on home to spend some time with the boys before he put them to bed.

Returning to the hotel that evening, Jana took Mr. Watson's package up to the room, then changed into a plain skirt and waist, before going down to the saloon to check on Greta. When she walked in, Greta was standing behind a table, ladling out dippers of stew from a black kettle. Just then, Tom McGowan came from the little kitchen carrying another kettle.

"Hi, Jana, have you tasted your sister's stew yet?"

"No, but I'd love to."

"You'd better get a bowl quick. I thought Greta was making way too much, but it's going like hot-cakes. When this pot's gone, it's gone," Tom said.

"It's that good?"

"It is now." Tom smiled. "Carl and me, why, we talked her into putting in a lot more black pepper than she was using, and this pot's got a whole bottle of red-pepper sauce. It's dang good, if I do say so myself."

Jana laughed. "You're scaring me, Tom. I'm not sure I want to taste this stuff."

Just then, Greta saw Jana, and a wide smile crossed her face. Jana thought she had never seen her sister look happier.

"Why don't you two go on back to the kitchen and sit a spell? I'll do the serving," Tom said.

"All right, thank you, Tom," Greta said. "Come on, Jana, I haven't eaten yet either." Greta ladled two bowls from the pot, and the sisters went to the little room behind the bar.

"I'm so tired, but it's a good tired," Greta said when she almost fell into a chair sitting beside a small table.

"You're sure this work isn't too hard for you?" Jana sat down beside her sister. She lifted a spoonful of the stew to her mouth and blew on it gently as Greta eagerly awaited her reaction. "Greta, this is good! I knew you could cook, but I didn't know you could cook this well."

"I didn't know it either," Greta replied with a big, proud smile. "But I can, and, oh, Jana, I actually enjoy it."

After the last of the stew was served to the saloon patrons, Jana helped Greta tidy up the kitchen. After the sisters washed and dried the bowls and spoons, Jana practically dragged Greta to their room.

"I've got to go get dressed," Jana said.

"Get dressed? For what?"

"I'm going down to the courthouse tonight for my job. Why don't you come with me? Mr. Watson says everyone will be there watching the election returns, and I'm going to be passing out discount cards to get customers to come to the store."

"He's making you work that late?"

"Oh, no, it's not him. This was my idea. I want him to think his store can't get along without me."

Jana untied the package Mr. Watson had given her and removed a beautiful outfit.

"This is absolutely gorgeous," Greta said as she picked up the dress. "Wouldn't you love to have a dress like this?"

"It is mine, can you believe it? Mr. Watson gave it to me."

"He gave it to you?"

"Yes, he did, so you can wear it, too. But right now, I need you to help me get into it." Jana removed her clothing.

The dress was an orange-tinted satin with a plush green velvet collar. The bodice had insets of silk folds that were embroidered with gold lace and green chenille. Contrasting with the tinted satin were shaped panels of the green velvet in both the sleeves and the skirt. Then in the back, Greta carefully arranged the heavy drapery so that the orange satin foot plaiting still showed.

"You certainly won't need a coat tonight," Greta said as she placed a green-lace-and-feather hat on Jana's head. "Mama could make three dresses out of the material that's in this one dress."

"I know. And to think that today I've had on seven outfits that are just as fine as this one."

"Seven! What do you do at that store?"

"Let me show you what I do. I stand in the window, and I do this." Jana began striking poses, making each new pose more extreme than the one before until she had Greta laughing so hard that tears were coming. But soon the laughter turned to wheezing and coughing spasms.

"Oh, Greta, I'm sorry." Jana got a cool cloth from the washbasin and began to wipe Greta's brow. "This is the first time I've heard you cough since we've come to Dakota."

"I think you're right. It must be the climate." Greta began to take deep breaths and the coughing began to subside. "It was worth it, though, because it was so good to laugh. But I think I'll lie down for a while. You go on to the courthouse and I'll stay here and rest."

"All right, but I'm going to tell Tom that you aren't feeling well, so he can check in on you."

"Please don't tell him. If he thinks I'm sick, he may not want me to be cooking."

"I understand." Jana stood at the door looking back at her sister, who looked so pale against the white sheet of their bed. "I don't know when I'll be back. Mr. Watson said they really don't know anything until about ten o'clock."

"I'm fine. Really. And, Jana, you look beautiful."

SEVEN

When Jana arrived at the courthouse at a little before ten o'clock, a small number of people had already assembled. She searched the crowd looking for Mr. Watson and found him standing on the courthouse steps.

"There you are. I was beginning to think you might have changed your mind."

"Oh, no, I just know we're going to sell a lot of clothes tonight. How can we not, when they see this beautiful dress?"

"Well, let's just see how good of an advertisement it is. There aren't many people right now, but when the band gets here, the excitement will step up."

"There'll be a band?"

"Oh, yes, indeed, the band that plays at Whitney's Opera House will be here soon. So when it does, you just start circulating and passing out those cards."

"Yes, sir."

"Oh, I saw you in the window today," a young woman who introduced herself as Mary Clark said, when Jana approached her. "And I thought what a clever way to advertise new dresses. I talked Mr. Clark into going into the store with me." Mary laughed. "He said if the dress would look as good on me as it did on you, he would buy it."

"Well, I'm sure it would. Did he buy it for you?"

The woman tittered demurely as she looked down. "Yes, he did."

"That's wonderful, and here is a way to save Mr. Clark some money. If you bring this card in by Saturday, Mr. Watson is giving a sale price on anything you buy."

"Oh, how wonderful!" Mary said enthusiastically.

Several of the other women who were standing nearby heard Jana's comment, and they asked for cards as well. Many had seen her in the window, and Jana felt a bit like stage actresses must feel when they are greeted by people they don't know. Although she would never have thought so, she was actually rather enjoying the attention, and the idea that she might even be selling more of Mr. Watson's dresses.

"My friends!" a man shouted, climbing up to the top of the steps in front of the courthouse. He stretched his hands out toward the crowd. "My friends!"

"What are you doing up there, Colonel Lounsberry?" someone called out to him. "It's a little late for speechifying, ain't it? The polls has all done closed."

The others in the crowd laughed, but someone shouted, "Let the colonel speak!"

Jana recognized the latter as Frank Allen, Drew Malone's law partner.

"My friends," Lounsberry began, "not all the results are yet in, but the early indications are that the people of Burleigh County aren't going to allow claptrap politics any longer. Two or three men didn't buy the vote this time. Not McLean, not Stoyell, not Griffin, not Richards—nobody but the people, irrespective of nationality or party, have the right to choose who shall serve them, and knowing their rights, they dare maintain them!"

Lounsberry literally shouted the last few words, and they were met by loud cheers and hurrahs from those gathered.

"I think we owe a debt of gratitude to Charles Healey and John Foley for the most excellent work they have done at the polls in the interest of the citizens' cause. They were ever on the alert, working from early this morning until tonight in our cause. They deserve every consideration, and the time may well come when this appreciation will be shown."

Again there were cheers.

"But the evening has just begun. There will be dancing in the streets tonight as the people of Bismarck take back their town—not with violence, but with the ballot box!"

"Good evening," Drew Malone said as he stepped

up beside Jana, who was standing near the back of the gathering.

"Drew," Jana replied with a big smile.

"I just got here. Has your friend Mr. Richards been defeated yet?"

Jana chuckled. "I checked his numbers, and so far, it looks bad for him."

"Let's hope the numbers hold up, not only against him, but against all the others who are just as corrupt as he is."

Just then the returns for the Galloway Precinct were posted, and a loud cheer went up.

"Ladies and gentlemen, let the music begin," a man said as he climbed up beside the slate board and pointed toward a band that had just come up. Immediately, the musicians began playing a rousing polka, and the dancing started.

Offering his arm to Jana, Drew asked, "May I have this dance with you, madam?"

"Yes, sir, but you may be sorry."

"And why do you say that?"

"Because I'm not that good of a dancer. In order to get the steps right for the polka, I have to say, 'Hippety-hop, to the barbershop, to buy a stick of candy.'"

"'One for you and one for me, and one for sister Mandy,'" Drew said, finishing the children's rhyme.

Jana stopped and stared at Drew. "How did you know what comes next?"

"I just know." Drew pulled Jana to him and once more started the fast-moving dance.

Drew felt guilty for not telling Jana about Sam and Benji. That would have been the perfect moment to mention that he read such verses to his children every night, but he didn't say a word. For the first time in two years he felt something for a woman, this woman. He liked that she had not tried to flirt with him, as did so many of the local women, who considered him to be one of the most eligible prospective husbands in town. Jana and he had spent practically the whole day together the day before, and she had impressed him not only by her intelligence, but by her persona. She was not flighty, as were so many of the young women he knew, but neither was she a boring stuffed shirt. She seemed to find just the right balance between the two extremes.

But he didn't want to tell her about the boys. Not yet, because he'd had more than a few women trying to get to him by buying presents for the boys. He would wait until he knew Jana better.

A man appeared at the board and wrote in some more numbers, adjusting the vote totals, and once more the totals were met with cheers from a crowd that now numbered at least two hundred Burleigh County residents. This time there was much backslapping and hugging as it appeared that the Citizens' Ticket was going to win.

In his exuberance, Drew grabbed Jana and pulled her to him in a big bear hug.

At first Jana was taken aback by Drew's action, but she saw that nearly every woman around her was being hugged by someone, so certainly nobody was paying any attention to them.

Drew pulled away quickly. "Oh, excuse me. I'm so sorry. I shouldn't have done that."

Jana adjusted her hat and then smiled. "No harm done. Anyway, hugging seems to be the thing to do tonight."

Drew looked around at the others around them, then brought his gaze back to Jana. "It just shows what a . . ." He stopped in midsentence. This woman was standing just inches away from him. Her eyes were shining bright as they reflected the twinkle of the many gaslights that had been strung for the occasion. But it was her lips—full, teasing lips—that looked so inviting. He lowered his head to hers. He knew he was going to kiss her, right here on Thayer Street, in front of the courthouse, in front of everybody.

"Drew. Drew, come over here for a moment. I want you to shake hands with our new justice of the peace," Frank Allen called.

"Uh . . . I'd better . . ." Drew turned quickly and walked over to his partner.

Jana was left staring after Drew. What had just happened? If she didn't know better, she would have thought Drew was about to kiss her. What did she mean, if she didn't know better? What was her experience with kissing? Jackie Schuler out behind the barn the summer she turned eleven? That was it.

"Hello, Jana, how are you doing?" Mr. Watson asked as he stepped up beside Jana. "Are you getting rid of your cards?"

"Yes, sir. I only have a few left," Jana said as she turned her attention away from Drew.

"I have to confess, this was a wonderful idea you had about tonight. Do you see that woman over there?" Mr. Watson pointed toward an attractive woman who was dressed exquisitely. "She is one of my best customers. See to it that she gets a card. In fact, give her two or three cards."

"She must be a special lady. What's her name?"

"Elizabeth McClellan, and she is special." Mr. Watson tipped his hat toward the woman and turned away.

Jana made her way through the crowd until she reached the woman. She was at least a head shorter than Jana, but up close she was even more attractive than she had been from afar. The lady seemed to be wearing makeup, but not the garish sort worn by theater people. "Elizabeth McClellan?" Jana asked, not knowing if she was a miss or Mrs.

"Yes, and you must be Jana Hartmann."

"I am. But how did you know my name?"

"My dear, just as you knew my name. I make it my business to know the name of any beautiful young woman who appears in Bismarck. I hear you are decorating Walter's window."

Jana laughed. "I guess you could say that. I'm not used to standing in windows and having people look at me, but it's actually sort of fun getting to wear all the beautiful clothes that Mr. Watson has for sale."

"You did a good job. Several of my . . . associates were the recipients of some of the clothes that you sold today, and we thank you."

"Oh, that reminds me. Mr. Watson asked me to give you several of these cards." Jana handed her a half dozen. "If you bring these into the store by Saturday, you get a discount."

The lady smiled as she put the cards in her reticule.

"You don't know who I am, do you?"

"If you're someone other than Elizabeth McClellan, no, I don't know."

"I'm known by another name." Elizabeth withdrew a calling card from her purse and handed it to Jana.

Jana looked at it, but it had no writing. It was a playing card, the two of spades. Jana looked quizzically at the woman.

"The deuce of spades is known as the 'little casino,' and that's what some folks call me. If you get into any kind of trouble, you come find me and I'll help you. My place of business is on the other side of the train tracks. You'll know which one it is because you'll see this card on my sign. Good night, Jana."

"Good night, Elizabeth, and thank you." Jana watched as the attractive, but rather mysterious, woman slipped into the crowd and disappeared.

After meeting with Frank and Hugh McDonald, the new justice of the peace, Drew was anxious to find Jana. She wasn't where he had left her, and he looked through the crowd until at last he saw her. But he didn't like what he saw.

Jana Hartmann, a woman he had thought might be someone he could care for, was talking to Little Casino. Respectable women didn't talk to the madam. He watched Jana pass something to Little Casino, and in turn Little Casino gave something to Jana. What was this? Surely Jana wasn't trying to go "on the line" at Little Casino's house of prostitution . . .

Or was she?

After Elizabeth McClellan left, Jana looked around for Drew, finding him in a group of men who were laughing and talking. She was sure the men were discussing the results of the election, since many of the races were now decided. She continued to hand out her cards.

Jana stayed around the courthouse until nearly one in the morning, and by that time most of the women had left. She was hoping that she would have a chance to speak to Drew again, but in all that time he never returned to talk to her. On the few occasions when Jana located him in the crowd, she tried to make eye contact with him, but when she may have caught his eye, it seemed as if he purposely looked away. It was almost as if Drew was avoiding her.

But why? What had she done?

Jana had never had any kind of relationship, not even a real friendship with a man, so she had no idea what she might have done to put him off. She could have sworn that Drew Malone was about to kiss her just before Frank called him away. But now he wouldn't come near her; he wouldn't even look at her. She wished she had a better understanding of courtship.

Jana felt her cheeks flame. *Courtship?* Why would she call this a courtship? She was definitely making assumptions unwarranted by the facts. Anyway, it was time she returned to the hotel. Tomorrow was a workday and she didn't want to make the mistake of arriving late, as she had today.

As she walked down the dimly lit street to the Custer Hotel, she experienced an eerie feeling. She didn't pass a single person, yet, just a couple of blocks behind her, she could hear the raucous celebration continuing. The band was playing, fireworks were exploding, and the din of the crowd was growing louder and louder. She was glad when she reached the hotel.

When she stepped into the lobby, she was surprised to see that two old gentlemen were playing cards.

"Good evening," she said. "Or, perhaps I should say, good morning."

"It's about time you got home, missy," one of them said in a gruff voice.

"Oh, I'm sorry. Were you waiting for me?"

"You bet. It's our job to close up and turn off the lights, 'cause you're not stayin' at just any hotel. We watch out for one another, and you're one of us now. We gotta take care of you and that little sister of yours."

Jana smiled. "That's good to know. If I'm ever late again, I'll be sure to let someone know. Good night."

When Jana entered the room, she went to the side of the bed to check on Gretà, who was now sleeping peacefully, her breathing normal. In the dim light of the kerosene lamp that was still burning, Greta resembled the wedding picture of Marta Kaiser.

What would her mother think if she knew her

baby daughter was cooking in a saloon, and that her other daughter was standing in a window like an exhibit at the fair?

"Mama, I promise you, I'll make us a better life," Jana whispered. "I'll not let anything happen to your baby." She knelt to kiss her sister on the forehead.

Greta opened her eyes. "Is it time to get up?" she asked sleepily.

"No, go back to sleep. I'll come to bed in a minute."

"Well, Drew," Walter Watson said, "it looks like a clean sweep, and you know what that means, don't you? We won't be able to live with Colonel Lounsberry. He'll claim victory for the whole Citizens' Ticket."

"He'll be crowing, that's for sure, but I guess he has a right to," Drew said. "He was the one who started preaching reform, and now everybody in Burleigh County will benefit, and that includes you."

"I suppose you're right, but I can't afford to let it be known that I support this ticket. I'm a merchant, and I have customers who vote on all sides. I have to keep myself neutral."

"I can see that. Oh, I saw your newest employee here tonight."

"Jana is quite a woman." Watson chuckled. "Do you know I had more men in my store in one day than I've had in the last six months? Yes, sir, she can certainly draw the men in and, not only that, persuade them to part with their money. She is a jim-dandy of a salesperson, and I've got you to thank for bringing her to me."

Drew didn't reply as he clenched his mouth in anger. He didn't like the thought of Jana Hartmann drawing the men in. If she could do that fully clothed, what could she do if she went to work for Little Casino?

He shook his head to clear the thought. Whatever she did, it wasn't any of his business. After all, she was a pretty woman, and she had a right to make a living any way she chose. Besides, he had no personal investment in the woman. He'd only met her yesterday.

Drew lay awake all night long. He was unable to get the image of Jana Hartmann out of his mind. Finally he decided what to do. He would go to Rimfire, and he would take his two boys with him.

Rimfire was his bonanza ranch, which Drew had initially acquired by buying Valentine script from the US government. The script allowed the holder to claim land of his choosing as long as it was public. Drew had chosen land along the Little Missouri River. In addition, the Northern Pacific had given him more land as compensation for deed work he had done for the railroad, and that brought his total holdings to twenty thousand acres.

Drew's ranch house, the small one that was there now, and the bigger one that was being built, stood just back from the river. He had chosen a spot, shaded by cottonwood trees, that looked across the river to a strip of meadowland. To the west rose a line of sheer cliffs and grassy plateaus.

As the sun set on the first day he came to see his land, it ignited a golden glow that stretched from end to end all along the rim of the cliffs. It looked as if the rim were on fire.

"Rimfire," he said. And the name of his ranch was born.

Rimfire was located in the Badlands, about 130 miles west of Bismarck. Since the railroad bridge had crossed the Missouri River, it was now an easy six- or seven-hour train trip to the small hamlet where he and the boys would get off. The railroad called the settlement Pyramid Park, but the locals called it Little Missouri, though some sages referred to it as Little Misery. But Drew didn't think it miserable, he thought it peaceful.

Yes, a trip to Rimfire would soothe his mind, indeed.

"It's grown cold outside!" Elfrieda informed him the next morning when Drew told her what he was going to do. "You can't take those babies out there in the cold like this. And besides, Sam is in school."

"We won't be gone long, and the boys love it at the ranch. I promise we'll be back before Thanksgiving," Drew said as he poured another cup of coffee.

"You'll bring 'em back with roaring head colds, I just know it," Elfrieda said as she went to awaken the boys.

Drew stood at the window looking out on the bleak landscape. His house was near the edge of town, and the view was rolling plains. Was Elfrieda right? Did he have a right to jeopardize his children just because he wanted to get away from a woman—a woman who didn't even know he wanted to get away from her? What was wrong with him? He who was always the rational one.

Well, he was going, and he had an excuse. His foreman, Devlin McCarthy, was building a new and larger house for him, and he should really check on its progress before hard winter set in.

"Daddy, Daddy, is it true?" Benji yelled as he came running into the kitchen in his pajamas. "Are we going to Rimfire?"

"It's true, Benji." Drew smiled at the boy's enthusiasm.

"Yeah, yeah, and I'm going to ride Africa."

"No, you're not." Drew picked his son up and threw him over his shoulder. "Africa is Mr. Carswell's horse."

"Toby let's me ride him. Toby said I could ride him, next time I came."

"We'll see."

Just then Sam walked into the kitchen fully dressed.

"What's the matter, Sam? Didn't Mrs. Considine tell you we're going to Rimfire?"

"Yes."

Putting Benji down, Drew moved to Sam and bent down to his six-year-old. "Don't you want to go, Son?"

"It makes me sad. I think about Mama when we're there."

"I know, Sam, I know, but Mama's in heaven, and she wants us to do all the things that we would do if she was with us." Drew pulled his son close to him and held him.

"Does she want us to have a new mama?"

Drew pulled back and looked directly at Sam. "Why do you ask that?"

"Because Miss Peterson said I need a new mama."

"Your teacher said that?"

"Uh-huh."

"What did you say?"

Sam blinked his eyes over and over, holding back tears. "I don't want a new mama."

"Are we going to get a new mama? I want a new mama, I want a new mama!" Benji said over and over as he ran round and round the table.

"Out of the mouths of babes," Elfrieda said as she entered the room.

"Get Benji dressed, and put a few things in a rucksack for us, would you, Elfrieda? I've got to tell Frank I'm going to be gone for a couple of weeks." Drew gave Sam one last squeeze.

Jana had arrived at the Emporium before eight o'clock and was standing out front when Mr. Watson showed up.

"You were outstanding last night. I can't tell you how many people came to compliment me on my method of advertising. Do you know, Eben Strauss asked me if you could wear some of his jewelry while you're in the window."

"And what did you tell him?"

Mr. Watson grinned widely. "Just what do you think I told him? As long as we get a commission on what you sell, you can wear all the diamonds and rubies he's got in his store. Would that be all right with you?"

"Oh, I don't know about all of this, Mr. Watson. It makes me a little uncomfortable. I feel a little like I'm duping people out of their money."

"Nonsense, girl, we're not making anybody buy anything. They just see something they think is pretty, and then they want it for themselves. But we don't want to overdo a good thing. Today, I think you should work in the store, maybe work in the stockroom, just so you know what all we have for sale."

"I think I'd like that." Jana took off her coat and hung it on a peg in the stockroom.

"Why don't you start straightening up back there? We were selling things so fast yesterday, everything got in a mess."

"I can see what you mean." Jana saw articles of clothing everywhere.

She spent most of the day in the stockroom, and while she was doing mindless work, she thought about Drew Malone. He was an enigma to her. She replayed everything that had happened when she had been with him—at the Sheridan House when he had praised her for rebuffing Richards when he'd tried to buy her vote, and when he had chided her for not knowing more about New Salem and Pastor Kling, and then when he had understood when she said she wanted to homestead.

Then she thought of the physical contact she had had with him, starting with when he had kept her from tripping on the boardwalk and offered her his arm as they walked to the telegraph office. Then after he had sold her skills to Mr. Watson, he had grabbed her hand as they left the store, and all these things seemed to be the most natural thing in the world for a man and a woman to do.

And then there was last night.

While she was dancing with Drew, she thought it was the first time in her life that she felt like a desirable woman. And finally there was a moment—*that* moment was how she thought of it—the moment when he almost . . . what? Was she reading too much into a reaction? He was looking at her with eyes that she thought were filled with passion, and then, when he lowered his head, his lips were but an inch away from her own. She felt, no she knew, he was going to kiss her. But he was interrupted.

For the rest of the evening, he avoided her. Why?

Then it hit her. Maybe he was married. She hadn't even thought of that. Yes, that must be it. He was probably married, and if he was, she had no business even thinking about him.

But even though she tried, his face with the captivating blue eyes kept reappearing in her mind. Pastor Kling couldn't get here fast enough.

"Are you nuts?" You're going to Rimfire today?" Frank Allen asked when Drew told him what he was going to do. "I've had three people in here already this morning because, after the election, they know they won't have to pay off a politician just to buy a piece of property."

"You can handle it, Frank. Besides, I'm not going to be gone that long. I need to see how the house is coming along."

"You can't kid me. That house has been going up since August and you've not even thought about it until now. I know you, something's happened."

"Will you drive us to the train?" Drew asked, cutting off the line of conversation.

"Ha, I see. You're not only going to run out on me at a time when we are going to be very busy, you want me to facilitate it by driving you to the depot. Is that it?"

Drew chuckled. "That's it."

With Sam and Benji loaded in the carriage, Drew and Frank headed for the railroad depot. They rode down Eighth Street turning onto Main. When they were in front of Watson's Emporium, Frank came to a complete stop.

"I thought we'd get a chance to see the canary in the cage," Frank said, "but she's not there."

"Maybe she flew to another nest," Drew said sarcastically.

Frank looked questioningly at Drew. Did Jana Hartmann figure into the decision for this quick trip?

Drew looked with pride on his two sons, four-year-old Benji sleeping soundly with his head nestled against Drew, and six-year-old Sam, his face pressed against the window of the train. For the first part of the ride, Sam had seldom taken his eyes off the landscape.

The boys were so different in personality. Benji was happy-go-lucky, never met anyone he considered a stranger, and Sam was reserved, always suspicious of anything that was new to him. The last two years had been difficult, and Drew knew that Sam still wasn't over the trauma of seeing his mother fall to the ground, dying before his very eyes. He begrudgingly accepted the few women who were in his life: his grandmother; Miss Peterson, his schoolteacher; and Elfrieda. Drew had hoped that Elfrieda might be more nurturing, but she was first a housekeeper, then a cook, and finally a caregiver to the boys. He should have been more careful when he hired her, but until Elfrieda, every woman he had considered was interested in only one thing—marriage.

Benji snuggled closer to Drew, and he put his arm around his son, holding him more tightly. Maybe he was wrong. Maybe it was time to take a wife. He knew that he could go for the rest of his life without ever getting married again, but maybe he owed it to his boys to find someone who would come into their house and make it a home.

He looked toward Sam, who seemed old beyond his years. The boy always seemed so sad, and it broke Drew's heart that Sam was always so distant. During this time at Rimfire, he wanted to find a way to talk to Sam about what he thought of Drew's bringing another woman into the house.

But who could that be?

The face of Jana Hartmann came to his mind. When he had first met her, he had been mentally attracted to her, and when he had seen her with her hair in a less severe style, and in clothing other than the plain clothes of an immigrant, he realized he was also physically attracted to her.

But what about Little Casino? Why was Jana talking to the most prominent prostitute in Bismarck? But what if it was an innocent conversation? When he got back, he would make it his business to find out what kind of relationship the two women had.

The train began to slow as they approached the settlement of Little Missouri, so named because it was located on the west bank of the Little Missouri River at the Northern Pacific crossing. It was known as one of the roughest communities in the territory. The permanent population was no more than a couple dozen people during the day, but at night all kinds of derelicts showed up, generally men, and a few wayward women, who had no desire to ever be counted. They were the horse thieves, escaped criminals, deserted soldiers, renegade Indians, and other hoodlums who roved the Badlands, and the prostitutes who plied their avocation among such men.

But when Addie died, Drew had come for solace to this land that she'd loved so. They had found Rimfire together, and he had planned to someday make this ranch their home.

"Benji, it's time to wake up," Drew said as the train rolled across the bridge. "We're here. Sam, put your coat on." Drew began gathering their belongings and herded the children toward the exit.

"Mister, are you sure you want off here?" the conductor asked as he opened the door and put down a step stool, carefully looking up and down the dirt road that ran in front of the depot. "This isn't a place for kids."

"We won't be here long," Drew said, wishing he had taken the time to wire Devlin McCarthy, his ranch foreman.

Sam was barely off the train when the conductor had the step picked up and the door closed. More than once, a conductor of the Pacific Express had been forced to dance as town rowdies shot at his feet, in what they considered great sport.

The town was originally the site of the Badlands Cantonment, a military installation where soldiers had been stationed to protect the railroad construction crews from the Indians. When the end of the track moved farther west, the soldiers moved, too, and the buildings were abandoned. Now a few shanties, a post office, a sutler's store, the Pyramid Park Hotel, a livery stable, and nine saloons all lined up in a row facing the Little Missouri River.

"Come on, boys," Drew said, trying to sound as cheerful as he could. "Let's go hire us a wagon and get to Rimfire. Won't Devlin be surprised when he sees us?"

Just then Drew heard yelling from the Blue Goose Saloon and then a volley of revolver shots. He held the boys close to him as a man came tumbling out the opened door.

"Get the hell out of my place," the man who was doing the tossing yelled.

"I'll go when I damn well want to," the man on the ground said as he crawled toward his gun. When he got to the gun, he began firing into the air.

Sam immediately began screaming.

Without stopping to think, Drew ran to the man, kicked the gun from his hand, and yanked him to his feet, only to land a punch knocking him back to the ground.

"You son of a bitch," Drew yelled. "What in the hell do you think you're doing, shooting like that in broad daylight?" He picked up the gun, emptying all chambers of ammunition and sticking the bullets in his pocket. Then he recovered his hat and, rubbing his hand, went back to the boys, who were now terror struck.

"I want to go back. I want to go home," Sam said, hiding behind Drew, while Benji sobbed uncontrollably.

Drew knelt to console the boys, hugging them to him. "When we get to Rimfire, everything will be fine. Let's go find Mr. Paddock. He'll have a fast team of horses for us and we'll be home in a half hour."

The three walked down the street, both boys staying as close to Drew as they could. Then it hit Drew what he had just done. He was foolish to have hit the man, not because he didn't need it, but what would have happened if a stray bullet had hit him? He was all the boys had.

EIGHT

Rimfire was about five miles from the Little Missouri settlement, and usually the ride was like a soothing balm for Drew. But today the maze of colorful buttes and far-flung hills that rose as a backdrop to the saffron-colored waters of the river did not work their magic. Frank, and even Elfrieda, had tried to convince him not to come, but he had done it anyway. He should have listened to them.

"Oh, look, boys. There's our new house," Drew said, trying to shake his own melancholy mood. "Let's bring our wagon in on the run, so everyone will come out to meet us." He flicked the team with the whip and the horses picked up speed.

"Well, if it ain't the boss man," Devlin said as he came out of the new house, a wide grin on his face. "You just couldn't stand it, could you?"

"I wanted to see how you're spending my money," Drew said as he jumped down from the wagon, shaking his foreman's hand. "I can't believe how much you have done. Come on, boys, let's go see what it looks like."

"You've brought me some new helpers," Devlin said as he mussed Benji's hair.

Benji ran ahead, going in the open door, but Sam stayed beside his father.

"Daddy, it's a big house. Can we move here?" Benji asked.

"Not now, but maybe sometime we will," Drew said.

"I don't want to come here," Sam said so quietly that only Drew heard him. Drew squeezed Sam's hand in reassurance.

They toured the house, a sprawling eight-room structure.

"Don't you like this site I picked out?" Devlin asked. "Right here on this little knoll back of the cottonwoods, you'll have a fine breeze in the summer when I get the porch finished, and you're far enough back that you won't get any water during the runoffs. That is, unless we have a fifty-year flood."

"It's perfect," Drew said, "but isn't that another cabin over there behind the shack?"

"It is. Ole Toby's brought his woman, and he built her a house."

"His woman?"

"Nobody knew. He says he's been married for more than thirty years, and not one time did he ever tell anybody he had a wife. She's a real peach."

"Well, let's go meet her."

When they reached the cabin, Toby Carswell opened the door. "Howdy, Mr. Malone. I knowed it was you come flying in here like a bat out of hell. Come on in and take a bite with me and the missus. She just took a batch of crullers out of the oven. You think these younguns could eat one of them?"

"Crullers, yummy!" Benji said as he climbed onto a bench next to the table.

"Hold up there, young fellow. I'll bet you've not washed your hands for a week of Sundays." A woman who appeared to be in her fifties brought a cloth to Benji and began wiping his hands and face.

"You must be Mrs. Carswell," Drew said.

"I wouldn't know how to answer to that Mr. Malone. I'm just Peach."

"Peach, nice to meet you." Drew stuck out his hand. "And I'm Drew. This is Sam, and that one is Benji, and I think by the smell of things, we're all going to get along just fine. What about you, Sam? Can you eat a cruller?"

Sam smiled as he sat down, and Peach handed the wiping cloth to him, respecting that he was older.

Drew watched Sam accept a cruller from Peach, thank her, then lift it to his mouth to take a bite. Sam was such a sensitive boy. Drew wished he could find some way to get through to him.

In the week since the night of the election returns, Jana had changed the way she displayed herself in the window. She convinced Mr. Watson that people would come by more often if they saw her doing something, rather than just standing *en tableau*.

Now she sat in the chair in front of an easel as she sketched, sometimes using a charcoal pencil and other times using a brush and a palette of watercolors. She had the easel turned so that her art could be seen from outside. Today, she was painting a vase of red carnations that had come from Fuller's Greenhouse, some of the winter-blooming plants that he grew for the Christmas season. Word of her activity spread through the town, and as on the first day, the crowd outside the window was large. And sales in the store were brisk, now expanding beyond the dresses that she modeled, including the jewelry from Eben Strauss, as well as vegetables and flowers from the greenhouse.

She was also selling her artwork, making nearly as much from it as Mr. Watson was paying her.

For the first time since she and Greta had left Illinois, Jana was beginning to feel less apprehensive about their situation. She was earning a living, and even Greta was helping by providing for their room and board. Jana enjoyed watching her savings mount and was pleased when she felt it was necessary to open a savings account at the bank. It was a good feeling, being self-sufficient.

Jana sat in the window most of the day now, changing clothing only a couple of times. Mr. Watson was trying to convince her to paint portraits of people, but she was reluctant to do that. She didn't think she could capture a good likeness in the limited amount of time she had to work, and if a subject had to sit for several days, the customers would lose interest. Still lifes of flowers or bowls of fruit were good sellers, and because she could do them quickly, she could paint more pieces.

When her day was over at the store, she went back to the hotel to start her second job. Tom had discovered that when Greta and Jana were in the saloon, it tended to do two things: help business, and keep the patrons calm and well behaved. Jana thought it was humorous that she was paid to sit in a window during the day and have people watch her every move, and that she was paid to sit in a bar every night and have people watch her eat.

"It looks like the hungry crowd is waiting for you," Jana said when she walked into the kitchen, putting her coat on a peg.

"How many are out there?" Greta asked as she lifted a tin basin from a pail of steaming water.

"I'd say at least twenty-five, maybe thirty. What did you make today?"

"Scotch broth. Last week, Hugh McDonald shot a bighorn sheep over in the Killdeers and he gave me the shinbones, so Tom showed me how to fix it."

"I don't think that's broth in the steamer," Jana said.

Greta smiled. "I wanted to fix something special tonight because it's Hank's birthday. I fixed him some tapioca, but if there are thirty people out there, I don't have enough."

"What you have is fine. After all, they're getting this for free." Jana grabbed some hot pads to carry the soup kettle into the bar.

When the two women had the soup set up on the serving table, the men lined up quickly.

"Hank's first," Greta said as she called to the old gentleman who was sitting in the corner.

"What's so special about him?" someone asked.

"It's his birthday today. How old are you, Hank?"

"Seventy-two." Hank stood with his cane and walked to the table. "In my day, nobody would've beat me to the mess line. Why, I followed old William Tecumseh all the way to Atlanta."

"I guess you was one of the Yankee scoundrels who burned my mama's house," a man in uniform said. He was about half Hank's age.

"I beg your pardon. General Sherman gave us strict orders not to destroy anything unless there was resistance."

"That's a bunch of hogwash," the soldier said. "I saw you steal and burn and rape anybody that got in your way." The younger man swung his fist at the old man, knocking him against the table, causing some of the soup to slosh out of the pot.

Immediately, three other men grabbed the belligerent soldier and ushered him out of the bar and into the street.

"Hank, I'm so sorry," Greta said as she knelt beside the old man, wiping his bloody lip on her apron.

"Girl, it wasn't your fault, and it sure ain't the first time I ever got my lip bloodied," Hank said as Greta and a couple of other men helped him to his feet.

"The rest of you men stand back," one of the other patrons said. He looked at Hank, then held his hand out invitingly. "This is Mr. Hank's birthday, and we're goin' to wait until he's served and seated."

"What gentlemen you men are," Jana said.

"Yes, ma'am, we try to be."

Jana refilled Hank's soup bowl, and Greta filled a second bowl, this one filled with tapioca, then walked with him, carrying it over to the table.

"Happy birthday, Hank," she said, leaning over to kiss him on the forehead.

"Whooee, Greta, do we all get a kiss on our birthday?" one of the men asked.

"Tell me, Ken, who would kiss your ugly mug?" Carl called over to him.

"Well, I ain't no uglier than Hank."

"I'll tell you what, Ken. On your seventy-second birthday I'll give you a kiss," Greta said, and the others laughed.

A couple of days later, Jana was on her way to the First National Bank with a painting for Asa Fisher. He had especially commissioned a painting of a cornucopia filled with pumpkins and squash, as a present for his wife. The canvas was much larger than what she usually painted, and she was having trouble getting through the bank door.

"Here, ma'am, let me help you," a man said, holding the door.

"Thank you," Jana said, then she recognized him. "Oh, Mr. Allen, how nice to see you again."

"Miss Hartmann," Allen replied with a nod of his head. "I've heard great things about your talents, and if this painting is an example, I can see why people are talking."

"I'm not accustomed to so much attention." Jana lowered her eyes. "I'm afraid the impression that some people have of a woman sitting in a window is not so good."

Allen chuckled. "Ignore what people say. Drew tells me that Walter couldn't be happier with what you're doing for his sales, and that's all that's important."

"Mr. Malone said that?"

"Yes, he did."

"I've not seen your partner for some time. Is he well?"

"I think he is now, but Elfrieda's going to skin him alive if he brings those kids back from the ranch with the sniffles."

"Kids?" Jana said weakly.

"Yeah, Sam and Benji. He took his boys to the Badlands for a couple weeks. I didn't think he'd stay the whole time, but I've not heard from him, so I'm guessing everything's all right."

"I'm sure he's fine. Thank you, Mr. Allen, for helping me with the door. Good day."

Jana hurried into the bank, taking a deep breath to steady her trembling hands.

Took his boys to the Badlands. The words hit Jana like a blow to the stomach.

Drew Malone was married.

Drew and the boys had been at Rimfire for over a week, and he had allowed the activity of the ranch to wash his soul. The pace of actual ranch work was slowed down in the crisp November air, as many of the hands were let go for the winter. All the horses, except the personal mounts of the cowboys, were turned loose on the open range. That allowed them to forage on the grass that had dried in the late-summer sun and now provided a natural hayrick for the animals that roamed the Badlands. The horses fared better than the cattle, as they were better able to paw through the snow and find the food.

The cattle required little work during the colder months. Some cowboys were assigned to the line shacks, which were put on a perceived line that would indicate how far the cattle would be allowed to drift. A few of the men did some line riding, looking for any cow or calf that they thought was weak. When they found such an animal, they would bring it back to the home ranch for temporary care, and when it had regained its strength, they would turn it back on the range.

Occasionally, if the herd began to wander off the open range, and especially if the cows were heading toward an Indian reservation or an area that was largely settled by grangers, cowboys from several ranches would band together to drive the herd back closer to the home ranches.

During the winter most of the work around the home ranch was in oiling and repairing leather harnesses or saddles, or building outbuildings or corral fences. But the men's favorite pastime was practicing roping. The cowboys would throw their forty-foot lariats at anything: a set of cow horns put on a sawhorse, a fence post, a stump, a deer that came down to the river for a drink, or, if they were in a particularly playful mood, they'd just lasso each other.

Drew was watching Toby trying to teach Sam and Benji how to make an overhand knot in a length of rope.

"Pull it tight," Toby said after Sam had put the loose end of the rope through a loop. "Now make another one, just below this one, but don't pull it tight."

Sam tried and tried to do as Toby said, but each time he failed. Finally he threw down the rope.

"I don't want to do this. I'm not ever gonna learn to throw the silly old rope." Sam walked away, his head down.

Drew jumped down off the ledge where he had been sitting and hurried over to his son. "Come on, Sam, let's saddle up Baldy and Santana and go for a ride. And Benji, you go see Miss Peach. I heard her say she was going to make molasses candy today, and I'll bet she can use some help."

"Oh, goody," Benji yelled as he started running toward the Carswell cabin.

"Tell Devlin we'll be gone a while," Drew said as he started toward the tack room.

Drew and Sam rode well over a half hour as they followed the twists of the Little Missouri River. Drew didn't know where this ride would take him, but he knew he had to talk to his son, and for now he was content to ride in silence. Around one bend in the river, they stopped their horses and watched as a dozen or more bison crossed the shallow river.

"Look, Daddy," Sam said with enthusiasm as he pointed out a particularly large animal that was rubbing his head on the bark of a cedar tree. "Do you think he wants to knock the tree down?"

"No, I think maybe he's just got an itch." Drew reached a hand out to Sam.

"It's a big itch."

"Come on, let's not bother him while he's getting a back rub." Drew turned his horse away from the river. "Let's go find Abraham Lincoln."

"Abraham Lincoln? Daddy, don't you know he was shot?"

"But everybody remembers him, and there's a butte somewhere out here that looks just like him. Or maybe we'll just find a castle or a turret to climb when the robbers come after us."

"Robbers? Are they going to come rob us?"

"Nah, not if we find a good place to be. That looks like a good one." Drew pointed to a nearby rock outcropping. "Let's climb to the top."

Dismounting, Drew ground-hobbled both of their horses, then they started climbing. When the two got to the top of the flat plateau, they sat down and looked out over the gorges and jagged hills that made up the rugged landscape. Everywhere the ocher and red scoria was fired by the sun's rays, and they watched as an eagle rode an air current, coming so close that Drew could have thrown a stone and hit it.

They were quiet for a long moment, then Sam moved closer to Drew. "Daddy, you won't leave me, will you?"

"What do you mean? Of course I won't leave you."

"Mama did."

Drew reached out to put his arm around his son. "Mama didn't leave us, Son. She's in heaven now, looking down on us."

"I wish she was here." Sam's sniff told Drew that he was close to crying.

"So do I, Son, so do I. But sometimes things happen that we don't like. It's not our fault they happen, they just do. And when they do happen, we have no choice but to live with it."

"What if something happens to you?"

"Sam, you can't be afraid. You have to be a brave young man. Think of Benji. Benji looks up to you. If you're afraid, then Benji will be, too."

"Benji doesn't even remember Mama."

"I'm sure that part of him remembers her. He was just so young that it's hard for him to remember."

"Will I ever have a new mama?"

"What do you mean?"

"Miss Peterson said if you'd get married, I'd have a mama."

"What do you think about that?"

"I don't want another mama. I want my mama."

"But you know that can never be, don't you?"

"Yes, sir. I know."

"Who knows, Sam? Maybe someday you'll have another mama. And if you do, why, I'll bet you could love her, too."

"Maybe. But I'll never love her as much as Mama."

"Well, it's not even something we have to think about now, is it?" Drew stood up, then held his hand down to pull Sam up.

Sam wrapped both his arms around Drew's leg. "Promise me you won't ever leave me like Mama did. Promise me, Daddy."

Drew wished he could say more to comfort the poor tormented soul of his son. He reached down to put his hand behind Sam's head and pulled it against his leg.

"I promise."

As the two rode back to Rimfire, Drew was deep in thought. He had refused to take an interest in any woman who pursued him, especially the ubiquitous Miss Peterson.

Maybe he should consider taking a wife. *Promise me you won't ever leave me like Mama did. Promise me, Daddy,* Sam had said. Drew owed his children some stability, and a woman—a wife— might give them that.

But who could that person be? The face of a blue-eyed, ash-blond German immigrant came to his mind, and in the same thought, he mouthed a silent prayer. *Please don't let Jana Hartmann be working for Little Casino.*

It was time to get back home.

Five days later, as Devlin McCarthy drove the spring wagon up to the small clapboard building that served as the depot in Little Missouri, Clem Pittman strolled out to greet them.

"You folks goin' east or west?"

"East," Drew said, taking their one bag out of the wagon. "Any idea what time the train will get here?"

"Nope. It'll be here when it gets here."

"All right." Drew took his watch out of his pocket. "What time is it supposed to be here?"

"Somewhere around eleven o'clock, I reckon. Depends on how long it takes 'em to get the train turned around at Glendive."

"I need tickets back to Bismarck for the two boys and me."

"All right, come on in, and I'll get you fixed right up."

"I'll be gettin' on back to Rimfire," Devlin said as he swung the team around. "I'm anxious to get the house done so you and the boys can spend Christmas here."

"Thanks, Devlin." Drew walked over to shake hands with his foreman. "I'm glad I came." Inside the depot a little potbellied stove pumped out heat, and both Sam and Benji went over to it, standing close and holding their arms out over it.

"Be careful you don't touch the stove," Drew called over to them.

"We'll be careful," Sam promised.

Drew bought the tickets, then sat on the single wooden bench that ran along the wall. Cold seeped in through the window, but the stove poured out heat from the front, so that the backside of him was cold while the front side was almost too warm.

"I'll have to get the semaphore arm out so's the engineer knows to stop," Pittman said. "We don't have a whole lot of passengers that get on or off here in Little Missouri, so most of the time the train just barrels on through. Oh, it'll pick up mail when we got some goin' out, but it don't even stop for that. I just put the mailbag out on the hook, and the train grabs it as it runs by."

"The train just grabs it as it goes by?" Sam asked.

"Yep. Just like this." Clem stuck out his arm, then closed his hand and drew his arm back. "It don't even slow down."

"That's funny," Sam said. "I'm goin' to watch that."

"Oh, it won't do it today because it'll be stopping to let you folks board, so I'll just hand the mail on up to the express messenger."

"Can I watch you put out the thing that tells the engineer to stop?"

"Sure, come along."

"Can I watch, too?" Benji asked.

Pittman looked over at Drew, and Drew nodded, so the two boys went outside with the station agent.

Drew watched through the window as the boys followed Clem. Again, he found himself thinking of Jana Hartmann. Would she like his new house? For some reason, he had been unable to get her out of his mind since the day he and Sam had gone for their ride.

As he sat here now, he visualized the look on her face, the gleam in her eyes, the purse of her lips as he held her close to him on election night. He was just about to kiss her, and he was almost certain she would have offered no resistance. More than that, he believed she would have been a willing participant.

He wished he had kissed her. He had not wanted

to kiss any other woman since Addie died. Two years.

That was a long time for a healthy thirty-year-old man to go without the comfort of a woman. It wasn't natural for a man his age not to have a woman to do for him, care for him, and, he admitted to himself, share a bed with him.

How would Jana be in that department? He believed that if he had kissed Jana, he would have known a lot more about her. He was of the opinion that you could learn a lot about a woman just by kissing her.

But whom was he kidding? Except for Addie, he had kissed few and had lain with no other woman. But now, just the thought of Jana Hartmann's looking at him expectantly caused a stirring in the front of his pants.

Clem and the two boys came back into the depot then.

"Daddy, I'm the one that's going to stop the train!" Sam said excitedly.

"How are you going to do that?"

"Mr. Pittman let me pull the lever, and this red board just popped out and it's sticking way out so the engineer will see it. Mr. Pittman says it's me that's going to make the engineer stop the train."

"You are indeed," Pittman said with a chuckle. At that precise moment, they heard a distant whistle, and Pittman took out his watch to look at it. "And, just in time, as it turns out. The train is a little early today."

As the train came closer, Drew, Sam, and Benji came out onto the platform and stood there, watching it approach. Black smoke curled up from the stack, and white, almost luminescent steam gushed from the actuating cylinders just before the driver wheels.

"Do you think he will see my signal?" Sam asked.

The train began to slow noticeably.

"He sees it all right," Drew said. "See, he's slowing down."

The train pulled into the station, the engine so powerful and heavy that Drew could feel the vibration. The fireman was leaning out the window of the engine cab, and he waved at the two boys.

"He's not stopping!" Sam said, his voice reflecting his concern.

"Yes, he is, he just needs to get far enough so that the cars are lined up with us," Drew explained.

With a hiss of air from the brakes, and the screech of metal on metal as the brake shoes were applied against the wheels, the train came to a halt. It sat there for a moment, then the conductor stepped down. As the train was stopped, Pittman took the mailbag out to the express car and handed it up to the messenger.

"Board!" the conductor called.

"That's us, boys. Let's get aboard," Drew said.

NINE

The meeting of the Ladies' Christian Union will be called to order," Linda Steward said as she banged the table with a small wooden gavel. "I, first of all, want to thank all of you women who made the New England supper such a success. And I am very proud to announce that the net receipts were ninety dollars."

This news was met with a round of applause from everyone present.

"But that is all the money we have in our treasury, and we must think of other fund-raisers so that we can continue to pay our rent for this fine building."

"We could start charging admission for any of the gentlemen who come to listen to the reading," Bessie McNeil said.

"No, that can't be," Fern Watson said. "This is a free reading room provided for the purpose of affording young gentlemen and strangers in Bismarck a place to spend a pleasant evening. We can't ask them to pay to come here."

"We could ask Reverend Jackson to read some more Dickens for us. He is especially good. The last time he brought women from his church to sing, and that was excellent entertainment," Bessie said.

"No," Mrs. Watson said again. "Many of these young men can't read, and this is their only opportunity to hear classic literature."

"Speaking of classics, I would like to see a melodrama that, even though it was written some time ago, has just become very popular in Europe," Clara Hollenbaugh said.

"A melodrama? Yes, that's a good idea. That may be something we could use to raise money. What is this play called?"

"*Menschenhass und Reue*. I have a copy," Clara said excitedly.

"Well, Clara, that's wonderful that you think it's so good, but some of us may have a problem with it. We don't all speak German like you do," Della Peterson said.

"In English I think it's called *The Stranger*, even though the translation is *Misanthropy and Repentance*. I suppose we could get the English version."

"If we need it to raise money, we don't have time for that," Linda Steward said. "Can you translate it for us?"

Clara blushed. "I—I don't think . . ."

"I know who we can get to do it," Fern Watson said. "Jana Hartmann."

"Jana Hartmann? You mean that woman who

displays herself so shamelessly in your husband's window? And then I hear she works in the Custer Saloon at night. I don't think that's the kind of woman we want affiliated with the Ladies' Christian Union," Della Peterson said.

"Do you think she's smart enough to handle the daunting task of translating a major literary work?" Linda Steward asked.

"There is absolutely nothing shameless about Miss Hartmann, neither in her work for my husband nor in helping to serve meals in the hotel. And she is probably more educated than any of us here. She has a degree from a Christian college in Illinois. I daresay that few among us have that much education," Fern Watson said.

"Fern, are you sure she has a degree? Or did she just tell you that? I hardly believe a college-educated woman would clear tables in a saloon," Della said.

"Well, we'll find out if she's lying," Linda Steward said. "Fern, you have an opportunity to see her. Will you ask her to do this for us? If the play is as interesting as Clara says it is, maybe Mr. Whitney will let us put on a local production at the Opera House."

Jana was surprised when Mrs. Watson came to the store specifically to see her, and when she asked Jana to translate a German play that was published more than eighty years ago, Jana was even more astonished. She had never read the playwright, August von Kotzebue, but she was pleased to have something stimulating to do. The novelty of her sitting in the window was beginning to wear off, and painting endless bowls of fruit or arrangements of flowers was getting boring.

She picked up the script and began to read through it rather quickly, silently thanking Sister Mary Kathleen for insisting that she learn to read German when she was in grammar school. When she was finished, she stepped out of the window in search of Mrs. Watson.

"Are you sure the ladies of the Christian Union want to put on this play?"

"Oh, yes," Fern Watson said. "Clara Hollenbaugh says it's a wonderful melodrama that's all the rave in Europe. Can you translate it for us?"

"Yes, I can do it, if you're sure that's what you want."

"Good, I'll tell Mrs. Steward, and she can pass the word around that you are who you say you are. Can you finish before Thanksgiving?"

"I don't think that will be a problem." Jana was puzzled by what Mrs. Watson had said: *you are who you say you are.* What did that mean? She hadn't spoken to anyone except the customers she had seen in the store or the patrons who came into the saloon, or to Frank Allen and Drew Malone.

Drew Malone. He could certainly be a cast member of this play. A play that was all about adultery. Except in this play the woman was the adulterer.

Jana took a pencil and wrote the words *Misanthropy and Repentance* across the top of the first page.

Misanthropy. That was a word she could take to heart. Not that she hated anyone, but she certainly did distrust certain people, and the number one candidate was Drew Malone. She would have let him kiss her the night of the election if he hadn't been interrupted by Frank Allen, and then Frank told her about Elfrieda and his children.

Elfrieda was a name that surely stuck in the memory, and when she heard Mr. Watson call out to someone with that name, she left the window to see what this Elfrieda looked like. A large woman at least twice Jana's age, she had come in to buy a seal hat. Jana was sure this was not Mrs. Malone. Maybe Mrs. Malone was the misanthrope because of her flirtatious husband.

If Drew Malone were her husband, he wouldn't . . . Jana's cheeks flamed with embarrassment. What was happening to her? Such thoughts about another woman's husband.

Jana went back to her translating, and the very next line spoke to her: *"I beseech you—There are strings in the human heart, which touched, will sometimes utter dreadful discord—I beseech you—"*

Jana Hartmann was in a state of dreadful discord. Right then she decided she would work for Mr. Watson only until Christmas. Then she would set the process in motion to find a plot of land to homestead. She did not come to Dakota to get involved with a married man. Another line from the play spoke to her: *Moments, which steal the roses from the cheek of health, and plow deep furrows in the brow of youth.*

This would not be her plight.

Drew, Sam, and Benji were on board the east-bound Pacific Express, returning from Rimfire. Drew smiled as he listened to the boys' lively conversation. He decided this had been a worth-while trip. The house was coming along nicely and would probably be finished by Christmas, but the most important thing was his talk with Sam. He needed that talk with Sam, as much for himself as for his son.

After Addie died, Drew had thrown himself into his work, withdrawing from anything that was social. Frank and his wife, Caroline, had tried to draw Drew out, but he had used the boys as an excuse not to do anything. Now it was time he accepted responsibility for how his behavior may have impacted Sam.

It was one thing to tell your son that things happen that we don't like, and when they do happen, we have no choice but to live with them, but it was completely different to have to live that. For the good of his children, he had to start living a normal life. At first he had hired Elfrieda to satisfy Addie's mother, but now he told himself he should take advantage of her presence and do some things—some things that were fun.

The train stopped at Dickinson to take on coal and water, and Drew and the boys stepped off the train to walk around for a moment. This town had a population of about fifteen hundred people, most of whom worked in some capacity for the Northern Pacific. There was a passenger depot, a freight warehouse, a commodious railroad shop, and a roundhouse that until recently had been the end of the track.

"Boys, we'd better get something to eat here," Drew said as he led the way across the street to one of the two hotels in town. "We'll only have about fifteen minutes before the train gets under way again."

When they walked into the restaurant, the proprietor had just taken out a batch of potato fritters, and the smell was tantalizing.

"We'll take a dozen of those," Drew said. "Oh, and put in a couple of cream cakes, too."

"You on the Pacific Express?"

"We are."

"Then I'd better put 'em in paper for you. That train don't stay here very long."

"I'd be much obliged if you'd do that."

When the train started rolling again, the boys, with bellies full, and rocked by the gentle motion of the train, fell asleep. Drew watched the afternoon slowly begin to fade as all the new little towns rolled by: Gladstone, Taylor, Richardton. No wonder he was so busy filing claims, since most of these towns were formed to accommodate the immigrants who were homesteading their section of land from the undulating hills of fertile soil.

And then he saw a small, insignificant sign saying NEW SALEM. There was only one building.

So this was where she was going. Drew checked

his watch to see what time it was. By his schedule, New Salem would only be about thirty miles from Bismarck. That would be an easy trip.

A little more than half an hour to go and they would be home. He settled back in his seat, intending to take a nap as well, but that was not to be. As they approached Bly's Mine, the track took a sharp turn.

Suddenly a loud crashing noise reverberated through all the train. No longer traveling smoothly on the rails, the car was now bucking badly, as if going over a lot of bumps. A couple of women in the car screamed, and some of them shouted.

The commotion awakened the boys as they were jostled about; Benji was thrown on the floor. Drew grabbed him and pulled the boy to him.

"Are we going to die?" Sam said with more calmness than Drew was sure his son felt. The boy held on to the armrest of his seat, his eyes opened wide in terror.

"No, Son," Drew said without conviction.

From the window, he saw that the tender had left the track and was now in the ditch. It sounded as if someone were outside, beating on the side of the car with a sledgehammer, until finally they stopped. All the cars had been thrown from the tracks, and the baggage cars were whirled diagonally across the roadbed. Two passenger coaches were at a precarious tilt, but miraculously, the wheels of the passenger coach Drew and his sons were in rested upright on the ties.

"What happened? Why did we stop?" Benji asked.

"We ran off the tracks," Sam said.

"You mean we had a train wreck?"

"I wouldn't say it was a wreck, because every-body is all right. I think the tender ran into the ditch, and then all the cars got off the track," Drew said as he pulled the boys closer to him.

"You know why we weren't hurt?" Sam asked.

"Why?"

"Mama. She's taking care of us."

Drew smiled. "That could very well be, Sam. She loved us more than anything else in the world, and she could still be looking out for all of us."

Jana was helping Greta set up the soup kettle when a whistle began blowing in several short toots. The sound galvanized everyone in the saloon, and many of the men got up and started toward the door.

"Carl, what's that?" Greta asked. "Where's every-one going?"

"Those whistles mean something's happened to a train someplace," Carl said.

"What do you think it is?"

"I don't know, but I imagine we'll find out soon enough. It could be engine trouble or the track is out or it could be a wreck. It's really hard to say."

Jana and Greta joined some of the Custer regu-lars at the front window of the hotel. They saw several people milling about the depot, some rail-road workers and townspeople as well.

After a while a couple of the men who had been having their supper returned.

"What is it, Mr. Dempsey?" Greta asked one of the men. "What happened?"

"It's the Bly's Mine curve again. The eastbound left the track," Dempsey said.

"Oh, dear, was anyone hurt?" Jana asked.

"I don't think so. Leastwise we haven't been told of none. It's just that curve is the worst one in all of Dakota, and somethin' happens there every little whipstitch. They're puttin' an engine and a passenger car on now to go get 'em."

It had gotten quite dark, and the dim lights inside the car caused the windows to act as mirrors so that Drew could see nothing but his own reflection when he tried to look outside. He knew what had happened, though, because shortly after the accident he had gone outside to have a look around.

Ironically, the locomotive had not left the track, though the tender had, breaking loose from the couplings and turning over in the ditch. Several people were walking around, a few dazed and disoriented.

"A fine thing this is!" one man was saying angrily. "I paid my fare and I expected to be transported, safely, to Chicago. But I didn't even get out of Dakota. A fine thing this is."

"Mister, don't take on so," another passenger said. "I've been in train wrecks where people were killed or badly injured. You don't have a scratch on you."

"A fine thing," the man said again, his grumbling unabated.

The conductor informed the passengers that word had gone forward, informing the authorities of the accident. "I've no doubt but that a rescue train will be here soon enough," he said.

That had been more than an hour ago, and the car was beginning to cool, as the steam heat was generated by the now-defunct locomotive. Several others in the car huddled together for warmth while a few, like Drew's two sons, were sleeping. Some conversed quietly, and at the back end of the car a card game had begun.

Drew looked at Sam and Benji. When the commotion had begun, Addie's image had come to his mind as well, but not as the guardian that Sam had voiced. Drew's thoughts had been about what would come of the boys if something happened to him.

And he knew the answer: Rose Denton. Growing up next door to the Dentons, he had never realized what a pain that woman was. He shuddered as he thought about his children having to go back to Evanston to live with her.

"Here it comes!" someone called. "I can see the light! A train's comin'."

"I hope it's the rescue train, and not some limited that's roaring down the tracks like a cannonball," someone said. "Why, it could plow right into us."

"What?" one of the women asked in concern.

"Oh, pay no attention to him," another passenger said. "He's just talkin' to hear himself talk."

"Anyhow, it's slowin' down now," someone else said. "He sees us, and he's come to get us."

By now the train was close enough that everyone could hear it, and the conductor, who had been in one of the other cars, came in.

"Folks, grab whatever you've got with you, and be ready to get on the train."

"Come on, boys," Drew said as he scooped Benji into his arms and guided Sam through the car.

The rescue train rolled into the Bismarck depot at eleven thirty that night. Ordinarily a train arriving in the middle of the night would be met only by those people who had business with it, but as Drew looked through the window, it seemed as if half the town had turned out. He searched through the crowd looking—looking for what?

Benji woke up and rubbed his eyes. "Why did we stop?"

"Because we're home," Drew said.

"I'm going to tell Mrs. Considine about our train wreck."

"It wasn't a train wreck," Sam said. "The cars got off the track. That's all."

"But that's a train wreck, isn't it, Daddy?"

"You're both right," Drew said. "The cars ran off the track, and that's not an actual train wreck, but it is sort of like one."

When Drew stepped off the train, he watched as many of the other passengers were met in joyous reunion, and with exclamations of love and thankfulness that no one was hurt.

But of course no one met him, or his two sons.

"Oh, Johnny, my sweet Johnny, Mama was so worried about you!" a woman gushed as she embraced a young boy, a few years older than Sam, who had been on one of the other cars.

Drew felt Sam squeeze his hand more tightly, and looking down at him, Drew saw Sam watching the reunion of the mother and son. Sam didn't say a word, but he didn't have to. His eyes, wide-open and gleaming in the depot platform lamps, were portals to show the ache that Drew knew was in his son's heart. Drew returned the squeeze.

"It's good to be home, safe and sound, isn't it?" Drew said, not only to get Sam's mind off the pain of not being met, but his own as well.

"Yes, sir. But I wish . . ."

"That Mama was here to meet us?"

"I know it's dumb."

Drew reached down and put his arm on Sam's shoulder to draw him closer. "No, Son, it's love. You don't stop loving someone just because they died. And love is never dumb. Come on, let's go home."

Elfrieda met them when a dray left them at the back door. She, like nearly everyone else in town, was aware that there had been an accident, but she had no idea that Drew and the boys had been on the train.

"We were in a train wreck!" Benji said excitedly as he ran toward Elfrieda. "And one of the cars was in the ditch."

"It was the tender," Sam said knowledgeably.

"My, my, that must have been frightening for you," Elfrieda said.

"We weren't 'a scared a bit," Benji said proudly. "Were we, Sam?"

"No," Sam agreed. "We weren't scared."

"That's because you are both brave boys," Elfrieda said. "But let me ask you this. Would you like a cup of hot chocolate and an apple croûte before you go to bed?"

"Yes, please," Sam said.

"Yes, please," Benji echoed.

"What about you, Mr. Malone?" she added.

"If you have any coffee, I'll have that."

"I'll make a fresh pot," Elfrieda said as she cut two slices of bread for the croûte.

"Slice off another piece of bread," Drew said.

"I'm already doing it," Elfrieda said with a chuckle. "I know you. When you smell the apples and the cinnamon, you'll be wanting one, too."

Drew and the boys watched as Elfrieda toasted the bread in butter and sugar and cinnamon, then cooked the slices of apple in the pan residue. When they were soft, she spooned them onto the bread and placed one in front of each of them.

"I'm so glad you came to live with us, Mrs. Considine. Daddy never fixes good things like this," Benji said as he took a bite of the croûte.

"Thank you, Benji, but do you know it's already tomorrow? You boys had best get some sleep," Elfrieda said. "If you don't need me for anything else, Mr. Malone, I'll go get their beds ready and then go on to bed myself."

"You go ahead. I'll wash these cups and plates."

"You don't have to do that. Just leave them be

and I'll take care of them in the morning. Come on, boys, let's get you ready for bed."

"Good night, Daddy," Sam said as he finished his hot chocolate.

"Good night, Son."

"I'm glad we didn't die," Benji said as he threw himself into his father's arms.

"I am, too," Drew said as he held his young son. Then Drew saw Sam standing back watching the two of them. "Come here, Sam. I need to hug you, too, because we're the three musketeers."

"What does that mean?" Benji asked as he cocked his head quizzically.

"It means we love each other." Drew kissed each of his sons on the top of his head. "Now off to bed with both of you."

Drew gathered the plates and the boys' cups and put them in the dishpan. He poured hot water from the copper teakettle that always sat on the back of the cookstove, then refilled it with water from the kitchen pump, which brought water up from the cistern under the house. He carefully washed and dried the dishes, then put them back on the shelf above the marble sink.

He smiled. Frank often said Drew would make some woman a good wife someday, because until he hired Elfrieda, he had tried to do everything himself. He had done none of it well. Probably Rose was right to goad him into getting help. Even she had suggested he should take a wife. Addie's mother. How could she even suggest such a thing?

He refilled his coffee cup and sat at the kitchen

table, holding his cup until the coffee grew tepid. Normally the kitchen was brightly lit by a gas chandelier, but at the moment a low-burning kerosene lamp dimly illuminated it.

In his mind, Drew was once again cradling the dying Addie in his arms, her blood soaking his shirt as he applied pressure to the wound, trying to stop the bleeding. Again he heard the words, as clearly as if she were lying here before him.

Get a good woman to take care of my boys. I love you.

It was time.

Sam's teacher wasn't the only single woman in town who, in Elfrieda's words, had "set her cap" for Drew. There was also Bessie McNiel, a young widow, the mother of a ten-year-old daughter. She had let Drew know, in no uncertain terms, that she was more than ready to find another husband, and father for her daughter.

Clara Hollenbaugh was a German immigrant who worked at A. Logan's Bakery and often brought pastries. Presumably they were for Sam and Benji, but she always brought them to the law office. Drew had finally convinced her that while he loved the honey-glazed krapfen and the fried Berliners filled with vanilla cream, "the boys" should not always have something sweet. So now, every Tuesday, as regular as clockwork, Clara delivered warm krautkrapfen for both Frank and Drew. The dough was rolled up jelly-roll fashion with a filling of sauerkraut, onions, and ham, and both men looked forward to their Tuesday lunch.

All three eligible women—teacher, widow, and

baker—were active in the Ladies' Christian Union, a group of ladies who did charitable work around Bismarck. They also managed the Reading Room, where single men of all ages, mainly soldiers from Fort Lincoln, transients, and newcomers, could come listen to readings of the classics. Drew himself had been invited to read on numerous occasions, and he had enjoyed the evenings, even though the joke around town was that the Reading Room should really be called the Marriage Market. It was said that after only four visits to the Reading Room you would find your name in Colonel Lounsberry's "Current Comments" section of the *Tribune* announcing your betrothal.

Jana Hartmann.

How would she be as a wife, and a mother to his children?

He had thought she could be the perfect package: attractive without being self-centered, intelligent without being overbearing, and effervescent without being gushy. But why would such a woman enter into a business arrangement with Elizabeth McClellan?

TEN

Did you go down to meet the rescue train last night?" Mr. Watson asked the next morning when Jana walked into the store.

"No, my sister and I were both in bed by ten o'clock."

"Well, it was nearly midnight when it finally pulled in. I and about half the town were at the depot, mainly to meet Phin Causey. He sent word ahead that he'd be on the train with a fine lot of Mercer County venison. Everybody wanted a hindquarter and nobody wanted to wait till morning, so we all were there to meet him."

"I'll bet the other people were pleased to see all of you out to meet them, too."

"I expect they were, but I was surprised how many prominent citizens were on that train. It would have been a blow to the community if it had been a bad accident. Billy Pye and his son, Johnny, were on it, and then Lulu Mason and Sadie Cole were coming back from Miles City. You know they're the favorites over at the Opera House. Oh, and Drew Malone and his two little boys were in the wreck, too. Somebody said he was coming back from Little Missouri. Must be he's defending some good-for-nothing over there, but why oh why would he subject those poor children to that riff-raff."

"Oh my! Was anyone hurt?"

"No, not even a scratch on anybody. Those cars could have all turned over you know, or worse, they could have telescoped. That's when folks get hurt bad, and most often killed, when the cars telescope in on each other."

"It sounds like it was a miracle," Jana said.

"I think it was. They say only the tender turned over. Say, what picture do you want to paint today?" Mr. Watson withdrew a stretched canvas from under the counter.

"I don't think I'm going to paint today. Mrs. Watson asked me to translate a melodrama from German into English, so I'll be doing that."

"Ah, yes, for the Reading Room. Well, since it's Fern askin' you to do it, go right ahead. But do change dresses at least a couple of times. You won't have to do any selling on the floor today; far be it from me to get in the way of one of my wife's projects." Mr. Watson chuckled.

Jana chose a comfortable morning wrapper to start the day. The marine-blue cashmere felt soft against her skin, and she hugged herself to feel the sensuousness of the fabric. The frog-looped gold braiding that stretched down the front from her neck to her hemline made her think of a uniform as she took her place in the window, and with the strong wind blowing, her perch was quite drafty. Before sitting, she rearranged her window, placing the table that held her art supplies in position as a desk.

As she was moving the furniture, a passing gentleman quickly came to assist her. "Miss Hartmann, it ain't fittin' for a lady to be movin' furniture, especially one as pretty as you are. Let me help ya."

"Why, thank you, sir." Jana moved aside, letting him put her table in place. "I don't think I've had the pleasure of meeting you."

"Liam Flannery's the name. I've been meanin' to get meself over to the Custer, but the little woman, she don't much want me to be doin' that." His face began to turn a shade of red as he looked toward his feet.

"It's good that you've got a good woman to take care of you, Liam, and thank you again for helping me."

"Ma'am, ye could be a doin' something to help me out, too, if you don't think I'm a might too bold to be a askin' ya such a thing."

"If it's something I can do, I'll be glad to help you. What do you need?"

"I'm one of the lads that hold back the fiend, and we're trying to raise some money to help the cause."

"The fiend? I don't understand."

"Just look around ya. Bismarck's pretty much a wooden town, and if a fire gets started, the whole town's gone. That's why me and the boys at the firehouse call fire the fiend. Once it gets started, it's hard to stop it."

"I see. I'll be happy to donate to that cause." Jana turned toward the store.

"No, no. I don't want money, least not your money as such. It's the dance. The one on Thanksgiving night. We're raising money to help pay the standin' reward. The first team that gets to the firehouse when the alarm bell rings gets a whole ten dollars, and that's real money."

"Oh, Mr. Flannery, I don't think I can give you ten dollars."

"No, no, the boys think ye'd be the one that raises the most money, if you took a turn in the— the, aw shucks, Miss Hartmann, the kissing booth."

"The kissing booth?" Jana gasped.

"I tol' 'em ye wouldna do it. Ye was a finer lady than that." Liam turned to leave, knocking over a chair.

"No, wait." Jana righted the chair. "I've never been asked to do something like that before. Thanksgiving's just a couple days away, so let me think about it for a while."

"That's fair enough. If you show up at the dance, I'll take it ye thought about it and said yea to me askin', and if ye don't come, there's no harm done."

"I agree. That's fair enough."

Jana smiled as she watched Liam walk down the street. She was thankful he had left her a graceful way out of the dilemma he had set for her. No way was she going to a dance. First of all, she had never been to a dance in her whole life, and second, she would not go alone. Though not brought up in a social environment, she certainly knew that a single woman who wanted any kind of a reputation did not attend a social function alone. And to be asked to participate in a kissing booth?

As she thought about it, she laughed out loud. She—the woman the firemen thought would bring the most money at a kissing booth. What would they pay if they knew she could winnow mowed hay with the best of them, or shock corn as fast as any man in Madison County, Illinois? Or even better, what would someone pay for a kiss from her if they saw her in a butcher shop behind "the Yards" stuffing wurst in casings? And now, some people were looking down their noses at her for displaying herself in a store window to sell fancy clothes, or, even worse, living in the Custer Hotel.

Drew Malone. He was one of those people. *I've never known a woman to stay there. That's for railroad workers and transient army officers. It's not a place for a woman.* Those were his words.

Maybe she would go to the dance and be a part of the kissing booth. Surely the dapper Mr. Malone and his darling wife, Elfrieda, would come to a charity dance to benefit the firemen. He had wanted to kiss her for free on the night of the election. Let him pay for the privilege.

When Drew went to work the next morning, he saw a new picture on the wall, a painting of a wheat field with a homesteader's shack in the background. One lone tree shaded the house, and colorful clothing fluttered on a wire stretched from the house to the tree, while a woman dressed in a white waist and a dark skirt surveyed the scene. The woman's hair was just a shade darker than the ripened wheat, and the tall, willowy figure reminded him of someone but he couldn't immediately place who it was.

"How do you like the new picture?" Frank asked.

"It's very nice." Drew examined it more closely. "It's more than very nice. It's quite good. Where'd you get it?"

Frank smiled. "I bought it from a local artist."

"A local artist?" Drew shook his head. "I didn't know we had somebody this talented living in Bismarck. Who is he?"

Frank laughed. "What makes you think it's a he?"

"You're right, I was making an assumption."

"An assumption, my learned friend, that you would never make in a courtroom, as it is not supported by fact."

"Touché," Drew said. "All right, who's the artist?"

"Jana Hartmann."

"What?" Drew was surprised by the answer. "You mean the woman . . ."

"Who works for Walter Watson. Yes, that's exactly who I mean."

"Well, how did you come by this painting? How'd you know she did such a thing?"

"It's not a big secret," Frank said. "While she's sitting in the window at Walter's store in his fancy clothes, she's started to paint pictures. Most of the time it's fruit or flowers that she paints, but when I saw this one, I thought it would be appropriate for the office, seeing as how we probably handle more land-claim business than any other law firm in town. It's sort of representative of the immigrant, don't you think?"

Drew touched the painting. "It's really quite good, isn't it? Where do you think Miss Hartmann learned to do this?"

"I think there's more to that lady than meets the eye. Caroline tells me Fern Watson's got her translating a classic play from German to English for the Ladies' Christian Union to present sometime soon. And besides all this stuff, with working for Walter and all, she's helping her sister serve meals in the saloon over at the Custer."

"No doubt she's making a lot of connections," Drew said, thinking of her work with the woman who called herself Little Casino.

"Evidently, she is. I know that Walter has been just real pleased with her."

"So"—Drew rubbed his hands together—"do I have some work piled up?"

"You do indeed. You've been off playin' cowboy for two weeks, but maybe that will come in handy. Have you ever heard of the Marquis de Morès?"

"No, I can't say that I have."

"He's someone you'll probably get to know quite well. He's a French nobleman, married to the daughter of a wealthy American. He's contacted the Northern Pacific about finding a tract of land for him, and they've contacted us because of you."

"Me? What do I have to do with all this?

"Because of Rimfire, or that's what the NP said, but I think the real reason is because of your father. This de Morès fellow intends to do things on a grand scale, and the Northern Pacific is just making sure he can get to a high muck-a-muck if he needs help from Congress."

"Well, that's just hunky-dory! That's all I need. To play nursemaid to some European dandy who thinks he's a bigwig. Especially now, when I've decided to . . ."

"When you've decided to do what?"

"Oh, nothing." Drew went into his office and closed the door.

Drew put in a full day of work, much of it in pouring over section maps, putting together a suitable piece of land for the marquis, whose full name was Antoine-Amédée-Marie-Vincent Manca de Vallombrosa, Marquis de Morès.

On a whim, Drew decided to drop in at the Custer Hotel Saloon. He had not visited the saloon since Addie's death, and from the moment he entered, the change in the atmosphere was noticeable.

The last time he was here, it had been filled with railroad workers, riverboat hands, and soldiers from Fort Lincoln. He recognized a few of the railroad employees who had stayed behind once the building of the track had advanced farther west, and he saw a couple of riverboat captains who were wintering over in Bismarck. In addition, there were some military officers from Fort Lincoln. When he had been here before, only the enlisted men had been customers.

Before, the atmosphere had been loud and often

crude, but the demeanor of the customers now was as refined as if it were a gentlemen's club. Drew saw two women present, Jana and another woman, who looked so much like Jana that he would have guessed the two were sisters, even if he didn't already know that she had a sister.

The two women were standing behind a table covered with a red-and-white-checked tablecloth. Jana was ladling soup into a bowl, and her sister was cutting off pieces of freshly baked bread, its aroma wafting throughout the saloon. A line of amiable men were filing by the women.

Drew joined the line and watched as Jana interacted with the men, smiling and calling most of them by name. She seemed to have some personal comment for just about everyone. When he got to the table, he picked up an empty bowl and held it out toward Jana, a big smile on his face. He wondered what her reaction to him would be when she saw him.

But if he had expected a joyous welcome, he was mistaken. The expression on Jana's face changed immediately, and she didn't speak at all.

"Ah, *Kartoffelsuppe.* I love potato soup. Elfrieda makes it often," Drew said to cover the awkwardness.

"I hope it measures up to what you're used to," Jana said curtly.

Drew found her action puzzling because, to the very next man, she was as friendly as she had been before Drew approached her. Her reaction was quite clearly intended just for him.

Jana's sister, on the other hand, flashed a bright smile as she sliced off a big piece of bread. "You're a newcomer."

"I am. And you must be Jana's sister."

"Yes, I'm Greta, but you know Jana?" Greta looked toward her sister with a questioning look.

"My name is Drew Malone, and I had the pleasure of meeting her very soon after you arrived."

"Oh, yes, you're the one who helped Jana get her job."

"I did," Drew said, looking back toward Jana.

"Sir, we have others waiting to be served," Jana said. "Will you please take a seat? If you'd like something to drink, you can get it at the bar."

Drew was puzzled. Why was she making it a point to be unfriendly toward him when she was so friendly to everyone else? If she was really working for Little Casino, maybe, because he was a lawyer, she saw him as a threat.

Drew found a table and ate his potato soup, all the while keeping an eye on Jana. If he had come here to talk to her, he certainly wasn't making any headway. As he watched her with the other men, he saw a warm, open woman, but with him it had been so different. What could he possibly have done to her?

The last man was served and Greta came to remove bowls and glasses from a table near Drew.

"Miss Hartmann, the soup and the bread were both delicious. Which did you make?"

"Why, thank you, Mr. Malone. I did both, but I am not Miss Hartmann. I am Greta Kaiser."

"Oh," Drew said, his eyebrows rising inquiringly,

"is there a Mr. Kaiser or perhaps a Mr. Hartmann?"

Greta laughed. "There is a Mr. Kaiser, but he's my father, and there was a Mr. Hartmann, but he passed when Jana was three years old."

"Well, that's useful information."

"That's a strange comment, Mr. Malone. How do you plan to use that information?" Greta asked, striking a coquettish pose.

"Oh, miss, I meant nothing by it," Drew said hurriedly. "I was just thinking about Tom McGowan. He must be well pleased with what you're doing for his business, and I'm sure having two unmarried, exceptionally attractive women is a big draw for his clientele."

This time Greta laughed infectiously. "I'm sure Hank Thompson is very glad we're both not married. He loses a lot of sleep when he has to look out for us. If Jana doesn't get home when he thinks she should, or if I have to go to the greenhouse to pick up some produce, he almost sets a watch on us."

"Don't sell Hank short," Drew said, picking up on Greta's banter. "A seventy-two-year-old man can still enjoy the scenery."

Jana, observing Greta's exchange with Drew, wanted to make certain her sister knew just what kind of man he was.

"What does Elfrieda think about you taking your supper here?" Jana asked as she approached the table to refill Drew's glass of water.

"What does Elfrieda think?" Drew chuckled. "I don't know. She's probably just as glad that she only had to prepare supper for the boys."

"That seems a strange way for a wife to act."

"A wife?" Drew replied, puzzled. Then, suddenly he laughed out loud. "Jana, you think Elfrieda is my wife?"

"I rather assumed she was. Of course, I've never met your wife, so I don't really know who she is."

The smile left Drew's face. "You've never met my wife, Jana, because . . ." Drew paused. "I don't have a wife. She was killed two years ago in July. Elfrieda Considine is my live-in housekeeper and nanny rolled into one."

"Oh!" Jana gasped, putting her hand to her mouth. "Forgive me for . . . oh, I'm so embarrassed. I feel like such a—"

"There's no need for that," Drew interrupted. "Because Addie's death was such a public event, I forget that not everyone knows what happened to her."

"I'm sorry for jumping to conclusions. When Frank told me you and your two sons had gone to the Badlands, I assumed you were . . ."

"Is that what this is all about?" Drew took Jana's hand in his.

"What do you mean?"

"You mean you don't know you've been ignoring me?"

"Oh, that." Jana lowered her eyes and a grin overtook her features.

"Why don't you join me?" Drew rose to pull out a chair for her.

"I should help Greta," Jana said, looking toward her sister.

"You should help me do what? We're out of

soup, so that means we're finished for the evening." Greta picked up Drew's bowl and turned away. "I'll have Hank help me clean the dishes."

Jana slipped into the chair, and Drew sat beside her. When Jana really looked at him, his deep blue eyes seemed to burn into her consciousness as the gaslight caused them to sparkle.

"What do you want to know?" he asked.

"The most obvious, I guess. What happened to her?"

"It was the Fourth of July. She was walking home alone with the boys while I was going to watch a shooting match. Someone—it's hard to say who—was shooting into the air, and when the bullet came down, it struck Addie. Within minutes she was dying in my arms."

"Oh, Drew, I am so sorry."

"It's been hard, but it's really been hard for Sam. He was four years old and he saw her die. Of course Benji did, too, but he doesn't remember it. I'm not even sure if he remembers his mother at all, because he was barely two at the time."

"I'll bet he does remember her, or at least when he sees a picture of her, there's a memory." Jana thought of the picture of her own father and mother that she had left back in Highland. "I was three when my father died, and I think I can remember him. At least I know about him because of the things my mother told me. Do you talk about her a lot with the boys?"

"No. Not as much as I should. I guess I feel guilty for letting it happen. If I hadn't left . . ."

"If you hadn't left, what? You just said there was no way of telling whose bullet hit her."

"You're right. I just avoid talking about the whole thing as much as I can. While we're clearing up conceptions we've had about one another, I have something I would like to ask you, if you don't mind?"

"Sure, if I can answer it."

"Do you work for Little Casino?"

Now it was Jana's turn to have a puzzled expression. "Little casino? What is a little casino?"

"It isn't a what, it's a who."

Then Jana remembered that when she had met Elizabeth McClellan, she had told her, if she ever needed anything, to look up Little Casino. Jana laughed. "Do you mean Elizabeth McClellan?"

"Yes. Yes, I do mean her."

"Why did you ask about her, of all people?"

"The night of the election. I saw you give her a piece of paper and then she withdrew something and gave it to you. I thought you were making a connection with her."

"Well, I guess I did, and it was a lucrative connection at that. My purpose for going to the courthouse that night was to pass out cards advertising a ten percent discount to any woman who bought a dress from Mr. Watson, and if they turned in the card, I got an extra commission on the dress. As it turned out, Elizabeth bought lots of dresses, but then she's always in the store buying clothes. I swear I have no idea why any one woman would need as many dresses as she buys."

"She's buying them for her girls."

"Her girls? My goodness, how many daughters does she have?"

"Not her daughters, her girls."

"Drew, you aren't making any sense."

Drew laughed. "You don't know, do you? You don't know who she is."

"Other than Elizabeth McClellan, no, I don't know."

"What was on the card she gave you?"

"It was a playing card, a two of spades I think."

"And it didn't say anything else?"

"No. What was it supposed to be, Drew? I don't understand at all."

"Elizabeth McClellan is Little Casino, and she runs"—Drew hesitated—"Little Casino runs a bordello."

Jana's eyes opened wide. "Oh, my goodness! And you just asked me if I worked for her? Drew Malone! How could you?"

Drew laughed again. "My dear, you could not have given me a better answer to my question if I had given you a twenty-dollar gold piece." He raised her hand to his lips and kissed it gently. "And now I have another question."

"Well, I hope it's better than the last one." Jana broke into a smile.

"My sons and I would love to have you come to our house for Thanksgiving. Will you come?"

"Drew—oh, I don't know. I appreciate the offer but . . ."

"Greta is invited, too."

"Greta can come as well?"

"Yes, of course she can."

Jana smiled. "All right. In that case, I will come."

"Oh, there's one thing I should tell you though. The Malone Thanksgiving is not the typical one, at least, it hasn't been for the last couple of years."

"You mean you don't bake a turkey?"

"Oh, yes, we do that. But we take Thanksgiving to the prisoners at the jail. So by inviting you, I'm actually asking you to help me—and Elfrieda—to get everything ready."

"You're a man with many facets, Mr. Malone. I'll be honored to enjoy Thanksgiving with you."

"Well, there's more. First, stop calling me Mr. Malone. It makes me feel like I'm older than Hank, and secondly, there's a fireman's ball on Thanksgiving night. Will you go with me to that, too?"

"Oh." Jana covered her mouth with her hand. "I already have an invitation to go to the ball."

A disappointed expression crossed Drew's face. "I'm sorry to hear that. I wanted to be the one to take you."

"I can see you there. I'm sure I won't be in the booth the whole night."

Drew looked confused. "The booth? What booth? What are you talking about?"

"Liam Flannery asked me if I would spend some time in the kissing booth. He thinks I may be able to raise money for their rewards fund."

"The kissing booth!" Drew laughed uproariously. "All right, look, you can still go with me if you want to. I'll even volunteer to be your chaperone if you need one."

"I accept your offer."

"Good. I'll come pick you up Thanksgiving morning. Ten o'clock?"

"I'll be ready."

ELEVEN

Jana remained at the table a long time after Drew left. What had she just agreed to? This was the first time a man—any man—had ever asked her to do anything, much less go to his home. And this man was Drew Malone. A man whose face she had drawn in the margin of the Kotzebue translation, in her mind affixing his likeness to "the stranger" character. A man she fantasized about, but what were those fantasies?

And then there was the dance, and the kissing booth. As she thought about both, her heart began to pound. Jana considered herself self-confident, but the prospect of dancing and kissing scared her to death. Anyone would soon find out she couldn't do either. Why had she ever said she would go?

She knew that men and women were supposed to love one another and get married and have children and live happily ever after, but she had no couple in her acquaintance who exemplified the perfect marriage, least of all her mother and Frederick Kaiser. If that was what marriage was all about, she would be better off staying single. She knew what she could accomplish. Hadn't she found a way to get an education? Hadn't she found a way to get Greta and herself away from Highland? Hadn't she found a way to make a living while waiting to homestead? The answer to all of those questions was a resounding yes.

That brought her back to the dance. She would find a way to get out of going. She couldn't let Drew know what a neophyte she really was.

The next morning the smell of roasting turkey permeated not only the small kitchen behind the bar, but also the saloon, the lobby, and every hallway of the upper stories of the Custer Hotel. The other residents were gathering in the dining area, and Jana thought it endearing the way they were taking such pride in setting the table. Mr. Dempsey had bought a gold-colored tablecloth, and the men had pushed tables together to make one long one, so they could sit together. Hank Thompson was putting small pumpkins and gourds on the table, then putting shafts of wheat between them, to create an artful table decoration.

"Hank, I do believe you've missed your calling. That's beautiful," Jana said.

"My mama used to do this and I always liked to see the orange pumpkins. She didn't put the wheat in it, but I thought that would look good, too, especially since we're here in Dakota."

"I think it's just the right touch, and I'm sorry I'm not going to be able to eat with you."

"I know. Greta told me you're going to eat with Malone, but she's not gonna leave us. And no offense to you, Jana, but if one of you is not gonna be here, I'd rather it be you than her, 'cause she's turned into some kind of cook. Did you know she's gonna make a mincemeat pie for us?"

"She told me that," Jana said. "You know she was invited, too, but she turned it down, just so she could cook for all of you."

"And that's why we love her. Don't get me wrong, we love you, too, but it's not the same. That little ole gal in the kitchen, now she's gonna make some man a mighty fine wife someday."

"I expect that's very true, Hank."

"You go on now. Get ready for your man. Don't worry about Greta; me and the boys will take care of her."

"Thanks, I know you will."

Jana climbed the stairs and went into the room she shared with Greta. Who would have thought Greta would have adapted so well? Her breathing problems had almost completely disappeared in the dry air of the northern plains of the Dakota Territory, and she looked and felt healthier than she had ever been in Illinois. Jana should be feeling so happy for her, but a part of her was melancholy. For her whole life, she had been Greta's protector, but now every day Greta was proving she didn't need her big sister. Jana's feelings were in turmoil as she gathered her clothes and headed for the bathing room at the end of the hall.

When she reached the room, she turned on the water, which in the winter months was actually too hot for a bath because it was interconnected with the steam heat. Two large oaken buckets of cold water sat nearby, and Jana spilled them into the copper tub, making sure the water was comfortable before stepping into it. She lowered herself, submerging to her neck, making certain not to get her hair wet, because Drew would be coming for her at ten, and it wouldn't have time to dry.

Get ready for your man.

That was what Hank had said.

A part of her wished that was true. Drew Malone seemed to be everything a woman would want in a man. Physically, she found him attractive. His eyes were a deep blue set against a perennially tanned face, and he had a strong, angular jawline, the kind an artist would likely draw.

And his hair. He kept it cropped shorter than most of the other men in Bismarck. She imagined that was because the thick brown hair would be unruly if it had any length at all, and she couldn't help but wonder if it would be curly if it was longer.

All of these thoughts about a man, about Drew Malone, caused Jana to experience strange and rather unsettling sensations as the warm water washed over her body.

What would he think of her body? she wondered.

She looked down at her breasts, visible beneath

the warm water. Her nipples stood erect, and she touched them gently at first, then took her breasts in her hands. What would it feel like if a man, if Drew, held her breasts in his hands? She began to knead the soft mounds, and then, with one hand, began to brush a nipple with the slightest touch. This caused the strangest sensation, and not just at the site of her ministration, but lower in her private area. A fullness began to build deep within her body, and her hand moved to that area. What was happening to her?

Tentatively, she touched herself, and her face flushed. She knew that this was not something that a good girl would do. Hadn't she once heard a sermon about the sin of concupiscence? What she was doing to herself was the very definition of that word. This was new territory for her. She was experiencing a sexual desire for Drew Malone.

Just then there was a light knock on the door.

"Jana? Are you in there?" Greta called quietly.

"Yes, I'm here," Jana replied breathlessly.

"Didn't you say Mr. Malone was coming for you at ten?"

"Oh, what time is it?" Jana jumped out of the copper tub, splashing water on the floor.

"It lacks fifteen minutes of ten. Hank thought I should tell you."

"I'm glad you did." Jana grabbed a bath sheet and wrapped it around her. "Is anybody in the hallway but you?"

"No, but what difference does that make?"

"None at all." Jana streaked down the hall holding the sheet in place, her clothing all in a bundle.

When she reached the room, she dropped the towel and grabbed for a dress. She had intended to wear one of the fine dresses Mr. Watson had given her, but instead she grabbed her old, trusty rose wool, which she had worn the first time she met Drew. She threw on a chemise made of pink washing silk, then pulled on some drawers, not taking the time to put on a petticoat. Finally she was dressed, buttoning the last of the fifteen buttons that closed the bodice. She had intended to do something special with her hair, but when she looked at the clock, she barely had five minutes to spare. Pulling her hair straight back, she tied it with a pink ribbon and let it hang down her back, much as she had done when she was a child. This was not the way she had intended to present herself to Drew and his children, but it would just have to do. If he wanted to see her done up like a mannequin, he could always stand in front of Watson's window.

Once dressed, she hurried down the stairs to the lobby of the hotel, and when she got there, Drew was standing with his back to her, looking out onto Meiggs Street. He was wearing black twill pants tucked into high boots, topped by a fringed leather jacket.

Hearing her approach, he turned to meet her, and immediately a broad smile crossed his face.

"Good. A woman ready to work."

"That's me," Jana said, thankful that she had not dressed the way she had intended. "Let me step into the saloon and get my coat."

"No hurry. I'll wait right here."

When Jana stepped into the saloon, which was growing even more crowded, Hank looked over at her and smiled. "Well, now, if you don't look prettier than a little pair of red shoes."

"Why, thank you for the compliment."

"It ain't just a compliment, it's the God's truth," Hank said.

Grabbing her coat from the peg near the kitchen, Jana stepped over to the serving table where Greta and Carl were getting things organized for the meal.

"Greta, Drew is here, so I'm going to leave now."

"I'm glad you're doing this," Greta said. "And I hope you have a great time today. Don't be nervous."

"Nervous? What do you mean?"

"You know exactly what I mean. They're just little boys. Just like the dozens of little boys you've had in classrooms before."

How perceptive Greta was. Without Jana's even voicing her trepidation, her sister had put her finger on what was bothering Jana about this day. Two little boys—one four and one six—could be instrumental in her future happiness.

Jana took a deep breath. How foolish. She was going to Drew's home to help him put together a Thanksgiving meal to be delivered to prisoners. Hadn't he just said "a woman ready to work"? That was all. There was no "future happiness" to even think about.

When Jana approached Drew, she overheard Hank Thompson addressing him.

"If you take our girl, you treat her with respect,

you hear me? Because if you don't, I'm here to tell you, you'll have me and a whole lot of other folks to answer to. Now don't forget what I've said."

"Hank, I promise you, you have nothing to worry about. I'll not only treat her with respect, I'll see to it that everyone else does, as well."

Hank smiled. "Heck, Mr. Malone, I ain't really worried none. From ever'thing I've heard about you, you are a good and decent man."

"Hank seems very concerned about your welfare," Drew said a moment later as they were walking from the hotel to Drew's house.

"It isn't just Hank. Everyone who lives at the Custer Hotel looks out for both Greta and me. If I recall, you made a comment the first time you learned that I was living there, something about it not being a fitting place for a woman to stay."

"I'm afraid I spoke without thinking. I really didn't know many of the gentlemen who live at the Custer. And I can see that they are gentlemen. You have my humble apology."

"The apology should be to the gentlemen you miscategorized, not to me."

Drew chuckled. "The apology is meant for them as well."

Drew's large, two-story house was at the edge of Bismarck, the only house on the block. Jana was surprised to see that it was brick, one of the few brick houses in town. Drew opened the cast-iron gate that matched the ornamental fencing surrounding the yard, then stepped aside to let Jana pass through it first.

"Are you ready?" Drew asked as he took her hand and led her up to the front porch with its imposing stained-glass-paneled door.

"Yes," Jana replied with a wan smile. "I think so."

"I have to admit that the boys are a handful, but I wouldn't trade them for all the gold in California, and that's saying a lot."

When the door opened, a miniature Drew came bounding toward them, throwing his arms around his father's legs, almost causing Drew to trip.

"Hold up there, little man, I have someone I want you to meet. Miss Hartmann, this is Benjamin Eli Malone, and he is four years old."

"I'm almost five, and my real name is Benji." The little boy held out his hand to Jana.

"I'm very happy to meet you, Benji. When will you be five?"

Benji looked toward Drew and asked, screwing up his face, "When is it?"

"January, Benji. It's in January."

"That's right. January comes right after Christmas. Isn't that right, Miss—what is your name again?"

"My name is Jana, so why don't you call me that?"

"All right, Jana. I like you." Benji hugged Jana's knees just as he had his father's.

Just then, Jana noticed a rather large woman standing in the hallway, her apron covered with a dusting of flour.

"You'd better come in, miss, before we heat up the whole town," the woman said.

"Oh, I'm sorry." Jana hurried inside.

Drew laughed as he closed the door behind them. "This is Elfrieda Considine. I don't know how I ever ran my household before she came to live with us. She's my sergeant major."

"Ha, sergeant major my foot. My Martin was a sergeant and that's good enough for me."

"Elfrieda's husband was killed with General Custer at the Little Big Horn," Drew said.

"Oh, I'm so sorry to hear that."

"It was six years ago, God rest his soul. Mr. Malone tells me you're a good cook come to help me get the food out for the jailbirds."

"I'm afraid Mr. Malone is mistaken. It's my sister who can cook, but I'm willing to try."

"That's good to know. Makes me think my job is secure."

"Elfrieda," Drew said, "let's not jump to any conclusions here."

"Well, how many times have you brought a lady into this house? I can tell you right quick."

"That's enough. Where's Sam?"

"He went to his room right after you left, Mr. Malone."

"I'll go get him."

When Drew went into Sam's room, he found him sitting on the window box looking out the window, holding a pillow against his chest.

"Sam, are you coming down?"

"No."

"You don't want to help take the food to the jail?"

"Not if she's going."

"I asked Miss Hartmann to help, and she's going to go with us."

"I don't like her."

"How can you say that? You haven't even met her. Why, I'm just sure you would like her if you met her."

Sam turned his face toward Drew, and he saw an angry little boy.

"I don't want to like her. She's not my mama."

Drew went to Sam and sat beside him. "Sam, nobody said she was your mama. Your mama is gone, and no matter how much we all want her to be here, she's never coming back. We can love her as much as we ever did, but that can't stop us from finding other people to be in our lives."

"Do you love Miss Hartmann?"

"No, I don't. I like her. I like being around her. She makes me laugh and she makes me feel good. And she would make you feel better, too, if you would let her. I think Benji likes her."

"Benji likes everybody. I'm not Benji."

Drew took Sam into his arms. "No, you're not, and I wouldn't want you to be. I have one Benji and I have one Sam, and I want both of you to be just who you are." Drew held his son for several minutes, with neither of them saying a word as both looked out at the empty prairie. "I have to go back downstairs. Will you come down and meet her? You can call her Jana if you'd like."

"Maybe."

"Good, because I need you to carry the pumpkin pies. Nobody can do that as well as you can." Drew gave Sam one last big hug and held him close. "I love you, Sam, and no matter what happens, I want you to always remember that."

"I love you, too, Daddy," Sam said as Drew stood to leave.

Drew closed the door to Sam's room, then walked slowly down the hall. How was he going to handle this? He could see right now that Sam was going to be a challenge to his new resolve to find the boys a mother. But was his interest in Jana Hartmann for the benefit of the boys, or for his?

He knew the answer without even thinking. He was hungry for a woman's companionship, not just any woman, but a woman who had substance. So far, Jana was the first to come along that seriously interested him, but could he ever really love another woman? He couldn't answer that question. And then, did it matter if he loved her or not?

When Drew returned to the parlor, Jana and Benji were sitting on the floor playing snakes and ladders, a board game that Benji loved. It was played with a die, and if your marker landed on a ladder where the virtues were, you moved forward, and if you landed on a snake, where the vices were, you went backward.

Jana had just thrown the die and counted as she moved her piece. "One, two, three—oh, no!"

"You have to go one more, you have to," Benji

said as he rolled on the floor in laughter. "You got drunkenness. You have to go all the way back."

"Drunkenness. Oh, Miss Hartmann, that is bad," Drew said when he came into the room, sitting down on the floor.

"Daddy, you don't have to call her Miss Hartmann. Her name is Jana."

"Yes, did you forget?" Jana teased.

"No, I've not forgotten," Drew said with a devastating grin. "But who's helping Mrs. Considine? I leave you two, and what do you do? You start playing when there's work to be done."

"Come on, Jana. Daddy will clean this mess up," Benji said as he pulled on her hand.

"He's right. Daddy cleans up." Drew began picking up the game.

Just as Jana stood, she saw another child sitting on the top step of the stairway. She stopped at the bottom of the stairs, wanting to say something, but she thought the child should be the first to speak. When he did not, she smiled and waved, then followed Benji through the swinging door that went into the kitchen.

"Oh, it smells lovely in here," Jana said.

"I'm just waiting on the gravy to thicken and everything will be ready," Elfrieda said. "Start putting the stuff in these crates."

Jana put the mashed potatoes and turnips in one crate while Benji put the pudding in another.

Just then Drew and Sam came through the door.

"The pie man's here," Drew said. "We can put the mince pies in the crates, but we have to carry the pumpkin pies, and Sam's the best there is."

"Hi, Sam," Jana said.

"Hi." Sam picked up a pie and went through the swinging door.

Drew looked toward Jana and shrugged his shoulders.

"It's all right," Jana said as she picked up the vegetable crate.

"Mr. Malone, you carry the turkey and the roast pork," Elfrieda said.

"Hey, what are we gonna eat?" Benji asked.

"Don't worry, there's plenty for us, and Mr. Malone and Miss Hartmann will eat at the church."

"We're eating at the church?" Jana asked.

"Yes. Oh, did I forget to tell you? The whole town has a potluck dinner on Thanksgiving, and then we all go to the dance. Elfrieda is making her oyster stew for us to take."

Drew hitched a horse to a wagon that was now loaded with food, and the four headed toward the jail.

"Daddy, I beat Jana in ladders and snakes," Benji said. "You know why I beat her?"

"No, why did you beat her?"

"Because I'm a very good player."

"That's right," Jana said. "You are a very good player because you've practiced. You're certainly a better player than I am."

Jana looked over at Sam, who seemed to find something interesting to look at outside the wagon.

When they reached the jail, Drew jumped down, leaving the boys and Jana in the wagon.

"Are you gonna stay with us?" Benji asked.

"No, I have to go home," Jana said.

"Where do you live?" Sam asked.

Jana was glad that Sam had spoken to her. "I live at the Custer Hotel."

"Why do you live there?" Benji asked.

"Because she doesn't have a house," Sam said.

"You mean you don't have a house to live in?"

"No."

"That's all right, we have a house, you could live with us," Benji said.

"Oh, I think it would be better if I stayed where I am. Besides, you have Mrs. Considine to take care of you."

"Yeah, it would be better if she stayed in the hotel. Where would Elfrieda go?" Sam asked. "Miss Hartmann can't live at our house, Benji."

Sheriff McKenzie and his deputy met Drew when he came into the jail.

"Well, now," McKenzie said. "The boys are certainly going to appreciate this. They've been waiting all day."

"How many prisoners do you have?"

"There are four. Of course, Deputy Ames and I plan to eat with them, if there's enough food."

"You don't have to worry, there's plenty of food," Drew said. "Come give me a hand bringing it in."

Sheriff McKenzie and Deputy Ames followed Drew back out to the spring wagon, where Jana, Sam, and Benji were waiting.

"Sam, you're going to have to carry the pumpkin pie in," Drew said. "I don't trust these guys with it."

"Can he carry it without dropping it?" Sheriff McKenzie asked.

"Are you kidding? He's the best pumpkin-pie carrier in the world," Drew said.

Sam climbed down from the wagon carefully and, with great attention to his responsibility, carried the pie into the jail.

The sheriff had put a table into one of the cells, and all the prisoners were brought into that cell for their dinner.

"Mr. Malone, I want you to know how much we appreciate this," one of the prisoners said. "Sometimes people forget about prisoners when the holidays come around. But you didn't."

"Well, just because you're in jail is no reason why you can't celebrate the holiday like the rest of us."

"And now, Sheriff, if you don't mind, I'd like to say a little blessin' before we eat," one of the prisoners said.

"I don't mind at all, Adam. You go right ahead." Sheriff McKenzie and Deputy Ames removed their hats, and all bowed their heads.

"Most gracious Father, we thank you for this food we are about to eat, and for those good people who prepared and are serving it to us. Look with pity on those of us who are housed here. Grant us true contrition for past sins, and strengthen us in our good resolutions. Amen."

After telling everyone good-bye, Drew and Sam returned to the wagon, where Jana and Benji had patiently been waiting.

"We made some hungry men very happy. Now let's hurry home and eat our dinner."

"Drew, I think I should go back to the hotel."

"Why?"

"I just think it would be better."

"You aren't changing your mind about dinner and the dance tonight, are you?"

"No, I haven't changed my mind. But I really do think I should go back for now."

"All right, but I'm going to pick you up at four o'clock."

When Jana returned to the hotel, she went straight upstairs, even though the sounds coming from the saloon were inviting. The men were singing patriotic songs and hymns, which seemed incongruous to Jana. Hymns and a bar just didn't seem to go together.

When she went into her room, she lay down on the bed and stared at the ceiling for a long time, thinking about Sam Malone. He was going to be a big problem.

She thought about her relationship with Frederick Kaiser. No matter how much her mother may have cared for him, if she ever did, Jana's life had been miserable.

She would see to it that any potential relationship between Drew and her would be nipped in the bud immediately. As she lay there, tears began to well in her eyes because he seemed to be such a perfect man.

TWELVE

Jana, Jana, wake up!" Greta was saying as she shook Jana's shoulder.

"What?" Jana responded groggily.

"Wake up. Drew is here, and you're not even dressed. Quick. Put this on." Greta pulled the orange satin dress with the green velvet collar out of the chest.

Jana took the dress without comment.

"What are you doing sleeping? Don't you want to go to the dance? That man is the most handsome man in town, and here you are taking a nap."

"Why don't you go with him?"

"Because I'm not the one he asked. You are." Greta quickly worked Jana's hair into a French braid. "Here. Put this on." She dabbed lip coloring on her sister's lips.

"What are you doing?"

"Making you look even prettier than usual. Now grab your cape and get out of here."

Jana did as she was told, moving down the hall-

way as slowly as she could. Of all things to do, she
least of all wanted to go to a potluck dinner at a
church with a man with whom she—with whom
she wanted to do what?

She saw Drew waiting for her at the foot of the
steps, his eyes glowing in the reflected light of the
gas chandeliers.

"You look beautiful," he said, his tone almost
reverential.

"I'm sorry I'm late."

"There's no problem. I took Elfrieda's oyster
stew by the fellowship hall already. Now, if that
had been late . . ."

"It's that good, huh?"

"Greta could probably make it better, but that's
what Elfrieda thinks she makes best, so that's
what I take. I hope you don't mind if we walk. I
just enjoy it."

Stepping out into the street, Drew took her arm
and held it snuggly against him. "You know what
you need? A seal hat. I'll get you one for Christmas."

"Drew, you can't do that."

"Why not? If it'll make you feel better, it'll be my
pay for your services."

"Sometimes you talk in riddles. I have no idea
what you mean."

"I need your help. I need a woman to help me
pick out furniture for Rimfire."

"Rimfire? That's your ranch, isn't it?"

"Yes, but how did you know?"

"Frank told me that's where you had gone."

"You were wondering about me," Drew said

with an easy smile. "That's the way it should be."

"What's Rimfire like?"

"It's beautiful. You'll have to see it someday."

"I'll bet the boys like it."

"They do, but they'll like it even more when I get their own horses for them. I'm waiting for them to be a little older though."

"Let me guess. Benji thinks he's ready for his own horse now, but Sam is a bit more cautious."

Drew chuckled. "You've got 'em figured out, all right. Benji's ready to try anything, anytime. Sam's a little more . . . well, I guess the word is *reserved.*"

"I could see that."

Drew stopped and looked at her, then he touched her lips with his finger as he pulled her closer to him.

Jana closed her eyes as she took a deep breath. Despite her best intentions, she knew she was falling in love. How could she be around this man and not fall in love with him? For just this one night she would forget her pledge to try to shield one little boy from the heartache she had experienced at the hands of a stepparent. She would enjoy being with Drew, who, as Greta had so rightly said, was the most handsome man in Bismarck.

When Jana and Drew walked into the church fellowship hall, there was a sudden lull in the conversation. Drew stepped forward and raised his hand.

"Ladies and gentlemen, for those of you who don't know her name, I would like to introduce

Miss Jana Hartmann, or, as most of you know her, the 'woman in Watson's window.'"

A loud cheering followed as several of the men stood up.

"She's the one who's costing me a bloody fortune," one man said as he yelled above the others.

"And I for one can't thank you enough," a white-haired lady said as she patted the man on the arm. "Thurlow hasn't bought me this many clothes in all forty years of marriage combined."

Although the Thanksgiving meal was held in the Methodist church, a great many non-Methodist townspeople were present for the nondenominational event. Four long tables had been prepared for the diners, with an array of native vegetation, pumpkins, fruits, and nuts interspersed with shafts of wheat running down the center length of the tables, each of which would accommodate fifty diners.

At one side of the room a long buffet table was filled with food, featuring stuffed turkey and roasted venison in addition to the oyster stew, countless vegetables, freshly baked bread and rolls. Finally there were the desserts: pumpkin, mincemeat, and pecan pies, almost too many to count.

Drew turned to Jana and took her hand. "Shall we get a plate of food and find a place to sit? I'm starved."

"I think that would be best, now that we've made an entrance worthy of the Opera House."

As Drew directed her toward the buffet table, Jana felt the light pressure of his hand on the small of her back, and the gesture sent rhythms of pleasure up her spine.

"Elfrieda says everybody likes her stew, and I guess she's right because it's all gone, but there's still enough food for an army," Drew said as he picked up a turkey drumstick. "I can't get this at home because drumsticks are the boys' favorites."

"Was Sam all right after I left?"

"I think so. Jana, I hope he didn't—"

"Drew, you forget. I haven't always been the 'woman in the window.' At one time, I was a teacher, and I've been around a lot of children."

"I guess that's why you were so patient with Sam today, and why you were so good at snakes and ladders." Drew laughed. "Benji said you explained what asceticism was when he landed on that block, but he's not convinced that doing without things is actually a virtue."

"I would rather explain that one than some of the others."

"You mean like lust."

"That would have been a bit challenging."

"I have changed the rules," Drew said. "Benji and I say that lust is a virtue rather than a vice because, the way I explain it, it's when you want too much ice cream."

"And when he gets older and some teacher tells him the real meaning of lust, he's going to say, 'My daddy says it's good.'"

All at once, Drew's expression changed, and Jana knew they were no longer talking about a child's game.

"Lust is good when you know what you want."

Jana looked down as her cheeks began to flush. She continued along the line, making her food choices silently.

"Oh my, the woman in the window out among the real people," someone said. Looking toward the sound of the voice, Jana saw an attractive, rather petite, blond-haired woman.

"Hello, Drew, aren't you going to introduce me to—your friend?" the woman asked, setting the words *your friend* apart for emphasis.

"Jana Hartmann, this is Della Peterson. Miss Peterson is Sam's teacher."

Jana smiled. "Well, Miss Peterson, I've very pleased to meet you. Sam's a special young man."

"A special young man who needs a lot of work," Della said. "I've tried to get Drew to meet with me so we can go over some things that could help the boy, but he's always too busy."

"Sam is sensitive," Jana said. "But I'm sure you can understand why."

"He was a very young child then. I don't see how he can even remember the incident."

"You would be surprised at how far back children can remember, and what vivid impressions traumatic events can make on them."

"Oh, so now a woman who displays her body in a window for all to see is going to tell me about children?"

"Della!" Drew said sharply.

"I'm sorry," Della said quickly, smiling and putting her hand on Jana's arm. "It's just that I have tried so hard with that child, and the results have been very frustrating. Please forgive me."

"Of course."

Della looked toward Drew and flashed her most coquettish smile. "And, Drew, my dance card is not yet filled for tonight, but it is filling rapidly."

"I've no doubt that it is," Drew said. Then, looking out over the dining area, he spoke to Jana, effectively dismissing Della.

"There's Frank. Come, I'd like you to meet Caroline. She's a good friend, and I think you'll like her."

"It was a pleasure to meet you, Miss Peterson," Jana said.

Della did not respond, and Jana couldn't help but notice the glaring expression on the schoolteacher's face as they moved through the crowd toward the Allens.

After the Thanksgiving feast the diners all moved to the Sheridan House. The tables in the dining room had been pushed to the side to make room for dancing. More than a hundred couples had congregated. The hall was decorated with flags and emblems of the Pioneer Fire Company Number 1, which both sponsored and profited from the event.

The members of the fire brigade were easy to pick out because they were all wearing their red shirts, creating a swirl of bright color among those who had come to the dance.

Jana and Drew were sitting with Frank and Caroline when Liam Flannery saw them.

"Miss Hartmann, sure 'n' I hope you haven't forgotten, now," he said as he approached their table with a broad smile.

"Oh, Mr. Flannery," Jana replied, remembering her comment about participating in the kissing booth if she attended the dance. "I don't think I can do this."

"But t'would be a fine thing for you to do. 'Tis not a single young lad here who'd not be for layin' down hard money for the chance of kissing such a lovely young lassie."

"How much hard money?" Drew asked.

"It'll be two bits a kiss, sir."

"And how long does she stay in the booth?"

"A quarter of the hour for each of our lovely ladies."

"So at the most, Miss Hartmann could raise about seven dollars. Is that what you're saying?"

"Aye, we're thinkin' somethin' like that."

Drew pulled a bill from his billfold and handed it to Liam. "Here's ten dollars. I'm buying all her kisses for myself."

"Oh, Drew, that's too much money," Jana said.

"Do you want to kiss somebody else?" Drew asked.

"No, I don't."

"Oh, Mr. Malone, I did no' know she was your special lady, or I would no' have asked her." Liam held up the $10 bill. "But 'tis thankful I am for the donation. And 'tis a promise to you that I'll be for makin' good use of it."

"I'm sure you will, Liam," Drew replied with a smile.

Caroline and Frank exchanged knowing glances as Drew took Jana's hand and led her onto the dance floor as the music began.

The first dance was the polka, and because Jana had danced the polka with Drew on the night of the election, she felt confident she could follow the steps without anxiety. But the next dance was different, a slow waltz, and Jana was more than a little apprehensive about it.

This was the first actual dance she had ever attended, and she felt awkward. Dancing had not been allowed at McKendree College, so her only prior experience was with the occasional community barn dances held in Highland, and those dances were more a form of exercise than a sensual experience.

It turned out, as she expected, that Drew was an excellent dancer, and with him leading, the steps seemed to fall into place. So easily did the movement come that Jana found herself concentrating less on the dance and more on her partner.

As they danced, he looked into her face, and the smoldering fire in his eyes caused a dizzying current to race through her. The tiniest trace of a smile was on his lips, as if he could read her thoughts, but he neither said nor did anything that was, in the slightest, unseemly.

The dancing continued far into the night, and she found herself giving a little prayer of thanks that the floor was so crowded that no one could observe any one couple individually. The evening progressed through the polka, waltz, schottische, the Portland, and the mazurka. It seemed, as Jana and Drew moved deeper into the evening, their physical contact during the dances grew much closer and more intense. By the wee hours of the morning, Jana could almost feel the beat of Drew's heart, so closely was he holding her, molding the soft curves of her body against his. She enjoyed the feel of his arms around her, strong and possessive.

At two o'clock in the morning the dance came to a close, a surprise to Jana, who had so enjoyed the evening that she thought it not yet midnight.

"Two? In the morning?" she gasped. "Oh, my goodness! Greta must be worried to death!"

Drew chuckled. "My bet is that Greta was so tired from all the work she did today that she's in bed, fast asleep, with no idea that you're not even there."

Jana laughed. "I suspect you may be right. It's just that I worry so much about Greta that I sometimes forget she has her own life to lead. I know she doesn't think about me nearly as much as I think about her."

"That's often the case with people who've taken the burden and responsibility of looking after someone else. And you've taken on that burden with your little sister, haven't you?"

"I—I suppose I have."

"Why is that? Greta seems to me to be perfectly capable of looking out for herself. The few times I've met her, she seems like a remarkably capable young woman."

"She is, isn't she?" Jana smiled. "I can't tell you how proud I am of her, for how she's adapted to this change in our lives."

"What kind of change do you mean?"

"Being uprooted from comfortable . . ." Jana

paused in midsentence. "I mean from familiar surroundings."

Drew knew that something in the way she amended her comment was significant, but he didn't press the question.

"Well," he said, "it seems the musicians are putting away their instruments, so that must mean it's time to go home. I'll walk you back to the hotel."

"You don't have to do that. It's so late and the Custer is right around the corner. I can make it by myself."

"I insist."

The night air was cold, considerably cooler than it had been earlier, so cold that the cape Jana had worn seemed insufficient, and she began to shiver.

"Allow me." Drew removed his coat and draped it over her shoulders.

"I can't take your coat. It'll be too cold for you."

"I'll find a way to keep warm," Drew said easily as he put his arm around her and pulled her closer to him.

Strangely, Jana was no longer aware of the cold, so heated was she from the feel of his arm around her. They passed out of the glow of a streetlamp and into the shadow of Beal's Hardware store. Then Drew stopped.

"What is it?" Jana asked.

"Something I've been wanting to do."

Drew pulled her against him in an all-encompassing embrace. A small warning voice told her that she should resist, but that voice was drowned out by the overpowering desire that was coursing through her body, a desire to be held by this man, to be consumed by him. His hands found the hollow of her back and pulled her to him, much closer than she had been at any time during the evening.

She knew he was going to kiss her, and because it would be her first real kiss, she was a little overwhelmed. Would he know how inexperienced she was and turn away, or would he be amused?

He tilted his head to hers, and his kiss was slow, nonthreatening, allowing her time to build some trust so that the apprehension changed to sweetness; then she felt shivers of desire as his tongue began to trace the soft fullness of her lips. Then, shocking and thrilling her both, he opened his lips on hers and pushed his tongue into her mouth. The kiss caused a swirling sensation in the pit of her stomach, and involuntarily a moan of passion began in her throat. Her body was warmed with a heat that put a lie to the surrounding temperature. His lips left hers to nibble at her earlobe, then his tongue left a searing heat down the side of her neck and around to her throat, before moving up again to recapture her lips. The kiss went on, longer than she had ever imagined such a thing could last, and her head grew so light that she feared she would swoon, and she fell into him, totally dependent upon his strength to keep her from falling at his feet. They were in the middle of Bismarck, but she was aware of nothing save the wave after wave of pleasure that was sweeping through her.

Then, for the first time in her life, she felt, firsthand, the result of a man's sexual excitation, for a hardness was pushing against her. Though she had no experience in such things, she knew what it was, and she knew she'd caused it.

Finally, the kiss ended, and he pulled away from her. The abrupt end of the kiss left her hanging on an edge, aching and unfulfilled. She stood there for a long moment with her eyes closed, her mouth upturned, not sure what she should do next.

Drew kissed her again, but this time the touch of his lips against hers was light as the brush of a butterfly's wing.

He smiled down at her. "I'm glad no one else got to kiss you tonight. Liam Flannery doesn't know it, but I would have paid a hundred dollars just to keep your kisses for myself." He lowered his head again, and this time he backed her up against the building, trapping her with his body as he kissed her again, demanding a reaction from her that equaled his own, and she willingly gave it.

"Did you know we're on the main street of town?" Jana asked in a bare whisper.

Drew chuckled lightly against her lips. "You're right. What would someone think of your improprieties, Miss Hartmann? The very idea of kissing a man in public. Why, it's scandalous."

"No one would notice. They'd just say, 'It's only that woman in Watson's window who works at the saloon.'"

"Oh, is that the same woman that someone thought worked at Little Casino's brothel?"

"I can't believe you actually thought that." Jana hit Drew's chest playfully.

He caught her hand and held it, looking into her eyes with a longing—no, a hunger.

No one had ever looked at Jana the way Drew looked at her. To Mr. Kaiser she had been nothing but a hired hand; her mother's looks were always tired, and touched with a bit of unspoken guilt for having brought Mr. Kaiser into her life. Greta had always looked at her with the affection of an admiring sister, but Drew's looks were slow, seductive appraisals.

Finally he took a deep breath. "Come. As much as I'd like to stand here for the rest of the night, I'd better get you back to the hotel."

When they reached the Custer Hotel and Drew opened the door, the lobby was softly lit by the low-burning, orange flames of the overhead chandeliers. Hank Thompson was sitting in one of the padded rocking chairs, his head thrown back and his mouth open. He was snoring softly.

"What's he doing here?" Drew asked in a whisper. "Doesn't he have a room?"

"He's waiting for me."

"What? Are you serious?"

"I'm very serious. He's sort of adopted Greta and me, and either he or someone he assigns is always on watch to see that we're where we're supposed to be. If I'm late getting home from the store, or if Greta has to go get meat or vegetables for the soup, he gets anxious."

"Then I'll bet he's had a very hard night with it being so late."

"I don't think so. A couple of hours ago I saw Mr. Dempsey stick his head in at the Sheridan. I'm sure he told Mr. Thompson that the dance was still in progress and that I was there."

"You don't think Mr. Dempsey followed us home, do you?"

"I hope not." Jana's whole face spread into a radiant smile. "Maybe we'd better awaken Hank and just let him know he's fulfilled his duty."

Jana and Drew both walked quietly over to the sleeping man. Jana leaned down and kissed him lightly on his forehead, then she moved away from him quickly as he brushed at his forehead with his hand.

"What?" he said, waking abruptly. "What is it?"

"Hank, I'm home."

"As you can see, I brought her back, all safe and sound," Drew said.

"You don't have to tell me that," Hank said. "I saw the two of you as soon as you came through the front door." He pointed to Drew. "I had my eye on you, young man. If you'd tried any shenanigans with this girl, why, I'd have been on you like a duck on a june bug."

"I don't doubt it for a minute," Drew said with a broad smile. "That's why I was every bit the gentleman with her."

"Yes, well, you'd better be."

"Did you have a good Thanksgiving dinner?" Jana asked.

"Did I ever! I'll have you know I'm stuffed plumb to the gills. I haven't eaten me a dinner like that since the last time my own mama fixed one for me, and that's nigh onto forty years ago. That sister of yours is one fine cook, I'll tell you. She's gonna make some man a fine wife."

"You mean some *lucky* man a fine wife, don't you?" Drew clarified.

"Yes, sir, that's exactly what I mean."

"Well, speaking of the cook, I'd better get up to the room and see how she's doing. I'm sure she's asleep by now, but just in case she isn't, she might be wondering what I've been up to."

"Are you going to tell her . . . about everything?" Drew asked, taking her hand in his.

"There are some things that even sisters don't need to share."

Drew nodded his head as a smile curved his lips. "I can see that. Jana, I want you to know that I can't remember the last time I've enjoyed a day as much as this one." He held her hand, preventing her from moving toward the staircase.

"I enjoyed it, too."

"Well, go ahead," Hank said.

Drew looked at Hank. What was the old man telling him?

"Kiss her good night," Hank said. "I can see right now that's what you want to do, and you're not gonna get out of here till you do. You know the girl's got to work tomorrow and she needs her rest. But mind you, you make like you're kissin' your sister, 'cause, remember, I'm here watchin'."

Drew chuckled, then kissed Jana lightly on the lips.

That kiss, as light as it was, and under Hank's scrutiny, fired Jana's senses once more. She knew she had to pull away from him and hurry up the stairs while she still had some control.

"Good night," she said as she turned away from him.

"Good night."

Drew watched as Jana hurried across the lobby, then started up the stairs.

Will she look back at me? he wondered.

When Jana reached the landing, she turned to look back. Drew smiled triumphantly and nodded at her before she turned again and disappeared as the stairs continued on up.

"I've got one thing to say to you, Mr. Malone. Most of the time the prettiest ones are the hardest to get a rope around," Hank said when Drew turned to leave.

"You sound like you're telling me that from experience."

"Don't let this old carcass fool you, young man. I've flung a few lariats in my day, and I've caught my fair share of pretty ones."

"Well, I intend to catch that one, mark my words. Take care of her, Hank." Drew smiled and waved as he stepped out of the hotel.

THIRTEEN

Greta was sound asleep when Jana let herself in the room, but she awakened as Jana began undressing.

"How was the dance?" Greta asked in a voice groggy with sleep.

"It was very—enjoyable. I saw Hank downstairs. He said your Thanksgiving dinner was a great success."

"It went very well. Everybody told me how much they enjoyed it, and guess what? Tom gave me a twenty-dollar tip. He said I earned it."

"Oh, how thoughtful of him!"

Dressed in her nightdress, Jana climbed into bed beside her sister, then turned onto her side and pulled the cover up over her shoulder. She could tell by her sister's deep and rhythmic breathing that Greta had gone back to sleep quickly, but for her, sleep was more elusive. She fixed her gaze upon the soft silver splash of moon glow on the far wall.

As she lay there, staring at the moon silver, Jana let her mind pass over the events of the day. This had been a day unlike anything else she had ever experienced in her life. She had never been invited to a man's home before—certainly not in the way she had been invited into Drew Malone's home.

And she knew it was an honor to be introduced to his sons, as well.

Then at the dinner, to be introduced to an entire crowd of people as the "woman in the window" was also new for her.

The dance had been wonderful. This was nothing like the occasional community dances back in Highland. Well, that wasn't exactly true; this was a community dance, but never before had she gone to a dance with a man. She had been frightened by the prospect, but she thought she had comported herself quite well, and she smiled in self-satisfaction.

What stood out most in her mind were the kisses, and her reaction to them. But she knew she was not the only one to react. As she lay in bed, she recalled the pressure she had felt poking against her, the pressure from a hardness under Drew's pants. Jana lacked experience, but she did not lack imagination, and unbidden, her mind extended the parameters of those kisses, imagining even that hardness unbound so that she could see and even touch it.

Such thoughts set her entire body aflame. Despite that the room was quite cool, she was on fire and felt a tingling in that most private part of her body that begged for something. But what?

To clear her mind Jana began making a mental inventory of the dresses in Watson's store. Finally, after she heard the clock strike four, she got to sleep.

Drew had looked in on his children when he got home. Benji had covers over his head, while Sam had his feet sticking out at the bottom. Drew used to see that and cover Sam's feet thinking he would want that, but he would soon have them uncovered again, so Drew decided that was what Sam preferred.

When he lay in his own bed, Drew thought about the day with Jana, and he realized that this was the first truly pleasant day he had had since Addie's death. He smiled when he pictured Jana playing snakes and ladders with Benji and seeing his son rolling on the floor with laughter. Even though Sam had been cool toward her, she had not shown any anxiety; she simply let Sam be himself without putting any pressure on him. Drew appreciated that. She had surmised, immediately, the best way to handle the situation.

He found himself comparing Jana to Della Peterson, recalling Miss Peterson's words to him one day when he had encountered her just outside the school.

"Sam is a very sensitive child," she'd told him. "I think he feels deprived."

"I'm doing the best I can," Drew had replied.

"Oh, Mr. Malone," Della had said as she reached out to put her hand on his arm and smiled flirtatiously. "This isn't directed at you. I just think that Sam needs a woman's influence in the home."

Miss Peterson was probably right; Sam and Benji needed a woman's influence, but not hers.

Yes, Jana would be good with his children. But was he being fair to her when he put consideration of the boys first? Or *was* he putting them first? Obviously, any relationship with a woman would have to take the children into account, but it wasn't just the children that drew him to her.

Drew thought of the kisses he had shared with her out on the street. That was the first time he had kissed a woman since Addie had died. And it had been more than just a kiss; it was a kiss so intimate that it gave him an erection. He had pulled her against him, enjoying the pressure of her body against his.

Had she felt that?

How could she not have felt it?

He had enjoyed her company, he couldn't deny that. But was she merely a diversion? He had decided he needed a wife, and so far, no woman had come close to attracting his attention.

Not until Jana Hartmann.

As he lay there, his mind pushing back sleep, he thought of the boys. He was using them as justification for finding a woman, but how would they react? Della Peterson was right about one thing: Sam was sensitive. Would he ever accept Jana, or would he always feel that she was an intrusion, usurping the place of his real mother?

And what about Benji? Sam was convinced that Benji couldn't even remember their mother. Drew had to be damned certain before he entered into any kind of relationship because so many conditions had to be met.

Yet even as he thought about the effect such a relationship would have on the boys, he could not push aside the real, physical, attraction he felt for Jana. He and Addie had enjoyed a robust sex life—but not since her death had Drew enjoyed the pleasures of a woman. Though he missed the sex, he had always thought of it in a rather amorphous way, not attached to any particular woman, but now his body was reacting to imagined images of Jana naked and writhing with pleasure beneath him.

Pushing those thoughts away with difficulty, he finally fell into a fitful and not very restful sleep.

For the first few days after Thanksgiving, Drew did not pass by Watson's window, at least not where he thought Jana could see him, and he didn't stop by the Custer Hotel Saloon. He was purposely avoiding her, not because he didn't want to see her again, but because he did.

One week after Thanksgiving, Drew was in his office handling some paperwork for a client when he looked up to see Charley Draper standing at his door.

"I've got a message for you," Charley said with a long face.

"You look like you're delivering bad news. What is it?"

"I'm afraid it's awful bad," Charley stepped into Drew's office and handed him a telegram.

Drew opened the yellow envelope with trepidation. Had something happened to one of his parents? Or was it something at Rimfire? He hated getting bad news.

The telegram read: HOUSE FINISHED. SEND FURNITURE. DEVLIN.

"You rascal." Drew looked toward Charley. "You had me thinking some catastrophe had happened, and here it's great news."

"It might be good news for you, but it won't be for Bismarck."

"Why do you say that?"

"We've grown rather used to you around here, but if you get out to the Badlands and you like where you're stayin', why, you might decide not to come back." Then Charley smiled. "That is, unless the Watson woman stays here. Then you'll be back."

"The Watson woman?"

"You know the one I'm talking about, the one you brought to me lookin' for a job. I hear she's just about got you roped and branded."

"That's what you hear, is it?" Drew asked with a lazy smile.

"I shouldn't tell you this, but after the firemen's dance last week, some of the guys got up a pool to see who gets the closest to the day you marry that little ole girl."

"What day did you pick?"

"I can't tell you that. It wouldn't be fittin' 'cause then you might pick my day just so as how I could win, or if you had a mind to, you could pick some other date, just so's I'd lose."

"Has anyone consulted Miss Hartmann about this pool?"

"Oh, no. It's like bettin' on what day the ice breaks up on the Missouri. It's just sportin' talk. We don't mean nothin' by it, but mind my words, we all think it's gonna happen."

"Well, maybe I'd better call it quits here and go see if I can rouse up Miss Hartmann."

"From the looks of the two of you Thanksgiving night, it don't look like it takes much to get that woman roused up when you're around."

"Just what are you saying, Charley?" Drew asked, the tone of his voice changing slightly.

"Don't you go gettin' all riled now. It's just that lots of folks walked home from the Sheridan. And they've all got eyes, so that's when we set up the pool."

"Get out of here." Drew chuckled as he stood. "Wait. Send Devlin a telegram and tell him we'll see him for Christmas."

"I'll do it." Charley put on his hat and headed for the door.

After Charley left, Drew walked directly to Watson's store. When he arrived, Jana wasn't in the window, but a nearly completed drawing sat on an easel. She had begun to shade in the brown and white of the skewbald pony, and the drawing was so accurate it was obviously Tom McGowan's horse. Drew stepped into the store, hoping Jana was still there. She would be just the one to help him furnish his house.

"Drew, it's good to see you. How may I help you?" Walter Watson asked.

"I'm looking for Jana. I'm hoping you can spare her for a couple of hours so she can help me with a personal matter."

"I suppose I could let her go, but I'd have to know that she wasn't going to be doing something improper."

"I want to drive her out in the country and ravish her, if that's all right with you," Drew said with obvious exasperation.

When Jana stepped out of the back storage room, she saw Drew, and her heart fluttered as she smiled broadly.

"I haven't seen you for a while," she said as she approached him and Walter. "I was beginning to think you had gone back to Rimfire."

"Well, Rimfire is the reason I'm here. I got word today that the house is ready for furniture, and I'd like you to help me pick some out. Does that meet with your standard of decorum, Walter?"

Walter flushed with embarrassment at Drew's chiding. "Of course. I can spare her for a couple of hours, if she wants to go."

Jana wasn't sure what had been said between Drew and Walter, but she did understand that she could be away from the store for a couple of hours.

"I would love to go with you. Let me get my cloak."

When they stepped out of the store, Drew took Jana's hand as if it were the most natural thing in the world for him to do.

"Where shall we go first?" he asked.

"You're asking me? The only thing I know is

that Watson's Ladies' Emporium doesn't sell furniture," Jana said, laughing easily.

"I suppose that was a dumb thing to say, but this will be my first time to look for furniture."

"You didn't help furnish your house?"

"Oh, no, everything that was put in our house had to have Rose Denton's approval, so every stick of furniture was shipped from Chicago. Even Addie didn't have much to say about it."

"I take it Rose was your mother-in-law?"

"She was, and in her mind, she still is." Drew rolled his eyes. "Come on. Let's see if Jim Cady has anything we like."

They entered a small store where several pieces of rustic furniture sat about, all made from the cottonwood trees that grew in the area. Jana saw several beds and chests as well as various chairs where the bark had been stripped from the logs, which were sanded smooth. The grain was attractive, and she ran her hand over the wood.

"We'll take that bed," Drew said, indicating the oversize, four-poster bed. "That will be our first purchase."

A beaming man stepped forward. "When do you want it, Drew?"

"Now."

"No. I mean, is there a specific date when you'll need it?"

Drew narrowed his eyes as he looked at the proprietor of the shop. "Jim Cady, are you in the pool?"

"I might be." Jim cast his glance toward Jana.

"This is for my cabin at the ranch. Miss Hartmann is just helping me select the furniture."

"Uh-huh, and the first thing you buy is a bed. I'm buyin' another day."

Drew laughed. "Don't waste your money. But seriously, could you get this and four more beds on the evening train for Little Missouri? I guess I need some ticks to go on the beds, so send those, too."

As Drew and Jim wandered around the shop selecting other pieces of furniture, Jana walked to the front of the store. She tried to decipher what the conversation between Jim Cady and Drew had meant.

"That's a start," Drew said when they left the store. "Now let's go to Eisenbach's. Sol will no doubt have more comfortable sofas and chairs than Jim had."

"What were you two talking about?" Jana asked, realizing that the "cabin" might be a bit larger than she'd envisioned.

"We were just haggling over the price. Five bedsteads was quite a sale for him."

"Not the beds—the pool. What was that about?"

"Oh, it was nothing."

"I don't believe you for one minute, Drew Malone. Why do I have the feeling that the pool has something to do with me? More specifically, something to do with us?"

The smile Drew gave her was absolutely dazzling. "I can't tell you about it because you'd cheat if you knew all the details. Come on, we've got work to do."

By the end of the day, Drew, with Jana's input, had selected furnishings for what Jana learned was an eight-room house, hardly a "cabin" by her estimation. He had consulted her on various pieces and was acquiescent on her suggestions. A part of her wanted to think she was selecting furniture for a house—no, a home—for her and Drew and the boys. But she knew that was only the figment of an active imagination.

When they were back on Main Street, Drew turned in the opposite direction.

"I should get back to help Greta," Jana said when she realized they were going away from the hotel.

"She can handle tonight's soup without you, and besides, I want to confuse Hank a little bit. Let's get a bite to eat at Le Bon Ton," Drew said as he ushered her toward the restaurant.

"I can't."

"Please, Jana. I want to spend as much time as I can with you. Will you join me?"

Jana took a deep breath. "I will."

The following morning, Jana was humming a little tune as she was selecting a dress from the new shipment that had arrived while she was out yesterday. Her thoughts were of Drew and the pleasant evening she had spent with him. Was it too much to hope that he enjoyed her company as much as she enjoyed his? She had never been happier in her life. When she stepped away, she was admiring the drape of the soft faille dress she had chosen to display on the mannequin when Hank Thompson and Carl Meunch came into the store.

"Why, hello, you two, what brings you here?"

she asked with a broad smile. Then suddenly the smile was replaced by a look of concern. "Oh, no, has something happened to Greta?" she asked, her voice tinged with fear.

"No, she's fine," Hank said quickly, putting his hand out to calm her. "But she's the reason we're here."

"Oh." Jana sighed with relief. "You had me a little worried. What can I do for you?"

"We want to buy something," Carl said, "but we don't know what we want."

"The boys 'n' me," Hank said, "that is, the boys who come to the Custer Saloon, well, we've took up a collection, and what we would like to do is buy Greta a dress. Not one to work in, but a dress she can wear at Sunday go to meetin's and such. We want to give it to her for Christmas."

"And we thought, bein' as Greta is your sister, and bein' as you work here and all, well, you'd be able to give us an idea on what she might like," Carl added.

"My, what a wonderful thing you're doing for her," Jana said, genuinely touched by the gesture. "I'd be honored to help pick out a dress for Greta. Her favorite color is blue, so we can start there."

"Since it's for Christmas, don't you think she would like something red?" Hank asked.

"That's a good idea, Hank." Jana went directly to a red chasseur jacket that was trimmed in black basket braid. "I think this would be useful if you paired it with a black cashmere skirt. What do you think?"

"I don't know. We sort of wanted a dress," Carl said.

Jana smiled. They were going to be more difficult than her usual customer. She pulled out stylish redingotes with pretty shoulder capes and suits of rough-finished English tweeds. They finally settled on a myrtle-green brocade dress with a mantle of brown velvet.

"This is the one," Carl said. "How much is it?"

"That one is a little more expensive," Jana said. "It'll be six dollars and fifty cents."

Both men began to smile broadly.

"We've got enough money for two outfits. We'll take the skirt and the red jacket if you don't think she'll think it looks like a soldier," Carl said.

"I think Greta will think it's wonderful, and she will love you even more for thinking of her."

The purchases made, the two men left with the dresses wrapped in a package. Jana took her place in the window, smiling as she thought of the pleasure her sister would take from the generosity of "her gentlemen."

Jana had been drawing for a couple of hours when she heard a light tap on the window. She looked up to see Drew. She waved as he turned to enter the store.

"I want you to know, Miss Hartmann, you aren't the only artist I know." He handed her a sheet of paper. "Benji wanted me to give you this." On the paper were two circles as heads with stick arms and legs. One was bigger with lines that indicated long hair, and the other was much smaller and standing alongside. The arms of the taller figure and the shorter figure were connected, as if holding hands.

"He says to ask you if you know who this is."

"I can guess if he asked you to give it to me. I think this beautiful creature with the flowing hair is me, and this handsome young gentleman is Benji, and the best part is that we're holding hands."

Drew shook his head. "That's right, but how did you know that?"

"When one is an *artiste*, one can recognize a fellow *artiste*," Jana said in an affected French accent.

"Well, I have another request of the *artiste*. You're invited for supper tonight, food to be prepared by the acclaimed French cook Elfrieda, and her two sous-chefs, Sam and Benji. May I escort madam to my home?"

"Drew, I ran out on Greta last night, and I can't leave her two nights in a row."

"Did she have a problem last night?

"No, she said Carl helped her."

"And he probably enjoyed doing it. Please come, Jana. I think the boys are fixing a special dessert just for you, and they'll be disappointed if you don't come."

Jana looked directly at Drew, pondering what had just happened. If she accepted his invitation, she was moving their relationship, if that was what it was, to another dimension. It was one thing to go to Drew's home to help prepare a Thanksgiving dinner for prisoners in the local jail, but it was a completely different thing to go to his home to have a supper—a family supper, for no reason at all, other than to spend some time with him and his sons.

"If it will help you make up your mind, Jana, I'll throw in an evening at the Opera House. Colonel Lounsberry said the show that's playing now is really funny. So now, will you consider it?"

Of course she would consider it.

But the picture of a little boy with a solemn face came into her mind. If she proceeded, she would have to win not only the hearts of Drew and Benji, but also convince Sam that she was not ever going to usurp his memory of and the love he felt for his mother.

Jana broke into a wide smile. "I'll come, but you might be embarrassed. Do you know I've never been to an opera house?"

"Then it will be my pleasure to introduce you to vaudeville. I'll come by the hotel at six, if that's all right with you."

"I'll be ready."

When Jana walked into the hotel, she apprehensively went into the saloon to tell Greta that, again tonight, she would not be around to help her.

"How was your day?" Greta asked as she brushed the fall of her hair away from her brow.

"It was busy," Jana said. "People are beginning to buy Christmas presents already. I can't believe this town has so much money."

"You mean people are getting more than the candy and nuts we always got for Christmas?" Greta asked with a chuckle.

"Don't forget, we got an orange, too. But it was the best Mama could do for us. I miss her, don't you?"

"I think about her all the time. Do you think we could send her some Swiss chocolate for Christmas? Maybe we could find some like Dewey Gehrig's cousin brought when he came from Zurich."

"She'd like that. I'll ask Drew if he knows where we could get some."

"Drew? Aren't we getting awfully familiar with Mr. Malone?"

Jana's face turned crimson. "Greta, I'm so sorry."

"Sorry? Why would you say that? I think it's wonderful. You deserve all the happiness you can get."

"I won't be here tonight. He's asked me to come to supper at his house, and . . ." Jana hesitated.

"And what?"

"And then I'm going to Whitney's Opera House with him."

Greta laughed at her sister's apparent discomfort in telling her the plans for the evening, but then she got a serious look on her face.

"Are you in love with Drew Malone?"

"What?" Jana asked with a little gasp. "Greta, how can you ask such a thing?"

"I don't know anything about love, but I can see how your eyes light up when you talk about him. I know what love is between us, and I know I love Mama. And Papa, well, I suppose I honor him because that's one of the Ten Commandments, but I can't say I love him. It's just that I don't know anything about the love between a man and a woman, so that's why I asked you. Are you in love with Drew?"

"I—no—I don't think so."

"You don't think so, but you might be?"

"I don't know, Greta. I don't know any more about falling in love than you do."

Greta started stirring the pot of soup, then looked directly at Jana. "If you do decide you're in love with Drew, will you tell me? And will you tell me what it feels like?"

Jana chuckled. "Yes, little sister. If I do decide I'm in love with Drew, you'll be the first person I tell. That is, after I tell him, of course."

Greta threw a dish towel at her sister. "Go. Go get pretty for your date."

FOURTEEN

As promised, Drew showed up at the hotel at six o'clock to meet Jana, who was waiting in the lobby for him. She was dressed in a black wool skirt with a cream-colored, tucked shirtwaist, but at the last minute, she had picked up a lace fichu and thrown it around her shoulders. Having never been to an opera house, she had no idea how people would be dressed, but she felt the magenta fichu would dress up her rather plain outfit, and it would provide warmth if the place was drafty.

"I hope I didn't keep you waiting," Drew said as he came into the lobby, removing his hat.

"No, I just came down."

"Do we need to check with Hank before we can leave?" Drew asked with a smile as he helped Jana into her cloak.

"Not tonight. I've already told him I'll be late."

Drew laughed. "I don't think it will be too

late because I don't want to get on Hank's bad side."

"Nor do I." Jana laughed as well.

Benji was the first to greet them when they stepped into Drew's house. As he had done before, he ran first to Drew, to wrap his arms around his legs, then to Jana, to do the same thing.

"Did Daddy give you the picture I drew for you?" Benji asked.

"Indeed he did. It's a fine picture, as fine a picture as I've seen in a long time."

"Did you hang it on your wall?"

"I haven't yet, but I certainly intend to do that."

Elfrieda came into the front room then. "Good evening, Miss Hartmann. I'm so glad you came tonight."

"Please call me Jana."

"All right—Jana. Benji, you show your daddy and his friend into the dining room, and I'll go finish up in the kitchen."

"You're my friend, too," Benji said, taking Jana's hand and leading her into the next room.

"Where's Sam?" Drew asked.

"He's in there." Benji pointed to the parlor.

"I'll get him."

Sam did not say a word throughout the dinner of roast venison, with homemade noodles, but Jana took comfort that he had sat with them to eat. The conversation was lively with Elfrieda joining them at the table, and when Drew announced that it was time to leave, Elfrieda prompted the boys to get the dessert that they had made for Jana.

"Come on, Sam," Benji said as he bounded into the kitchen. They came back with a tin and handed the box to Jana.

"Look inside," Benji said excitedly. "We made these for you, and Sam made a card."

Jana opened the tin and saw the snaps, which were obviously cut by the boys. She opened the folded piece of paper that lay on the top of the cookies.

"Is this your card, Sam?" Jana asked as she smiled toward him.

He looked away quickly as Jana opened it and looked at the drawing. Because Sam was older, his drawing was more carefully drawn than Benji's. It was obviously a picture of Drew with Sam and Benji beside him. Written across the bottom in all capital letters was HATE, SAM.

Jana put the card in the pocket of her skirt. "I know I'm going to enjoy my cookies, but there are so many. Will you help me eat a few?" She offered the box to Benji and then Sam.

"We made them for you," Benji said, "but we'll help you if you want us to, won't we, Sam?"

Sam turned and ran from the room.

"I've never seen him turn down Elfrieda's snaps," Drew said, grabbing a cookie for himself.

"He had a big supper. Maybe he's full," Jana said as she began taking out a few cookies. "I'll leave the box behind with a few cookies in it. Maybe Sam will want a glass of milk and a cookie before he goes to bed."

"Speaking of which, it's time for you to get your nightshirt on, young man." Drew picked Benji up and threw him over his shoulder and carried the squealing little boy up the stairs.

"I want to say good-bye to Jana," he was yelling.

"Good night," Jana said as she stood by the door waiting for Drew. Then she saw Sam's head peeking around the doorframe of the parlor.

"I think your daddy needs you." Jana tried to use her most pleasant schoolteacher voice. She did not want to be stern, but neither did she want Sam to think what he had done was acceptable. She knew it was not her place to say or do anything, and she would make certain Drew did not find out what his son had done. She watched as Sam passed by her, his head lowered to avoid any eye contact with her. Jana was convinced that the boy knew he had done something wrong.

Just then, Drew came to the head of the stairs, meeting Sam. He knelt to give him a big hug, and when he did, Sam raised his face to stare angrily at Jana. Then he kissed his father and ran off to his room.

"Are you ready for this big evening?" Drew asked as he grabbed his coat from the hall tree and slipped it on.

"I am," Jana said as Drew took her arm in his. They went to a waiting buggy and climbed inside.

"I thought we might like the warmth tonight." Drew put a large buffalo robe over the two of them, which of necessity caused them to sit close together.

"Do you like the theater?" Drew asked as they

drove through town, the hoofbeats of the horse echoing back loudly from the buildings that fronted the streets.

"I don't know. I meant it when I said I've never been before."

"Good."

"Why good?"

"Because that means I'll be the first one to ever take you to the theater. And it'll be fun for me to experience something for the first time again, through your eyes."

"Drew, you'll find that I'm a person of very little experience in anything. I was born in Germany, I came to America when I was eight, and I was raised on a small farm. The only time I've ever been out on my own was when I went to college, and that was only fifteen miles away from home."

Drew reached over to take her hand. "You're on your own now though. But don't worry. I'll be here to guide you through the rough spots."

Jana didn't know what, exactly, Drew meant by that. But she did like the feel of her hand in his, and his words did make her feel protected.

Two hundred people were in the audience at Whitney's Opera House as the show opened with a duet by a man and a woman. That was followed by a comedic routine by John Coburn. Drew had told her that Coburn was quite well-known, having appeared in theaters all over the States. Next was a song-and-dance number, followed by Coburn's making another appearance. The night continued like that with songs followed by dance routines, with Coburn performing between each act.

When the curtain came down for the final time and the applause finally ended, the gas lamps in the hall were turned up bright enough for the theatergoers to exit the auditorium. Drew put his hand on Jana's arm to help her up the inclined aisle, which was crowded with people.

"What did you think of your first theater experience?" Drew asked.

"Oh, I've never had a more enjoyable evening! What a delight to hear the music, to watch the dancing, and Mr. Coburn"—Jana shook her head— "I've never laughed so hard in my life!"

Drew held up a finger, then began to sing one of John Coburn's ditties. "'Bless the wives who fill our lives with little bees and honey. They ease life's shocks, they mend our socks—but, oh, how they spend our money!'"

Jana laughed. "That's very good; you should be on the stage."

"Why, thank you."

"'There's one leaving in half an hour,'" Jana added, quoting one of the jokes she had heard, and they both laughed.

"I don't think you would, though," Drew said more seriously.

"You don't think I would what?"

"Be the kind of wife who would recklessly spend my money."

Jana stared at Drew. "Believe me, Mr. Malone, if there is one thing I do have, it's an appreciation for frugality." She turned and hurried to the standing buggy.

Drew was sorry for his comment. He thought he had said it in a joking way, but he didn't think that was how Jana had taken it.

When Drew stopped the buggy in front of the hotel, he hopped out to tie off the horse, then came around to help Jana down.

"Thank you for an enjoyable evening," Jana said.

"Oh, I'll walk you inside. I want Hank to know what a responsible citizen I am."

Taking her arm, Drew led her into the hotel lobby, where, once again, they found Hank sleeping in the chair.

"Let's not wake him," Drew whispered. "I'll walk you up to your room."

"You don't need to do that."

"I want to do it."

They walked arm in arm up the stairway until they reached the third floor.

"This is my floor," Jana said, turning to Drew.

He looked down the long, narrow hallway flanked on both sides by closed doors. A couple of wall-mounted gas lamps hissed quietly and emitted an orange light that lit the way. Behind the stairway Drew saw a small alcove that was dark save for the dim splash of light that did little to illuminate it. Drew stepped into the alcove and pulled Jana in with him, though not forcefully so.

As Drew looked at her, Jana saw a smoldering flame in his eyes, and she felt a tingling in the pit of her stomach. He moved toward her, paused for a moment, and, encountering no resistance, entangled his hand in her hair and pulled her lips to his. The kiss began innocently enough, no more than the brush of lips soft and tentative, as if he were exploring the bounds, but when she offered no resistance, the kiss deepened. She felt his tongue trace the soft fullness of her lips, and the kiss sent the pit of her stomach into a wild swirl. His mouth covered hers hungrily, then, as it had when they kissed in front of the hardware store after the Thanksgiving dance, his tongue slipped through her lips to explore her mouth.

At first she was concerned that here, in the hall of the very hotel where she lived, they might be discovered, and she thought to resist. But then she felt new spirals of ecstasy racing through her, leaving her mouth burning with fire, and she knew she would offer no resistance whatsoever. When his tongue withdrew from her mouth, she followed it with her own tongue, returning the kiss with reckless abandon.

During the kiss his hands were busy; one moved down from her hair to massage the back of her neck, the other went farther down to begin gathering up folds of the black material and, by so doing, began to lift the hem of the skirt. Jana could feel the soft touch of air as more and more of her leg was exposed until, finally, Drew was able to slip his hand under the skirt to her hips and thighs, the touch of his fingers on her bare skin sending pleasant jolts through her.

Jana lost all control of herself, becoming totally subservient to Drew's will and demand. She could no more break off this kiss than she could fly, and though a weak cry, far back in her mind, warned her against going too far, every emotion and sensation in her body silenced that voice.

Drew had not expected such easy acquiescence and was now torn between two conflicting emotions: the one to avoid taking unfair advantage of this woman, whose naïveté was such that he feared she wasn't quite aware of where this could lead, and the other to explore the parameters of this kiss. How far would she let him go before she asked him to stop? Would she ask him to stop, or was she as caught up in the maelstrom of sensations as he?

It was dark enough here, they could move back, deeper into the alcove, and no one would ever be the wiser. Why not give in to the need that was clearly driving them both?

Drew moved his mouth to her throat to kiss the pulsing hollow. He felt her trembling against him— or was he trembling against her? It was a most unusual sensation for him; he had been married, and he had fathered two children, yet he couldn't recall ever experiencing a craving this intense.

Was Jana feeling a desire as great as his? He was certain that she was, and he cast aside all caution as he undid the clasp of her cloak and began moving his lips down, searing a path across her shoulders, then untying the triangle of cloth that covered her shoulders, he opened the top buttons of her blouse and moved his lips onto the creamy tops of her breasts, feeling, as much as hearing, her rapturous moan.

Then he heard footfalls coming up the steps!

Although every part of Drew's body ached to go forward, somehow he found enough control to stop before compromising the delightful creature over whom he now had complete mastery.

***Oh, why did** he stop?* Jana screamed in her mind so loudly that she must surely have spoken them. But she knew that she had not, and even as she realized that, she knew why he had stopped, for now she, too, could hear footsteps.

Quickly they stepped back out into the hall and started toward her room, Jana refastening her buttons as she walked.

"Here!" Hank's voice challenged. "What are you doing up here on this floor?"

Her buttons now back in place, Jana turned toward Hank with a big smile on her face. "Hello, Hank. When Mr. Malone brought me home from the Opera House, you had fallen asleep in your chair and we didn't want to disturb you."

"So I offered to see her safely to her room," Drew added.

"Oh, Hank, I wish you'd gone to the theater with us. It was one of the most delightful things I've ever done," Jana said.

Hank smiled. "Now you're just bein' polite. I know you wouldn't really want me to go with you and your young man, but I do appreciate your sayin' that." He looked at Drew. "You said somethin' about walkin' her to her room?"

"Yes."

"All right, go ahead and do it. I'll wait here for

you, and we can go back down the stairs together; then I can see you out."

Drew smiled. "Yes, I sort of expected you'd say that."

Drew walked Jana to her room, then stopped and looked back toward Hank. Jana's self-appointed guardian was standing in the middle of the hall with his arms folded across his chest, staring down toward them.

"Who made him your bodyguard?"

"I think it's sweet."

Drew kissed her lightly on the lips, then pulled away from her. "What if I went into your room with you? What do you think he would do?"

"He'd probably come through the door with an ax."

Drew chuckled. "I think you might be right. Good night, Jana."

"Good night, Drew."

Drew walked back down the hall to Hank. "Hank, do you know where I can get a ladder tall enough to reach her bedroom window?"

"What?" Hank nearly shouted. "Why would you want a ladder to reach her window?"

Drew laughed. "You're right. It's probably not a good idea."

"All right, boys and girls, please close your copybooks and put them in your desks. Be careful to clean your nib before you put your pen away, and make certain the top is tightly placed on your ink and the bottle is resting in its well," Della Peterson said as she erased the blackboard at the front of the room. "I will expect you to write the letter *P* twenty times on your slate and show it to me tomorrow. When the counting sticks are put away and the readers are in their place, we shall prepare for dismissal."

The children cleared off their desks and put their things away, then waited quietly for the dismissal.

"First row may rise."

The children in the first row stood by their desks.

"Pass," Della said, and the children went to get their coats off the hooks in the long, narrow cloakroom behind the classroom.

She went through the same regimen with the subsequent rows, but when Sam Malone started into the cloakroom, she called out to him, "Samuel, would you come to my desk please?"

"Yes, ma'am." Sam walked to the teacher's big desk. He purposefully shuffled his feet along the boards of the classroom, making a sound as he moved slowly to the front.

"Your reading recitation was not very good today. I would like for you to recite today's lesson again for me." Della opened the *Swinton's Reader* to the page the beginners had read earlier in the day. "Read this for me, please."

Sam began to read: "'A big pig and six little pigs. Do not whip the pigs with the big whip! No, I will not whip them. Run, little pigs! Run, big pig!'"

He read the page without missing a single word, waiting for Miss Peterson's comment.

"Your father has been seeing a lot of that woman who poses in Mr. Watson's window, hasn't he?"

"You mean Jana?"

"I've been told her name is Miss Hartmann. That would be the polite way to address her."

"She said to call her Jana."

"Do you like Miss Hartmann?"

"She's all right, I guess."

"But you don't like her very much. Is that right?"

"I don't want a new mama." Tears welled in Sam's eyes.

"Oh, dear, has it come to that? You loved your mother very much, didn't you?"

With his chin quivering, Sam nodded.

"You loved your mama, and now here comes a woman who wants to take her place. But you and I both know that nobody can ever take your mama's place. Now, what does your father have to say about this?"

Sam didn't answer.

"Does he know you don't want that woman in your house?"

Again Sam nodded. "I told him."

"And what did he say?"

The child did not answer. He began tracing circles on the floor with the toe of his shoe.

Della took a piece of paper from her desk, dipped a pen into the inkwell, and began to write in clear, easy-to-read cursive. When she was finished, she took out a blotter and dried the ink, then folded the paper over and put it in an envelope.

"Give this note to your father as soon as he comes home."

"Yes, ma'am."

When Sam arrived home after school, he said nothing to Elfrieda about the note, but as soon as Drew came in, Sam gave it to him.

"What's this?" Drew unsealed the envelope and withdrew the note.

"It's from Miss Peterson."

"Well, let's see what she has to say about her very best scholar."

> *Dear Mr. Malone,*
>
> *It is with some trepidation that I address you with my concerns for Samuel. For some time now, he has been distracted and withdrawn. I assumed that it was because he still missed his mother, although as it has been nearly two years, and he was so young when the tragedy occurred, I could not understand why his melancholy has lingered so.*
>
> *But now, after a brief conversation with him, I am able to see the problem more clearly. I believe you are making a grave mistake by carrying on so with Miss Hartmann. I'm sure that you can see that a woman who exposes herself so shamelessly for all to see, is hardly the kind of person you want to introduce to a boy as sensitive as Samuel.*

*I would very much like for you to visit
with me so we can discuss this issue,
because I am sure that you, as well as I,
want only what is best for Samuel. I will be
available this evening until six p.m.*
    Sincerely,
    Della Peterson
    Teacher, Bismarck Primary School

Ten minutes later, Drew strode into the classroom, where he saw Della writing on the chalkboard.

"Miss Peterson," he said rather sharply. "I would have a few words with you, if you please."

Della turned away from the chalkboard, then flashed a broad smile. "Ah, Drew, how good of you to come!"

Drew held up the crushed note. "What's the meaning of this?" he asked between clinched teeth.

"Well, Drew, I thought I made that quite clear," Della said with a forced smile. "Samuel's schoolwork has been suffering for some time now, and I've been trying to get you to come talk to me about it. I'm glad you've finally found the time."

"I can understand if you're concerned about his schoolwork, but what's this crap about Miss Hartmann?" Drew said angrily.

"Mr. Malone! A gentleman does not use that kind of language in the presence of a lady." Della raised her hand to her lips.

"And a lady does not interject herself into somebody else's business. Now, what possible business is it of yours who I see?"

"My only concern is for Samuel. You have no

idea how upset he is, because he thinks she's trying to replace his mother. Now, I know that fear is foolish, but really, Drew, it must be dealt with if Samuel is ever to succeed in his schoolwork. I know Miss Hartmann is a very attractive woman—in a garish sort of way. After all, if she weren't, she wouldn't be daily exposing herself for commercial gain. It's only natural that you'd be attracted to her, but really, you should think of your children. Samuel is such a sensitive child. I worry about his home life."

"Look, you teach him his letters and his numbers. That's all you have to do, and I'll worry about his home life. And as for my seeing Miss Hartmann, that's absolutely none of your business. Do I make myself understood?"

"Well, I . . . I was only trying to help. That's what I think a good teacher should do."

"Then teach. But stay out of my affairs," Drew said angrily. Then, before she could respond, Drew turned and walked purposefully out of the classroom.

FIFTEEN

Two days later, Drew invited Jana to go to Rimfire for Christmas.

"What? Why, I couldn't possibly do that!" Jana said, though every sinew in her body urged her to say yes. "We'd both be scandalized!"

"No, we won't. The boys will be with us, and of course, Elfrieda will be there as well. Oh, and I want Greta to come, too, if she will. And then there's Peach."

Jana chuckled. "Peach?"

"She's Toby's wife. So there'll be a chaperone in every alcove even if Hank's not around." Drew kissed Jana lightly. "You don't have to worry about your reputation because nobody dares question Elfrieda."

"But, Christmas. I can't abandon Mr. Watson during Christmas. He's been so good to me, and that will surely be his busiest time of the year."

"Christmas comes on Monday. We won't leave

until the evening train on Saturday, so that way you'll be there for his busiest time."

"I don't know."

"I'll teach you to ride a horse. I know you'll have a good time. And, all right, I didn't want it to come to this, but, Jana, I need you. The house is finished, and all the furniture we bought is there. Devlin says they just piled it in the great room without even trying to put it in any of the rooms. I can't even remember what we bought, let alone try to decide where to put stuff. I'm serious. I really do need you to go with me."

Jana could feel her reserves breaking down. "How long would we be there?"

"Probably no more than two weeks."

"Two weeks? I can't stay that long."

"Why not? Walter's busy time will be over by then. And anyway, I'll talk to him. He'll let you go."

"All right." A big smile crossed Jana's face. "Why can't I ever say no to you?"

Drew's eyebrows shot up as his eyes began to twinkle with amusement. "Miss Hartmann, I can guarantee I'll remind you of your words again sometime, and I can tell you this: you won't be sorry."

"I'd love to go with you, but I can't," Greta said after Jana had extended the invitation to Rimfire.

"Why not? Greta, it's Christmas. We should be together."

"I promised Tom I'd be here to fix a Christmas dinner, and I can't let everybody down. Most of these men who live here don't have any family at all, and they think of us as their daughters. In all my life, I've never made such close friendships, and to be honest, I really do want to stay here and make their Christmas a little bit happier."

"Of course, I understand." Jana's voice showed her disappointment. "I'll tell Drew we can't come."

"What do you mean you'll tell him *we* can't come? I can't go, but there's no reason why you shouldn't go."

"Sure, there is. Half the town already thinks I'm scandalous because of my job. If they found out I spent Christmas with Drew and his family, it would just add fuel to the fire."

"Do you want to go?"

"Of course I do."

"Then think about this. To the half that already think you're scandalous, it won't make any difference whether you go to the ranch with Drew or not, they will still think you are scandalous. And the other half of the town knows you well enough by now that your reputation will be safe, no matter what you do. Besides, won't Elfrieda go with you?"

"Yes, she's going."

"Then I don't think anyone would dare question you if Elfrieda is there. Not unless they want to make an enemy of her, and from what I've seen of that woman, she's not someone you want for an enemy." Greta laughed.

"Oh, Greta, are you sure you think it's all right?" Jana realized that, for the moment, their roles had changed. She was now looking to her younger sister for guidance and validation.

"I'm positive," Greta said, also recognizing the reversal of their usual roles.

The Pacific Express was supposed to leave at seven thirty in the evening for its westward run, but the schedule on the chalkboard said that the train from the east had been delayed and wouldn't depart the Bismarck station until almost midnight. It would be an eight-hour trip to Little Missouri, which meant the train should arrive at eight o'clock the following morning. Drew wired instructions for Devlin McCarthy to meet the train.

In the Northern Pacific Railway depot, Jana, Drew, the two boys, and Elfrieda waited for the train to arrive, taking seats near the little potbellied stove. It radiated enough heat from the coal fire to keep them comfortable when they were close, but if one wandered away from the stove, the heat began to dissipate and the cold took over.

Drew got a checkerboard from the agent, and the boys entertained themselves by playing checkers as they waited.

Jana saw another family waiting, husband, wife, and a young girl who looked to be about twelve. Jana smiled as she realized that she had thought of them as "another family," as though she was part of this family.

And why not? She certainly felt more a part of this family than she had ever felt with her mother and Mr. Kaiser.

No, that wasn't entirely true. Greta and her mother had been family to her. But it wasn't quite the same as the sense of acceptance surrounding her now, except for maybe Sam, who remained a little reticent around her.

Finally, at a few minutes before nine, the building began to shake and rumble as the train from the east drew into the station.

"Here's the train!" Benji said excitedly.

"We all heard it, you don't have to tell everyone," Sam said.

"I know, but I wanted to tell everyone. Daddy, do you think we'll have another train wreck?"

"Heavens, child, I certainly hope not!" Elfrieda said.

"But it was fun, wasn't it, Daddy?"

"I'd just as soon not have another one," Drew said.

"It wasn't a wreck," Sam said.

"It was, too."

"Please, boys, let's not go through all that again. Sam, take the board and checkers back to Mr. Emerson, then let's go out on the platform. They'll be boarding soon."

As they boarded the train, Jana couldn't help but compare this car with the cars she and Greta had ridden in on the way out to the Dakota Territory. Those seats had been hard, uncomfortable benches crowded close to each other. These seats were comfortably padded, with plenty of legroom. Also, an enclosed necessary room was at each end of the car, one for the gentlemen and one for the ladies. She grimaced at the remembrance of the horrible odors emanating from the filthy corner on the emigrant car.

Elfrieda sat first, and Jana sat beside her, thinking the boys would want to sit with their father.

"Guys, why don't you sit next to Mrs. Considine, and let Jana sit beside me. You two will fall asleep before long, and then I won't have anybody to talk to all the way to Little Missouri," Drew said.

"You're gonna talk all night long?" Benji asked as he jumped down and sat next to the window.

"Maybe."

"Don't grown-ups need any sleep?" Benji asked.

"This grown-up needs sleep," Elfrieda said. "Come on, Sam, get over here."

Jana took the seat next to the window, and Drew sat beside her, his leg just barely touching hers. A moment after they were all settled, the train started forward, first with a few jerks, then evening out as the car began to build speed.

Through the window, Jana watched the lights of the town flash by until soon they were out of town, and all she could see was a long, flat prairie, stretching out and gleaming under the full moon of the cloudless night sky.

"We're on our way," Benji said.

"Yes," Drew answered.

"We're really on our way," Benji repeated.

Jana had to smile to herself at his excitement, which mirrored her own, unspoken feelings.

As the train rolled through the night, the lamps were turned down so that the inside of the car was nearly dark. Before long both Sam and Benji were sound asleep, their heads resting on Elfrieda's ample lap, their coats placed over them as blankets. Then Elfrieda's head began to bob, and Drew rolled his wool scarf so as to cradle her neck against the seat.

"Are you sleepy?" Drew asked Jana.

"No. I'm much too excited."

Drew reached over to take her hand in his. He did it casually, without asking, and as if not anticipating any resistance. Jana offered no protest because having her hand in his seemed perfectly natural.

"I'm glad you came with me," Drew said.

Jana became keenly aware of the pressure of Drew's leg against hers, a pressure that increased whenever the train rounded a curve. She should try to reposition her leg, but she did not.

She stared out onto the night landscape as they passed through a little town not far from Bismarck. She thought about the path her life had taken until she arrived at this precise moment, sitting next to Drew Malone, her hand in his. She had committed herself to spend Christmas with this man and his family—people she had never even heard of as recently as two months ago.

"November fifth," Jana said.

"I beg your pardon."

"November fifth was the night I arrived in Bismarck to start a new life."

Drew squeezed her hand. "And how has your new life been?"

"Interesting, so far."

"Just interesting?"

Jana chuckled. "How would you have it be?"

"Well, you've met me," Drew teased. "I would have your new life be exciting."

"There's been some excitement. And I'm looking forward to seeing this 'cabin' that you're furnishing."

"I hope you have no regrets when you see it."

"My only regret is that Greta isn't here with me. I don't really understand why Greta wanted to stay at the hotel over Christmas."

"Sure, you do," Drew said. "Greta has adopted the men who live there, she feels an obligation toward them, and they feel just as big an obligation toward her."

"I have to confess that Greta has really blossomed since we left Illinois; not only has her health greatly improved, but her whole personality has changed."

"What do you mean? Changed in what way?"

"I've always thought of Greta as the shy, reserved one, but that certainly isn't the case now."

Drew chuckled. "I'll say it's not. She's absolutely effervescent the way she interacts with the residents at the hotel."

"I only have one regret. I wish our mother could see us now, especially Greta, and how well she's doing."

"I'm sure she'd be very proud of you both."

"This will be the first Christmas either one of us has ever spent away from our mother. I can't help but wonder what sort of Christmas she'll have, with both her daughters gone." Jana smiled. "She loves Swiss chocolate, so that's what Greta and I sent her for Christmas. I want her to know that we haven't forgotten her, and how much we love her."

"I have a feeling that she knows."

"I can't tell you how proud I am of Greta for the way she is taking to this new life."

Jana thought, but didn't say aloud, that she felt pride for her part in bringing Greta's new life about. But, what about her? She was also starting a new life, and—a new relationship. Relationship? Was that what she had with Drew?

She couldn't really call it new, could she? It was more than just new. It was a first, and here she was, on a train, rushing through the night, bound for a place called Rimfire.

She not only knew little about Rimfire, the place they were going, she realized that she didn't know that much about Drew. It was time to find out a few things.

"Drew?"

"Yes."

"How did you meet your wife?"

"I don't really remember meeting Addie."

"What?"

Drew chuckled. "What I mean is, we lived next door to one another, and when it was time to go to college, her father convinced me to stay in Evanston and go to Northwestern University. He was a little biased, I guess, because Eli is a professor there."

"What about your father? What does he do?"

Drew was silent for a moment. "My father is a United States congressman."

"What?" Jana gasped, jerking her hand back.

"What's wrong?"

"Your father is a congressman? I—I had no idea."

Drew chuckled. "What does that have to do with the price of eggs in China?" Once more he took her hand in his. "Jana, my father is the congressman, I'm not. To me, politics is a perfidious profession."

"It's just that I'm so—so . . ."

"You're so what?"

"Pedestrian."

Drew laughed out loud, and his outburst caused Sam to stir in his sleep. Drew covered his mouth with his hand.

"Why do you laugh?"

"Believe me, Jana, anyone who would use the word *pedestrian* out here, on the frontier, is anything but ordinary, or dull. On the contrary, I find you quite intriguing."

"I'm a farm girl from Illinois. There's nothing intriguing about me."

Drew put his finger on Jana's cheek, then gently turned her face toward his.

"Don't underestimate yourself," he said quietly, his lips so close to hers that she could feel his breath. "You're the most fascinating, exciting, and stimulating woman I've ever met." Now he was so close to her that as he spoke, she could feel his lips moving against hers. "Did I say stimulating?"

"Yes," she said almost breathlessly.

"Stimulating," he said again, the word smothering her lips.

Jana felt a quick sense of fear; they were kissing here, on the train, not three feet away from

Benji, Sam, and Elfrieda. For that matter, they weren't that far from anyone else in the car, and though the car was relatively dark, she was sure that anyone looking toward them could see what was going on.

What was going on?

Nothing was going on. That they were in a car with several others, and so close to Elfrieda and the children, made her self-conscious, but it also gave her a sense of security because she knew that nothing more than a simple kiss could happen.

But a simple kiss? Absolutely nothing about these kisses was simple. They were urgent, and as she parted her lips to give his tongue entry, the kiss left her mouth aflame with an aching need for more.

But there could be no more, not here.

Could there?

His lips nibbled at her earlobe, then moved down to the hollow of her neck. She was glad she didn't have to stand now because her knees were so weak that standing would be impossible.

At that moment the car ran over a rough section of track, and it jarred about. Drew and Jana separated.

"Is it another wreck?" Benji asked, waking abruptly.

"No, Son, it was just a rough section of track," Drew said. "Everything is fine."

"Daddy, I want to sit with you and Jana."

"You won't have as much room on our side."

"Come on over," Jana invited. "You can lean against me."

Smiling, Benji left his seat, then hopped across to crawl up between Drew and Jana.

Jana was glad Benji had joined them. She wasn't sure how much longer she could maintain control if Drew continued kissing her the way he had been doing. Before long, Benji had crawled up into Jana's lap, laid his head against her chest, and was asleep. She held him close to her, running her fingers through his fine hair, and imagining what it would be like if he were her child.

The train stopped twice during the long night to take on water. Jana woke up both times, but Drew and the others, used to these overnight trips, slept through the stops. Jana could hear voices from outside, and she felt a little guilty as she thought of how warm and comfortable she was in the heated car, compared to what the men must be dealing with outside in the cold night air.

The next morning the train made a long curve to the right, and the morning sun, now full disk up, sent its bright rays in through the window, waking Jana. When she opened her eyes, it took her a second to realize where she was, but then she felt Benji snuggled up beside her. When she looked across at Elfrieda and Sam, she saw that Sam was staring at her.

"Good morning," she said softly, not wanting to wake the others.

"We're almost there," Sam said.

"Good. I can hardly wait."

"You won't like it."

"Oh? Why not?"

"Little Missouri's not like Bismarck. It doesn't have stores. It just has saloons where people shoot one another."

"Oh, that's not good. But we won't be in that town very long, will we?"

"Rimfire's not very far away. What are you going to do there?" Sam asked.

"Your daddy asked me to help him put his new furniture in place."

"You can't do that because you aren't strong enough. You're a girl."

Jana laughed. "Oh, I'm not going to actually move the furniture; I'm just going to tell him where I think things should go."

"Couldn't Elfrieda do that?"

"No, honey, that takes someone who knows how to arrange such things so that it looks pretty," Elfrieda chimed in. "I'm afraid I couldn't do anything like that, and neither could your daddy. You need someone who has an artist's eye, and Jana has that."

"I have an artist's eye, too, but I'm glad you're here," Benji said as he turned his face up to Jana.

Jana swallowed hard to keep the knot that was forming in her throat from causing her to cry.

"I'm glad, too," Drew said. He reached across the gap between the seats and took Sam's hand. "Come over here and sit on my lap. Have you forgotten tonight is Christmas Eve?"

"Oh, no!" Benji said, loud enough to awaken some of the other passengers. "Daddy, I just thought of something. Something awful!"

"What's that?"

"Santa Claus won't know where to find us! He thinks we live in Bismarck. What's he gonna do when he goes to our house and we're not home?"

"He'll know where you are," Drew said.

"How will he know?"

"Because I sent him a letter."

"You did?"

"Yes, and I kept a copy. Would you like to hear it?"

"Uh-huh."

Jana thought Drew was teasing, but he pulled a piece of paper from his pocket and handed it to her. "Jana, will you read it for us?"

Jana smiled as she took the letter from Drew, then cleared her throat and began to read.

"'Dear Santa Claus, I'm writing to tell you that my two sons, Sam and Benji Malone, will not be found at 112 East Street, in Bismarck, DT. Instead, you will find them at Rimfire Ranch, which is five miles north of the settlement of Little Missouri, on the Little Missouri River.

"'Sam and Benji have both been exceptionally good boys this year, and I would not want you to forget them this Christmas. You will find some cookies under our tree that Mrs. Considine will make for you.

"'I hope you have a very nice trip on Christmas Eve and get home safely.

"'Your friend, Drew Malone, father of Sam and Benji.'"

Jana finished reading the letter and handed it back to Drew.

"Oh, Daddy, thank you, thank you. He will find us, won't he?"

"I don't think he'll have any trouble at all."

The train began squeaking to a halt, and Sam looked through the window. "Daddy, I see Devlin. He's here to meet us."

"Good, then we won't waste any time in getting to the ranch."

"Jana, are you excited?" Benji asked as he grabbed Jana's hand and pulled her into the aisle as the train slowed to a stop.

"Yes, I'm very excited." *And a little frightened,* Jana thought, but she didn't say that aloud.

As soon as the boys stepped off the train, they ran happily to a wagon that was standing nearby.

"Devlin!" Benji called. "We came to visit you! I'll bet you didn't know we were coming for Christmas!"

"Yes, he did," Sam said. "If he didn't know we were coming, he wouldn't be here to meet us."

"Where's Africa?" Benji asked as, using the spokes of the front wheel, he climbed up into the wagon. When he got near the top, Devlin reached down and lifted him the rest of the way. Sam followed and also got a lift.

"Africa's not a pullin' horse; he's a ridin' horse," Devlin said as he jumped down off the wagon, pulling a gun and holster from under the seat.

Drew extended his hand to Devlin, and after shaking hands, Devlin handed the holster to Drew and he strapped it on.

"I thought it looked like we were going to rustle

up a snowflake or two this morning, and I could come get you in the sleigh, but it didn't happen."

"Maybe, we'll get some yet." Drew looked toward the sky. "Devlin, you remember Elfrieda."

"Yes, sir, I do. Mrs. Considine," Devlin said, touching the brim of his hat.

"And this is—" Drew stopped and took Jana's hand as he drew her to him. "Miss Jana Hartmann. Jana, this unsavory character is Devlin McCarthy. I'm warning you about him; believe only half of what he shows you, and none of what he says," Drew teased.

Devlin looked at Drew, then at Jana, as a broad smile spread across his face. Again he touched the brim of his hat. "It's just real nice to meet you, ma'am."

"And it's nice to meet you, Mr. McCarthy." Jana noticed that Devlin, too, was wearing a holster and pistol.

"Aw, shucks, ma'am, there's nobody calls me Mr. McCarthy. Even the boys here call me Devlin."

As the train pulled away, Drew looked around quickly. "I hope they set our baggage off."

"Yes, sir, there's a pile there, near where the baggage car was," Devlin said.

"Good, pull the wagon up close to it, and we'll throw it on the back."

"Yes, sir." Devlin got back on the wagon, clucked at the team, and drove the wagon up to where several suitcases and some boxes sat. As Sam and Benji remained seated on the front seat, Devlin helped Drew put the freight behind the last seat.

"I think that's all we brought, so let's get the

women on board and head for home. I'm anxious to see what you've built for me."

"I'm proud of the house, and I know you're gonna like it." Devlin removed a two-step bench from the back of the wagon. "This'll make it easier, ladies."

Drew offered his hand first to Elfrieda and then to Jana as the women climbed into the wagon. It had been fitted with two more seats, and Elfrieda settled in the last one as she searched through the freight for some fresh produce she had brought from Bismarck. When she found what she was looking for, she put it under her coat to keep it from freezing during the short ride to Rimfire.

"Daddy, we're goin' to ride up front with Devlin," Sam said as he and Benji remained ensconced in the front seat.

"Well, now, that would be up to Devlin, wouldn't it?"

"Devlin doesn't mind," Sam said. "Do you, Devlin?"

"No indeed. Why, I'm not sure I could even drive this wagon back home if I didn't have some help."

"See, Daddy?" Benji said. "Devlin needs us."

"Then by all means, help him," Drew said as he sat on the second seat beside Jana.

Not even during the trip by train from Chicago had Jana ever seen scenery like this. She saw an accumulation of hills ranging from rounded tops, to knife edges, to obelisks. Then, looking out across the horizon, she saw, glistening in the bright sun, what could have been a city in ruins, surrounded by walls and bulwarks, and highlighted by a palace of huge domes. The colors ranged from soil that was white as snow, through yellows and browns, to the brick-red pyramids with their sharp-pointed summits.

"What do you think of your first trip to the Badlands?" Drew asked.

"I don't know what I expected, but it's both wild and fearsome looking, and yet beautiful in a bizarre and untamed way."

Drew smiled. "I knew you'd like it here."

SIXTEEN

There it is," Drew said, a broad smile crossing his face. "My house. Devlin, it looks fantastic!"

"I knew you'd like it, boss. The green was Toby's idea."

The house was made of clapboard and looked to be a long, single-story structure with chimneys at each end, as well as one in the back where a kitchen wing had been added. Dormer windows sprouting from the roof added a functional second story for additional rooms. The boards had been painted a light gray, with window shutters and a tin roof painted a dark green. It was on a small bluff facing the Little Missouri River to the south, with a covered front porch that ran from one end to the other. Jana saw at once what a wonderful place it would make to sit in the long summer evenings, listening to the rushing water and watching the western hills set ablaze with the dying sun.

"What do you think?"

"I think it's the most beautiful thing I've ever seen," Jana said. "The setting is perfect. It's too bad I didn't bring my art supplies because I could have painted you a picture."

"There'll be time for that later." The tone of Drew's voice and his expression said more than the words, and Jana wondered what he meant, as the wagon stopped in front of the big house.

"Devlin, did Peach make any crullers?" Benji asked as he jumped from the seat of the wagon to the ground.

"She may have," Devlin said. "But don't you want to see your new house before you go and find out?"

"All right. I'll come in, but it's only gonna be a minute, 'cause if she made crullers, and I think she did make 'em for us, it wouldn't be polite if we didn't eat them. Isn't that right, Mrs. Considine?"

Elfrieda laughed. "I suppose you're right, but come on. Let's look first. I want to find the kitchen and put my groceries in place, that is, if you want Santa to have cookies tonight."

"Who gets to go in first?" Sam asked.

"I think it should be you, since you're the big brother," Drew said. "Come on, Jana, I'm anxious for you to see the place."

Jana followed Sam in through the front door to a huge room. Here, most of the furniture she and Drew had bought had been pushed together in the middle. A fireplace was at the far end of the room, and yellow and blue flames were curling up around the logs in it. A gas bubble in one of the logs ignited and popped rather loudly, sending up a shower of sparks.

"This is a big house," Jana said, drawing out the sentence as she looked around at the huge room.

"You'll have to blame Devlin for that." Drew chuckled. "I tried to hold him back, but he just kept thinking of something else to build."

"It wasn't me who kept shipping more lumber," Devlin said. "You can't find this kind of wood in Little Missouri." He ran his hand over the smooth boards that formed the door facing. "But don't you think it's pretty?"

"It's more than that. It truly is beautiful," Jana said.

"Well, it'll really look good when we get all this furniture in place. We need to get it ready so we can have Christmas tomorrow," Drew said.

"You're right. I wish we would have come yesterday," Jana said. "How many rooms are there?"

"Eight. Right?" Drew asked as he turned to Devlin.

"Technically, that's right, but I did add some spaces where I thought you'd need it. There are closets and pantries and alcoves all over this place. It'll take you a week of Sundays to find all the little things I put in here. You're gonna like it so much, you'll never go back to Bismarck."

"You know, I'd stay right now," Drew said.

"Not me," Sam said. "This place looks like a big, empty barn."

"Ah, you just wait until your dad goes to work on it," Devlin said. "But for now, why don't we go see if Peach has anything for us. In the meantime, I'll send some of the hands over to get this furniture moved."

"Thanks, Devlin," Drew said. "Now let's help Elfrieda find the kitchen."

After the cowboys got there, they were able to put the furniture in place almost faster than Jana could decide where the pieces should go. Sooner than she would have thought possible, every room in the house was presentable.

Suddenly, the door opened and Sam and Benji ran in, the dusting of cinnamon around their mouths evidence of the crullers they had eaten.

"What do you think, boys?" Drew asked, taking in the newly placed furniture with a wave of his hand.

"Oh, I like it!" Benji said excitedly as he ran to the sofa that sat in front of the fireplace.

The sofa was covered in a smooth, tan jute fabric that imitated the look of the Turkish goat's hair that was on more expensive lounges. The inlaid floor was covered with a red Turcoman carpet, picking up the red paint above the wainscoting. A frescoed panel was on either side of the fireplace, just waiting for an artist's brush.

"What about you, Sam?" Drew asked.

"It looks a lot better now."

"Really? Well, I'm glad you see it that way, since I didn't think you were all that enthused about the house when you first saw it."

"Well, frankly, I thought the situation was hopeless," Sam said, speaking beyond his years.

Drew laughed, then ran his hand through his oldest son's hair. "It will really look good when we get the Christmas tree up, but we'd better hurry. We won't have many more hours of daylight. Now, who's going with me?"

"These boys can't go," Elfrieda said as she came into the room carrying a large bowl of popcorn. "I've got to have help making a rope to go on the tree, and if I made too much corn, somebody's got to help eat it."

"I'll help you," Sam said as he took a handful of the just-popped corn.

"Good, and, Benji, what about you?"

"Can you get the tree without me?" Benji asked his father.

"I think so—that is, if Jana will go with me."

"I'd love to." Jana went to the hall tree to get her coat.

When they stepped outside, Drew headed to the bunkhouse. "Wait here a minute; I'll get someone to go with us."

Jana waited as Drew stepped into the bunkhouse. A moment later he came back with a young-looking, towheaded cowboy.

"Jana, this is Charley. He's not much more than a sprout himself, so he's more than willing to help us find a tree."

"Ahh, I ain't all that young, Mr. Malone. I'm sixteen, most near seventeen."

"Well, it's very nice to meet you, Charley. And thank you for coming to help us."

"It's my pleasure, ma'am."

"Get a harness put on Harry and hitch him up to

the cart," Drew said, indicating a mule standing in the corral. "There's no sense in us lugging the tree back as long as we have him."

"All right," Charley said.

Ten minutes later they were near one of the buttes on Drew's property. Drew looked over several small juniper trees carefully. Finally he selected one that was about five feet tall and had a good shape.

"What do you think?" he asked.

"I think it will make a great Christmas tree," Jana said, leaning in to smell the pungent fragrance.

Charley quickly chopped the trunk of the tree while Drew held it upright.

When they got back to the house, Devlin had brought in a butter keg. They trimmed off the bottom branches of the tree and stuck it down into the dirt Devlin had put in the keg.

They had also brought back a few limbs cut from some of the other trees, and Jana picked them up. "These branches will look pretty on the mantelpiece." She began arranging them on the board. "I wish we had some red ribbon."

"We don't have any ribbon, but we have some red calico," Elfrieda said as she opened a box and began to search through it. She brought out a square of cloth that was printed with green holly.

"That's Mama's," Sam said as he snatched the cloth out of Elfrieda's hand.

"It was Mama's, but don't you think she would want us to use it?" Drew asked.

"That's for our house, not for this one."

"But, Sam, this is our house, too, and this is where we're going to have Christmas, so we're going to decorate." Drew took the cloth from Sam and handed it to Jana. "Now, let's put the rest of the ornaments on the tree."

The box was filled with cloth ornaments, many in the shape of apples and pears, as well as balls that were quilted together with small pieces of fabric and then filled with batting.

At first Sam held back and would not help, but as all the others seemed to be enjoying themselves, he eventually joined in. He put on the string of popcorn and a few of the gingerbread cookies that the boys had helped Elfrieda make while Jana and Drew had been out getting the tree. Soon the tree was trimmed, except for one final ornament. That was an angel with oversize wings. She had blond hair and was wearing a dress made from the same red cloth that was now on the mantel. Drew picked Benji up, so he could place the angel on the top of the tree.

"Did your mama make the angel?" Jana asked Sam quietly as they were picking up some of the berries that had fallen off the juniper.

"She made all the ornaments. They've been on every Christmas tree I've ever had," Sam said.

"Then I'm glad Mrs. Considine didn't forget to bring them. I'll bet you wouldn't think it was Christmas if you didn't have them."

"I miss my mama."

"I know you do." Jana gave Sam a gentle hug.

He did not hug her back, but he didn't seem to mind that she had put her arms around him.

✎✎✎

After supper, during which all the cowboys along with Devlin and Toby and Peach shared some of Elfrieda's oyster stew, everyone came back into the keeping room to admire the Christmas tree, which now glowed with lit candles. They sang carols and Peach read the story of how the baby Jesus was born in a manger. As the cowboys were leaving, Drew passed out envelopes containing money, and everyone left in high spirits. Elfrieda went to the kitchen, and then to a room that adjoined the kitchen that she had claimed as her bedroom.

Jana and the boys sat on the sofa, and Drew joined them.

"Is it Christmas yet?" Benji asked.

"No, silly. It's the night before Christmas," Sam said. "Tonight is when Santa Claus comes."

"I don't understand," Benji said. "How does Santa get here?"

"He comes in his sleigh," Drew said.

"He can't come in his sleigh because we don't have any snow."

"He doesn't need snow. His reindeer know how to fly," Jana said.

"I don't believe that," Sam said.

"That's what the poem says."

"What poem?"

"'Twas the Night Before Christmas,'" Jana said. "Do you mean you've never heard that poem?"

"No."

"Oh, it's a wonderful poem!" Jana began to quote the famous lines.

*'Twas the night before Christmas, when all
    through the house*
*Not a creature was stirring, not even a
    mouse.*
*The stockings were hung by the chimney
    with care*
*In hopes that St. Nicholas soon would be
    there.*

"Do you know the whole poem?" Drew asked.

"Yes, I do. I used to have my class recite it every Christmas."

"Are you a teacher?" Sam asked as he pulled up from his position.

"I used to be. Would you like to hear the whole poem?"

"Yes, but start over. I want to hear all of it," Benji said as he snuggled under the crook of Jana's arm.

As Jana recited the poem, both children seemed enraptured. Benji leaned closer to her, and Sam fell back upon Drew's chest.

She continued with the poem, putting great emphasis on certain passages, eliciting laughter from Benji and even Sam when she spoke the lines *He had a broad face and a little round belly, that shook when he laughed, like a bowlful of jelly.*

Jana recited the poem to the very end, then Benji repeated the last line. "'Happy Christmas to all, and to all a good night,'" he said, laughing.

"And it *is* time for good night to all," Drew said. "Santa won't come if you aren't in bed."

"But I want to see Santa come down the chimney," Benji said.

"He'll just fly right by our house if you're awake," Drew said.

"Aww. Is that true, Jana?"

"I'm afraid so."

"And you do want Santa Claus to come, don't you?" Drew asked.

"Yes."

"Then you'd better go to bed."

"Can I sleep with Sam?"

"You'd better ask him," Drew said, "but right now, let's get you to your new room."

"All right. Good night, Daddy, good night Jana," Benji said as he got down from the sofa. He started for the bedroom, but then he turned around and came back to give Jana a hug. "I'm glad you told us about Santa Claus."

"I'm glad, too. Good night."

"Come on, Sam. I'll tuck you in," Drew said as he headed down the hall to the boys' bedroom.

Sam smiled shyly at Jana, but he didn't say good night.

While Jana waited for Drew to return, she moved around the big room, putting chairs back in place that the cowboys had moved, and picking up anything that needed to be put away.

"That was easier than I expected," Drew said when he came back into the great room. "They're two tuckered-out little boys, and I guess I'm a little tired myself. Come sit beside me, and let's just look at the tree before we blow out the candles."

Jana joined him on the sofa, and he placed his arm so as to invite her to put her head on his shoulder. When she did, he draped his arm around her casually and laid his cheek against her hair. Neither said anything as they sat for several minutes watching the flames flicker in the fireplace, as the candles burned down.

"I could stay like this forever," Drew said as he turned his face to her hair. He placed a gentle kiss on the top of her head. "I want you to know, I've not been this happy for a long time."

Jana turned her face up to his and initiated a kiss—not on his cheek, but directly on the lips.

Drew pulled back and looked down at her with a seductive gaze, causing her pulse to pound. As he lowered his head to kiss her again, they heard the door opening in the entryway.

"Boss, are you ready for these?" Devlin called softly.

Drew jumped up from the sofa. "I almost forgot that Santa's coming. Bring in the saddles and put them under the tree."

"Tim Murchison did a heck of a nice job on these things. Look at this tooled leather. Why, he even put their names on them," Devlin said as he and Charley brought in the small saddles.

"What about the ponies?" Drew asked. "Are you pleased with them?"

"They came from the Custer Trail Ranch, and Howard Eaton picked them out himself. He says they're bred from the gentlest broodmare he's got."

"They are broken, aren't they? Sam and Benji aren't going to want to wait until we can gentle them."

"They're as gentle as lambs right now," Devlin said.

Drew smiled. "Good, they'll love that."

Jana remembered the gifts she had brought, so she went back to the room that had been designated for guests, where her valise had been put. She had a slate board and colored chalk for Benji, and a cup-and-ball game for Sam, and a shawl for Elfrieda. Drew's gift had been difficult to choose. She had seen many things that she wanted to get for him, but most were either too expensive or too personal for a woman to give to a man who wasn't her husband, so she had finally decided on an English tweed neck scarf.

Greta's present had been the easiest to pick out. She hoped Tom McGowan would not forget to give Greta the hat Jana had selected to go with the dresses the men had bought. Jana had considered giving it to Greta herself, but she thought it would be more fun if Greta actually got her present on Christmas morning.

The packages Jana had brought with her were neatly wrapped with brown paper and bright red ribbon and tucked among her garments in her luggage, so she retrieved them and took them out to place under the tree. Drew and Devlin were still conversing near the door, so Jana made certain the candles were extinguished and made her way to her room.

She took off the easy-flowing, gray worsted skirt she had worn, thankful that she didn't have to wear the bustle Mr. Watson had insisted she wear under many of the fashionable dresses she modeled. She folded the skirt and put it in a drawer of the wardrobe, then removed her cotton waist, folding it as well. She was glad she had worn her flannel vest under her blouse because with it she had not needed a jacket. Drew had not told her exactly how many days they would be staying at Rimfire, but she knew she would be wearing this outfit on numerous occasions.

Mrs. Watson had given her a new nightdress as payment for her translation of *The Stranger*, as Mrs. Watson called Kotzebue's play, and Jana had brought it with her. Slipping out of her vest and drawers, she pulled out the foulard gown and reveled in the feel of the soft fabric against her body. She had never worn a nightdress that had the opening trimmed with a frill all the way down to the hem, and it made her feel a little bit special. While she was attempting to close the long opening, she heard a light knock on the door.

"Jana," Drew said softly. "Are you awake?"

"Yes." Jana crossed to the door.

"Can you help me for a minute? When Devlin put my bedstead together, he didn't tighten the tie rods, and now one end of the footboard has come loose. I can't hold it and put the tie rod through at the same time. Will you come hold it for me?"

"Of course." Jana opened the door at once.

Drew's gaze fell immediately to the open front of Jana's nightdress, and she clutched frantically at the closure. When she looked down, she realized that the whole front of the gown was agape.

"I'm sorry."

"I'm not," Drew said with a devastating grin.

"I must get dressed." Jana turned toward the wardrobe.

Drew caught her hand. "Don't, Jana." His voice was husky. "I'll only need you for a minute, and besides . . ."

Jana took a deep breath as she looked down the hallway. "Is everyone asleep?"

"With visions of sugarplums dancing in their heads."

She scurried across the hallway and into Drew's bedroom much as a child would do if getting into some sort of mischief.

"Now what do you need?"

"If you only knew what I need." Drew cupped her face gently.

A shiver rippled through her as she visualized the intimacy of this scene. She was with Drew, the most virile man she had ever known, in his bedroom, alone, in a nightdress that was not securely closed.

"I must go back."

Drew dropped his hand. "All right. But while you're here, will you hold up the footboard? Otherwise, I will get no sleep tonight."

Jana stepped farther into the room and steadied the heavy footboard, all the while holding her gown closed as best she could.

Drew tried to slip the tie rod through the bed rail and the footboard, but he couldn't line up the hole.

"I'm going to have to take the thing out and get everything lined up properly. Can you hold it?"

"I think so."

When Drew removed the rod, the heavy foot-board, made of intertwined cottonwood posts and branches, started to fall against Jana as the bed rails fell to the floor with a loud noise. Jana instinctively, grabbed the footboard, preventing it from falling, but in doing so, she had to use both hands. That caused the nightdress to fall open, and the front of her body was fully exposed.

Drew held the rod in his hand, not even attempting to put the bed together. She could hear his breathing quicken as he openly stared at her.

"Mr. Malone, have you forgotten why I am here?" Jana asked with more levity than she could have imagined possible in the circumstance.

"No, ma'am. I need to get this bed put together as quickly as possible because I think I'm going to need someone to test its strength. I certainly don't want this to happen again."

"Nor do I," Jana said, realizing that it was now too late to even attempt to cover herself.

Drew had the tie rod in place and the bolt securely fastened within an instant.

Jana began arranging the feather bed that had slipped when the side rails had fallen, and she smoothed the sheets and counterpane, as though it were the most natural thing in the world to do. When she looked toward Drew, she saw that he was removing his shirt. He stood before her bare chested, a sheen of perspiration causing his chest to glisten in the light of the lamp that stood on the table near the head of the bed.

"Shall I go any further?"

Jana knew she should get out of this room, but

she could not make her legs move. She stood mesmerized by the scene before her. The mystery of the coupling of a man and a woman was before her very eyes, and she knew that she wanted this man to be her first.

Drew moved toward her, his arms encircling her as he held her tightly against him, kissing her in a deep, tongue-tangling kiss. The offending nightdress fell away, and proudly Jana stood naked, the texture of his chest causing her nipples to harden against him. Suddenly she was lifted into his arms and he carried her to the bed and placed her on the downy comfort of the tick.

She watched as he dropped his pants, and for the first time in her life, she saw a male member, large and engorged, standing erect from his body. She could not avert her gaze as Drew climbed into the bed with her. "Jana," he whispered, "do you know how much I have wanted this?" He kissed her again, this time trailing kisses down to her belly, flicking his tongue inside her navel. When she thought she could take no more, he moved his head farther down her body into the soft down that was at the juncture of her legs. He began to kiss her as he moved toward the most private part of her body, that which no man had ever touched, which no man had ever seen. Jana could hardly believe what was happening.

And then it all stopped.

The doorknob was turning as both Jana and Drew heard Benji's voice.

"Daddy, I heard a loud noise. Do you think Santa Claus is on the roof?"

Drew quickly covered Jana, including her head, with the counterpane.

"Just a minute, Son. Let me get my pants on," Drew said as he jumped out of bed, throwing on his drawers before he opened the door.

"Did you hear it?" Benji asked. "It was a while ago, and I tried to listen but I couldn't hear the prancing hoofs of the reindeer."

"Let me come to your room and I'll listen with you," Drew said as he led Benji down the hall.

Jana slipped out of the bed and found her nightdress. She put it on quickly, and without even trying to secure it, she hurried across the hall to the safety of her own room.

When Drew returned from Benji's room, he knocked lightly on her door, but Jana didn't answer him. More than anything, she wanted to be in his bed, feeling the exquisite sensations that Drew had awakened in her, but she couldn't recapture what they had just shared. She lay in bed looking through the window. The moon was full and the cloudless sky was filled with stars. Sleep would not come no matter how hard she tried.

What had she done? What would Drew think of her? She had wantonly gone to him, and she would have allowed him to do anything he wanted to do to her body. She pictured him as he stood before her, his chest gleaming, his member erect. Never had she visualized what the male physique would look like, and Drew Malone was the perfect specimen. She thought of Michelangelo's *David* and the desire to chisel a perfect man. She could draw Drew as a perfect man—a perfect man with an erect phallus.

I've got to get these prurient thoughts out of my mind! She turned into her pillow and hit it with her fist.

What would the morning bring? Could she face Drew after what she had done? Could she face his sons? Thank heavens Benji had interrupted when he did.

Back in his bedroom, Drew was dealing with his own thoughts. He had not felt this way toward a woman since Addie. And if he was honest with himself, he hadn't really felt about Addie the way he did about Jana. With Addie, their intimacy was comfortable and familiar. But when he was around Jana, his blood seemed to boil, his skin tingled, and with every ounce of his being, he wanted to possess her fully.

But was it just a sexual attraction?

He didn't think so. He also appreciated her intelligence, her self-confidence, her sense of humor, and the way she interacted with his children. He was sure it was more than a physical attraction, but he needed to be certain. He couldn't risk a relationship based just on physical attraction, not for himself, and not for his children. It needed to be more, and he needed to be sure.

"Jana, wake up. Daddy says come see what Santa brought us. I got a saddle with my name on it," Benji yelled excitedly, waking Jana.

"I'm hurrying. I'll be there as fast as I can."

Jana was not aware that she had fallen asleep at all, but when she looked out the window, the first sliver of daylight was breaking, causing the ice that covered the Little Missouri River to reflect the pink light. She had planned to wear a festive dress this morning, but when she thought about the last evening with Drew, she pulled out her trusty rose wool, which she had worn to Dakota. The dress was a visible reminder to her of who she really was.

When she entered the great room, Drew was sitting on the sofa, his feet bare and his hair tousled.

"Good morning, sleepyhead," Drew said, a boyish smile crossing his lips. "Did you forget? Santa came and he brought the boys saddles. I don't know why he did that, do you?"

"If you have a saddle, you need a pony. Do you think he might have brought one for these boys?" Jana asked, getting into the spirit.

"We didn't even think of that, now did we?" Drew said. "We should go see if there's one in the barn. Come on."

"Daddy, we can't do that. We don't have our clothes on," Sam said.

"Jana's dressed. She could go look."

"All right," Jana said, and grabbed her coat from the hook.

When she opened the door, two ponies were tied to the porch railing.

"Oh, my goodness, they're right here." She held the door open wide for both boys to see the little brown-and-white-spotted ponies. "I guess Santa Claus didn't want to leave them in the house."

"I can't believe it," Sam yelled as he ran out onto the porch. "This is exactly what I wanted!" He threw his arms around the first horse, and it whinnied and tossed its head. Benji, not to be denied, ran out onto the porch to the second pony.

"You two better get back in here before you get sick and then you won't be able to ride them. We've got other presents to open now that Jana's here." Drew took her hand, and when he did, he winked at her. They walked hand in hand back to the Christmas tree.

Jana had never had a more blissful morning, and her gifts were a great success. Elfrieda sat by the fire and seemed to really like the shawl Jana had gotten her. Drew was as warm to her as any person had ever been in her life. He made her feel like an integral part of his family, and because of the way he was acting, Benji and Sam were both demonstrative toward her, making sure she saw and understood how to play with the gifts they received.

Jana couldn't help but contrast her own meager Christmases over the years with the abundance that these children received. There were gifts from both sets of grandparents, as well as from Elfrieda and the cowboys. But in spite of all that they got, they seemed genuinely appreciative of each new gift they opened.

"I see two more packages under the tree," Drew said when everything else was opened. "Shall I see whose name is on them?"

Jana nodded, not wanting to say anything.

"This one's for you, and it looks like the other one

is for me," Drew said as he handed a package to Jana.

She opened the package with trembling fingers as her eyes welled with tears of happiness. "You said you were going to get me a seal hat. Oh, Drew, thank you for the hat, but most of all thank you for letting me share this day with you and your family."

Drew looked at her with smoldering eyes. "I'd like you to share more than this day. I'd like you to share my life." He leaned forward and gave her a gentle kiss on the lips.

Sam saw the kiss. He didn't say anything, but he didn't look away.

SEVENTEEN

The day after Christmas, the mild weather in the Badlands changed, and a fierce wind and blowing snow came from the north, causing Sam and Benji much distress.

"Can we bring Spotty into the house?" Benji asked. "He'll be too cold outside."

"No, he's safe in the barn, and anyway you saw your pony's heavy coat. He'll stay warmer than we will, and Toby will see to it that he has plenty of hay from the rick that's right beside the barn," Drew said.

"What about Buster?"

"Both ponies will be fine. Just think about it, the stock horses fend for themselves all winter and they find food, but Spotty and Buster are in the barn, and they're being well fed. They'll be ready when the weather warms up and we get to ride."

"Did you say the stock horses have to fend for themselves?" Jana asked.

"That's right, but it's not as bad as you think. If we don't have much snow, the dried grass is like a hayfield, just ready for the horses to graze."

"Benji, do you smell cinnamon buns?" Sam asked as he ran into the kitchen with Benji close behind him.

"Elfrieda spoils those two," Drew said.

"How could anyone not want to spoil them? Besides, you seem to benefit from Elfrieda's treats as well. Say, how would you like to play a game of chess? I've been thinking, maybe this time I can beat you," Jana challenged as she headed toward the room that was to be Drew's office and library when the books were shipped.

On Thursday the weather broke, and the boys were anxious to ride their ponies after being in the house for several days. Drew asked Charley, the young cowboy whom Jana had met, if she could borrow some trousers, a shirt, and a shearling coat, and when she was outfitted, the four of them rode horses for at least a couple of hours every day. The snow made the Badlands seem like a fairyland, and Jana could easily imagine that she was indeed in her own fairy tale.

A mother, a father, and two children, all loving one another. But of the four people, only one openly expressed those sentiments, and that was Benji—sweet, lovable, cherubic Benji—who told Jana at least once a day how much he loved her.

Sam didn't say anything, and much to Jana's disappointment, neither did Drew. After their intimacy on Christmas Eve, and then his saying he would like her to share his life, he had become more distant.

They stayed at Rimfire until after New Year's, returning to Bismarck on the late-evening train of the fifth. By the time Jana reached the hotel, Greta was already in bed.

"Greta, it's me," Jana called softly as she opened the door to the room.

"I was thinking it was about time you came back," Greta said, turning up the lamp and hopping out of bed to give her sister a welcoming hug. "I've missed you."

"And I've missed you, too. Did you have a good Christmas?" Jana set down her valise.

"It was wonderful! You can't believe what I got for Christmas." Then Greta laughed. "Oh, wait, I guess you do know. Tom told me you helped pick out the beautiful clothes the men bought for me."

"Oh, no, I didn't. It was Carl and Hank who chose the dresses for you. I told them your favorite color was blue, but did you get a blue dress? No, they had their own ideas what you should have. Those men are so funny."

"They really are, but they're so appreciative. Jana, some of them told me they hadn't celebrated Christmas in years. I was so tired after fixing the dinner for them, but it made me feel good to know I was doing something special for all of them."

"And you should. Mama would be very proud of you, Greta, and so am I."

"Listen to me going on about my Christmas. I haven't even asked about yours."

Jana smiled broadly, and her eyes gleamed so brightly, it seemed more than a mere reflection of the lamplight. "This may have been the most wonderful time of my entire life!" she said excitedly.

"Tell me everything that happened and don't leave out even the smallest detail."

"Wait until I get in bed." Jana began removing her clothes.

For what seemed like hours, the two sisters lay in the dark as Jana told about the house, the furniture, the cowboys, and Christmas.

"Some people just know how to celebrate Christmas. I wish we would've had a tree when we were little, because you should have seen how excited Benji and Sam were when they found new saddles under the tree. And then when they got new ponies, they were really happy."

"They got ponies for Christmas? Drew must be very rich."

"I don't know. I suppose he might be. But I do know he's the nicest man I've ever known. You should see the way he treats his children, and the people who work for him, too. He is kind and gentle and understanding."

"How does he treat you?"

"Oh, he . . ." Jana thought back to Christmas Eve, and she was glad the room was dark. She fell silent.

Disturbed by her silence, Greta sat up in bed and turned up the light.

"Jana Hartmann, look at me. He didn't do anything to you, did he?"

A smile crossed Jana's face. "He did. He claimed my heart."

"You're in love!"

"I am."

"You said you would tell me what it was like."

"I don't know how to tell you, other than to say it's the most wonderful feeling. I love him more than I can say, and I can't tell you how happy I've been for the last two weeks. We didn't do anything out of the ordinary, other than ride horses, or play games, or sit by the fire and talk. We just enjoyed one another's company."

"Did he ask you to marry him?"

"No, he did not."

"Jana, does Drew love you?"

"I don't know. One time he said he'd like me to share his life with him, but he never said anything more."

"If he said that, I think that's a proposal for marriage and you should tell him so."

"Greta, it's more complicated than that. Whoever marries Drew Malone also marries Sam and Benji. I think Benji would have me as his stepmother tomorrow, but Sam—well, let's just say I'm going to have to prove myself to him."

"If anybody can do that, it's you. Who would've thought two little farm girls from Illinois could be working themselves into the hearts of total strangers so many miles from home?"

"We do seem to be doing that, don't we? That is, except for one."

"Don't worry, Jana, one little boy isn't going to

stand between you and the man you love. Sam will come around. You just wait and see."

"I hope you're right, Greta. I can't tell you how much I love Drew."

Greta chuckled as she turned out the lamp. "It's not me you have to tell. It sounds like it's Sam you have to convince. And Drew, of course, if you haven't already."

For the rest of the night, Jana thought about what she had told Greta. She did love Drew, but she hadn't ever said as much. The kisses, even the time in Drew's bed, was that love to a man? Or was that just lust?

And then there was Addie. Could Drew ever love again? She didn't know, but she decided that night, January 5, 1883, she would set out to prove that he could. She would do whatever it took to make him love her, because no matter how comforting it was to be with him, just being comfortable wasn't enough. She had to have his love.

The next morning Jana got dressed and went to the Emporium. Now that the holiday season was over, she wasn't sure if she still had a job, especially since she had been away for so long.

But when she walked in, she was met by an exuberant Fern Watson.

"Jana, you'll never guess," Mrs. Watson said. "The play you translated for the Ladies' Christian Union, *The Stranger,* is going to be performed on January twentieth, and Sam Whitney has given us permission to use the Opera House. Isn't that wonderful? We've been rehearsing, and I just know it's going to be absolutely magnificent." Mrs. Watson lowered her head. "Although, I suppose I shouldn't say that because that may be boasting. You see, I'm playing the part of Countess Wintersen."

"That's wonderful news, Mrs. Watson," Jana said enthusiastically. "And I'm sure you'll make a perfect countess."

"Well, don't forget. You must come to see it. Mr. Whitney says if we get a big enough audience, he may let us use the Opera House again."

"I'll be there."

For the rest of the day Jana was busy working around the store. There was no suggestion that she take her place in the window, but Mr. Watson didn't say her job was over, either. She was rearranging the hats when she heard a familiar voice.

"Where's the lady in the window?" Drew called.

"She's working, now that you finally brought her back," Mr. Watson said jokingly. "I missed her."

"And you should." Drew headed toward Jana. "I'm going to miss her, too."

"What do you mean you're going to miss me?" Jana asked when he reached her.

"Because I'm going to be out of town for a while. I wonder if you would mind dropping in on Elfrieda and helping out with the boys, not that she needs any help, but I'm sure Sam and Benji would love to see you."

"And I'd love to see them, but where are you going and for how long?"

"I'm not sure how long I'll be gone. I'm going with Colonel Lounsberry and Sheriff McKenzie down to Yankton. With all the talk of statehood now, we think the capital should be moved to a more central location than Yankton is. And of course, it's our opinion that the best place for the capital is Bismarck. But the people in Yankton don't agree with us, so it's our job to convince the legislature to see it our way."

"I have no doubt that you can do that, but tell me, Mr. Malone, isn't this"—Jana paused—"politics? And didn't you tell me once that you had no interest in the, I believe you called it, 'perfidious profession'?"

Drew laughed. "You have a memory like an elephant. But this isn't really politics—it's business. When Bismarck becomes the capital, everybody's business will boom even more than it is now. Seriously, will you visit the boys a time or two while I'm gone?"

"I will. But you have to promise me one thing."

"What's that?"

"If you're back by the twentieth, you have to go with me to see *The Stranger*."

"And who might he be?" Drew's eyebrows shot up.

"It's not a *who*, it's an *it*. That's the play I translated. It's going to be put on that night at the Whitney, and I've been invited to go see it. Will you take me?"

"I do believe this is the first time a lady has ever asked me for a date."

"Oh!" Jana gasped, putting her hand over her mouth. "That isn't very ladylike, is it?"

Drew laughed out loud. "You could wear a ten-

gallon hat and smoke cigars, and you'd still be a
lady to me. I'd love to take you to the play." He
kissed her lightly on the lips and turned to leave.
"Don't forget. Go see the boys."

"I will," Jana said as she waved good-bye.

Jana was amazed at how much she missed Drew,
especially when she dropped in to see Sam and
Benji. She read to them and played games and
drew pictures, and both boys seemed to enjoy it
as much as she did. She almost breathed a sigh of
relief at her tentative acceptance by Sam.

Working at the store and helping Greta at the
hotel also helped to pass the time. But she decided
to start another project as a special surprise for
Drew when he returned.

She began an oil painting of Rimfire Ranch.
Unlike her other drawings and paintings, though,
she didn't work on this one at the store. Instead,
she did it in the privacy of her room.

"Jana, that's spectacular!" Greta said as enough
of the house became visible for Greta to get an
idea. "I think it's the best work you've ever done."

Jana captured the river and the surrounding
scenery perfectly, but the home ranch, as Drew
called it, was the primary focus: the long front
porch, the green of the shutters and the roof, the
bunkhouse and the barn. She even put four horses
in the corral.

"This is Dancer," Jana said, pointing to one of
the horses. "He's mine, and that's Santana, Drew's
horse. This is Sam's pony, Buster, and this is Spotty,
Benji's pony."

"Spotty," Greta said with a chuckle.

"Now, don't laugh. I think Benji chose a good name. The pony does have spots, wouldn't you say?"

The final touch to the painting was to add the golden reflection of the setting sun to the western windows of the house, as well as a corona of red light to the rim of the cliffs surrounding Rimfire Ranch. Those touches gave credence to its name and, Jana thought, were the finishing touches to an accurate painting.

Late one morning, Jana was working in the store when Charley Draper came in.

"Mr. Draper," Jana said.

"I have a telegram for you." Draper handed her an envelope.

Jana was startled. Never before in her life had she received a telegram, and she took it with some apprehension, wondering if it might be bad news from home.

"It's from Drew Malone," Draper said, relieving her anxiety.

Curious now, she opened it eagerly.

ARRIVING TONIGHT 7:30. MEET ME WITH BOYS. LOVE DREW.

Love Drew. She was happy he wanted her to meet him at the train station, but the last two words sang in her heart.

She put the telegram back in the envelope, then held it to her chest and smiled at Draper. "Thank you, Mr. Draper."

"My pleasure. You're getting a fine man there, Miss Hartmann."

"I think so, too."

When Walter Watson came into the store, he brought a copy of the *Bismarck Tribune* folded in such a way as to highlight one story.

"It looks like our boys did a good job down in Yankton," he said. "You might want to read this."

CAPITAL TO BISMARCK?

Special to the Tribune *by telegraph from Yankton: Bismarck sent three of its finest citizens to the territorial legislature in Yankton to plead the case that the capital be moved from Yankton to Bismarck. Our delegation, composed of Colonel Clement Lounsberry, the editor of this newspaper, Sheriff Alex McKenzie, Bismarck's leading advocate, and Andrew Malone, an attorney with the firm of Allen and Malone, were aided in their presentation by the enthusiastic support of Governor Nehemiah Ordway. If Dakota is to become a state, as surely it shall, then Bismarck should be the capital.*

There has been a proposal bandied about that the Dakota Territory enter the union as two states, this idea strongly supported by Senator Hale of Maine, whose reasoning is that two states will

mean four new senators, all of whom,
he believes, will be Republicans. This
would insure the party's majority status should Virginia's Readjuster Party
throw in with the Democrats, making
the Senate in the 48th Congress tied at
38 Senators for each party.

In seeking the honor, and responsibility, of becoming the capital one has but
to look to a recent editorial in The Cin-
cinnati Commercial to find enumerated
the many reasons why Bismarck should
be so selected. The article reads thus:

"Situated on the east bank of the Mis-
souri River, at the crossing of the North
Pacific Railway, is the thriving city of
Bismarck, the county seat of Burleigh
County, and perfect for the capital city
of the Dakota Territory.

"Bismarck is the center of the great
stage routes to Deadwood, Keogh, Yates,
Fort Lincoln, Buford, and Mandan, and
the steamboat trade. Already the Northwestern and St. Paul roads are heading
toward Bismarck, being now but 125
miles distant, with their surveys completed. Work will be rapidly pushed this
coming spring.

"Among the improvements of the city
are a flouring mill with a capacity of
100 barrels per day, a grain elevator
with a storage capacity of 100,000

bushels, seven churches, schools, and a fine courthouse."

These attributes, put forth by our delegation to the territorial capital meeting in Yankton, and validated by newspapers from the East, have to have a positive effect on the final outcome as to where our capital should rightly be. It is our desire and belief that the time will come, and soon, when Bismarck assumes its role as one of the nation's guiding cities, by virtue of being the capital of a state, equal in authority and prestige with all the other states in the union.

When Jana stopped by Drew's house, Benji shouted happily as he ran to meet her with his usual exuberance, and, as always, he threw his arms around her legs.

"Benji, have you been an extra-good boy today?" Jana asked, bending down to his level.

"Yes, ma'am, I've been so good. You can ask Mrs. Considine."

Elfrieda chuckled. "He's been asking all day what time you'd come by, but I didn't expect you until later. There's plenty for lunch if you'd like to eat a bite with us."

"I can't stay now, but I'll be back. Guess who's coming home today?"

"Daddy!" Benji yelled enthusiastically.

"That's right." Jana and Benji exchanged hugs.

"And he wants us to meet him at the depot. Will you tell Sam when he gets home from school?"

"Goodie, goodie, goodie! My daddy's coming home!"

"I think that one's excited," Elfrieda said. "What time does Mr. Malone's train get in?"

"It should be about seven thirty, so I'll come by at seven."

"I'll have them ready for you," Elfrieda promised.

Jana returned to the store and was almost as euphoric as Benji at the prospect of Drew's returning. She was waiting on a customer when Mrs. Watson entered the store. She busied herself straightening the glove box until Jana was free.

"My dear, you haven't forgotten—tomorrow is the date for *The Stranger*."

"Yes, ma'am," Jana said. "I can hardly wait, but I'm sure if August von Kotzebue were alive, he would have a right to take umbrage with me because I do feel a little proprietary over his words. I must admit, I'm looking forward to seeing the production."

"You should feel proud. You did a wonderful job, and because of that, I want you to choose any dress in the store to wear tomorrow night," Mrs. Watson said. "On second thought, this is the one you should wear."

Mrs. Watson pulled a plain black velvet dress from a hanger. "Put this on. I want to see you in it."

Jana went to the back room and put on the dress. The long, slender torso fit tightly through the hips. The low-necked polonaise was trimmed with appliqués and jet beads, and the underskirt was made of black moiré. This dress was the most elegant garment Jana had ever seen, and she would never have chosen it herself, but when she stepped into the store, Mr. Watson gave her an admiring look.

"You'll be the talk of the town when anyone sees you in that dress. I only wish you were entering the Opera House on the arm of Drew Malone," Mr. Watson said.

"Oh, I will be. He's coming in on the evening train."

"Good. Then I want you to wear this, too." Mr. Watson withdrew what could only be described as a black velvet dog collar. But this was dotted with diamonds, pearls, and fine flowers made of colored stones. "What do you think, Fern?"

"Perfect," Mrs. Watson said as she smoothed the dress over Jana's hips. "Do you think she should wear gloves?"

"I don't think so. Jana has such lovely hands. Let them show against the black. You do look beautiful, my dear," Mr. Watson said. "Oh, and one more thing. I want you to wear your hair like this." He took a drawing he had torn from a newspaper of Empress Elisabeth of Austria, and as he did so, he handed Jana a pearl band. The empress's hair was falling loose in the back, but the pearl band kept her hair away from her face.

"Mr. Watson, I'm not sure I can do this," Jana said.

"Nonsense, my dear. How is this any different from what you've done for me all along? With the Christmas season behind us, we need to gin up more business."

❧

Jana took what she preferred to think of as finery back to her room at the Custer Hotel. For some reason, she did not want Greta to see what she would be wearing, so she hid the dress behind her other clothes.

Mr. Watson was right. What she was being asked to do wasn't that much different from what she had done before, but for some reason she felt uncomfortable. She felt like a fraud.

The fancy dress had taken away some of her anticipated pleasure from knowing that the actual words to be said at the play were hers. Yes, she had merely translated from the German, but the interpretation was how she had envisioned it. And now, her every move would be scrutinized. She wished she could sit in the poorest seat in the highest location wearing her rose wool dress.

But then she thought of Drew. How would his face look when he saw her in the dress?

At seven o'clock, Jana opened the iron gate and walked up the path to Drew's house. Before she reached the door it opened, and Benji and Sam came rushing down to meet her.

"What did you bring?" Benji asked when he spied a large package wrapped in paper.

"It's a gift."

"For me?"

"Yes, but it's also for Sam and for your father. It's for all of you."

"How can it be for everybody?"

"Let me show you." Jana stepped into the foyer and began removing the paper. It was the painting she had been working on, and she showed it to Benji, and to Sam, who was just as curious.

"It's Rimfire!" Benji said excitedly. "Did you draw that picture?"

"Yes."

"That's a real good picture. You can really draw good."

"Thank you, I'm glad you like it. I just hope your father likes it."

"He won't," Sam said.

"Yes, he will," Benji insisted.

"He won't like it. I know he won't," Sam said.

"I think he'll love it," Elfrieda said. "While you're gone to the depot, I'll find just the right place to hang it, and when your daddy sees it—"

"Thank you, Elfrieda," Jana interrupted gently, so as not to exacerbate Sam, "but now we'd better hurry. We don't want to be late, in case the train is early."

As Jana and the boys waited in the depot, night had already fallen, and the kerosene lamps, mounted on brackets, cast light on the railroad advertising posters and wanted bills.

The building was pleasantly warmed by a red-glowing, potbellied stove with high-backed benches around it. The room smelled of smoke and tobacco juice, emanating from the spittoons, which were strategically placed on the wide-planked, wooden floor, though that the chewers were less strategic in the placement of their tobacco quid was strongly indicated.

Jana and the boys were seated near the stove

to keep warm. The boys could hardly contain their excitement. Even normally reticent Sam was animated over Drew's returning home.

"Daddy's been gone for two whole weeks," Sam said. "I don't like it when he's gone."

"I don't like it either," Benji said. "How many days is two weeks?"

"I don't know," Sam said.

"Sure you do," Jana said. "How many days are in one week?"

"Seven."

"So if you have seven days two times, how many days is that?"

"Fourteen!" Sam said, rewarding Jana with what, for him, was a rare smile.

"Let's go see if we can see the train coming!" Benji suggested, and he and Sam ran to the window that protruded out in a bay with a view of the tracks from both directions.

As the boys stood by the window, Jana looked around the waiting room. A few people seemed to be waiting to board, but others were there, like Jana, to meet someone on the arriving train. Jana had seen such people in depots before, lovingly greeting a spouse or a family member, and always before, that scene had left her feeling profoundly lonely.

But not tonight. Tonight she was one of the people welcoming home a loved one.

Yes, she thought. *A loved one.*

"Jana!" Benji called excitedly. "Here comes the train! I see the light! Can we go outside to wait?"

"It's cold out there."

"I don't care. I want him to see us when he gets off the train."

"All right. We'll all wait outside."

A few minutes later the train rolled into the station, the engine gushing steam and trailing glowing cinders from the firebox. Metal screeched on metal as the great driver wheels were braked and the train came to a stop, the kerosene head-light casting a glistening reflection on the rails.

The conductor was the first one down, then the passengers began to egress. Jana watched a woman greet a male passenger with a hug and a kiss; then an older couple embraced a young woman, who she supposed was their daughter.

Then Colonel Lounsberry and Sheriff McKenzie got off.

"Where's Daddy?" Benji asked worriedly. "Did he miss the train?"

"No," Jana said. "There he is. See?"

Drew stood on the top step for just an instant as he looked out over the people gathered on the platform; then, when he saw Jana and his two sons, he smiled and started toward them.

"Daddy!" Benji yelled, running toward him, and Sam went as well.

Drew hugged both boys. "Oh, I can't tell you how happy I am to be home, and how much I missed you two."

Then, seeing Jana, he walked over to her as well. "They aren't the only ones I missed." He hugged and kissed her, just as all the returning husbands hugged and kissed their wives.

EIGHTEEN

Jana dressed quickly in the black velvet gown. It was as if she thought she could ignore what she looked like if she didn't dwell on it. She had stepped out into the hall when she remembered that she was to wear her hair like the empress. Returning to the room, she released her chignon, letting her ash-blond hair fall down her back, then she worked some waves around her face, anchoring them in place with the pearl band. As she looked at herself in the mirror over the dresser, she was struck by how different she looked.

She thought she actually looked pretty, an adjective she seldom applied to herself. Jana began to pinch her cheeks to add some color, then she applied a little petroleum jelly onto her eyelids, causing them to glisten. Grabbing her cloak and taking a deep breath, she stepped into the hallway.

When she went down the stairs, she had planned to gauge Drew's reaction to her, but she couldn't. She was too busy reacting to him. Drew was wearing a black tailcoat and trousers, a gray vest, a wingtip shirt, and a silk puff tie. This was the first time Jana had ever seen any man in formal attire, and surely there could be no one more handsome and more elegant than this man standing before her.

Jana was so struck by it that she stopped at the bottom step to stare for a long moment. Gradually she realized that he was appraising her with the same intensity and appreciation as she was him.

Drew spoke first. "Jana, no princess in any fairy tale could possibly be more beautiful than you. I feel sorry for the poor player who struts and frets his brief hour upon the stage tonight, for surely all eyes in the house will be on you."

"Well, thank you, Mr. Shakespeare." Jana smiled, thankful that the repartee had eased her nervousness. "And surely the great bard was never as well turned out as the gentleman who is to be my escort tonight."

Drew helped Jana into her cloak, then put on his coat and offered his arm. "Come, princess, your carriage awaits."

"My carriage?"

"Yes, I hired a carriage and driver for the night. I'm sure that you would agree with me that one shouldn't attend an event like this in a mere wagon."

As they rode to the Opera House, Drew took Jana's hand in his, then raised it to his lips and kissed it. "Thank you," he said.

"For what?"

"Thank you for asking me to attend the play with you. Thank you for bringing the boys to the depot to meet me. Thank you for looking as beautiful as you do tonight, which fills me with pride to be your escort. And thank you for that wonderful painting of Rimfire. Jana, you could not have imagined a better gift. It will always have a place of honor, not only in my home, but in my heart."

"And I thank you for the invitation to the ranch that inspired me to do the painting."

"Inspired, yes. The painting is truly an inspired work." Drew put his arm around her shoulders and pulled her closer to him, and they rode like that for the rest of the way to the theater.

After a few minutes the coach stopped, then the driver jumped down and opened the door to the carriage.

"Chancy, I think this shindig is over at ten. Will you pick us up then?"

"Yes, sir, Mr. Malone, I'll be here," the driver replied.

Drew and Jana followed the others into the theater. They started toward the orchestra level, but Linda Steward, the president of the Ladies' Christian Union, stopped them.

"No, dear," she said, smiling. "We have a box seat reserved for you."

The box was the one nearest the stage, affording them an excellent view of both the play and the audience.

Della Peterson had the leading role, that of Mrs. Haller, and she was costumed so as to show off her figure. Foster Suett, a post-office employee, was playing the role of Peter. Late in the second act now, they were the only two onstage.

The play described the miseries that the dishonor of an adulterous wife can cause. It continued for three acts, with Della projecting her dialogue loudly, with self-importance, until her final line.

The curtain closed to thunderous applause; then, one by one, the players came to take their curtain calls, with Della Peterson being last.

As she stood there, making what seemed to be endless curtsies and blowing kisses to the audience, Sam Whitney came onstage to present her with a large bouquet of roses.

After the play, Jana was told of the reception for the cast and staff of the production, and Linda Steward insisted that Jana should attend.

"Oh, no, I appreciate the invitation," Jana said, "but the reception should be for the actors who made this such a success, and for those who worked behind the scenes and produced the play."

"Nonsense," Mrs. Steward said. "There wouldn't have been a play without you. You should be at the party."

"I'm here with Mr. Malone."

"But of course, he's invited, too."

"Drew?" Jana asked.

"Mrs. Steward is right, Jana. You did have a part in the success of the evening. If you hadn't been able to translate the script, this play may not have been the one produced."

"Good. Then that's settled. Come to my house as

soon as you can. My husband will be there to greet you if I'm not able to get away quick enough."

When Jana and Drew stepped into the rather commodious parlor of the Steward home, several people were gathered around Della Peterson, all of them complimenting her on her performance. She was accepting all the accolades as if they were her due, occasionally condescending to bestow her own congratulations to the other actors, without whom, as she pointed out, her own role would have had no meaning.

"I may have been the bright moon, but what is a night without the twinkling of starlight, which but adds only more to the beauty of the moon's luster?"

She had just completed her paean to the lesser luminaries of the play when she saw Jana and Drew come into the room.

"Miss Hartmann," Della called out. "I'm sorry, but this is a private celebration for those of us who had speaking roles or were stagehands. The audience was not invited, dear. I'm afraid you'll have to leave."

"Oh, no, Della, I invited Miss Hartmann," Linda Steward said. "For without her, we wouldn't have had a translation of the script. By sharing her talent with us, she contributed as much to the success of our production as anyone did."

"Talent? What talent? From what I understand, she was born in Germany. What talent does it take for a German to speak German?"

Linda laughed nervously. "This *is* my party, and *I* invited her, and she *is* welcome."

"Of course," Della said, forcing a smile. "I guess I just misunderstood. Please accept my apology, and thank you for what you did for us."

"There's no apology needed," Jana said graciously. "Working on the play was my pleasure, and by the way, you were a wonderful Mrs. Haller. Have you had theatrical training?"

Della smiled condescendingly. "I was the lead in three plays when I attended Vassar College. That's in New York."

"How wonderful. I'm sure you were as good in those plays as you were in this one."

"Della," someone called. "Could you come here for a moment, please? We have a photographer, and he would like a photograph of you, alone, before he takes the whole cast."

"Of course." Della smiled at Jana and Drew, though Jana got the impression that the smile didn't go much beyond a stretch of her lips. "If you will excuse me?"

After the pictures were taken, Fern Watson called for everyone's attention.

"We have been heaping praise upon everyone tonight, especially our star, Della Peterson, and she so rightly deserves it. But let's not forget Jana Hartmann." Fern looked over at Jana and smiled. "I'm sure most of you have seen Miss Hartmann, who has been somewhat of a star herself." Fern paused. "I would like to point out, the beautiful gown Jana is wearing tonight came from my husband's store. As you all know, Watson's Emporium is the place to go for the finest in women's attire."

"Oh, I hardly think that one who displays herself in a window could ever be called a star," Della said. Then, realizing that what she had said might have come across as a bit shrewish, Della smiled. "Still, she is a beautiful woman, and it requires a certain finesse to be able to seduce—excuse me, I mean, *in*duce—men into purchasing dresses for their wives."

The others applauded, but Jana was mortified. She felt her cheeks flaming as she was pointed out as little more than a walking mannequin.

When a sufferable amount of time had passed, enough that would satisfy Mrs. Watson, Jana asked Drew to please take her home.

Once they were in the carriage, Drew turned to Jana, and with his hand poised under her chin, he lowered his lips to hers and kissed her with a gentleness that was a godsend for Jana. He knew exactly how she was feeling without her having to say one word.

"Soon, very soon, my love, you won't ever have to be put in that position again. I'm sorry." He kissed her again.

When they were within a couple of blocks of the hotel, Drew asked the driver to stop. "Thanks, Chancy, but I think Miss Hartmann and I would like to walk for a few blocks."

"Shall I follow along behind you?"

"No, you're discharged. Good night, Chancy."

Hand in hand, Drew and Jana walked slowly toward the hotel.

"You know you were the most beautiful woman there tonight." Drew squeezed her hand reassuringly.

"It's the dress, and tomorrow Cinderella's coach will be returned to the fairy godmother, and I'll just be me again," Jana said wistfully.

"That's not so bad. The prince fell in love with Cinderella, not her trappings. Do you recognize where we are?"

Jana looked around and smiled. "If it's Beal's Hardware, this must be our doorway." She remembered the night after the firemen's ball.

Drew started to kiss her, but then he looked around to make certain no one was observing them.

"Why, Mr. Malone, I do believe it is you who has become sensitive to scandal."

"It's not that. I just don't want to influence the pool." This time he kissed her with passion. "Will that one last for a while?"

"Until tomorrow." Jana wrapped her arms around Drew's neck, drawing him to her for another kiss.

"Unfortunately, I won't see you tomorrow." Drew started walking toward the hotel. "Antoine-Amédée-Marie-Vincent Manca de Vallombrosa, Marquis de Morès is here, and I must go with him to Little Missouri."

"That's impressive. How long did it take you to memorize his name?"

Drew laughed. "That's why he's known as the Marquis de Morès or just de Morès. I've been trying to find land for him all winter, and I think we've found a way for him to take over a large tract very near Rimfire. Anyway, I'm going to Little Missouri in the morning."

"I'll miss you."

"I'll miss you, too, but when I get back, I want to have a very serious talk with you. Are you ready for that?"

"It all depends on what you have to say, Mr. Malone."

"I'll just say the name Malone will figure prominently in our discussion." A broad smile crossed his face as he opened the door to the hotel.

When Drew and Jana walked into the lobby, they were both surprised to see the space filled with the residents, including Greta.

"I told you boys!" Hank said. "Have any of you ever seen anythin' more regal than our girl, Jana, and her man?"

"Never, and she's purty, too," someone said, and everyone applauded.

Drew chuckled. "Well, I see I'm leaving you in good hands." He kissed her lightly, on the lips, as the men whooped and hawed in appreciation.

"Good night," he said.

"Good night," Jana called to him as he started toward the door.

Drew expected to be gone for about two weeks, but fortunately he came back sooner. When he arrived, Elfrieda was beside herself.

"What's wrong?" he asked when he saw how distraught she was.

"It's my sister. Her husband is near death's door

with diphtheria, and now my cousin writes that Ethyl has it, too. Nobody will take care of her five little ones because they're all in quarantine. I wish I was there to take care of the poor little souls." Elfrieda wiped her tears.

"Where is there?"

"She's on the Mississippi at Cape Girardeau, Missouri. Oh, Mr. Malone, what are those poor babies gonna do?"

"They're going to have their aunt to take care of them, Elfrieda. You have no choice. Your sister needs you and you must go to her."

"But what about Sam and Benji? Who will take care of them?"

"Don't worry about the boys. They'll be taken care of. Do you have enough money to get there?"

"Yes, sir, I do. I can't thank you enough for letting me go help Ethyl. I haven't seen her since the Little Bighorn. You know, she came to see me after Martin was killed."

"Then you must go to her now." Drew withdrew a money clip from his pocket. "Take this." He handed her some money.

"Mr. Malone, do you know there's over three hundred dollars here? I can't take this."

"Then consider it a loan. But right now, you have no idea what you'll need when you get to Missouri. There could be expenses you aren't expecting."

"You don't have to do this."

"I know I don't have to, Elfrieda. But I want to. You've been a wonderful addition to my house and to my family. The boys love you, and I'm very appreciative of what you do."

While Elfrieda was packing for her trip, Drew dropped by the Emporium to talk to Jana. "I know it would be asking a lot of you," Drew said, "but I wonder if you would think about staying with Benji during the day, and also with Sam when he comes home from school. They know you, and I think it would be less of a disruption for them while Elfrieda is gone. That is, if you would consider leaving your job here at the store for a while."

"I would love to do it, but what would the boys think about me coming to their home every day?"

Drew chuckled. "Well, now, just how do you think Benji will feel about it? You won him over the first day he ever saw you."

"He's not the one I'm worried about. It's Sam that may have trouble with the arrangement."

"He'll accept it. First of all, he'll be in school most of the day, and secondly, you know he really is a good boy. It's just that he's so sensitive, but I have no doubt that with Benji's help you'll win Sam over in no time at all."

"Drew, if I agree to this, I want you to know I'm not going to make any overt effort to win Sam over. If he accepts me, it will have to be of his own volition. If it is to happen, it will happen."

"I understand. When can you come?"

"When is Elfrieda leaving?"

"She'll be leaving tonight."

"Then if it's all right with Mr. Watson, I'll come tomorrow. I think he's been creating work for me ever since Christmas, but his business has slowed considerably. I'll tell him this afternoon."

"Good. If you would, come for supper this evening, and we can tell the boys together."

The first few days of looking after the boys were pure pleasure for Jana. She felt like a little girl playing house with real live dolls. Every day, she tried to think of a new activity to do with Benji, and when Sam came home, Benji was anxious to show him what they had done. Drew came home every couple of hours whenever he could, just to make sure everything was going well. Then, on the fourth day, when Jana arrived, Drew met her at the door with a concerned look.

"What's wrong?" Jana asked as she stepped into the house.

"It's Sam. He says he has a sore throat."

"Oh, dear." Jana went into the boy's bedroom and felt Sam's forehead. It was warm, and she noticed also that his cheeks were puffy.

"Are you hurting anywhere?"

"Yes, ma'am. My head hurts, and my ears hurt."

"What about when you swallow?"

"That makes my throat hurt really bad."

Jana bent down and kissed Sam on the forehead, and he made no move to resist it.

"Drew, I think Sam should stay home today. Do you know if anyone in his classroom has had the mumps recently?"

"Miss Peterson said Jamie Wilcox has the mumps," Sam said.

"There's the answer," Jana said. "He'll be out of school for at least ten days."

"Should I ask Dr. Pinkstaff to stop by?" Drew asked.

"I don't think so. There's really nothing that can be done for mumps. When his jaws begin to really swell in a couple of days, it's going to be painful. Then we'll just need to have a lot of cold compresses handy."

"What about Benji?"

"I'll try to keep him away from Sam as much as possible, but I'm sure he is exposed as well."

When Jana and Drew stepped out of Sam's room, Drew took her in his arms and held her. "I'm sorry, Jana. Nursing wasn't something you signed on for, was it?"

"Sam didn't ask to get sick. I'll do my best, and who knows, the mumps may be just the thing that breaks the ice between us."

"Did anyone ever tell you, you're wonderful? That's what I love about you. You always see the bright side. I'll come home as often as I can, but I know the boys are in good hands." Drew kissed her lightly on her brow, much as a husband would kiss his wife before he left for his day.

For the next few days, Jana made certain she had cool cloths to apply to Sam's swollen jaws and warm cloths to ease the pain of his ears. Benji tried to stay out of the room, but when Jana read stories to Sam, Benji crawled up on her lap and listened. At first Jana had insisted that he stay away, but then she decided it was useless. Benji would have the mumps in two to three weeks, if not before.

When Sam's swelling began to subside and he began to feel better, Drew asked Jana if she would tutor him, so that he didn't fall farther behind in his schoolwork than he already was. Drew showed her some of the notes Della Peterson had sent him, detailing Sam's difficulties. Jana picked up the latest note and read: *Sam is falling behind in his schoolwork. He needs extra attention if he is to stay up with the others in his grade.*

Jana thought it strange that a teacher would send such a note to a parent. Wasn't it her job to see that a child learned what he could?

"Oh," Sam said when Jana picked out *Swinton's Third Reader* for him. "Miss Peterson says I can't read that book."

"Why not? Let's try it." Jana opened the book near its middle.

Sam began reading. "'I am going to tell you about Daniel Weh . . . Web . . . '"

"Webster," Jana said.

"'I am going to tell you about Daniel Webster's first case. It was his very first, for Daniel was at this time only ten years old.

"'Webster's father was a poor farmer, and besides Daniel, he had an older son, E . . . '"

"Ezekiel."

"'Ezekiel. Both boys used to help in the farmwork.'"

Sam read the entire story of how when they trapped a woodchuck who had been eating from their garden, Ezekiel had wanted to kill him, but Daniel wanted to set him free. Their father established a court, appointing Ezekiel as the prosecutor, and Daniel the woodchuck's defense counsel. Daniel did a good job explaining that the woodchuck wasn't violating any laws but was, instead, following the law of nature to feed himself.

Acting as the judge in the story, Daniel's father set the animal free.

"Well," Jana said when Sam had finished, having read the story perfectly, stumbling only over the two names, "what do you think?"

Sam was smiling from ear to ear. "It's a wonderful story, and you know what? Daddy's a lawyer, too, so I'm going to read it to him because he doesn't know I can read."

"He will be so proud of you."

"May I read it again?"

"Of course you can." Jana pulled Sam closer to her, but before he started to read, he climbed onto her lap and laid his head back against her chest. Then he opened the book and began.

Jana didn't say a word, but she put her arm around him to pull Sam a little closer as she listened to him read. She was glad he couldn't see the tears streaming down her cheeks.

NINETEEN

When Jana came to Drew's house one morning, she was met by an exhausted Drew.

"Benji's not going to be as good a patient as Sam's been," Drew said. "I've been up most of the night with the little guy while he's been crying that he can't swallow. He finally fell asleep about an hour ago, but now Sam's awake, so I've tied a wet cloth around his head. He says his ears hurt."

"That does it," Jana said. "I'm moving into Elfrieda's room until the boys are better. You can't stay up all night and then expect to work all day."

Drew smiled tiredly. "I'm not even going to try to talk you out of it. I'll stop by the hotel and have Greta gather some of your things, so you won't have to leave."

So it was that Jana moved into Drew's house.

Dinner that first night seemed strange to Jana. She had sat at the dinner table with Drew before, she had slept in the same house with him before, but this time, everything was different. This time there were only the four of them, no Elfrieda to act as an unofficial chaperone, no Devlin nor Toby nor Peach nearby to lend a sense of propriety.

Not only Benji but Sam accepted her presence as if she was a part of their family. But with both of them ill, and in their beds, it made for an extremely intimate situation. And because of what had happened at Rimfire, sexual tension hung in the air.

After putting the boys to bed, Drew and Jana went into the parlor, where they sat together on the sofa. Jana stared absently into the fireplace as the logs burned down. While the fireplace was no longer necessary for heating the house, having been replaced by a coal furnace and hot-water radiators, Drew kept the fireplace burning. He liked to watch the flames lick up around the logs, blue at the base, then yellow, then orange at the dancing tips.

Drew reached out to touch Jana's cheek, then her lips. Her lips were quivering as he moved his hand down over her chin to tilt back her head. She stared into his eyes, smoldering with fire though whether from within or the fireplace she didn't know. She pursed her lips to meet his, and they shared a deep and demanding kiss. She closed her eyes, surrendering herself totally to the sensations she was experiencing.

"No," she said, breaking off the kiss and pulling away from him. "I can't do this."

Now the eyes that had been filled with fire but a moment before were hurt and confused. Jana knew that based upon what had nearly happened while they were at Rimfire, Drew could think he had license to pick up where that incident had left off.

"Please, Drew, not here, not now."

"All right." Drew moved away from her slightly. "I've no intention, nor wish, to force myself on you."

"You don't understand. I'm the one using force here, for I must force myself not to give in to something that I so badly want."

He smiled at her, the smile as intimate as the kiss they had just shared. "Well, I'm glad it's something you want, and not all one-sided."

"Believe me, it isn't one-sided. But, I can't afford to let myself go tonight. Can you understand that?"

Drew shook his head. "I don't understand it at all. But I will respect it. You'll be getting no unwelcome advances from me, Jana."

As Jana lay in bed that night, she replayed the events and the conversation of the evening. The closeness on the sofa, the mesmerizing effect of the flames in the fireplace, the stimulation of the kiss . . . the combination was nearly more than she could resist. Had Drew taken it but one small step further, she would have given in to him.

She found herself wishing that he had been just a bit more insistent.

After about a month, Drew told Sam that he was no longer contagious and that he would be returning to school on Monday. Both Jana and Drew thought Sam would be excited, but he turned and ran quickly to his room.

Then, on Monday morning, Drew went into Sam's room to find him hiding under his bed.

"What's the matter with you, boy? Don't you know, today's the day you go back to school." Drew knelt on the floor to look under the bed.

"I'm sick. I can't go to school."

"Sure you can. You just want to stay home with Jana and Benji."

All at once, Sam slid out from under the bed. "Can I please, Daddy? Can I stay with Jana?"

"You have to go to school. You don't want to be a bumpkin all your life, do you?" Drew smiled.

"No, sir, that's why I don't want to go to school. Jana knows I can read, but Miss Peterson doesn't. Can't Jana be my teacher?"

"I can't ask Jana to do that," Drew said just as Jana entered the room.

"What can't you ask me to do?"

"Be my teacher," Sam said. "You can do it, can't you, Jana?"

"I would love to teach a boy as smart as you are, Sam."

Sam put his arms around her and smiled. "See, Daddy. Jana says I'm smart. Miss Peterson never says that."

"No, she doesn't," Drew agreed. "All right, Jana, if you don't mind. I'll hire you as a private tutor."

"I'd love the job."

"Can she teach me, too, Daddy?" Benji asked.

"Well, first, don't you think you should get well?" Drew replied.

Benji had a bandage wrapped around him from below his chin to the top of his head. It wasn't really necessary, but Benji thought that to heal he should have a bandage.

"But if I just sit here and be quiet while Jana is teaching Sam, can I come to school, too?"

"Of course you can, can't he, Sam?" Jana said.

Sam smiled. "Yes. But I'll be ahead of him in reading."

Sam's homeschooling was going well, and Benji had recovered from the mumps much faster than Sam did. One evening while the boys and Drew and Jana were seated around the supper table discussing what each of the boys had learned that day, there was a knock at the front door.

"I'll get it," Sam said, hopping down from his chair.

"All right," Drew said.

A moment later, Sam brought Della Peterson into the dining room.

"Drew, I came to see why Sam hasn't returned to . . . we . . . oh," Della said, seeing Jana seated at the table with the others. "I'm sorry, I didn't know you had a guest."

"Jana isn't a guest," Benji said. "She lives here."

"Oh?"

Drew laughed nervously. "It isn't what you think. Mrs. Considine was called back to Missouri, so Jana kindly agreed to take her place for a while.

And it's a good thing she was here. Both boys have had the mumps."

"But I'm not sick anymore," Sam said.

"That's why I'm here. Mr. Malone, when will Sam be coming back to school? You do understand that it is your obligation to educate your son?"

"That's what I'm doing. I've hired Miss Hartmann as a private tutor for Sam."

Della shook her head. "With all due respect, Mr. Malone, a private tutor hardly takes the place of a trained teacher. I was educated at Vasser."

"Oh, yes, I remember," Jana said. "You had the lead in three plays if I recall. Well, I was educated at McKendree." She knew Della Peterson had no idea where or what McKendree was, but Jana wouldn't give her the satisfaction of being told.

"I'm sure the child has lost every bit of learning I have drilled into his head. He will undoubtedly be asked to repeat the primary session thanks to your ignorance, Miss Hartmann."

"That's enough," Drew said. "Sam, go get your book. I think Miss Peterson should hear you read."

"Yes, sir." Sam ran into another room. A moment later he returned with *Swinton's Third Reader*.

Jana took the book from Sam, then handed it to Della. "Select any story."

"That's impossible," Della said as she glanced at the book. "Not even my best readers can read from this book." She threw the book on the table.

Then, without taking her gaze off Della, Jana picked up the book and opened it to a random page.

"Read from this page, Sam," Jana said, handing

the book to him and keeping her eyes steadily on Miss Peterson.

Sam began reading: "'What a pretty custom! And how kind and thoughtful! For in that country the winter is very long and the snow lies on the ground for eight or nine months: So the poor little birds have hard work to pick up food.'"

"I think that's enough, Sam, thank you," Jana said.

"I thank you for your interest, Miss Peterson," Drew said as he rose from the table. "But as you can see, Sam is progressing quite nicely." Drew smiled. "You have yourself to thank. After all, it was your suggestion that all he needed was more personal attention."

"Yes, but I didn't mean . . ." With a sigh of frustration Della stopped. "I do not think you are raising your children in a moral home. When people begin to talk, it will be these two precious boys who will suffer. And you—a pillar of Bismarck society. What will people think?"

"I don't care what people think, Miss Peterson," Drew said coldly. "And I especially don't give a damn what you think. Now, if you don't mind, our supper is getting cold."

"Well, I never!"

"Miss Peterson, you know where the door is," Drew said, turning his back to the woman and taking his seat at the table.

The teacher turned in a huff and slammed the door as she left.

"I fear that woman will make trouble," Jana said.

"Don't worry about her," Drew said. "As long as you're tutoring Sam, no one can say he's truant. I'm sure we've heard the last of Miss Peterson."

Della Peterson could hardly contain her anger when she returned to the boardinghouse where she lived. How could Drew Malone dare speak to her in such a fashion! She—the best-educated woman in Bismarck!

She had gone to his home with only the best interest of his son at stake. She told herself her only concern was for Samuel, and his prolonged absence from school. She had been willing to offer whatever assistance she could in helping him catch up with the other students. But when she fully investigated the situation, she discovered that the problem was much larger than mere truancy. Those two innocent children were being exposed to indecent—no, scandalous—behavior.

She knew immediately how she would take care of Drew Malone. He would rue the day he had ever thrown Della Peterson out of his house. She sat down at her desk and began to compose a letter.

About a week after Della Peterson's unexpected—and unwanted—visit, Drew came home in the middle of the afternoon. Accompanying him was a tall, handsome man, standing ramrod straight. He had piercing dark eyes, and a perfectly waxed, tightly curled mustache that stretched easily four inches, ending in needle-pointed, waxed tips. He was wearing a uniform of blue and gold, festooned with so many medals that Jana wondered how he found enough room on the tunic to wear them all.

"Jana, this is the Marquis de Morès. He is the gentleman who has been keeping me so busy of late, and, Antoine, this is Jana Hartmann."

De Morès clicked his heels and made a slight bow. "Good afternoon, Mademoiselle Hartmann. It is my pleasure to meet you."

"Le plaisir est pour moi, monsieur, Marquis de Morès," Jana replied.

De Morès smiled broadly as he turned to Drew. "A charming young lady, the most cosmopolitan I have met on the frontier." He held up his finger. "As the husband of a beautiful, intelligent, and educated woman, I advise you to . . . *accrochez-vous à son.* That is, hang on to her."

"I intend to," Drew said with a smile that Jana could only call possessive. "Jana, I'm going to see that the marquis and his valet are settled at the Sheridan House, where Frank's joining us for dinner. Will you explain to the boys that I won't read to them tonight?"

"How I envy you, my friend. The Marquise de Morès would be by my side this very day if we were not awaiting the birth of our first child. Miss Hartmann, I hope that you and Medora can become friends, just as Drew and I are."

"Please, I am Jana, and I look forward to meeting the marquise."

Drew clasped Jana's hand in his as he pulled her toward the door. "I'll see you tonight," Drew said, and put her hand to his lips as he and de Morès left the house.

After Drew left, Jana decided to make potato dumplings for her and the boys' supper. As she was forming the balls, she felt close to her mother, envisioning her doing the same thing. Potato dumplings had been a favorite dish that Marta had often made for Jana when she was a child. She wondered if Sam and Benji would ever think back and remember her making these for them. Or would they even remember her at all?

After supper Jana played a game of checkers with Sam, then as Sam read to them, she helped Benji draw pictures on his slate. Near eight o'clock both boys began yawning, so she suggested they go to bed, which they agreed to do so if she would read a chapter from the book that Drew usually read to them. When she noticed both boys' eyes were closed, she tiptoed out and closed their door.

Jana was in the kitchen setting the sourdough bread to rise when Drew came in. He stepped up behind her and put his arms around her waist as he nuzzled the back of her neck.

"Are the boys in bed?"

"Yes, and asleep."

"You are so good with them, Jana, and it's only because of that, that I feel comfortable doing what I have to do."

"And what would that be, Mr. Malone?" Jana turned to face him, putting her arms around his neck.

"Frank was planning to go with de Morès to Little Missouri, but the venue for the case he's defending has been moved to Jamestown, so he'll be gone for at least a week, maybe more. Anyway, tonight, we decided that I'll go with de Morès instead of Frank, and except for leaving the boys with you, it makes more sense for me to go. I'll be gone for a couple of weeks at a minimum, and we can stay at Rimfire while we're out there."

"Oh, Drew, do you have to go with him? It seemed to me like the marquis could take care of just about anything that might come up."

"Would you rather not stay with the boys?" Drew asked, drawing back from Jana.

"It's not that . . . it's just . . . I'll miss you."

"And I'll miss you, too." Drew kissed her dismissively on the tip of her nose, then turned to go to his office. "I've got a lot of work to do tonight before I'm ready to go. You'll be up before I have to leave in the morning, won't you?"

"Yes, Drew. I'll be up."

As Jana watched Drew go toward his office, she couldn't help but feel a sense of abandonment. He was going to be gone for at least two weeks. Surely, their relationship had advanced beyond a simple peck on the nose.

He had told her the night of the play that when he returned from Little Missouri he wanted to have a very serious talk with her—one that would involve the name Malone. It was now the middle of March and no meaningful discussion had yet come up.

Jana went into Elfrieda's room, where she was staying, and removed her clothes, folding them and putting them in the chest she was using. She withdrew her nightgown, put it on, and climbed into bed.

But she was unable to clear her mind.

What did Drew really think of her? Was she only a convenient caretaker for his children? The worst of all thoughts came to her as she recalled the words Della Peterson had thrown out the night she came to the house.

I do not think you are raising your children in a moral home. When people begin to talk, it will be these two precious boys who will suffer.

Had Drew taken those words to heart? Did he think she was a "loose woman"? Is that why he had never approached her with the serious discussion he had hinted that he wanted to have?

Jana could take it no longer. She had to know what he thought of her, and there was only one way to find out. Quickly, she left her bed, going down the steps as quietly as she could. She didn't want to awaken the boys and also didn't want Drew to be forewarned that she was coming.

When she reached the door of his office, she put her hand on the knob, but for a moment, she couldn't make herself turn it. What if the answer she got to her question was one she didn't want to hear?

Then, summoning her nerve, she opened the door and stepped inside, seeing Drew sitting at his desk, his shirtsleeves rolled up, and papers strewn about. His hair was disheveled where he had been running his fingers through it, and the stubble of a beard was beginning to form.

As she stood there looking at him, her anger fell

away. The truth was, she loved this man, and she had to know how he felt about her.

But she was afraid. What if he told her he didn't want her? What would she do?

"What is it, Jana?"

She looked at him, and though she wanted desperately to run to him, she was quite unable to move.

"Jana?"

"Drew, I—" Jana could go no further.

Drew rose from his chair and started toward her. He held his arms out, and with a small cry, she rushed to him, wrapping her arms around his neck and pressing her body against his, lifting her head and parting her lips.

For just a moment Drew tried to hold his body in check, telling himself that he could not compromise Jana while she was staying in his house, but feeling this soft, beautiful woman pressed against him, he was powerless to obey his own sense of propriety. When he felt her lips part under his, felt her tongue dart into his mouth, his blood ran hot and he knew there would be no turning back.

"Come," he said quietly. It was more of a command than an invitation, and Jana obeyed it willingly, eagerly. He led her up the stairs to his room and shut the door behind her; then, after turning up the lamp, he pulled her to him in a body-molding embrace, and a tongue-tangling kiss.

Within a few minutes Jana was naked, but Drew wasn't sure when it had happened or even how it had happened. He had not undressed her and he couldn't remember seeing her take off her gown. But there she was, standing nude before him, with the lamp causing her skin to gleam softly. Without a word of explanation or apology for her nakedness, Jana started toward him.

She put her arms around Drew, then kissed him, again sending her tongue probing deep into his mouth. After the kiss he pulled his head away from her for a moment, then spoke softly.

"Jana, do you know what you're doing? There can be no turning back—not now."

"Drew, if I didn't want this to happen, I wouldn't have stepped into this room," Jana murmured. She kissed him again, even more deeply than before. This time he reacted more actively. He began to stroke her back and massage her buttocks.

Within seconds his own clothes were on the floor, his eyes feasting on the beauty that was before him, from the beautiful and delicate features of her face, to the graceful neck, the thrust of her breasts, the flat stomach swelling to the flare of her hips, then down her shapely legs.

He ached with the need for her, a need that he realized, now, had been there from the first moment he saw her in the dining room of the Sheridan House.

Intuitively, in Jana's innocence, she knew the power she had over this man, and for a fleeting moment it was a heady feeling, until she realized that he had the same power over her. She lifted her hand to his cheek, feeling the texture of his skin and the stubble of a day-old beard.

Drew turned his head toward her hand, kissing the palm, a seemingly benign kiss, yet one that sent thrills through her body. Bringing her other hand up, she framed his face.

Jana brought her hands down from his cheeks, to his shoulders, then to his chest. Her lips followed her hands, and Drew inhaled deeply, then pressed Jana's naked body against his own. She could feel the heat of his body, and she lifted her mouth to his, to connect in a flood of passion. She felt his hand in the hollow of her back.

The bright hunger in Drew's eyes told her, in no uncertain terms, that he was now single-minded. He would have her tonight, nothing would deny that.

"My beautiful one," Drew murmured as she felt his hands go to the pins that held her hair. As he removed them, her soft, silky tresses fell forward across her shoulders, shielding her breasts so that only the nipples poked through.

Drew caressed Jana as though he were admiring a sculptor's work in marble. He moved his hands over her body, tracing the curves, the concave of her stomach, the indentation of her belly button, then moved up to her breasts, brushing aside the covering tendrils before taking each of them in his hands, and letting his thumbs tweak the nipples, delighting in her reactions to his ministrations. He looked into her eyes with a deep and triumphant smile, lowered his lips to one of her nipples, sucking at it, as if tasting sweet nectar.

Jana gasped as she felt Drew's mouth at her breast, both sucking at her nipple and flipping his tongue across it. Involuntarily, as if it were a conditioned reflex, she arched her back and thrust her breast farther into his mouth, groaning softly with the pleasure of it all.

Now Jana began her own exploration as her hand trailed down across his hard, muscled body until she discovered a steel-hard shaft, throbbing with a pulse of its own, and so hot to the touch that it seemed to be on fire. It became a sensual exploration, one that both instructed and thrilled her.

"No, Jana."

She was both surprised and disappointed to feel Drew reach down to gently push her hand away.

"I can't let you do that, or we'll be done before we've started." A muffled laugh escaped his lips. "I've not denied myself this moment only to be cheated out of the pleasure of knowing that we'll be doing this together."

"But, we are doing this together."

"Not yet, my love. Not yet. But soon. Very soon now."

She'd already anticipated joining with Drew with far more yearning than she'd ever imagined possible. His mere touch had brought her to readiness, and when she'd felt the liquid warmth spreading within her, she'd quite naturally thought he would bring their closeness to a culmination. But that culmination was not to be, at least not yet.

Drew swept her into his arms, then stepped over to the bed and laid her on it. Climbing in beside her, he again lowered his mouth to her breast, and as he suckled her nipple, it was almost as if she could feel the blood racing through her veins, tingling on its way to her breast and Drew's supplication.

Drew was caught up in his own overpowering sensations. His hands slid over Jana's smooth, naked skin, down to her waist, then into that welcoming, bushy mound at the juncture of her legs. His lips followed his hands, and he kissed his way across her chest. His thumbs locked on her hip bones while his mouth followed her concave belly down to the juncture of her legs, to that same bushy mound that his hand and fingers had just discovered.

When Drew's tongue followed his fingers into that hot, damp center of all her sensation, Jana gasped and arched her back up from the bed. She put her hands on the back of his head to what? Stop him? Urge him on?

She opened her mouth, intending to tell him to stop, that she couldn't take any more, but all that came out was a feverish moan. She thrust her hips toward him, grabbing him with her hands, pulling him to her, not knowing what was going to happen next, but knowing that Drew was in complete control of her. Finally the building tension exploded within her, sending her into a shaking, shuddering climax that enveloped her in a whirlwind of passion.

Lifting his head, Drew smiled at her slowly, lazily, almost insolently. "Jana?"

Was it a question? If so, she couldn't answer. All she could do now was take in deep, gasping breaths, like that of an animal that had been run to ground and was now helpless before its predator.

Drew lifted himself up, spread her knees apart, then moved between her legs. He braced himself with the palms of his hand to either side of her head and looked down at her. Jana realized then that Drew had not experienced anything compared to the pleasure he had given her, but she knew he was bound to do so now, and as he stretched his body out, full length over hers, she waited . . . and wondered.

Before entering her, Drew bent down to kiss her, not the deep, tongue-probing kisses of before, but soft, gentle kisses that somehow Jana knew were the calm before the storm.

"Drew?" Just saying his name was all the question that was needed.

"My sweet, beloved Jana. The best is yet to come."

Drew let his weight down onto his forearms, then his engorged, hot, pulsating shaft probed at the entrance. He pushed harder, and she opened up to him, letting it come in—then, suddenly, and unexpectedly, she felt a sharp pain and she cried out, though it was more of a quiet moan than a cry.

"It's all right, my darling." Drew stopped and held her close to him, inching ever so slowly into her moist cavity.

Even as Drew was soothing her, the pain was gone, replaced by the most delightful sensations Jana had ever experienced. She felt him thrust into her, taking him deeper than she thought possible as she arched her body up to meet his, wanting to keep him there forever, but she soon found as much pleasure in when his shaft slid out as when he thrust it back into her.

His thrusts were powerful and deep, and she clung to him, taking him wantonly, delighting in the powerful, sensory-laden strokes that were setting her body aflame.

Then it happened! Everything Drew had wanted for her began. A feeling burst over her like a sudden storm, lifting her to the heavens, then letting her float back down, only to feel a second lightning strike, then a third, then a fourth.

Were these powerful sensations ever going to stop? She wanted them to go on and on, but knew that they couldn't; her body simply could not take any more! She felt Drew's own release, felt him jerking in pleasure, felt the warmth in her womb, then gradually, slowly, finally, she came back to earth.

When the last ripples of pleasure had subsided, they lay together, her head on his shoulder, his arm around her, his hand resting on her naked buttock as her leg curled over his body. The feeling was total contentment. Outside, the wind had started blowing, and Jana could hear the dry rattle of the leafless limbs of an ancient cottonwood tree.

"Jana, as soon as I get back from this trip with de Morès—"

"—you have something you want to discuss with me," Jana finished.

"No, we're discussing it now."

"Discussing what now?"

"Our wedding."

Jana lifted her head off his shoulder and looked

directly into his eyes. "You're not teasing me, are you?"

"I love you, Jana. I want you to be my wife."

"Oh, Drew, yes, yes. I want to be your wife, and I've never been so happy in my whole life." She rolled on top of his hard body, allowing her own to mold with his as she kissed him deeply.

"I don't think I'll have to worry that I won't see you before I leave in the morning," Drew said with a chuckle. "You're going to stay right here with me the whole night."

"Are you sure you have to go?" Jana asked between kisses.

"I have to, but you'll have something to think about while I'm gone." He rolled her over and placed her beneath his body as once again he began to make love to the woman he would have by his side for the rest of his life.

TWENTY

Drew had been gone for a week when Greta came over to visit Jana, bringing a pot of soup.

"You didn't have to do that," Jana said.

"I wanted to. I figure you're busy enough entertaining Sam and Benji, and I thought you wouldn't mind having a meal you didn't cook. Besides, now that you're getting married, we won't have as many opportunities to eat together anymore."

"Oh, Greta, I can't wait to marry Drew. Benji and I went down to the Emporium, and Mr. Watson showed me the ready-made wedding dresses in *Godey's Lady's Book*. I marked one that I like, but I'm not sure I can afford it."

"When Drew gets back, have him buy it."

"No, he can't do that. It's bad luck if the groom sees the wedding dress before the wedding day." The two sisters laughed together. "Anyway, I want it to be a surprise for him."

"Am I going to be your maid of honor?"

"I haven't made up my mind yet. I was thinking of asking Little Casino, or better yet, Della Peterson," Jana said with a twinkle in her eye. "Of course you're my maid of honor."

"Well then, I'll have a reason to get a special dress, too. I'll just see what's in *Godey's* for me."

"Oh, Greta, the only thing that makes me sad is that I wish Mama could come and see us. She would be so proud of us, and I know she would love Drew."

"Well, when the date is set, we'll have to send for her. Do you think she will come?"

"The question is, would Mr. Kaiser let her come?"

"Jana, if it doesn't cost him anything, even my father isn't that mean that he would keep Mama from coming to see us. We won't tell her about the wedding until we're sure of the date, but when we do know, I'll bet all our friends at the Custer Hotel will help pay for her ticket."

"I'm so glad we came here. Both of us are going to have such good lives," Jana said.

"Oh, that reminds me. Guess who came in the saloon the other day looking for you?"

"For me? I have no idea."

"Reverend Kling and his group from Chicago. He said he was coming in March, and sure enough, he did, but I don't think he felt too comfortable looking for members of his flock—especially female members—in a bar. He looked relieved when I told him we were going to stay in Bismarck. That is what we're going to do, isn't it?"

Jana screwed up her face as if she were contemplating the question. "Let me decide. What shall I do? Go to New Salem and live in an eight-by-ten tarpaper shack while I pull a plow just to eat, or stay in Bismarck and live in this house with two beautiful children and the most wonderful man in the world? Shack or Drew? It's such a hard decision. I can't make up my mind."

"No matter what happens, don't ever lose your sense of humor. It's no wonder Drew Malone loves you so much. I wonder if I'll ever find a good man."

"What do you mean? Why, you have at least a dozen men. What about Hank and the others?

"They're all wonderful, aren't they? But I'm not likely to marry any one of them."

"Not even Hank? He'd marry you in a minute," Jana teased.

Greta laughed. "Yes, he would, wouldn't he? But if you don't mind, I'm going to try to land one just a bit younger. And when I finally do find the man I'm going to marry, I hope he's as good as Drew. Well, maybe that's not possible. I don't think there is anyone else as good as Drew."

"That's not true, Greta, I know there's someone. And I know that he's out there, somewhere, looking for a good woman." Jana embraced Greta. "He just doesn't know how lucky he's going to be when he finds you."

"Jana, I'm so glad I have you for my sister," Greta said as the two women embraced.

The next day Jana received a letter from Drew. In the same envelope was a letter for Sam and Benji.

Jana read her letter first.

My Dearest Jana,

    *Never has time dragged by so slowly
as have these interminable days of our
separation. Often, though I may appear to
be looking at land for the Marquis de Morès,
I am in fact looking just over the horizon
where I see your sweet face, calling to me.*

    *I can think of nothing but our wedding
to come, and the love that we will share
forever after. Keep me in your heart, as you
are in mine, and the time will come when,
once more, we are together.*

    With all my love, your husband to be,
    Drew

"Sam," Jana called. "You and Benji have a letter from your daddy."

Sam and Benji came running into the parlor, where Jana gave them the letter. Sam started reading it.

"Sam, read it out loud," Benji yelled. "You know I can't read yet."

Sam read aloud:

Dear Sam and Benji,

    *I miss you. But I am not the only one who
misses you. I saw Buster and Spotty and
they looked very sad. I am sure they miss
you as well, and they want you to hurry
back to Rimfire so you can ride them again.*

    *Peach made crullers yesterday. She says
she will make them every day when you
are here. You know the other cowboys want*

*you to hurry and get here, so they can have
some, too.*

*Be good boys for Jana. I will be home
very soon.*

. *Love,*
Daddy

"Well, now, wasn't that a wonderful letter?"
Jana asked.

"Yes, but he didn't say anything about Dancer,"
Benji said. "Do you think Dancer misses you?"

"I think Dancer misses you," Sam said. "Don't
you think so, too, Jana?"

"I know he does because I miss him."

"When do you think we'll get to go back to Rimfire and ride our ponies?"

"I'm sure it won't be too much longer. I heard
your daddy talking about the cattle roundup.
I know he wants to be there for that, don't you
think?"

"Oh, yeah! That's my favorite time of the year,"
Benji said.

At that moment there was a knock at the door,
not a gentle knock, but loud and insistent.

"Goodness, who could that be?" Jana asked.

"I'll get it," Sam said.

"Sam, no, wait." Jana found something about
the texture of the knock disturbing. She held her
hand out toward the children. "I think I'd better
answer the door."

When Jana opened the door, she saw two
strangers, a man and a woman, standing on the
porch.

340 · SARA LUCK

"Who are you?" the woman asked, the tone of her voice anything but friendly.

"Perhaps it would be proper if I asked you that question," Jana said.

"Where are my grandchildren?" the woman demanded.

"I beg your pardon?"

"Yoo-hoo! Samuel! Benjamin! Where are you?" the woman called.

"Grandmother?" Sam's voice replied.

"Oh!" Jana said with a broad smile on her face. "Please excuse me. Had I known you were the boys' grandparents, I wouldn't have been so curt. Please come in." She stepped back out of the way.

"I hardly need to be invited into my own daughter's home," the woman said as she pushed past Jana

"Daughter?"

"Yes, I'm Addie's mother. I daresay you've heard her name. Come, Eli, we have much to do. Boys, aren't you excited? You're coming to live in Evanston with us."

"What! What did you say? You can't do that." Jana went to stand between the children and their grandmother.

"Oh, yes, I can. Tell her, Eli."

"I am Eli Denton, the boys' grandfather. We have a court order, authorizing us to take these two children,"

"Why? Their father is a wonderful man who takes excellent care of his children."

"And where is he now?" Rose Denton asked.

"He's in Billings County, attending to some legal work."

"I am told that you are staying here."

"Yes, I am. I'm looking after the children."

"I have also been informed that Samuel has been withdrawn from school. Is that correct?"

Jana shook her head. "Not exactly. I mean, he has quit attending the public school, but he hasn't stopped his schooling. I tutor him every day."

"You? And what qualifications do you have to do that?" Professor Denton asked.

"I am a certified teacher with a certificate to teach in Illinois. I graduated from McKendree College."

"Well, there you have it," Mrs. Denton said. "This isn't Illinois. You don't have any legal right to teach this child."

"Grandmother, I have a pony!" Benji said. "And when Daddy comes back, we're going to go to our ranch so I can ride him. Sam has a pony, too."

"That's sweet, dear," Rose Denton said, dismissing Benji as she was clearly concentrating on Jana. "I received a letter that says you are cohabitating with the father of my grandchildren. Is that true?"

"Well, I don't know who sent the letter, or what it had to say, but I wouldn't put it that way."

"Is it also true that you display yourself in provocative clothing for the enjoyment of gawking men?"

"That's not true. For a while I was modeling dresses for Mr. Watson, a very respectable Bismarck businessman, but there was absolutely nothing untoward about it."

"Are you, or are you not, living in this house?"

"I don't deny that because I am living here. But the way you are putting it implies that . . ."

Jana stopped in midsentence. What, exactly, does it imply? She knew that she could not, in good conscience, deny what it implied because she had shared Drew's bed.

"Mrs. Denton, perhaps I should tell you that Drew and I are engaged to be married."

"Let me make myself clear. I don't have the slightest interest in what goes on between you and Drew Malone. I do, however, care very deeply about the moral character of my grandchildren. They will be returning to Illinois with me and their grandfather."

"You can't do that!" Jana said.

"Oh, can't I? Eli, read the court order to her."

Professor Denton pulled a paper from his pocket and, clearing his throat, began to read: "'Pursuant to the minor children of the late Adelaide Denton Malone, it has been reported that they are exposed to the immoral behavior of their father, Andrew Malone. Therefore I, John Bobe, Federal Judge of the District of Dakota Territory, issue this court order that they be remanded to the custody of their maternal grandparents, Eli Denton, and his married wife, Rose Denton."

"Jana, what does that mean?" Sam asked.

Rose Denton bent down to be at face level with Sam. "Why, darling, it means that you and your little brother, Benjamin, are going to be going on a trip. You're coming back to Evanston where your sweet mother used to live. Now, you tell me what you want to bring with you."

"We can't leave," Sam cried. "Daddy isn't here. He won't know where we are."

"Don't worry, he'll know, and he'll be so happy that you'll have a good home to live in. Do you remember? We live close to the water and you can watch all the boats. You used to like to do that," Rose Denton said.

"No!" Benji wrapped his arms around Jana's legs. "I don't want to go! Jana, don't make me go!"

"Don't be silly. Jana"—Rose said the name with a sneer—"will be happy to have you gone."

"No! No! No!" Benji cried as he lay on the floor and kicked his feet at his grandmother. "I don't want to go."

"A perfect example. No discipline. Stop that this instant," Mrs. Denton said as she jerked Benji to his feet.

"Please, Mrs. Denton, I beg of you. Drew will be back in a few days. Couldn't you at least wait until he returns? I don't feel I have the authority to turn these children over to you."

"That's just it," Rose said. "You have no authority at all, certainly not enough authority to defy a federal court order."

"I won't let you have these children."

"Young lady," Professor Denton said, "you just intimated that you are an educated woman. If that is true, you know the power of a court order. There's nothing you can do to prevent us from taking the children. And if you make any attempt to stop us, you'll be found in contempt and possibly put in jail, and the children will still be taken. So what will you have gained? My advice to you is to stay out of the way."

"Jana, are they going to take us?" Sam asked. Unlike Benji, Sam wasn't crying, but he couldn't keep his voice from breaking.

"No, not if I can help it. Come on, boys, we'll go find Mr. Allen. He'll know what to do."

Jana grabbed the hands of both boys, and when Rose Denton stepped in her way, Jana pushed her aside.

"You can't defy a court order," Mrs. Denton insisted.

"Maybe not, but I'm going to have a lawyer tell me that. I'm not turning these children over to you based solely on your word, court order or not."

Jana, with both boys in tow, ran out of the house headed for Drew's office.

When she reached the law office, it was closed, and then Jana remembered that originally Frank was to have gone with de Morès, but had been called to Jamestown. Her next thought was of Sheriff McKenzie, but she learned he was in Yankton. She went to the Emporium to see if Mr. Watson could help her, but was told that he was at the depot, picking up a new shipment of freight.

Jana hurried to the depot, Sam and Benji in tow, only to learn that Mr. Watson wasn't there.

But Professor and Mrs. Denton were there, and now they had someone with them. The tall man had a handlebar mustache, a high-crowned hat, and, most important, a star pinned to his shirt.

"There they are, Marshal," Rose said. "Those are my two grandchildren, and that's the woman who took them from us."

"I didn't take them from you," Jana said. "I'm trying to keep you from taking them from their father."

"Young woman, I am Curt Wallace, a duly appointed US marshal. You were informed of the court order granting custody of these children to their grandparents?"

"It was read to me, yes."

"Then, I'm sure you are aware that you have no choice but to hand these boys over. If you do not, I will personally take the children in my charge and put you in jail."

"No!" Sam said, as he stood closer to Jana. "I don't want to go to Evanston. I want to stay with Jana."

"I want my daddy!" Benji said, now sobbing loudly.

"Stop acting like babies," Rose Denton said, pulling the boys away from Jana. "Eli, get them on the train."

"Come with me, boys."

"No! No!" both Sam and Benji shouted. "We don't want to go."

"Sam, Benji!" Jana called, stepping toward them with her arms outstretched.

"Madam, cease and desist your interference now!" Marshal Wallace ordered, stepping in front of her.

The scene was playing out, vividly, before everyone else at the depot.

Jana felt her stomach retching, and she watched

Sam and Benji as the marshal took them onto the
train. When all were aboard, the train began to
move. Jana ran along the track until she could run
no farther. Both boys were at the window of the
car, visibly upset as she heard their cries. The train
began to gain speed, and Jana could do nothing
but stand helplessly on the platform and watch as
the engine pulled away, black smoke pouring from
the stack.

Jana put her hands over her face and wept bit-
ter tears. How had she let this happen? How could
she face Drew?

Slowly, she walked to Charley Draper's office.
Sending this telegram would be the hardest thing
she had ever done in her life.

"What did you say they call this place?" de Morès
asked. Drew and de Morès had spent the last several days exploring the land that was to be de
Morès's ranch. Now they were standing in front of
the train depot.

"Little Misery," Drew said.

"It's an apt name for this filthy place. Medora.
That's what I'm going to call my town."

"Medora?"

"Yes. I will name my town for my beautiful wife."

Drew laughed. "Well, now, Antoine, I'm not sure
even you can change the name of a town just by
saying you're going to."

"Little Missouri can stay right where it is, until
it withers and dies. I'm going to build a fine town
on the opposite side of the river. My workers will
need houses, and stores, and a saloon that they

can enter without gagging from the smell. You'll see. When my abattoir is up and running, Medora will become the most important settlement in the Badlands."

Drew laughed. "I'll give you this, Antoine, you don't think small."

"My dear boy, you have no idea. I need money—more than you can imagine—because my ultimate goal is to revive the royal house in France, with me as the monarch."

Drew whistled and shook his head. "Like I said, you don't think small."

"Drew?" The summons came from the station master, who had stepped out of the depot to call him.

"Yes, Clem?"

"There was a telegram come for you, a couple of days ago. Did you get it?"

"No. Did it get to Rimfire?"

"It did. But I expected you to be outa here on last night's train."

"It was that bad?"

"It was. I'll get it for you."

Drew followed Clem Pittman into the depot with a feeling of trepidation. Something was very wrong.

Clem shook his head as he handed the telegram to Drew. "It's too bad, Mr. Malone. I've seen those two little tykes, and they're good boys."

Drew read the telegram, his heart beating wildly.

"That damn woman! I'll tear her apart limb by limb." He stomped out of the depot.

"Is there a problem?" de Morès asked.

"You're damned right there's a problem. My boys are on their way to Evanston, Illinois, and I'll go to hell and back to bring them home."

Jana was standing at the front window when Drew returned, arriving in front of the house in a hired spring wagon. He jumped down from the wagon before it actually stopped and strode quickly up to the house. Jana moved away from the window and was standing just inside the door when Drew came in. The expression on his face was unlike anything she had ever before seen, a cross between anger and despair.

Jana's throat felt tight and her lips were dry. Nervously she moistened them.

"How could you let this happen? Where are my sons?" Drew demanded, a chill to his words.

"They're with the Dentons."

"And you just gave them to them? How could you do that?"

"I didn't just give them Sam and Benji."

"Well, what would you call it then? They aren't here, are they?"

"Drew, I'm so sorry."

Drew's jaw was clenched, and his eyes were narrowed. "And you think that's enough. Elfrieda would have stood up to those people. I know she wouldn't have given them up."

"I didn't just give them up. I went to get Frank, and I tried to find Sheriff McKenzie, but neither of them was in his office."

"I can't tell you how disappointed I am with you, Jana."

"Drew," Jana said as a knot formed in her throat, "I'm sorry. I can't begin to tell you how sorry I am."

"You're sorry, but they're gone. Well, they won't be gone long."

"What do you mean?"

"I mean, I'm going to go get them and bring them home." Drew sighed and ran his hand through his hair. His mouth was tightly drawn, and a little throb was in his cheek. "It's my fault. I shouldn't have left them with you."

"Drew, you aren't being fair."

"Fair? What's fair about it? My children have been taken from me, and you stood by and watched it happen."

"I didn't just stand by and watch it happen."

"Well, Miss Hartmann, what would you say happened?" Drew turned and headed for the stairs. When he was midway up, he stopped and turned to look at Jana. "I'm going to Evanston to get my kids. There's no need for you to be here when we get back."

With tears streaming down her cheeks and the raw hurt of a broken heart, Jana left the house.

"But it wasn't your fault," Greta said when Jana told her everything that had happened and about Drew's reaction to it. "You did explain it to him that you had no choice?"

"I couldn't. He wouldn't let me. Oh, Greta, what hurts the most is that he actually believes I could just let the boys go without trying to stop it."

"Oh, honey." Greta put her arms around her sister to comfort her as Jana sobbed uncontrollably. "You'll get this all worked out. I know it. Drew Malone *will* get his kids back."

Jana began to cry even harder. "I've lost everything—the boys, Drew—whatever I may have thought I had. What am I going to do?"

"You can't give up. Two days ago, you were in love with this man, and you have to ask yourself if he's worth fighting for."

Jana looked at Greta with a forlorn expression. "It's not my fight to win. Drew doesn't ever want to see me again."

"You can believe what you want, but I don't believe that. When he finds out you had no choice, he'll understand, and if he loves you as much as I think he does, everything will work out."

"No, Greta. It cannot be."

That night, Jana was restless, her eyes too swollen to sleep. Fearful that she would keep Greta awake, she dressed and went down to the lobby.

"I've been expecting you," Hank Thompson said when he saw Jana. "Come, sit with an old man for a while."

"Thanks, Hank," Jana said with a semblance of a smile.

"You look like you've been rode hard and put away wet," Hank said as he took her hand in his and began to pat it.

"That's probably the kindest thing anybody's ever said to me."

"Do you want to tell me everything that happened?"

For the rest of the night, Jana poured out her

tale to Hank, and he offered comments without condemning either her or Drew.

"Sometimes people just have misunderstandings, and the only thing that will heal them is time. Right now, we need to figure out just what it is you can do to pass the time," Hank said reassuringly.

"You can't do that!" Greta exclaimed when Jana told her what she was planning to do.

"Why not? We came out here to homestead, and I'm going to do just that. I'm going to New Salem and join Reverend Kling's group. Hank says they left a few days ago with a couple of boxcars loaded with supplies, so they'll already be there when I get off the train."

"Jana, I . . . I don't want to leave Bismarck."

Jana smiled and, with her eyes welled with tears, put her hand on Greta's cheek. "Oh, my sweet sister. Just because my life is in chaos is no reason I should make a mess of yours. I want you to stay here. You've established yourself here, and I couldn't be more proud of you. Now, I have to know that there is some happiness left in the world, and who better for it to be than you?"

Greta hugged her sister. "I'm going to miss you."

"It's not like we won't see one another as often as we can. New Salem is only a two-hour train ride, and I'll expect you to come visit me anytime you can get away. You'll have to bring me Swiss chocolate when you have extra."

"You're going to need a lot more than chocolate."

"I know, but Hank helped me choose what I'll

need, and I should be able to survive quite nicely for at least a year."

"Don't say that!" Greta said emphatically.

"What did I say?"

"*Survive*. That's not a word I want to hear. It makes me think of all sorts of things."

Jana laughed. "All right, *exist* may be a better word. Now I have something I'm going to demand of you. Under no circumstances are you to tell anyone where I've gone—not Tom, not somebody who lives in this hotel, not the Watsons, not anyone you might see on the street—absolutely no one—do you understand?"

"I guess that includes Drew?"

"Especially Drew. Now come up to our room and help me get ready. I want you to have all my fancy dresses because I can't see myself wearing any of them when I'm plowing behind a mule."

TWENTY-ONE

Evanston, Illinois

When the hired carriage turned onto Foster Street, Drew saw the houses of his youth and was able to recall the people who'd lived in each of them. When he was a child, Foster Street had been a dirt road going through the Foster farm property, which was the site of Northwestern, his alma mater. Now the street was paved with cobblestones, which echoed back the clopping sound of the horse's hooves, and the village had grown to a population of at least ten thousand. When the carriage stopped in front of 726 Foster, Drew sat there for a moment, looking at the familiar two-story brick home with the wide, covered porch running across the front.

The house where he had grown up was next door, number 728, but his family was no longer there. His parents spent all their time now in Washington, DC, and only kept a small cottage on Orrington, just to maintain residency in his father's district.

"This is it, sir, seven twenty-six," the driver called down.

"Thank you. Would you mind standing here for a while?"

"For how long, sir?"

"For as long as it takes," Drew said. "You'll be compensated."

"Yes, sir."

When Drew knocked on the door, it was answered by the Dentons' longtime housekeeper.

"Drew," she said, recognizing him at once. "I've been expecting you, dearie."

"Hello, Mrs. Billings. Is the professor in?"

"No, sir, he's at the university, but Mrs. Denton is in residence. I'll tell her you're here."

At Mrs. Billings's invitation, Drew waited in the parlor until Rose Denton appeared.

"You have no reason to be here," Mrs. Denton said.

"I've come for my sons."

"You can't have them. Tell me, Drew, did you think for one moment we would stand by and let the children live in that environment?"

"You mean in an environment where they are loved and cared for?"

"Cared for? Drew, don't play me for a fool? I could see with my own eyes what a charlatan that hussy is. And in Addie's bed no less. You're despicable."

"Woman, you don't know what you're talking about."

"Before you say anything else, I have proof. Proof that would hold up in a court of law should you try to take these children away from me. Shall I produce it for the lawyer to peruse?"

"That would be right Christian of you." Drew tried to keep the bile from his response.

Rose left the parlor, and as Drew waited, he saw over the fireplace, suspended from the picture rail, a large, oval photograph of Addie. He walked over to stand in front of it. The expression on her face was familiar to him, and he felt a sudden pang over her loss.

"Did you ever love Addie?" Mrs. Denton asked, returning to the room.

"Of course I loved her. What a stupid thing to ask."

"Then how could you subject her children to this?" Mrs. Denton extended an envelope toward Drew, and he removed a letter:

Dear Mrs. Denton:
   I am sure that you may remember me. When you were last in Bismarck, you visited with me to ascertain the quality of the education that Samuel Malone was receiving. I have had the privilege of instructing your talented grandson for the past several months. But I regret to inform you that he has been withdrawn from the fine educational system that is in our fair city. His father has perceived that Samuel's educational needs should be left to that of his paramour, whom Mr. Malone has taken into his home, subjecting his children to the tortures of living in an illicit environment.

*To add insult to injury, I feel it is my
duty to inform you that the woman whom
Mr. Malone has left in charge of the
children had as previous employment, the
position of posing provocatively in the
front window of a store and, in so doing,
enticing the men of this community to make
purchases.*

*There is no doubt that she is a most
attractive woman, and one can hardly
blame Mr. Malone for being beguiled by her,
but I cannot help but feel that his immoral
behavior with this woman can only create
an undesirable environment for young boys
who are at such an impressionable age.*

*I'm sure that you will wish to rectify this
situation at your earliest convenience.*

With kindest regards,
Della Peterson
Bismarck Public School System
Vassar, class of 1878

When Drew finished reading, he very deliberately
folded the letter and put it back in the envelope. He
placed it on the mantel, then turned to Rose.

"And you think this will hold up in a court of law?
This gossip?"

"Do you deny that it's true?"

"Parts of it are true, but there's nothing illegal
about anything that I'm doing. Miss Hartmann is
highly qualified to care for Benji and tutor Sam.
Now, I want to see my boys, and I want to be on

the next train to St. Paul with them by my side. Where are they?"

Rose Denton glared at Drew. "Did you conveniently forget the court order, Mr. Malone?"

"What court order?"

"Don't play dumb, Drew. Surely your very competent housekeeper didn't fail to tell you we came armed with a court order and a US marshal?"

Drew stood there for a long moment, staring at the woman who had been his mother-in-law, fighting to control his temper. Every vile word he had ever heard in the most flea-bitten saloon was on the tip of his tongue just waiting to be yelled at this woman. He raised his gaze to the picture on the wall, and out of respect for the memory of Addie, he said nothing. With clenched teeth and a muscle jerking painfully in his jaw, he turned and left the room, returning to the waiting coach.

"Which way, sir," the driver asked.

"Washington, DC."

The driver did a quick turn to look at Drew. "What did I hear you say?"

"To the train station on Central," Drew amended.

New Salem, Dakota Territory

When Jana got off the train, her carefully selected supplies were strewn along the track because there was no depot in New Salem. In fact, there was nothing in New Salem. As she began gathering her belongings, a man rode up on a horse.

"Ma'am," he said, as he tipped his hat. "Are you sure you're in the right place?"

"I'm not sure. Is this New Salem?"

"It is. Or at least it soon will be. Did you come from the Colonization Bureau?"

"I don't know what that is. I'm looking for Reverend Kling. Is he here?"

"Do you see him?"

Jana was beginning to get irritated with this man. "Look, mister, I'm not here to play games. Do you know Reverend Kling?"

"I'm sorry, ma'am. I didn't mean to ruffle your feathers. The reverend's down at the Bluegrass Siding. That's where the immigrant cars are, and we're waiting on the NP to build a new siding so we can move the cars here." The man jumped off his horse and walked toward her, extending his hand. "I forgot my manners. I'm John Christiansen, late of Ripon, Wisconsin, and once we get your stuff policed up, I'll take you to him."

"I will appreciate that, Mr. Christiansen. I'm Jana Hartmann, late of Bismarck."

The man gave her a strange look. "I think I heard Reverend Kling mention a couple of women who were supposed to join us in Bismarck. Would you be one of those women?"

"Perhaps. I made a connection with him in Chicago when I realized Dakota allowed women homesteaders."

"Were you working in a saloon?"

Jana swallowed hard. "I lived at the Custer Hotel while I was waiting for your group to come through. I did not work in the saloon." She said this with all honesty. Didn't *working* mean one was earning money?

"Uh-huh." Christiansen helped stack Jana's things in a neat pile, then started off toward the west, leading his horse. When he had gone about fifty feet, he turned to Jana. "Well, are you coming or not?"

Jana ran to catch up with him as she followed him through the tall grass.

When she got to the Bluegrass Siding, she saw two boxcars and was told they were serving as shelter until the Northern Pacific could build an immigrant house in New Salem. The women, numbering eleven by Jana's count, were staying in one, and about ninety men were in the other.

Dear God, what had she gotten herself into? She tried to think, but her mind was numb.

"Miss Hartmann," Reverend Kling said as he approached her. "I was told you wouldn't be joining us when I encountered your sister in the saloon."

"You lied," John Christiansen said. "'Thou shalt not bear false witness.'"

"He encountered my sister, but she isn't here. If you will have me, Reverend Kling, I would like to join your group."

"That is not my decision to make. It will be up to the other ministers of our colony. For tonight, you may stay."

That night Jana lay on the floor of the boxcar with no blanket or pillow. Not one woman spoke to her. It had never occurred to her that the German Evangelical Synod of North America would reject her. And what would they say if they knew she wasn't a virgin?

As she lay in the dark, the most comforting sound was the howling of the neighboring coyotes.

Washington, DC, the Capitol

"And who may I tell the congressman is calling?" a young man in a suit and string tie asked. He was sitting at a desk applying stamps to a pile of envelopes.

"Drew Malone."

"Malone? Are you kin to the congressman?"

"I'm his son."

"Please forgive me. I didn't know he was expecting you." The man stumbled to his feet, almost tipping the chair.

"He's not expecting me. But please tell him I'm here."

"Yes, sir!" The secretary stepped into an inner office for a moment, then returned with a smile on his face. "The congressman will see you now."

When Drew entered the office, his father was on the telephone and lifted his hand, both in greeting and to indicate that he would be with Drew shortly.

"I didn't say I don't like the Pendleton Bill; I do like it. That's why I voted for it. But you mark my words: this bill's going to be nothing but trouble for the president. Why, you know these party bigwigs like handing out patronage. When we get civil service jobs based on merit, you know it's going to cut into their power base, and they're going to raise bloody hell with Arthur."

Drew could hear a tinny sound coming from the receiver, though he couldn't understand the words.

"Yes, well, you convey my sentiments to Chester, and tell Speaker Keifer he can count on my support. Look, I've got someone in my office, Shelby. I've got to go. . . . I'll do it."

Sam Malone hung up the phone, then greeted his son with a broad smile and an extended hand. "Drew! What brings you to Washington? And where are the boys?" he asked, glancing toward the door.

"The boys are in Evanston, and that's why I'm here."

The smile on the elder Malone's face left, to be replaced by an expression of concern. "Drew, what's happened?"

"They've been kidnapped by your best friends, Eli and Rose Denton."

"Oh." Sam took a deep breath. "For a minute there you had me going."

"That is what they did, Dad. They came to Bismarck while I was in the Badlands on a business trip and they took Sam and Benji."

"I'm sure you're overreacting. They probably just want to spend some time with their grandsons. Eli and Rose would never do anything to hurt those boys, and you know it. They love them, as do your mother and I."

"Does removing them by a US marshal with a signed court order sound like I'm overreacting?"

Sam Malone frowned and fell back in his chair. "There's something you're not telling me. What is it?"

"I am their father, and Sam and Benji belong with me, not the Dentons."

"You didn't answer my question. Now sit down and tell me what's going on."

Drew sat down and told his father as much as he knew about what had happened. While he was talking, he realized that he had not allowed Jana to tell her side of the story. Otherwise, he would have known about the court order before he got to Evanston.

She had no choice. She had to let the boys go, and when she went to find either Frank or Alex McKenzie, that was the prudent thing to do. He realized now that only the authorities could have pleaded with a US marshal to wait until Drew could get there before allowing his sons to be abducted.

When he had finished, his father said, "Well, we'll have to get them back."

"That's why I came to you, Dad. What do I do?"

"The court order had to have been signed by Judge John Bobe. I helped get him his appointment."

"I think you're right. His circuit is the whole Dakota Territory."

"But I can trump his order," Sam Malone said as he reached for the phone.

Drew heard a ring in the outer office.

"Robert, will you ring up my good friend, Justice Stanley Matthews? I have a favor to call in."

Drew sat idly by while he listened to his father talk to a justice of the Supreme Court of the United States. When the conversation was over, Sam was assured that he had a court order that superseded Judge Bobe's order. And this time, there would be no higher authority.

TWENTY-TWO

Drew and the boys had been on the train for a little more than two days, and they would get into Bismarck within ten hours. For the long trip Drew had taken passage on a Pullman car, and as the two boys slept in the upper berth, Drew lay in the lower, listening to the click of the wheels over the rail joints, rocked by the gentle swaying of the car. As he looked out the window, the darkness was only occasionally interrupted by a twinkle of light in some remote farmhouse.

He thought of Jana, and how this would be perfect if he had her head lying on his shoulder. He closed his eyes and visualized her standing naked before him in his bedroom, and how he had carried her to his bed where they had explored each other's body. With just these thoughts he could feel the quiver of an arousal. He wished she were here to make love.

Love. That was how he felt about Jana.

Then he thought about Addie. This whole fiasco with the Dentons had had a happy ending. He had left Rose and Eli on reasonably good terms, even after what they had tried to do to him. They would always be the boys' grandparents, and he had tried to impress upon them that they were welcome to visit whenever they could.

But the best thing that had happened was a feeling of catharsis. For the first time since Addie's death, Drew truly felt free to love again. It was as if she had set him free—free to love someone else.

Tomorrow he would go to Jana and beg her forgiveness for what he had done to her. He would not take the boys. He had to do this alone.

He turned away from the window and closed his eyes. Where would she want to have the wedding? Bismarck? Surely not in Illinois? Then he smiled as he thought of her painting. Rimfire. The wedding would be at Rimfire Ranch.

New Salem

Jana was dumbfounded when she heard the decision of the colony ministers. She would be allowed to stay in New Salem if she became the wife of one of the men. With over ninety men in the colony, those who had not left wives behind cast lots to see who would be obligated to marry her.

The dubious honor fell to one Johan Seethoff, who approached her with barely concealed desire.

"Miss Hartmann, as it has fallen upon me to

set aside all thoughts of selfish aggrandizement, I have accepted my responsibility to procreate for the growth of this colony. At the behest of the ministers, I have consented to marry you, and you shall become Mrs. Johan Seethoff."

The blood drained from Jana's head and she reeled, grabbing the side of the boxcar for support. Countless thoughts coursed through her mind, not the least of which was that this man would immediately know that she did not come to the marriage bed chaste. In the Bible, didn't they stone adulterous women?

Jana turned and ran as fast as she could back to where her belongings were piled. As she ran, all she could think of was the word *survival*. How prophetic it was that Greta had seized upon that word in their last conversation.

Bismarck

Drew and the boys stepped off the train excitedly as each child jubilantly clung to their father's hands. Their first stop was the law office. Drew intended to leave the boys with Frank while he went immediately to the Custer Hotel to find Jana. If all went as planned, she would be with him and the boys when they entered the house.

"It's good to see you guys," Frank said as he hugged both boys. "And welcome home to you, too." He extended his hand to Drew.

"Would you mind keeping an eye on these two for a while? I've got to mend a pretty big hole I've made," Drew said.

"Sure, they can stay here, but Elfrieda's at your house. She came home about a week ago, and I let her in."

"That's great. I'll take the boys home first and then take care of my business."

"Daddy, if Mrs. Considine is back, where will Jana stay?" Benji asked.

"Silly. She'll be with Daddy," Sam said.

"I hope so, Son. Let's go, so I can bring her home as quick as I can."

"Take the rig. I just came in and old Joy's still hitched up," Frank said.

"I'll do it, and I'll take that mare's name as a good omen."

The reunion with Elfrieda was bittersweet. The boys were happy to be home, and they were happy to see her, but both of them went running through the house looking everywhere for Jana.

"I thought she'd be here. I looked in all the places where we play hide-and-seek and she's not anywhere," Benji said.

"How would she know we're back?" Sam asked.

"Sam's right. We didn't tell her. You stay here and I'll go find her," Drew said. "I'm really glad you're home, Elfrieda. We've missed you."

"Thanks, Mr. Malone, and thanks for what you did for my sister. The money you sent buried her man."

"I'm sorry."

"It couldn't be helped, but Ethyl's pulled through, and none of the little ones got the diphtheria, God be praised."

෧෨෨෨

Finding Jana proved to be more difficult than Drew had imagined. He hit his first stumbling block when he went to the Custer Hotel.

"I wouldn't think you'd want to show your face around here," Hank Thompson said when Drew entered the lobby.

"Where is she?" Drew asked.

"She's not here."

Drew took a deep breath. He should have expected Jana's friends to close ranks around her.

"Do you know where she is?"

"I do."

"But you're not going to tell me."

Hank rocked back and forth in his chair as he glared openly, never taking his eyes off Drew's face. Drew decided that it was useless to probe this old man any further. He would have to find Jana himself.

When he stepped into the saloon, it was empty, but he heard sounds coming from the little room off from the bar. Someone was preparing the evening's soup, so he pushed through the batwing doors and entered. He was disappointed that Jana wasn't there, but was gratified to see Greta. If one sister was still in Bismarck, the odds the other one was still here were greater.

"She's not here," Greta said when she saw Drew.

"I can see that, but can you tell me where I can find her?"

"No."

"I don't believe that. As close as you and Jana are, I'm sure you know where she is."

"You didn't ask me that, Drew. You asked if I could tell you where she is, and the answer is no. Jana made me promise I wouldn't tell anyone where she went, and most of all, she didn't want me to tell you, so . . ."

"You're not going to tell me."

"And don't try to get it out of me. If you don't already know the meaning of the German proverb *Blut ist dicker als Wasser*, then, buster, you're about to learn. Good day, Mr. Malone."

"Greta, you can't do this. You have to tell me where she is. I love her and I want to marry her. I have to find her," Drew pleaded.

Greta laid down the knife she was using to cut potatoes for the soup and said with cold and exact words, "You should have thought of that when you sent her away. She took it quite literally when you said there was no need for her to be here when you got back. Now, I don't expect to ever speak to you again." Greta picked up the knife and bent her head back to her task.

When Drew left the Custer, he climbed into the buggy and started for home. Out of habit, he headed for Eighth Street, but as he passed Sixth, he turned left. When he got to where Addie had died, he stopped. For a while afterward, her bloodstains had been on the cinders that hardened the path, and he couldn't bring himself to go there. Even though the stains had faded away over the last two years, he'd continued to avoid the place—until now.

Climbing down from the buggy, he walked over

to stand on the exact spot, and as he looked down, he could see Addie lying there. And he could hear her last words to him, as clearly as if she were speaking them.

Get a good woman to take care of my boys. I love you.

"I did what you asked, Addie, but then I did something stupid." Drew chuckled. "I know what you'd say. 'Stupid? You?' You'd be a little sarcastic about it. All right, I admit it, I was wrong.

"Her name is Jana Hartmann, and she *is* a good woman. The boys love her, even Sam. He hasn't changed. He's still the little cynic, but she won him over with her patience and kindness. And she won me over, too. I love her, Addie, and I'm going to find her wherever she is. I can't lose the second woman I love, too."

Drew looked around to make certain no one had been around to hear his talk with Addie. He walked slowly back to Joy, Frank's mare, who had stood so patiently, waiting for him. When he climbed into the buggy, he sat there for a moment looking at the spot on the path.

"Good-bye," he said softly, before he snapped the reins.

Now came the hard part. How would he tell the boys?

New Salem

Jana pulled a shawl tightly around her as she sat on her pile of belongings. She had been there for most of the day, and not one person had come from the Bluegrass Siding to check on her whereabouts.

For the first time in her life, she really didn't know what she was going to do.

The logical thing would be to go back to Bismarck, but what about Drew? He might well not be able to get Sam and Benji away from their grandparents. Even for an attorney, a court order could not easily be dismissed. It might be necessary for him to stay in Evanston for a long time and maybe never come back to Bismarck.

If he came back without the boys, he would always blame her for his loss, and he would grow to hate her if he didn't already. And if he came back with the boys, he would never trust her to be with them again.

But what about her? Did she even want to be in Bismarck? Over and over she heard Drew's last words:

There's no need for you to be here when we get back.

No, she could not go back to Bismarck. And more than likely she would not be allowed to stay here.

But what was farther west?

She closed her eyes to blot out what she knew was farther west. Rimfire.

That thought triggered an avalanche of tears and she let them flow freely, not even trying to control them. But after she had no idea how long, she sensed a presence, and when she opened her eyes, she saw a shadow in this treeless landscape.

Then she saw the man who had won the lottery, the man who was to be her husband. A man whose name she couldn't remember.

"Do you mind if I sit a spell?" he asked.

Jana didn't answer, but she moved to the side, making room for him to sit beside her.

"Which is it, a man or the law?" he asked.

"I don't—"

He cut her off. "Yes, you do. You're either runnin' from the law or you're runnin' from a man. Now, which is it?"

Jana looked at this stout, blond-haired man who was about her own height. He could have been Dewey Gehrig or Gus Kosmeyer or Hiram Helgen or any of a dozen other German or Swiss immigrants whom she'd grown up with in Highland, Illinois. In that instant, she decided to trust him.

"A man."

"Is he your husband?"

"No."

"Are you with child?"

Jana was silent.

"You heard the decree that was handed down by the ruling body. You and I are to be married, or you will be forced to leave the colony."

"I cannot marry you."

"Am I that displeasing to you?"

"You have been most gracious, but, sir, I don't even know your name."

"I spoke it to you. I am called Johan Seethoff."

"That should have been easy for me to remember." Jana laughed nervously. "My father's name was Johann and my mother's maiden name was Saathoff."

"They are German?"

"Yes, I was born in Geldersheim."

Johan smiled. "I know it well. I was born in Nie-derwerrn."

"Really? My mother's cousin lived there before she came to America."

"And what was her name?"

"Marie Gunter, and now she lives in—"

"Chicago. Back of the Yards," Johan finished.

"Yes, but how did you know that?"

"I call her Tante Marie."

"Mama's cousin is your aunt? But your name?" Jana asked.

"It was misspelled at Castle Garden when I was processed. What's the difference in America if one is a *Saathoff* or a *Seethoff*?"

"Well, Cousin, you've just solved my problem. The reverends will never let us have a consan-guineous marriage." Jana laughed for the first time since Sam and Benji had been abducted.

"I don't know what that word means, but it must be good. I like to hear you laugh."

"It means that the church frowns if you marry a relative, and you, Johan, must be my cousin, somewhere along the line."

"Oh." Johan was crestfallen.

Bismarck

For the rest of April and most of the month of May, Drew tried to keep busy both at work and doing things with the boys. Sam was enrolled at St. Mary's Academy, and Elfrieda took up where she had left off when she went to Missouri.

For a while, Drew had stopped by the Custer Hotel almost every day, varying the times, so that if Jana was still in Bismarck and she came to call on her friends, he would run into her.

At first, Greta was openly hostile to him, but over the weeks she softened and began to talk with him a little. No matter how much he cajoled her though, she never once mentioned her sister's name in his presence. And Hank Thompson was even worse. Drew finally had to concede that Jana was not in Bismarck, and that as far as he could tell, only Hank and Greta had any inkling where she was.

He went to see Foster Suett, the postmaster, and convinced him to keep an eye open for any mail to or from Greta Kaiser. Charley Draper was also on the alert for anything that came across his desk, and the station agent would tell him if any freight was shipped to Jana Hartmann. As a last resort, Drew visited Elizabeth McClellan to see if she knew of a new girl working anywhere in town, or any-where in the Dakota Territory that some of her clients might know of. Every avenue proved a dead end. There was not a trace of Jana Hartmann.

Drew thought perhaps she'd contacted Walter Watson, so he called at the Ladies' Emporium.

"I've not seen hide nor hair of her since the day she came in to look at wedding dresses," Walter said.

"Wedding dresses? Did she buy one?" Drew asked.

"Oh, I don't have them here. Most women sew their own or else have one of Dan Eisenberg's seamstresses make one. I just don't have much call for a ready-made wedding dress."

"Do you know which one she picked out?"

"It was in my *Godey's* catalog. I expect I could find it. Not that it's any of my business, but are you planning a wedding?"

"Yes, I am." Drew took out his money clip and peeled off several bills. "You know her size. Find the dress Jana wanted and have it here for her when she needs it. Oh, and have Fern pick out something she thinks Jana's sister would like for a bridesmaid's dress. Will this cover it?"

Walter smiled when he looked at the pile of bills. "Yes, sir. That would cover the finest wedding Bismarck has ever seen, and that includes the cake and the flowers."

"Would you handle that, too?"

"Well, I don't know. We don't normally do anything but clothes. But now if there was a commission . . . ?"

"When the time comes, you can count on it. In the meantime, get the dress here."

"You've got it."

New Salem

Thanks to Hank's help in equipping her before she left, Jana had the biggest tent in New Salem, and Johan had chosen the best place to raise it. The spot was far enough away from the two boxcars that sat on the new siding track, yet close enough to the water car that was brought in, to make it convenient for her. Like most of the men, Johan was sleeping in the open country because the men's boxcar was so crowded. He did sleep just outside the tent though, and for that Jana was grateful because his presence provided her with a sense of security.

The construction of New Salem went slowly. The railroad had provided enough lumber for an adequate immigrant house, but the leaders had decided to divert it to the building of a church. Jana was appalled at this lack of foresight, but no one asked her opinion.

The supplies, too, were running short because the people who had brought food with them were reluctant to share with those who had not.

Again the reverends had a solution. The next time the water tank was delivered, they arranged with the conductor for bread to be bought in Bismarck and delivered to them. But this posed a problem. New Salem was on one of the few inclines in Morton County, and the train from the east would not stop unless it was an emergency. Consequently, the bread was thrown from the train as it passed on its way west, and there was never enough to go around.

So amid much grumbling among the colony, Jana proposed a solution to Johan: "Why don't we bake the bread here?"

"Because nobody has any flour," Johan said.

"If they can throw bread off the train, they can throw flour. I have a Dutch oven and I'm sure the other women have one as well, and John Christiansen has a horse to go hunt for a vein of coal for fuel. That means we could bake twelve loaves of bread at one time."

"How are we going to pay for flour?"

"I'll take care of that. The next time the water

is delivered, I'll send a message to my friend in Bismarck, and he'll see to it that we get all the supplies we need to make bread. But, Johan, I can't use my real name."

"All right. What name will you use?"

"Hester Prynne. Hank will know it's me." Jana laughed at her own joke.

So it was that Johan and Jana became the most popular residents in New Salem, as they probably prevented the colony from disintegrating before it ever got started. Every day the westbound train threw off the supplies, and Jana supervised the bread-making, while Johan was made the keeper of the sourdough starter. Across the prairie, sod houses began to form, and one by one, people began to move out of the boxcar. That is, all except Johan and Jana, who were too busy with the bread.

Bismarck

"I'm not going to Medora," Drew said emphatically. "I don't care what kind of mess the marquis has gotten himself into. If you can't take care of it, then it's his problem."

"Drew, you know you're being ridiculous. You can't just live for the rest of your life hoping to hear from a woman who has apparently fallen off the face of the earth. You've been watching Greta Kaiser like a hawk, and you've struck out there, too," Frank said. "The woman doesn't want you to find her, or she would have done something to let you know where she is."

Drew sighed. "I'm not going. The last time I went, when I got back, my whole world was turned topsy-turvy. The boys were gone—I lost Jana. I won't risk it again."

"If you don't go, you're going to lose me as your partner. The Marquis de Morès is our client, and he's gotten off on the wrong foot with Gregor Lang. Now I have a telegram from his . . . valet saying three hunters are threatening to string up foreigners if they don't get out of town, and you know the marquis. He's not budging. He thinks he's back in Algiers or some other godforsaken place."

"And what do you expect me to do about it? That man listens to nobody."

"Well, you know those people out there a whole lot better than I do, and if you can't soothe the waters, maybe you can get Devlin or Toby to calm things down. Are you going or not?"

"I'll go, but if anything happens while I'm gone, I'm holding you personally responsible. Send a telegram telling Devlin to meet the train tomorrow."

Frank smiled broadly. "I already did."

Drew picked up a book and threw it at Frank.

Drew had been at the depot all night. The westbound train was late and didn't pull into Bismarck until almost five o'clock in the morning. He was tired and irritable and found a seat near the window away from everyone. He leaned back, pulled his hat over his face to keep out the morning sun, but was unable to fall asleep. At best he wouldn't get to Medora until after lunch and what would he find? The marquis in an uproar, and Devlin either drunk on Forty-Mile Red Eye or madly in love with some whore in Little Misery. Oh, no, he was not looking forward to this trip. A far cry from the trip at Christmas, when he had his boys across from him and Jana's sweet head on his shoulder.

Unable to sleep, Drew sat there watching the barren landscape, then noticed some construction and some soddies going up that he hadn't noticed before. What was this place?

Then he saw her. A woman standing beside the tracks. Her hair blowing in the wind, her face brown from the sun. She bent to roll some sacks of freight away from the track.

Was that Jana? He couldn't be sure, but his heart began to race. He wanted off this train, but what if he was hallucinating? He wanted it to be her, but what if it wasn't? He would be stuck in the middle of nowhere, and what would the boys think if it took him a week or more to get home?

The freight that was thrown off the train! What was the name on the freight? He rose from his seat and made his way to the express car.

"What was the name of the settlement we just passed, and whose name was on that freight that you just kicked out?" Drew asked.

"It's a new one—not likely to survive. Lots of squabbling goin' on there."

"The name? What's it called?"

"They're calling it New Salem."

"Damn, why didn't I think of that? Of course she went there." Drew pumped his fist in jubilation. He turned and almost ran back to his car.

"Don't you want to know the name on the freight?" the express messenger called out.

"Yeah, do you know it?"

"Do I? Every trip west there's three bags of flour for Hester Prynne."

Drew laughed uproariously. "Does she ever ask for a scarlet letter?"

He threw himself back into his seat, a grin stretched wide across his face and his heart practically singing.

For the rest of the trip, Drew could barely contain himself. He was more excited than Sam or Benji could ever be, and he began planning his next move.

The wedding would be at Rimfire as soon as he could get everybody there, and that included Jana's mother. He figured Jana's mother could get to Medora in a good week. By the time they reached Dickinson, he had a lengthy telegram ready to be sent to Walter Watson with exact details. Whom he was to invite and what he was to bring and when he was to be there.

To Frank he wrote three words: I FOUND HER.

At Dickinson, he tipped the telegrapher generously to make certain the two dispatches took precedence over everything else. The rest of the trip seemed like an eternity for Drew until, finally, the train stopped at the newly built depot in Medora.

"Howdy, Boss," Devlin said as he stepped up to shake Drew's hand. "Quite an improvement over the last time you were here. Look at what the marquis has done." Devlin swept his hand around, showing all the construction that had been done since March.

On an ordinary day, Drew would have been impressed, but that was not the case today. "I'm going back on the eastbound train. I've got to check to see what time they expect it. Is Clem still the stationmaster or is he across the river?"

"He's here, but why are you going back so soon? You won't have time to even ride out to Rimfire."

"Get it ready for a wedding. I'm bringing Jana and a few of her friends from Bismarck, and we'll be back in a week."

"A wedding? Hot damn, boss, didn't that come up sort of quick?"

"Devlin, if you only knew."

Clem Pittman checked the wires and told Drew the eastbound would be in Medora in a little less than two hours, so Drew felt honorbound to call on de Morès. Devlin drove him up the hill to de Morès's "cabin," which was finished and almost completely furnished. That was a major accomplishment because the cabin, or the château, as Devlin called it, had twenty-six rooms.

When Drew arrived, de Morès was the consummate host, providing cheese and fresh fruit along with French wine for their lunch. After Drew was satisfied that the marquis's incident with the local ruffians was under control, Drew briefly told him about Jana.

With de Morès, Drew did not express the same bravado that he had shown in either the telegram to Walter Watson or even his words to Devlin. He thought he could convince Jana to marry him, but what if after all he had said, she had changed her mind?

De Morès sensed the kernel of doubt in Drew's plans. "This woman. Do you love her?"

"I do."

"But do I gather you have not seen her since you left here in March?"

"This is true."

"My friend, a lot can happen in a short time. With my beautiful wife it was a *coup de foudre*, or, as you say, love at first sight. We knew one another less than six weeks when we were wed. Has it occurred to you that your Jana may have wed another?"

Drew's face paled. That thought had never occurred to him, but was that why she had kept her whereabouts from him when she was only thirty miles from Bismarck?

"I can see that this thought troubles you, but I have a suggestion. Come with me."

De Morès rose and led Drew down to the stable that stood at the bottom of the hill. He threw open the door, and standing in a bay were a beautiful pair of Shire horses at least sixteen hands tall, their black coats shining.

"My God, Antoine, what beautiful animals, but why on earth do you have these?"

"To pull Napoléon's coach." De Morès directed Drew to an oversize wagon with six wheels. It had a covering much like a Conestoga wagon, but with grommets laced with rope that when pulled would allow the covering to be withdrawn. "And for you, my friend, it can be a love wagon."

"I don't understand what you mean."

"We must hurry. We have less than an hour to get them to the train."

"What?"

De Morès clapped his hands, and at once several grooms appeared. "Hitch up Nate and Bob. They're going for a train ride. And make the coach ready for a week's journey with an overabundance of champagne and the finest food on board. My friend needs to ply his lady."

Just before three on the afternoon of June 2, 1883, Drew Malone was on the eastbound Pacific Express with two horses that were worth thousands of dollars and a coach that was a one-of-a-kind replica of the hunting wagon Napoléon used during his campaign against the Russians. De Morès had explained that if Jana agreed to the marriage, the trip back to Medora could be a veritable paradise, as Jana and Drew traveled as many or as few miles a day as they chose, and if she refused, Drew would have the solace of the many bottles of champagne to drown his sorrow.

As the miles flew by, and the hours ticked along, Drew's stomach began to churn. He tried to take deep breaths to calm himself, but the closer he got to Jana, the faster his heart beat. He checked his watch against the conductor's, and when it had been nearly six hours, he rose to make certain the conductor knew to stop at New Salem.

But when the train stopped and Drew stepped off, not a structure was in sight.

"What the hell! Where are we? Didn't I tell you to stop in New Salem?" Drew yelled, his nerves now almost shot.

"Hold your fire, partner," the conductor said. "This is the Bluegrass Siding. The engineer thought it might be a bit easier to unload that monstrosity the marquis is shipping on the flat instead of on a grade. New Salem's only another couple of miles down the track."

Drew smiled sheepishly. "Sorry. I'm a little anxious, and I want to make sure I get there before dark."

"Mister, are you new to these parts? You know you got more'n fifteen hours of daylight this time of year. Surely you can get that rig two miles before the sun goes down."

Drew chuckled. "I deserved that."

Drew sat in the coach watching the train until the caboose was out of sight and the smoke was but a thin wisp drawn across a bright blue sky. This was the moment. In less than fifteen minutes, he would know if he was either the happiest man alive, or . . . he refused to think of the opposite.

"Come on Nate, Bob, let's get going," Drew said, then he laughed out loud. Couldn't a man whose name was Antoine-Amédée-Marie-Vincent Manca de Vallombrosa, Marquis de Morès, come up with better names for horses than Nate and Bob?

But the laughter was good for him. All his tension was gone. He was going to see his Jana as soon as he crested the hill.

Jana was exhausted. The day had been hot, and two of the younger women had gone off with their husbands to spend the day on the prairie. She realized that they needed privacy to "couple" as they called it, but that could be done at night. She had taken over their bread duties, in addition to her own job of keeping the coals hot on the Dutch ovens for most of the day, because Johan had taken one of the horses to the vein to gather more coal.

Even though the water supply was low, Johan had brought two pails of water to the tent to warm during the heat of the day, and Jana had washed her hair and her body as best she could. Now she was sitting outside the tent brushing out her hair.

She had not seen Johan for most of the day. He was a good man, and a hard worker, who would make a dependable husband for some woman someday.

It is Drew Malone's fault, she thought, and she thought about him often. Did he come back to Bismarck? Did he get the kids back? Did he ever really love . . . ? She closed her eyes. She would not allow that thought to surface.

Just then, she looked up to a bit of a commotion. Most of the men who still lived in the boxcar were shielding their eyes from the sun, which was now low in the western sky. Something was coming, and at this hour that was unusual. Few people traveled this way except on the train, and it only stopped when the water car was exchanged. Occasionally, a Sioux Indian would wander into the colony, but they were friendly now, so there was seldom any activity.

When Jana stood up, she thought she saw an unusual coach that probably belonged to a drummer hawking his wares to the homesteaders. She had made it a habit to stay out of sight when any stranger was in the colony. But why? No one had tried to find her. Nonetheless, she stepped into the tent and lowered the flap.

She lay back on her pallet and closed her eyes, but in a minute she heard voices. At first they seemed to be far away, but then they came closer to her tent. She sat up, grabbing her flannel wrapper.

And then she heard it.

"Hester Prynne? Are you in there?" The voice was laced with humor, but she would recognize that voice anywhere. "Come out, come out, wherever you are."

"Drew!" she yelled as she dropped her wrapper and pulled back the flap of the tent, almost falling as her foot caught on the center pole.

He was standing not ten feet from her.

"What are you doing here?"

"I've come to apologize. I didn't even give you a chance to tell your side. I don't know what to say."

"All you have to do, Drew, is say you are sorry."

"I have no right to ask for your forgiveness, my dear Jana, but . . ."

"All you have to do, Drew, is say—"

"I'm sorry, I'm sorry."

"That's all it takes." Jana bounded into his arms and he lifted her off her feet, kissing her as only he could kiss her.

She wound her arms around him and returned the kiss with all the pent-up passion she had felt for these many weeks.

Then she heard a clearing of a throat. Beside Drew stood Johan. "I take it this is not a consanguineous relationship," he said, a smile crossing his face.

"No, no. This is him. This is the man I was going to marry."

Drew stopped her as he put her feet back on the ground. "You've made a mistake, miss. I'm not the man you *going* to marry."

Jana looked at him, confused.

Drew smiled broadly. "I am the man you *will* marry, one week from tomorrow at Rimfire Ranch, assuming, of course, that the answer is yes."

"Oh, yes, Drew, yes! You've made me the happiest woman in the world."

Rimfire Ranch—One week later

Jana stood on the porch that stretched across the front of the house watching Greta, wearing a peacock-blue dress and a hat trimmed with feathers, move slowly toward the wedding guests. Jana had to smile. Her little sister, no more a frail child, was radiant. If only her mother could see her now.

A lump lodged in Jana's throat as she thought back to the night when their mother had sent them out to steal a ride in a pig wagon to catch a train to the unknown. She recalled the cacophonous noise of the bawling livestock, coupled with the stench of the Yard where Greta had nearly died from the burning hell that was Chicago. And from that despair the dear girl had brought home the pamphlet that had led them to this place and this time.

The Dakota Territory. Who would have thought that a place called the Badlands could be the source of such unbelievable happiness?

"Are you ready?"

Jana looked toward her dear friend. "Oh, Hank, am I doing the right thing?"

"Of course you are, darlin'. If I was your blood daddy, I'd say the same thing. No man has suffered as much as Drew—losin' Addie the way he did—and then thinkin' he lost you. Just look at him, standin' there watchin' your ever' move. I know he loves you, but the question you have to answer is, do you love him?"

Jana kissed Hank on the cheek. "Yes, I love him. With all my heart."

"Then let's not keep him waiting."

Just then there was a commotion as a wagon pulled into the yard and two people jumped out and hurried toward the small group.

Jana clasped her hand to her mouth as she let out a gasp.

"Do you know those folks?"

"It's Mama! Johan brought my mama to my wedding!"

"I'm happy for you girl, and if I don't miss my bet, it was Drew who made it happen. Now, we'd better get going 'fore that orchestra has to play the 'Wedding March' again."

As Drew watched Jana and Hank coming down the path toward him, he thought his bride was the most beautiful woman he had ever seen. Her dress was all white satin and lace, while the orange blossoms that held her hair in place scented the spring air. Just as Jana approached the gathering, two little boys rose from their seats and went running to her. In spite of the billowing dress, both grabbed her legs and buried their heads in the folds of satin.

"We thought you had left and weren't coming back," Sam said as both boys held her so tightly that she couldn't move.

Jana leaned down to embrace them, smothering each boy with kisses.

Father Cotes, who was to celebrate the marriage, spoke up then. "Folks, I know we've set up the altar and flowers here, but it seems that there are a couple of young boys who have their own ideas. Drew, shall we move this marriage rite to your family?"

"Yes, sir," Drew said as he went swiftly to Jana's side.

"Daddy, can we marry Jana, too?" Sam asked.

"I don't know why not," Drew replied with a smile.

The guests, who had been facing the river, now turned toward the priest and the wedding party.

Father Cotes began the service. "Dearly beloved, we are gathered together here in the sight of God, and in the face of this company, to join together this man and this woman in holy matrimony."

As the priest intoned the marriage rites, Jana could barely hear the words, so overcome was she with happiness. Then she heard him ask, "Do you take this woman to be your lawfully wedded wife?"

"I do," Drew said.

"Me, too," Benji said.

"So do I," Sam added.

Tears of happiness streamed down Jana's face. "And I take all three of thee," she said. She had a family.

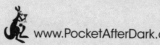

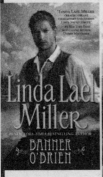 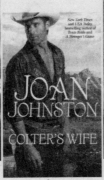 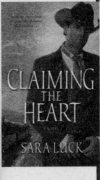